THE
AUSTRALiAN
LONG
STORY

Mandy Sayer is the acclaimed author of eight books, including the *Australian*/Vogel Award-winning novel *Mood Indigo*, and the memoirs *Dreamtime Alice*, which won the 2000 National Biography Award, and *Velocity*, which won the 2006 South Australian Premier's Award for Non-Fiction and the 2006 *Age* Non-Fiction Book of the Year Award. Her work has been translated into several European and Asian languages. In 2002, she received her Doctorate in the short story from University of Technology, Sydney, and is the current Scholar in Writing at the same institution.

THE AUSTRALIAN
LONG STORY

Edited by
Mandy Sayer

HAMISH HAMILTON
an imprint of
PENGUIN BOOKS

HAMISH HAMILTON

Published by the Penguin Group
Penguin Group (Australia)
250 Camberwell Road, Camberwell, Victoria 3124, Australia
(a division of Pearson Australia Group Pty Ltd)
Penguin Group (USA) Inc.
375 Hudson Street, New York, New York 10014, USA
Penguin Group (Canada)
90 Eglinton Avenue East, Suite 700, Toronto, Canada ON M4P 2Y3
(a division of Pearson Penguin Canada Inc.)
Penguin Books Ltd
80 Strand, London, WC2R 0RL, England
Penguin Ireland
25 St Stephen's Green, Dublin 2, Ireland
(a division of Penguin Books Ltd)
Penguin Books India Pvt Ltd
11 Community Centre, Panchsheel Park, New Delhi – 110 017, India
Penguin Group (NZ)
67 Apollo Drive, Rosedale, North Shore 0632, New Zealand
(a division of Pearson New Zealand Ltd)
Penguin Books (South Africa) (Pty) Ltd
24 Sturdee Avenue, Rosebank, Johannesburg 2196, South Africa

Penguin Books Ltd, Registered Offices: 80 Strand, London, WC2R 0RL, England

First published by Penguin Group (Australia), 2009

1 3 5 7 9 10 8 6 4 2

Copyright in this collection and the Introduction © Mandy Sayer 2009
Copyright © in individual stories retained by individual copyright holders

The moral right of the authors has been asserted

All rights reserved. Without limiting the rights under copyright reserved above, no part of this publication may be reproduced, stored in or introduced into a retrieval system, or transmitted, in any form or by any means (electronic, mechanical, photocopying, recording or otherwise), without the prior written permission of both the copyright owner and the above publisher of this book.

Cover and text design by Tony Palmer © Penguin Group (Australia)
Cover photograph by Jan Bruggeman / Getty Images
Typeset in Adobe Garamond by Post Pre-Press Group, Brisbane, Queensland
Printed and bound in Australia by McPherson's Printing Group, Maryborough, Victoria

National Library of Australia
Cataloguing-in-Publication data:

The Australian long story / editor, Mandy Sayer.
9781926428000 (pbk.)
Short stories, Australian
Sayer, Mandy
A823.0108

penguin.com.au

CONTENTS

Introduction 1

The Valley of Lagoons
David Malouf 13

Jesus Wants Me for a Sunbeam
Peter Goldsworthy 77

Ten Anecdotes About
Lord Howe Island
Louis Nowra 131

Honour
Helen Garner 183

Boner McPharlin's Moll
Tim Winton 251

Grasshoppers
Elizabeth Jolley 299

The Chance
Peter Carey 357

The Childhood Gland
Gillian Mears 407

Halflead Bay
Nam Le 451

Notes on the Authors 533

Acknowledgements 537

INTRODUCTION

AUSTRALIA HAS A RICH and lengthy storytelling tradition, dating back thousands of years to the myths of the Aboriginal Dreamtime. After European settlement, this oral storytelling ritual found expression around campfires and in pubs, with outback workers and itinerate labourers telling tall tales and yarns that staved off loneliness and provided entertainment in a harsh bush environment. Henry Lawson, considered 'the father' of the Australian short story, was one of our first writers to make a successful transition from oral to written storytelling, honing the yarn into a literary form in the 1890s and early twentieth century. Since then, the Australian short story has flourished, embracing the voices of women, migrants, children and refugees.

The idea for this collection of long stories was inspired by three sources. The first was my own foray into the form; the second was Richard Ford's 1998 anthology, *The Granta Book of the American Long Story*; and the third was my reaction to the most recently published collections of Tim Winton (*The Turning*, 2004) and David Malouf (*Every Move You Make,* 2006), both of which contained unusually long and extremely accomplished stories (between 10 and 20 000 words). It made me wonder if there was such a thing as an Australian long story.

But first I had to contemplate the definition: what distinguishes a short story from a long one, and at what point does a long story become a novella? Ford states in the introduction to his anthology that neither he nor his writer colleagues could come up with a concrete definition of the novella as a form, and therefore he regards all of the works selected for his collection as 'long stories' – even those that are over 50 000 words and were initially published as individual books.

Although Ford makes a compelling case for abandoning the title 'novella', for me, it didn't feel right. At the beginning of this inquiry I didn't know why – it was just a hunch. My research for this collection ranged widely, roaming through literary history around the world. It soon became obvious that many of the great international short story writers had also written stories of considerable length, many of which have become a part of the literary canon: Heinrich Von Kleist's 'The Marquise of O', Anton Chekhov's 'Ward No. 6', James Joyce's 'The Dead', Ernest Hemingway's 'The Short Happy Life of Francis Macomber', Eudora Welty's 'June Recital', William Faulkner's 'The Bear', Peter Taylor's 'The Old Forest', and just about everything Alice Munro has ever written. Having said that, there are also numerous masters of the short story form who never wrote a lengthy story; Raymond Carver comes to mind, as does Henry Lawson.

It was Edgar Allan Poe who first came up with a working definition of the modern short story: 'a story short enough to be read in one sitting', which seems reasonable to me. Other theorists have claimed, in one way or another, that short stories should be brief, have a single, compressed storyline, and contain an epiphany or turning point, however slight. This, too, seems more than reasonable. I don't believe that a character sketch, a slice of life, or a chapter of a novel can be published as or even called a short story. For me, narrative equals *change*, usually in the fusion of character and plot, and this idea is most purely realised in the structure of the modern short story. In a novel, a narrative can meander, falter, misstep or hiccup and still be forgiven – even celebrated – by its readers if it is interesting and entertaining enough. The short story, however, is an unforgiving form: any flaws or transgressions are immediately apparent.

After reading scores of longer narratives – some labelled stories, others novellas – interesting patterns began to emerge. Those published as novellas contained some formal features that seemed to allow them to stand on their own, while those published as part of a larger collection usually did not. And these formal features had nothing to do with length.

For me, the difference lies in complexity. One of Ford's inclusions in *The American Long Story*, 'Goodbye, Columbus' by Philip Roth, was initially published as a full-length, independent work. At around 50 000 words, this humorous gem about manipulation and class has a main storyline and two little offshoot narratives – or subplots – woven within it. This is indeed a novella.

On the other hand, Jane Smiley's 'The Age of Grief' (another of Ford's inclusions) was first published as part of a collection of stories, all based on the complementary themes of love and marriage. 'The Age of Grief' is billed as a novella on the cover of the original book, but while it is a beautifully crafted piece of work, it actually contains all the formal structures of the short story: it has various turning points that escalate into crisis, epiphany and resolution, but all through a single storyline, without any subplots.

Once I had unravelled some differences between a long story and a novella, I began to wonder what features, if any, distinguish a long story from a short one. The obvious answer is length. But are there technical differences between the two? What can the long story achieve easily that the short story finds more difficult? Going back to Poe, I found that like the short story, the long story 'could be read in one sitting' – but didn't necessarily need to be. Again, this is more to do with complexity than length. The lengthy story is complicated enough to sustain more than one sitting because, if successful, it gives readers enough to chew on mentally during the intervals.

After reading so many long stories – both Australian and international – two other features began to emerge that set the form apart from the traditional short story. The first and probably most significant difference is the way it can negotiate the passing of time. Generally, the short story is accomplished at covering a modest amount of time through a compressed storyline. It can be a single, dramatic scene (Ernest Hemingway's 'Hills Like White Elephants'); span a few hours (Katherine Mansfield's 'Her First Ball'); or be narrated over period of days or weeks (Eudora Welty's 'Why I Live at the P.O.'). While not impossible, it is difficult for a short story to span a year or more, though it demands the technical dexterity of a writer like Anton Chekhov ('Lady with a Toy Dog') or Richard Yates ('Liars in Love').

The long story, however, is able to incorporate vast passages of time. It can narrate passing years, even decades, without seeming forced or rushed. Naturally, because of its length, the long story has the luxury of broader context and exposition, but it also has the leg room to forge through narrative time and space. (I should stress that while the long story *can* do this if the events in narrative demand it, it of course doesn't *have* to.)

The second feature distinguishing the long story from the short is point of view. The short story is generally confined to a single perspective. Again, it is *possible* to narrate a short story from multiple points of view but to be quite honest I can't find any superlative examples. Even in my own practice of short story writing, any attempts to do so have fallen, well, *short*. A broadening of the perspective tends to either lessen the potency of the story or increase its length until it falls into the long story category. The long story is able to embrace more than one point of view without becoming a novella: that is, without diverging into subplots. An early example of this is Kleist's 1803 story, 'The Marquise of O'. It is narrated from an omniscient point of view (we are inside the minds of many of the characters, rather than one), but each character's point of view fuses into one storyline, one climax, one resolution. Another example is Eudora Welty's 'June Recital', which effectively alternates in point of view between a young brother and sister. This story is also a fine example of the long story's ability to transcend time: not only does it use flashbacks (difficult to achieve with the short story's need for compression), it also employs flashbacks within flashbacks. Again, even though there is a mosaic of time frames and points of view, every piece of the story contributes to the one narrative.

When I began my reading for this collection, however, most of these ideas and theories were set to one side. My only selection criteria were excellent quality, an Australian author and an Australian setting. Furthermore, the story had to justify the length. Some long stories were not included because they seemed overwritten: what was narrated in eighty pages, for example, could have been narrated in forty-five.

Initially, I imagined that the stories in the collection might span from the nineteenth century to the present day, providing a historical and literary overview. The further my reading delved into the past, however, the shorter the stories became. Sure, there were one or two longer stories from the nineteenth century, like Marcus Clarke's 'The Mystery of Major Molineux' (1881), but they were genre rather than literary works, and not of a high enough standard. The early to mid-twentieth century didn't provide many more examples, well written or otherwise. The great practitioners of the Australian storytelling tradition – Henry Lawson, Barbara Baynton, Dal Stivens, Hal Porter, to name a few – all concentrated on shorter versions of the form.

I suspect this phenomenon had more to do with practicalities than aesthetics. A long story was not complex enough to be published independently as a book, and not short enough to be published in a journal or magazine (a regular source of income for twentieth-century authors). On the other hand, it could be said that this preference for brevity mirrors what we've come to think of as a trait of our national character: a restrained, laconic voice that refuses to call too much attention to itself. The seeming simplicity of the short story also sits well with our Australian preference for the appearance of equality. As Christina Stead noted in the introduction to her uncollected short fiction, *Ocean of Story* (1985), 'What is unique about the short story is that we can all tell one, live one, write one down.' The Irish author

INTRODUCTION

and critic Frank O'Connor believes that the short form attracts stories from any given country's underdogs – what he calls a 'submerged population group'. He cites James Joyce's working-class Dubliners, Ivan Turgenev's serfs, and Guy de Maupassant's prostitutes, to name a few. The same could be said for Lawson's bush heroes and swaggies, Baynton's isolated and abused heroines and, later, Peter Cowan's farm labourers and Judah Waten's immigrants.

I did discover a few examples of the longer story written before the 1970s, but again, not many. In 1968, Christina Stead published *The Puzzleheaded Girl: Four Novellas*, but they were all set overseas. In the 1960s, Patrick White produced several long stories, for example 'Down at the Dump', 'Dead Roses' and 'The Burnt Ones', but I found his supposed satirising of the working class distinctly unfunny. He also, in my view, commits the cardinal literary sin of patronising his characters. Shirley Hazzard initially published the long story 'A Place in the Country' in two instalments in *The New Yorker* (illustrating my earlier point about the difficulty of placing long stories in magazines) but the unnamed 1950s setting (most likely the US) had no references to Australia and, to me, read as slightly clichéd.

The one long story from the earlier part of the twentieth century that I seriously considered was Frank Hardy's 'The Cockie in Bungaree', published in the 1964 anthology *Australians Have a Word for It*, edited by Gertrude Gelbin. Originally adapted from an Australian folk song that Hardy first heard in a Gippsland pub, it is a riotous account of masculine rivalry and class distinctions set in the harsh Victorian countryside of the 1930s. The problem with including it in this collection, however, was that it was too different in terms of tone, style and setting (the 1930s) to keep company with what would become the final selection.

The 1970s brought enormous changes to the Australian cultural and political landscape: feminism, arts funding, social welfare, free tertiary education, and the recognition of Aboriginal land rights, to name a few. Australia was emerging from its isolated, colonial identity and becoming part of the wider international community, demonstrated by the strengthening of the Australian film industry and how well our cinematic stories began travelling overseas. At the same time, short story writers like Peter Carey, Murray Bail, Frank Moorhouse and Michael Wilding, influenced by international writers like Jorge Luis Borges and Donald Barthelme, were shaking off the Australian story's tradition of realism in favour of more experimental, even surreal, narratives. These formal innovations led to a significant expansion in Australian short story writing, with an increase of publishing in both in magazines and full-length collections.

The proliferation of full-length collections, unrestrained by expectations of realism, gave short story writers more elbow room. No longer bound by the national story tradition of laconic brevity, long stories began to appear in the late 1970s in unprecedented numbers. (Two such stories are republished in this anthology: Peter Carey's 'The Chance' and Elizabeth Jolley's 'Grasshoppers'.) Furthermore, these and other writers, such as David Foster, Antigone Kefala, Thea Astley and Helen Garner, no longer felt obliged to articulate what it means to be 'Australian' – previously a significant expectation placed on Australian writers. By the 1980s the Australian short story had grown up and, for some, grown long. It seemed natural, therefore, to restrict this

INTRODUCTION

collection to the past four decades – a rich and compelling era for the form.

Making the final selection involved some tough decisions. My only regret is that I could not find a long story written by, or from the point of view of, an Indigenous Australian. Perhaps this is because the storytelling tradition of Indigenous Australians is oral, and therefore necessarily short, or because their written literary history is comparatively brief when measured against the British and European traditions. Yet another could be that they are attracted to other mediums of storytelling, particularly filmmaking, dance, music and painting. Whatever the reason, I hope in possible subsequent editions of this collection the omission may be rectified.

As an organising principle, I decided to begin the collection with the elder master of the group, David Malouf, whose story is set in the lush forests of Queensland during the earlier part of the twentieth century, and complete it with the up-and-coming young gun of Australian literature, Nam Le, whose story about a boy dealing with both his first love and his dying mother is set in contemporary times. Curiously, both are coming-of-age stories, as is Tim Winton's breathtaking 'Boner McPharlin's Moll', which details, over many years, a teenage girl's relationship with the bad boy of a small coastal town and her eventual and unwitting betrayal of him. Not one, but four girls come of age in Gillian Mears' 'The Childhood Gland', an elegant, funny and heartbreaking tale about the lifelong bond between sisters. Narrated non-chronologically and with radiant lyricism, 'The Childhood Gland' is yet another example of how the long story can play with time.

Louis Nowra's 'Ten Anecdotes About Lord Howe Island' is a delightful, rare example of the comedic long story. (And yes, I would have chosen it even if I weren't married to the author, though we did argue over his fee.) In my reading for this collection I found that the long story tends to be highly dramatic and, for some mysterious reason, rarely humorous. But this particular story is wonderfully whimsical and funny, and adds variety to the tone of the collection. Helen Garner is at her peak exploring the nuances of domesticity and jealousy in 'Honour', where relationships shift as subtly as tectonic plates, while Elizabeth Jolley is at her brutal best in 'Grasshoppers', exploring selfishness and casual cruelty – with devastating results. Peter Carey's 'The Chance', though non-realistic and set in a surreal environment, can be read as a very Australian yarn about our 'tall poppy syndrome', while Peter Goldsworthy's 'Jesus Wants Me for a Sunbeam' is an excoriating tale about the limits (or non-limits) of parental love and mortality, a story stunning for both its bravery and restraint.

Several of the stories in this collection may be already familiar to some readers; indeed, some of them are already deemed classics. My hope is that, say, fans of Helen Garner's 'Honour' might be introduced to the lesser-known stories of the late Elizabeth Jolley, or that Tim Winton enthusiasts may delight in the work of the comparatively younger Nam Le.

Every one of these stories has something utterly unique to offer, both in writing style and subject matter. It has been an honour and a pleasure to collect them into one volume. I trust you'll enjoy reading them as much as I did.

– Mandy Sayer, March 2009

THE VALLEY OF LAGOONS

David Malouf

When I was in the third grade at primary school it was the magic of the name itself that drew me.

Just five hours south off a good dirt highway, it is where all the river systems in our quarter of the state have their rising: the big, rain-swollen streams that begin in a thousand threadlike runnels and falls in the rainforests of the Great Divide, then plunge and gather and flow wide-banked and muddy-watered to the coast; the leisurely water-courses that make their way inland across plains stacked with anthills, and run north-west and north to the Channel Country, where they break up and lose themselves in the mudflats and mangrove swamps of the Gulf.

I knew it was there and had been hearing stories about it for as long as I could remember. Three or four hunting parties, some of them large, went out each year at the start of August, and since August was the school holidays, a good many among them were my class-mates. By the time he was sixteen, my best friend Braden, who was just my age, had been going with his father and his two older brothers, Stuart and Glen, for the past five years. But it was not marked on the wall-map in our third-grade schoolroom and I could not find it in any atlas; which gave it the status of a secret place, accessible only in the winter when the big rains eased off and the tracks that led into it were dry enough for a ute loaded down with tarpaulins, cook-pots, carbide lamps, emergency cans of petrol, and bags of flour, potatoes, onions and other provisions, to get in without sinking to the axle: a thousand square miles of virgin country known only to the few dozen families of our little township and the surrounding cane and dairy farms that made up the shire.

It was there, but only in our heads. It had a history, but only in the telling: in stories I heard from fellows in the playground at school, or from their older brothers at the barbershop or at the edge of an oval or on the bleachers at the town pool.

These stories were all of record 'bags' or of the comic mishaps and organised buffoonery of camp life – plus, of course, the occasional shocking accident – but had something more behind them, I thought, than mere facts.

Fellows who went out there were changed – that's what I saw. Kids who had been swaggering and loud were quiet when they spoke of it, as if they knew more now than they were ready to let on, or had words for or were permitted to tell. This impressed me, since it chimed with my own expectations of what I might discover, or be let into, when I too got there.

I stood in the shadows at the edge of what was being told, tuning my ear to the clamour, off in the scrub, of a wild pig being cornered while a kid no older than I was stood with an old Lee Enfield .303 jammed into the soft of his shoulder, holding his breath.

An occasion that was sacred in its way, though no one, least of all the kid who was now retelling it, would ever speak of it that way.

All that side of things you had to catch at a glance as you looked away. From the slight, almost imperceptible warping upwards of a deliberately flattened voice.

In the first freshening days of June, and increasingly as July came on, all the talk around town, in schoolyards and changing sheds, across the counter at Kendrick's Seed and Hardware, along the verandah rails and in the dark public bars of the town's three hotels, where jurymen were put up when the district court was in session, and commercial travellers and bonded schoolteachers and bank clerks roomed, was about who, this year, would be going, and in which party and when.

In the old days, which were still within living memory, they had gone out on horseback, a four-day ride, the last of it through buffel grass that came right to the horses' ears, so that all you had to go on was bush sense, and the smell in the horses' nostrils of an expanse of water up ahead.

Nowadays there were last year's wheel-marks. A man with a keen eye, crouched on the running-board of a ute or hanging halfway out the offside cabin window, could indicate to the driver which way to turn in the whisper of high grassheads, till the swishing abruptly fell away and you were out in the shimmering, insect-swarming midst of it: sheet after sheet of brimming water, all lit with sky and alive, like a page of Genesis, with spur-winged plover, masked plover, eastern swamphen, marshy moorhen, white-headed shelldrake, plumed tree duck, gargery teal, and clattering skyward as, like young bulls loose in pasture, the utes swerved and roared among them, flocks of fruit pigeon, squatters, topknots, forest bronzewings . . .

My father was not a hunting man. The town's only solicitor, his business was with wills and inheritance, with land contracts, boundary lines between neighbours, and the quarrels, sometimes fierce, that gave rise to marriage break-ups, divorce, custody battles and, every two or three years, the odd case of criminal assault or murder that will arise even in the quietest community. He knew more of the history of the shire, including its secret history, its unrecorded and unspoken connections and disconnections, than any other man, and more than his clients themselves did of how this or that parcel of their eighty- or hundred-acre holdings had been taken up out of what, less than a hundred years ago, had been uncharted wilderness, and how, in covert deals with the bank or in deathbed codicils, out of spite or through long years of plotting, this or that paddock, or canebrake, or spinney, had passed from one neighbour or one first or second cousin to another.

When he and my mother first came here in the late thirties, he'd been invited out, when August came round, on one of the parties – it was a courtesy, an act of neighbourliness, that any one of a dozen locals would have extended to an acceptable newcomer, if only to see how he might fit in.

'Thanks, Gerry,' I imagine him saying in his easy way – or Jake, or Wes. 'Not this time, I reckon. Ask me again next year, eh?' And had said that again the following year, and the year after, until they stopped asking.

He wasn't being stand-offish or condescending. It was simply that hunting, and the grand rigmarole, as he saw it, of gun talk and game talk and dog talk, was not his style. He had been a soldier in New Guinea and had seen enough perhaps, for one lifetime, of killing. It was an oddness in him that was accepted like any other, humorously, and was perhaps not entirely unexpected in a man who had more books in his house than could be found in the shire library. He was a respected figure in the town. He was even liked. But he wore a collar and tie even on weekdays, and men who were used to consulting him in a friendly way about a dispute with a neighbour, or the adding of a clause to their will, developed a sudden interest in their boots when they ran into him away from his desk.

My mother too was an outsider. Despite heavy hints, she had not joined the fancy-workers and jam- and chutney-makers at the CWA, and in defiance of local custom sent all three of us to school in shoes. This was understandable in the case of my sisters. They were older and would grow up one day to be ladies. It was regarded as unnecessary and even, perhaps, damaging in a boy.

After more than twenty years in the district my father had never been to the Lagoons, and till I was sixteen I had not been there either, except in the dreamtime of my own imaginings and in what I had overheard from others.

I might have gone. Each year, in the first week of August, Braden's father, Wes McGowan, got up a party. I was always invited. My father, after a good deal of humming and ha-ing and using my mother as an excuse, would tell me I was too young and decline to let me go. But I knew he was uneasy about it, and all through the last weeks of July, as talk in the town grew, I waited in the hope he might relent. When the day came at last, I would get up early, pull on a sweater against the cold and, in the misty half-light just before dawn, jog down the deserted main street, past the last service station at the edge of town, to the river park where the McGowans' Bedford ute would be waiting for the rest of the party to appear, its tray piled high with tarpaulins, bedrolls, cook-pots, a gauze meat safe, and my friend Braden settled among them with the McGowan dogs at his feet, two Labrador retrievers.

Old Wes McGowan and his crony, Henry Denkler, who was also the town mayor, would be out stretching their legs, stamping their boots on the frosty ground or bending to inspect the tyres or the canvas water bag that hung from the front bumper-bar. The older McGowan boys, Stuart and Glen, would be squatting on their heels over a smoke. I would stand at the gate of the ute chatting to Braden for a bit and petting the dogs.

When the second vehicle drew up, with Matt Riley, the 'professional', and his nephew Jem, Matt too would get down and a second inspection would be made – of the tyres, of the load – while Jem, with not much more than a nod, joined the McGowan boys. Then, with all the rituals of meeting done, Henry Denkler and Wes McGowan would climb back into the cabin, Glen into the driver's seat beside them, Stuart into the back with Braden and the dogs, and I would be left standing to wave them off; and then, freezing even in my sweater, jog slowly back home.

The break came in the year after I turned sixteen. When I went for the third or fourth year running to tell my father that the McGowans had offered to take me out to the Lagoons and to ask if I could go, he surprised me by looking up over the top of his glasses and saying, 'That's up to you, son. You're old enough, I reckon, to make your own decisions.' It was to be Braden's last trip before he went south to university. Most of the shooting would be birds, but to mark the occasion as special Braden would also get a go at a pig.

'So,' my father said quietly, though he already knew the answer, 'what's it to be?'

'I'd really like to go,' I told him.

'Good,' he said, not sounding regretful. 'I want you to look out and be careful, that's all. Braden's a sensible enough young fellow. But your mother will worry her soul case out till you're home again.'

What he meant was, *he* would.

Braden McGowan had been my best friend since I was five years old. We started school on the same day, sharing a desk and keeping pace with one another through pot-hooks and the alphabet, times tables, cursive, and those scrolled and curlicued capitals demanded by our Queensland State School copybooks. We dawdled to and from school on our own circuitous route. Past the Vulcan Can Company, where long shiny cut-offs of raw tin were to be had, which we carted off in bundles to be turned into weapons and aids of our own devising, past the crushing-mill where we got sticks of sugar cane to chew. Narrow gauge lines ran to the mill from the many outlying farms, and you heard at all hours in the crushing season the noise of trundling, and the shrill whistle of the engine as a line of carts approached a crossing, and rumbled through or clanked to a halt.

In the afternoons after school and in the holidays, we played together in the paddocks and canebrakes of the McGowans' farm, being, as the mood took us, explorers, pirates, commandos, bushrangers, scouts on the track of outlaws or of renegade Navaho braves.

Usually we had a troop of the McGowan dogs with us, who followed out of doggy curiosity and sometimes, in the belief that they had got the scent of what the game was, moiled around us or leapt adventurously ahead. But for the most part they simply lay and watched from the shade, till we stretched out beside them and let the game take its freer form of untrammelled thinking-aloud that was also, with its range of wild and rambling surmise, the revelation — even to ourselves, though we were too young as yet to know it — of bright, conjectural futures we would have admitted to no one else.

'You two are weird,' Braden's brother Stuart told us with a disgusted look, having caught on his way to the bails some extravagant passage of our talk. '*God*, you're weird. You're *weird*!'

Stuart was four years older. He and the eldest of the three brothers, Glen, had farm work to do in the afternoons after school. Braden in those days was still little and free to play.

They were rough kids, the McGowans, and Stuart was not just rowdy, I thought, but unpredictably vicious. He scared me.

I had come late into a family of girls, two sisters who, from the beginning, had made a pet of me. Going over to the McGowans' was an escape to another world. Different laws were in operation there from the ones I was used to. Old Mr McGowan had a different notion of authority from the one my father followed. Quiet but firmer. His sons, who were so noisy and undisciplined outside, were subdued in his presence. Mrs McGowan, unlike my mother, had no interests beyond the piles of food she brought to the table and the washing – her men's overalls and shirts and singlets, and the loads of sheets and pillowcases I saw her hoist out of the copper boiler when I came to collect Braden on Monday mornings.

She too had a softening influence on the boys. They might complain when she called them in from kicking a football round the yard, or working on a bike, to fetch in an armful of wood for the stove or to carry a basket of wet sheets to the line, and they squirmed when she tried to settle an upturned collar or hug them. But they did do what she asked in the end, and even submitted, with a good show of masculine reluctance, to hugging.

I liked the roughness and ease I found at the McGowans', but even more the formality, which was of a kind my parents would have wondered at and found odd, old-fashioned.

My sisters, Katie and Meg, were exuberantly opinionated. Our mealtimes were loud with argument in which we all talked over one another, our parents included, and the food itself was forgotten.

There was no arguing at the McGowans'. Glen and Stuart, rough and barefooted as they were, showed their hands before they were allowed to table, sat up straight, kept their elbows in, and lowered their heads for grace – the McGowans said grace!

They passed things without speaking. Barely spoke at all unless their father asked a question, or in response to a story he told, or to tell their mother how good the stew was in hope of a second helping.

I loved all this. When Braden began to have his own jobs to do after school, I stayed to help. I learned to milk, to clean out the bails, to handle a gun and shoot sparrows in the yard, and rabbits in the brush, then stayed for the McGowans' early tea. I wanted to be one of them, or at least to be like them. Like Glen. Like Stuart even. I wasn't of course, but then neither was Braden.

When we were very young it did not occur to me that Braden might be odd. He was often in trouble at home for being 'dreamy', but then so was I. 'What's the matter with you,' Stuart would demand of him, genuinely exasperated, 'are you dumb or something?'

He wasn't, but he found a problem at times where the rest of us did not, and to a point of inertia that infuriated Stuart (who suspected him, I think, of doing it deliberately) was puzzled by circumstances, quite ordinary ones, that the rest of us took for granted. Other kids found him slow. Some of them called him a dill.

I understood Braden's puzzlement because I shared it at times, and since we were always together, I took it that we were puzzled in the same way. I had for so long been paired with Braden, we had shared so many discoveries and first thoughts, that I had assumed we were in every way alike; that in all the hours we had spent spinning fantasies and creating other lives for ourselves, we had been moving through the same landscape and weather, and were one. When Stuart told us, 'You two are weird. You're weird,' I was pleased to see in his savage contempt the confirmation that in Stuart's eyes at least we were indistinguishable.

I did not want to know what I had already begun in some part of me to suspect. That Braden's oddness might be quite different from anything I could lay claim to.

For as long as I could remember, we had known, each one, what the other was thinking. The same things amused or excited or scared us. Now, almost overnight, it seemed, Braden knew stuff I had never dreamed of. His mind was engaged by questions that had never occurred to me, and the answers he came up with I could not follow. It was a habit of mind, I thought, that must have been there from the start, but moving underground in him and hidden from me; a music, behind the rambling stories he told, that I had all along been deaf to.

At the same time, in the six months before he turned fifteen, he put on height, six inches, and bulked up to twelve and a half stone. He was suddenly a big fellow. Bigger than either of his brothers. Not heavy, but big.

Then one day he showed me, in a copy of *Scientific American*, what it was that he was into. Cybernetics. I had never heard the word, and when he tried to explain it to me in his usual style, all jumps and sideways leaps into a silence I had believed I could interpret, I was lost.

I understood the science well enough. Even the figures. What I could not grasp was the excited vision of what he saw in it: a realm of action he saw himself moving through as if it had come into existence precisely for him. And this was the opening of a gap between us. Not of affection – no question of that – but of where our lives might take us. Braden, who had always been so vague and out of it, was suddenly the most focused person I knew. Utterly single-minded and sure of what he wanted and what he was for.

For the first time in my life I felt lonely. But not so lonely, I think, so finally set apart as *he* felt. From his family. His brothers. Who were still puzzled by him but in a new way.

Here he was, a big boy who had outgrown them and his own

strength, and ought, in springing up and filling out, to have become a fellow they could deal with at last on equal terms. Instead he seemed odder than ever. More difficult to get through to. Content to be away there in his own incommunicable universe.

Glen, who had always had a soft spot for the boy, was confused, but also I think impressed. He still teased him, but in a soft-handed affectionate way. As if Braden's difference, which had always intrigued him, had turned out to be something he might respect.

Glen, because he was so much older, had for the most part left us alone. We had always been a source of mild amusement to him, but except for the odd burst of impatience he had, in a condescending, big-brotherly way, ignored us. Stuart could not.

In the early days the mere sight of us drove him to fury. All jeers and knuckles, he was always twisting our arms and jerking them up under our shoulder blades to see how much we could take before we turned into crybabies and cissies.

He felt easier with me, I think, because I fought back. Braden disarmed him by taking whatever he could dish out with scornful defiance, never once, after our baby years, yielding to tears.

All this, I knew, belonged to a side of their life together that I had no part in, to hostilities and accommodations, spaces shared or passionately disputed, in rooms, at the table, in their mother's affection or their father's regard or interest.

But the fullness of the change in Braden, when it finally revealed itself, dismayed Stuart. He simply did not know what to do with it.

I think it scared him to have someone who was close, and who ought therefore to have been knowable, turn out to be so far from anything he could get a hold on. It suggested that the world itself might be beyond his comprehension, but also beyond his control. The only way he could deal with Braden was by avoiding him. Which made it all the more odd, I thought, that he began at the same time to latch on to me.

He had left school by now, was working in a garage and ran with a set of older fellows, all of whom were wild, as he was, and had 'reputations'. But suddenly we were always in one another's path.

He would appear out of nowhere, it seemed, on my way back from the pool, and offer me dinks on his bike. And when he exchanged his Malvern Star for a Tiger Cub he would stop, talk a bit, and offer to take me pillion.

I was wary. I had too often been on the wrong side of Stuart's roughness to be easy with him. It was flattering to be treated, in my own right, as a grown-up, but I did not trust him. He was trying to win me over. Why? Because he had seen the little gap that had opened up between Braden and me and wanted to widen it? To bring home to me that if Braden was odder than any of us had thought, then I had proved to be, like Stuart himself, more ordinary?

I resented his attention on both counts, and suspected that his unlikely interest in me was a form of mockery. It took me a while to see that mockery was not Stuart's style, and that by seeking me out, a younger boy and the brother of a girl he was sweet on (I learned this amazing fact from a bit of conversation overheard while I was sunbaking on the bleachers at the pool), he was putting himself helplessly in my power; making himself vulnerable to the worst mockery of all. That he trusted me not to take advantage of it meant that I never would of course, but I hated the familiarity with which he now greeted me as 'Angus, old son', or 'Angus, old horse', as if there was already some special relationship between us, or as if getting close to me brought him closer somehow to her. My own belief was that Stuart McGowan was just the sort of rough, loud fellow she wouldn't even look at. Then suddenly he and Katie were going out together, and he was at our house every night of the week.

Taking a break from my homework or the book I was absorbed in, and going through to the kitchen to get a glass of water or cold milk from the fridge, I would hear them whispering together on the couch in our darkened front room, and would turn the tap on hard to warn them I was about.

Or if it was late enough, and Stuart was leaving, I would run into them in the hall: Stuart looking smug but also, somehow, crestfallen, Katie hot and angry, ready I thought to snap my head off if I said more in reply to his ''lo, Angus, how's it going?' than a 'Hi, Stuart,' and ducked back into my room.

The truth was, I had no wish to know what was going on between them. I did not like the look of shy complicity that Stuart cast me, as if I had caught him out in something, but in something that as another male I must naturally approve.

Two or three nights each week he ate with us. I have no idea what he thought of the noisy arguments that marked our mealtimes. Perhaps it attracted him, as I was attracted by the old-fashioned formality I found at the McGowans'.

Occasionally, to kill time while Katie was helping in the kitchen, he would drift to the sleepout on the side verandah where I would be sprawled on my bed deep in a book. I would look up, thinking, 'God, not again,' and there he would be, hanging awkwardly in the open doorway, waiting for me to acknowledge him and taking my grunt of recognition as an invitation to come in.

Oddly restrained and self-conscious, he would settle at the foot of the bed, take a book from the pile on the floor, and say, with what I thought of as a leer, 'So what's this one about?' The way he handled the book, his half-embarrassed, half-suggestive tone, the painful attempt to meet me, as I saw it, on unfamiliar ground, made me uncomfortable. 'You don't have to pretend you're interested,' I wanted to tell him, 'just because you're going out with my sister.' On the whole, I preferred the old Stuart. I thought I knew better what he was about. It did not occur to me that what I was reading, and what I found there, might be a genuine mystery to him; which disturbed his sense of himself, and had to do with how, in this strange new household he had blundered into, with its unfamiliar views and distinctions, he might learn to fit in.

He would run his eyes over a few pages of the book he had in hand and shake his head. Thinking, I see now, of her, of Katie, and waiting for me to provide some clue – to me, I mean, to *us* — that would help him find common ground with her.

I would make a rambling attempt to explain who Raskolnikov was, and Sonia, and about the horse that had fallen down in the street. He would look puzzled, then stricken, then, trying to make the best of it, say, 'Interesting, eh?' Waiting for some sign perhaps that I recognised the effort he was making to enter my world, and what this might reveal about *him*: about some other Stuart than the one I thought I knew, and knew only as a 'bad influence'. After about ten minutes of this, I would swing my legs off the bed and say, 'Tea must be about ready, we'd better go out,' and to the relief of both of us, or so I thought, it would be over.

I had begun to dread these occasions of false intimacy between us that were intended, I thought, to be rehearsals for a time when we would be youthful brothers-in-law, close, bluff, easily affectionate. If he could get me to accept him in this role, then maybe she would.

Once, as he moved towards the door, I caught him, out of the corner of my eye, making a quick appraisal of himself in the wardrobe mirror. Starched white shirt with the sleeves rolled high to show off his biceps. Hair slicked down with Potter and Moore jelly. In the hollow of his underlip the squared-off, dandified growth of hair he had begun to affect in recent weeks, a tuft, two or three degrees darker than his hair colour but with flecks of gingery gold, that I had overlooked at first – I thought he had simply neglected to shave there. When I realised it was deliberate I was confused. It seemed so out of character.

Now, watching him take in at a casual glance the effect he made in my wardrobe mirror, I thought again. What a bundle of contradictions he is, I told myself.

He gave me a sheepish grin, and stopped, pretending to examine his chin for a shaving nick. But what his look said was, Well, that's how it is, you can see that, eh, old son? That's what they do to us.

When Katie first began to go out with him I'd felt I should warn her. That he was wild. That he had a 'reputation'. Only I did not know how to begin. We had always been close, and had grown more so since my older sister Meg got married, but for all that, and the boldness in our household with which we were willing to air issues and deliver an opinion, there were subjects, back then, that we kept clear of, areas of experience we could not admit knowledge of.

And it seemed to me that Katie must know as well as I did, or better, what Stuart was like. She was the one who spent all those hours of fierce whispering with him in the dark of our front room.

For weeks at a time they would move together in what seemed like a single glow. Then I would feel an anger in her that needed only a word on my part, or a look, to make her blaze out, though the real object of her fury, I thought, was herself. Stuart, for a time, would no longer be there, on the back verandah or in the lounge after tea. Things were off between them. When I ran into him at the baths, or when he stopped and offered me a lift on the Triumph, he would look hangdog and miserable. 'How are you, Angus, old son?' he'd ask, hoping I would return the question.

I didn't. The last thing I wanted was to be his confidant; to listen to his complaints about Katie or have him ask what she was saying about him, what I thought she wanted. These periods would last for days, for a whole week sometimes. Then he would be back, all scrubbed and spruced up and smelling like a sweet shop. Narrow-eyed and watchful. Like a cat, I thought. But also, in a way he could not help and could not help showing, happily full of himself and of his power over her. Couldn't he see, I thought, how mad it made her, and that it was this in the long run that would bring him down?

The crisis came a year or so after they first began.

Nothing was said – my parents were the very spirit of tact in such matters – but I guessed Katie had given him his marching orders. Again. *Again.* Because for two nights running he did not appear. Then, late on the second night, I looked out and the little Anglia he sometimes ran around in was parked under the street light opposite.

It was there at nine and was still there at half past ten. What was he doing? Just sitting there, I guessed, hunched and unhappy, chewing on his bitten-down nails.

To see if she had some other fellow calling?

More likely, I thought, just to be close to her. Or if not her, the house itself. To reassure himself that since we were all in and going about our customary routine, no serious breach had occurred. Then, remembering the old Stuart, I thought, No, it's his way of intimidating her. It's a kind of bullying. Didn't he know the first thing about her? Had he learned nothing in all those hours in the dark of the lounge room or the back verandah? Did he think that because she had sent him packing on previous occasions, all he had to do now was apply pressure and wait?

I could have told him something about those other occasions. That she was the sort of girl who did not forgive such demonstrations of her own weakness or those who caused them. There was only a limited number of times she would allow herself to be so shamefully humiliated. I stood hidden behind the slats of my sleepout and watched him there. Was she watching too?

I was surprised. That he should just drive up like that and park under the street light where everyone could see him. Was he more inventive than I'd guessed?

It seemed out of character too. Melodramatic. The sort of thing people did in the movies. Was that where he had got it?

Next morning at breakfast I glanced across at Katie to see if she too had seen him, and got a defiant glare. Then that night, late, when I went out to the kitchen to get a drink, she confronted me.

'So what do *you* think?' she demanded.

It was a clammy night. Airless. Without a breath. She was barefoot, her hair stuck to her brow with sweat. We stood side by side for a moment at the kitchen window.

'He's been there now for three nights running,' she said. 'It's ridiculous!'

I passed behind her and opened the fridge.

'Maybe you should go down,' she said, 'and sit with him.'

'What? What would I want to do that for?'

'Well, you're mates, aren't you?'

I had turned with the cold-water bottle. She took it from me and rolled it, with its fog of moisture, across her damp forehead, then her throat and chest.

'Is that what Stuart says?'

'Not what he *says*. Stuart never says anything, you know that.'

'What then? What do you mean?'

'Oh, nothing,' she said wearily. She handed the bottle back. 'Let's drop it.'

'Braden's my friend,' I told her. 'If Stuart wasn't here every night I wouldn't even see him from one week's end to the next.'

'OK,' she said, let's drop it. Maybe I don't understand these things.'

'What things?'

'Oh, boys. Men. You're all so – *tight* with one another.'

'No we're not. Stuart and I aren't – tight.'

'I thought you were.'

'Well, we're not.' I finished my glass of water, rinsed it at the sink and went to pass her.

Suddenly, from behind, her arms came round me. I felt the damp of her forearms on my chest, her face nuzzling the back of my neck.

'Your hair smells nice,' she said. 'Like when you were little.'

I squirmed and pretended to wriggle free, but only pretended. 'Stop,' I said, 'you're tickling,' as she held me tighter and laughed.

'There,' she said, glancing away to the window, 'he's gone.'

Neither of us had heard the car move off. She continued to hold me. 'Stay a minute, Angus,' she said. 'Stay and talk.'

'What about?'

'Oh, not him.' She let go of me. 'That wouldn't get us far.'

I sat at the kitchen table, awkward but expectant, and she sat opposite.

In the old days we had been close. When I came out of my room at night to get a glass of water or milk from the fridge, she would join me and we would sit for a bit, joking, exchanging stories, larking about. Stuart's arrival had ended that. He was always there, and when he wasn't she avoided me. Either way, I missed her and blamed Stuart for coming between us. We liked each other. She made me happy, and I made her happy too.

'I know you're on his side,' she said now. 'But there are things you don't know about.'

'I'm not on his side,' I told her. 'Are there sides?'

She laughed. 'No, Angus, there are no sides. There never will be for you. That's what I love about you.'

I was defensive. 'What's that supposed to mean?'

'It means you're nicer than I am. Maybe than any of us. And I love you. Listen,' she said, leaning closer, 'I'm going away.'

'Where to?'

'I don't know yet. Maybe I'll go and stay with Meg and Jack for a bit. Or I'll take the plunge and just go to Brisbane.'

'What would you do down there?'

'Get an office job, work in a shop – what do other girls do? I'm doing nothing here: Reading a lot of silly novels – what's the use of that? You know what this place is like. You won't stay here either.'

'Won't I?'

It pleased me at that time when people told me things about myself. Sometimes they surprised me, sometimes they didn't. Even when they confirmed what I already knew I was filled with interest.

'I've *got* to get out,' she told me passionately, 'I've *got* to. Nothing will ever happen if I stay here. I'd end up marrying Stuart, or someone just like him, and it'd kill me. It doesn't matter that he wants me, or thinks he does, or what I think of *him*. Even if he was kind – which he wouldn't be in fact. He'd be a rotten husband. What he really loves is himself. Maybe I won't get married at all. I don't know why everyone goes on all the time about marriage, as if it was the only thing there is.'

I was bewildered. She was telling me more than I could take in.

'So when?' I asked. 'When will you go?'

'I don't know,' she said miserably. 'I've got no money.'

'I have. I've got forty pounds.'

She leaned across the table and took my hand. 'I love you, Angus. More than anyone. Did you know that?' Then, after a pause, 'But you should hang on to your money, you'll need it yourself if you're ever going to get out of this dump. I'll get it some other way. Now go to bed or you won't be able to get up in the morning. It's after eleven.'

I got up obediently, and was at the door when she said, 'I suppose you'll be inseparable now.'

'Why?' I asked her. 'Why should we be?'

'Because that's the way he is. Once he realises this is the end, really this time, he'll want you to see what a bitch I am and how miserable he is.'

'That's all right,' I said. 'I won't listen.'

'Yes you will. But don't worry —'

'Katie —'

'No, no,' she said. 'Go to bed now.'

She came and kissed me very lightly on the cheek.

'We'll talk about it some other time. I told you, I love you. And thanks, eh? For the offer of the money. You sleep well now.'

That was in mid-April. The weeks passed. There was no reconciliation. Stuart stopped driving up to keep a watch on the house. Katie did not go away.

But she was right about one thing. Despite my reluctance, Stuart and I did become mates of a sort. Hangdog and subdued, he was in no mood to go out on the town with his mates, the daredevil rowdies he normally ran with, who did shift work at the cane mill, or were plumber's mates, apprentice builders, counter-jumpers in drapery shops or hardware stores, or helped out in their father's accounting business. Fellows whose wildness, which involved a lot of haring around late at night, scaring old ladies and Chinamen or the occasional black, was winked at as a relatively harmless way of letting off steam; the sort of larrikin high jinks that on another occasion might take the form of dashing into a burning house to rescue a kiddie from the flames or dragging a cat from a flooded creek or, if there was another war, performing feats of quicksilver courage that would get their names on the town memorial.

What Stuart needed me for, I decided, was to be a witness to his sorrows. Which he thought I might best be able to confirm because so much of what he gave himself up to came out of books. He was literary in the odd way of a fellow who did not read and who trusted my capacity to appreciate what he was feeling because I did. Perhaps he believed that if I took him seriously, then she would; though with a fineness of feeling I had not expected, he never once, in all our times together, mentioned her. Which made me more uneasy than if he had, since at every moment she was there as an unasked question between us, and as the only reason, really, why I was there at all.

He would pick me up in the Anglia at the bottom of our street, usually around nine when I had finished my homework, and we would drive out to some hilltop and just sit there in the cool night air, with the windows down, the sweet smell of cane flowers coming in heady wafts and the night crickets shrilling.

Stuart's self-pitying tone, and his self-conscious half-jokey way of addressing me as 'Angus, old boot', or 'Angus, old son', suggested more than ever, I thought, a character out of some movie, or a book he had been impressed by, and had more to do with the way he wanted me to see him, or the way he wanted to see himself, than with anything he really was.

Then it was July at last. The McGowans asked me to go out to the Lagoons. And I was going.

Just before sun-up the McGowans' heavy-duty Bedford ute swung uphill to where I was waiting with my duffel bag and bedroll on our front verandah. Behind me, the lights were on in our front room and my mother was there in her dressing gown, with a mug of tea to warm her hands, just inside the screen door. I was glad the others could not see her, and hoped she would not come out at the last moment to kiss me or to tuck my scarf into my windcheater. But in fact, 'Look after Braden,' was all she said as I waved to the ute, shouted 'See you' over my shoulder, and took three leaps down to the front gate.

Glen was driving, with his father and Henry Denkler in the cabin beside him. Braden, Stuart and the dogs were in the back. Stuart leapt down, took my bedroll, and swung it up into the tray where Braden, on his feet now, was barely managing the dogs. 'Hi, Angus,' Stuart said, 'all set for the boat race?' He laid his hand on my shoulder, but his glance, I saw, went to the house, in case *she* was there.

If she was, she did not make herself visible.

I climbed over the gate of the truck and Stuart followed. We staggered, the dogs around our legs, and Braden, to make room for us, settled on the pile of bedrolls at the back.

'Get down, you stupid buggers,' Stuart told the dogs, and grabbing the head of one of them under his right arm, plumped down heavily next to Braden.

I sat opposite, drawing the other dog, Tilly, between my knees. Braden banged the flat of his hand on the cabin roof and we were off.

He had said nothing as yet. Now he looked at me, grinned, and pulled his hat down firmly over his ears.

'Hi,' I said. 'Cold, eh?' was all he said in return.

Stuart laughed. 'He's always cold, aren't you, Brade? The warm blood in this family ran out with me.'

Stuart was wearing an old plaid shirt frayed at the collar and with the sleeves rolled loosely at the elbow. No jacket, no woolly.

Braden, hunched into his thick turtle-necked sweater, made a face and looked away. A draught of cold air streamed over us as we rolled down to the town bridge with its drift of bluish mist and up to where the other ute, with Matt Riley and his nephew Jem and their dogs, was parked at the petrol station before the entrance to the highway. Matt Riley, the white breath streaming from his mouth, was out of the ute, checking one of the offside tyres. Jem was driving.

I had known Matt Riley for as long as I could remember, though we had never had a proper conversation. His wife Eileen was our ironing lady. Every Monday morning he dropped her off in his ute, and he was there when I got home, silent, drinking tea at our kitchen table, waiting to take her back again. She ignored his presence, laying aside the shirt she was working on to make me a malted milk.

I was fond of Eileen. She was full of stories, told in a language, all jumps and starts, that I had got so used to at last that it seemed the only language for what she had to tell. I had never asked myself what might be peculiar about it, or where it came from. As I never asked myself why Matt Riley was so subdued and retiring in our kitchen and yet so quietly sure of himself, and so readily deferred to, when he was inspecting tyres or setting right an unbalanced load.

As for Jem, he had been one of the big boys when I started school. In the same class as Glen McGowan. A dark, sulky fellow, I thought. Although he was a big boy he could neither read properly nor write. At fourteen he had gone off to become a roo-shooter like his uncle.

He was no longer sulky. Just big and silent, almost invisible. His Uncle Matt's shadow.

An hour later we had left the bitumen and were bouncing due west on a clay highway cut clean through the scrub. The sun was up and had burned off the early-morning chill. The dogs were alert but quiet. Braden, his knees drawn up, one of the dog leads round his wrist, was dozing, his head toppled forward under his hat. Stuart, after a bit, leaned across, unwound the lead and passed it to me. The big dog, Jigger, turned its head in my direction but did not stir. 'Good dog, Jigger,' I told him, roughening the gingery ears, 'good old boy.' He lowered his head and settled.

I was beginning to feel good. We were riding high up on the camber of the yellow-clay road, which had been washed by the rains so that it was all exposed pebbles with eroded channels on either side, then tough grass, then forest.

Stuart shook a cigarette out of the packet in the breast pocket of his shirt, dipped his head to take it between his lips. He offered me one. I shook my head. Smoke blew towards me. Sharp and sweet.

'Big day, eh, Angus?'

It was. He knew how long I had wanted this. To come out here, be one with the others, part at last of whatever it was. The sky above us was high and cloudless, as it is up here in winter. Stuart followed my gaze as if there was something up there that I had caught a glimpse of, a hawk maybe; but there was nothing. Just the huge expanse of blue that made the air so clean as it tumbled over us; as if all this – sky, forest, the warmth of the big dog between my knees – was part of the one thing, a consciousness – not simply my own — that belonged not only to the body I was in, back hard against the metal side of the truck, muscles flexed in my calves and thighs, belly empty, but also to something out there that I had melted into as one melts into sleep, and was infinite.

I did sleep, and was woken by Stuart punching me lightly in the shoulder. 'Wake up, Australia!'

We climbed down. The other ute was already parked.

We were at the little junction station where the Chillagoe line branches west into anthill country: a water tank and pump, a general store, and the two-roomed cottage-cum-stationmaster's hut. It was the established custom for parties going out to the Lagoons to stop here for breakfast, before going down to the general store to fill the emergency petrol cans.

'I'm famished,' Braden announced. It was after eight.

I agreed.

'Don't worry, son, you'll get a good feed here,' Matt Riley told me. 'Trust Miss Appin, eh, Jem?'

Like most of the older members of the party, Matt Riley had been stopping here for nearly forty years.

Suddenly in a storm of dust a dozen or so guineafowl darted out from under the house, which stood on three-foot stumps, and got between our legs and began to peck around the tyres of the trucks. There was a clatter of hooves, and a young nanny goat skittered down the stairs from Miss Appin's dining room, with three more guineafowl at her heels, and behind them Miss Appin herself flourishing a tea towel in her fist.

'Morning, Millie,' Henry Denkler called across to her, and took the hat from his stack of white hair and made a decent sweep with it. 'Mornin', Millie,' Wes McGowan echoed.

'Drat the thing,' Miss Appin shouted after the goat, which had propped in the yard ten paces off and with its wide-set, sad-looking eyes stood its ground looking offended.

'Garn,' Jem told it, and at something in his unfamiliar growl it started and fled.

'Good on you, lad,' Miss Appin told him. Then, reverting to her role as hostess, 'It's all ready, gentlemen. Eight of you – is that right?'

I knew about Miss Appin. She had been described to me a dozen times by kids at school who had been out here and known what to expect, but had still, when they came face to face with her, been startled.

Forty years before she had been a beauty. Her family ran the biggest spread in this part of the state. She was one of those girls that a young Wes McGowan or Henry Denkler might dream of but could not aspire to. The best horsewoman in the district, she had been to school in Europe, spoke French and had been 'presented' at Government House in Brisbane.

But at twenty, in a single moment, fate had exploded out of a trusted corner and turned her whole world upside down. A horse had kicked in all one side of her face, flattening the bony ridge above her right eye, shattering her cheekbone and jaw. Over the years, the damaged side of her face had aged differently it seemed from the other, so that they appeared to belong to different women, or to women who had lived very different lives. Only one of these faces smiled, but you saw then why a girl who had been so lively and pleased with herself might have chosen to live in a place where she saw no more than a few dozen people each week, and most of them the same people, over and over.

Miss Appin was responsible for changing the points on the line, and had turned her front room into the station buffet, where twice a week, while the two-carriage train waited and took on water, she served freshly baked scones and tea out of thick white Railway crockery, and in winter, breakfast to shooting parties like ours that called up beforehand and put in their order.

Two tables with chequered cloths had been laid for us. Otherwise, the small neat room was a front room like any other. There was an upright piano with brass candelabra and the walls were covered from floor to picture rail with photographs of Miss Appin's nephews and nieces, all of them known, it seemed, to Henry Denkler and Wes McGowan and even, though he was shy to admit it, to Matt Riley: family parties on lawns, the ladies with their skirts spread; young men with axes at wood-chopping shows or looking solemn in studio poses in the uniforms of the two Wars; other boys (or the same ones when younger) in eights on a sunlit river or standing at ease beside their oars; five-year-olds in communion suits with bow ties, or like baby brides in a cloud of tulle. Three or four guineafowl crept back, and flitted about under the tables. There was a smell of bacon.

'Come on now, Braden,' Miss Appin jollied, 'and you too – what's-your-name – Angus, was it? – I need a couple of willing hands.'

She ushered us into the little blackened scullery and we fetched back plates of eggs, a great platter of sizzling rashers, bread, butter, scones. We were ravenous, all of us. But when we were seated even Jem Riley, who was a rough fellow, ate in a restrained, almost dainty way, swallowing quietly, blushing at every mouthful in an effort to keep up to the standard set by Henry Denkler and Wes McGowan, which was clearly what they thought was due to Miss Appin's 'background'. As soon as he had gulped the last of his tea, Jem excused himself and bolted. He would drive their ute down to the store and fill the emergency cans.

Glen, in a high state of amusement at Jem's confusion, got to his feet, thanked Miss Appin with an old-world formality that delighted his father and which the McGowan boys could turn on quite effortlessly when occasion demanded, and went after Jem to help.

'So then, Millie,' Wes McGowan began, pushing back from the

remains of his breakfast while Braden and I tucked into seconds, 'what have you got to tell us about this *pig*?'

A seven-mile drive south of Miss Appin's, the old Jeffries place where the boar had been sighted was no more now than an isolated chimney stack in a pile of rubble and a steel windmill whose spindly tower and blades could be seen in the long grass off the north–south highway.

We drove in slowly – there was no longer a track – and parked in a clump of water gums. I was directed to take charge of the McGowan dogs, Jigger and Tilly, but also of Matt Riley's dog, Archer, an Irish setter as new to all this as I was and very nervous, though Jem assured me, as the dog rubbed against him and licked his hand, that he was sweet-natured enough if you handled him right. And it was true. When I leaned down and hugged him a little, he immediately shoved his nose into my groin. I settled in the shade of the water gums, but the three dogs, excited by the sense that something was about to begin, remained standing, heads raised, lean flanks trembling, pulling hard at the leash. It was just after ten. The sun was fierce, the long grass a wave of cicada-voices rising and skirling, then lapsing, then rising again.

Matt, with Jem as usual at his side, went off to do some scouting and it was confirmed. There was a pig, a good-sized one.

Wes McGowan, whose party this was, had ceded authority for the moment to the professional. He was seated now, sweating under his hat, in the shade of the Bedford, having a quiet smoke.

Matt Riley, meanwhile, had taken Braden aside and was giving him instructions, pointing across the open grassland to where the boar was holed up and sleeping in the sun, somewhere between the windmill and the darker treeline that marked the course of a creek.

The other old-timer of the party, Henry Denkler, had set up a folding stool, and with his hat drawn down and his .303 across his arm, was dozing, for all the world as if he was having a quiet snooze in his own backyard in town.

The others, Glen, Stuart, Jem, were squatting on their heels in the shadows behind me. Not speaking. All their attention, like mine, was on the group Matt Riley and Braden made, Braden the taller by a head, which was all Matt-talk, low-voiced and slow, no more, as I strained my ears to catch it, than a few broken sibilants at moments when the cicadas cut out.

Braden was nodding. Allowing himself to be sweet-talked into a kind of high-pitched ease. Yet another area in which Matt was a professional.

I glanced back quickly at the others.

They too had been gathered in. A moment ago, Glen and Stuart had been as tense almost as the dogs, out of concern perhaps for Braden — more family business. They were subdued now. Almost dreamy. As if Matt had worked his spell on them also, as he had done three or four years back, when they had been where Braden stood now.

I too had a place made for me, but it was up to me what I made of it. I held fast to the dogs, watching their shoulders quiver in expectation. Something of their animal sense that we were set down now in a single world of muscle and nerve, mind both present and dreamlike afloat, communicated itself to me, entered my fists, where they held fast to the twined leashes and took the strain of the dogs' forelegs and rump, ran back down my forearms to my chest and belly, set my heart steadily beating.

Matt had his hand now on Braden's shoulder and was singing to him – that's how I heard it. Slowing him down. Creating in him a steady state of being inside himself. In the eye that would sight along the barrel of the rifle. In the index finger that would gently squeeze the trigger. In the softness of his shoulder that would take the impact of the shot down through his spine, his buttocks, the muscles at the back of his calves to the balls of his feet where they were spread just wide enough to balance the six feet two of him squarely on the earth.

I wished that Matt was singing, in that low voice whose words I missed but whose tune I was straining to catch, to me, or to something *in* me. That he was discovering for me that state of detachment but deep immersion, beyond mere attention or nerve, that, once I had hit upon it, I might go back and back to – the sureness of something centred that I lacked.

I watched Braden and thought I saw it entering him. When Matt nodded and released his shoulder at last he would be fully equipped. They would go forward and the others would get up and follow, even Henry Denkler, waking abruptly from his doze as if even in sleep he too had been quietly listening. Twenty minutes from now, Braden would have it for ever. Even if he never returned to any of this, it would be his.

It was this, rather than the business of simply putting a shot into the brain of a maddened beast, that he had come out here to get hold of so that these witnesses to it – his father, his brothers, the professional, Matt Riley, Henry Denkler – would know he had it, that they had passed it on.

On some signal from Matt Riley that I failed, for all my tenseness, to register, Wes McGowan got to his feet, came to where I was sitting and leaned down. His big hand covered Tilly's skull, tickling her with his finger behind the ears. 'Angus,' he told me, 'I want you to stay back here with the dogs.'

I swallowed hard, nodded glumly. I'd known this was coming, and Mr McGowan, not to embarrass me by witnessing my youthful disappointment, turned away. I knew what he was doing. He was keeping me out of harm's way. But there was something else as well. If anything went wrong out there my inexperience might be dangerous, and not only to myself.

'Come on, boys,' I told the dogs, and I put my arms around Tilly, who turned and licked my face.

Glen and the others were on their feet now. Braden cast me a quick look and I nodded. I too got to my feet. The little party formed in three lines, Matt Riley and Jem in front to do the tracking, Braden, Glen and Stuart behind. They set off through the waist-high grass. Once again I would be on the sidelines watching, as I had been so often before when it was a matter only of the telling. I urged the dogs up into the tray of the Bedford and, scrambling up behind them, stood straining my eyes for a better view.

The shoulders and hats, which were all I could see above the sunlit grasstops, moved slowly forward. Twenty, thirty yards further and Matt Riley sheered off to the left. The rest of the party came to a stop. Waited. I could hear the silence like a hotter space at the centre of the late-morning heat. Big grasshoppers were blundering about. Flies simmered and swarmed. The dogs, on tensed hind legs, leaned into the still air, tautening the leash. 'Easy, Jigger,' I whispered to the younger dog, though he paid no attention. His mind was away up ahead, low down in the grass roots, close to the earth. 'Tilly,' I told the other, 'quiet, eh? Be quiet now.' My own mind too was out there somewhere. Beside Braden. Who would be sweating hard now, every muscle tense, preparing for the moment when he would move on out of himself. I saw Matt Riley, without looking behind, raise his arm.

'Quiet now, Tilly.'

I laid my hand on the old dog's quivering flank. The sky hung above like a giant breath suspended over the shifting light and shadow of the grass and I watched the hats, and below them the upper bodies, part the still grassheads as they waded towards the treeline. They were moving in dreamlike slow motion, Matt Riley still in front. 'What can you see now, Tilly?' I whispered.

They had stopped again. I saw Matt, still without turning, beckon to Braden.

He moved forward and Matt passed to his right. Braden was half a head taller than anyone else among them except Henry Denkler, who towered above the rest.

Matt raised an open hand, and I saw Braden lift the .303 very slowly to his shoulder.

The cicadas stopped dead in the heat. There was a sound, more like a happening in the sky I thought than a shot, and dozens of birds that had been invisible in the grass were suddenly in the air, wildly flapping.

There was a swift movement among the hats, then another shot, and the dogs were barking and straining so hard at the leash that I was almost pulled out of the truck, too busy shouting at them to shut up, and cursing and jerking at the leash, to see what was happening off in the distance, till there was another shot and I risked it, and saw the knot around what I knew must be the kill.

At that moment, a quarter of a mile to my left and well out of the vision of the others, I saw the two ancient carriages of the Chillagoe train come puffing across the horizon, pouring out smuts. It would have made its mid-morning stop at Miss Appin's, taken on water, and was now heading west into anthill country.

I could see Wattie McCorkindale, the driver, in the cabin, a tough nut of a man with tight grey curls like a woolly cap. I passed him each morning on my way to school, always in the same faded, washed-out overalls and carrying his black lunch tin. Beside him, in the cabin, was his mate, Bill Yates.

For a moment, as it swung close, I heard the hammering of the wheels on the track, then it swung back again, and it was the little gated platform at the rear that was facing me, and a woman was there, shading her eyes as she peered into the sunlight. She must have heard the shots. I was tempted to wave. I wondered what she must be making of all this. The shots, then a lone boy standing in the tray of a ute, in a grassfield in the middle of nowhere, holding hard to a mob of crazy hounds. Meanwhile, the party of pig-shooters, in a tight bunch now, was coming back.

Braden was flushed and looked innocently pleased with himself. Stuart and Glen were on either side of him. They had never seemed such a close and affectionate group.

I let the dogs loose. They leapt down from the ute and went running in excited circles around him. He dropped to one knee; happy, I thought, to be in a group where he could be the focus of another sort and exhibit an easier and more exuberant affection. He hugged Tilly, then Jigger, who was jostling to be gathered in, and they licked at his face and hands. Perhaps they could smell the pig on him, or some other smell he carried that was whatever had passed between him and the three hundred pounds of malevolent fury, in beast form, that had come hurtling towards him in the blood-knowledge and small-eyed, large-brained premonition of its imminent death.

He looked up, with his arms round Tilly, who for the past eight years had shared so many of our games and excursions, and in her own way, with doggy intuition, so many of our secrets. I saw then what a relief it was to him that all this was done with at last, and done well.

He had wanted it to go well for his father's sake as much as his own; out of a wish, just this once and for this time only, to be all that his father wanted him to be. All that Glen wanted him to be as well, and Stuart, because this was the last time they would be together in this way. When he left at the beginning of the new year it would be for a life he would never come back from; even if he did, physically, come back.

Except for Braden himself, I was the only one among us, I thought, who knew this. And because I knew it, I felt, as he must have, the sadness that was in Wes McGowan's pride in him, and in what he had shown of himself in front of Henry Denkler and Matt Riley, whose good opinion the old man set such store on. Had it crossed his mind, I wondered, that Braden, even in this moment of being most immediately one with them, was already lost to him?

I glanced at Stuart. He knew Braden just well enough to see what was at stake for the boy in that other world he was about to give himself to, though not perhaps how commanding it might be, or how clearly Braden understood that there was no other way he could go.

Glen saw nothing at all. It was inconceivable to him that a fellow of Braden's sort, his brother, who had grown up in the same household with him, could imagine anything finer or more real than what had just been revealed to him: the deep connection between himself and these men he was with; his even deeper connection with that force out there, animal, ancient, darkly close and mysterious, which, when he had stood against it and taken upon himself the solemn distinction of cancelling it out, he had also taken in, as a new and profounder being.

What surprised me, and must have surprised Braden too, was the glow all this gave him. It was real, in a way I think that even he had not expected: the abundant energy surging through him that lit his smile when he glanced up at me, then gave himself, all overflowing warmth and affection, to the dogs.

An hour later, with Matt Riley's battered ute in front and Matt himself hanging out the cabin window to guide us, we bumped and lurched into the Valley. Which wasn't a valley in fact but a waterland

THE VALLEY OF LAGOONS

of drowned savannah forest, reedy lagoons stained brownish in the shallows, sunlit beyond, or swampy places, half-earth, half-ooze, above which ti-trees stood stripping their bark or rotting slowly from the roots up. We parked beside an expanse of water wide enough to suggest a lake and with a good deal of leg-stretching, and expressions of satisfaction at the number of game birds in evidence, made camp, Matt directing.

Matt's precedence out here, I saw, had nothing to do with Braden's business with the pig or his 'professionalism'. It was something else. Very lightly ceded, the authority that Wes McGowan might have claimed as the getter-up of our party, or old Henry Denkler as its senior member and as mayor, had passed naturally, and with no need for explanation, to the younger man. And though no one had spelled it out I knew immediately what it was. I looked at Matt – at Jem too – with new eyes.

The land out here was Matt's grandmother's country, and the moment he entered it he had a different status: that was the accepted but unspoken ground of his authority. That and the knowledge of the place and all its workings that came with the land itself.

I had heard of this business of 'grandmothers'. The grandfathers were something else. Overdressed men with beards and side whiskers – farmers, saddlers, blacksmiths, proprietors of drapery shops and general stores – they had given their names to streets, towns, shires all over the North. You saw their photographs, looking sternly soulful and patriarchal, round the walls of shire halls and in mouldy council chambers; men who, in defiance of conditions so hard that to survive at all a man had to be equally hard in return (in defiance too of the niceties of law as it might be established fifteen hundred miles away, in Brisbane), had carved out of the rainforest a world we took for granted now, since it had all the familiar amenities and might have been here for ever.

In fact, they had made it with their bare hands, and with axes and bullock-wagons. Doing whatever had to be done to make it theirs in spirit as well as in fact. Brooking no question, and suffering, one guesses, no regrets, since such work was an arm of progress and of God's good muscular plan for the world. All that so short a time ago that Wes McGowan might well have been one of the children in long clothes you saw seated on the knee of one of those bearded ancients, or in the arms of one of the pallid women in ruched and ribboned silk who sat stolidly beside him flanked by her brood.

No one would ever have spoken of Matt Riley's 'grandfather'. That would have given something away that in those days was still buried where family history meant it to stay, in the realm of the unspoken. 'His grandmother's country' was a phrase that referred, without raising too precisely the question of blood, to the relationship a man might stand in to a particular tract of land, that went deeper and further back than legal possession. When used in town it had 'implications', easy to pick up but not to be articulated. A nod to the knowing.

Out here, in the country itself, though what it referred to was still discreetly unspecified, it was actual. From the moment we climbed down out of the trucks and let the light of its broken waters enter us, and breathed in its sweetish water-smelling air, and took its dampness on our skins – from that moment something was added to Matt Riley, or given back; and he took it, with no sign of change in the quietness with which he went about things, or in his understated way of offering his own opinion or disagreeing with another's. He had re-entered a part of himself that was continuous with the place, and with a history the rest of us had forgotten or never known.

It was a place he both knew and was a stranger to; so deep in him that only rarely perhaps, save in sleep or half-sleep, did he catch a whisper of it out of some old story he had heard from one side of his family – the other would have a different story altogether – and which, the moment he stepped into it, became a language he understood in his bones and through the soles of his feet, though he had no other tongue in his head, or his memory, than the one we all spoke.

At home I had been shy of Matt – mostly, I think, because he was so shy of me. Out here things were different. All those afternoons in our kitchen when, with Eileen at the ironing board, I had sat at the table and drunk the milkshake she had stopped to make for me, and ate my biscuit or slice of cake, though we had barely addressed a word to one another, constituted a kind of intimacy, out here, that could be drawn on and made to bloom. 'Com'on, son,' he'd tell me, 'I got somethin' you oughta take a look at.'

Alone, or with Braden, and always with Jem in tow, he would uncover for me some small fact about the world we were in – a sight or ordinary but hidden wonder that I might otherwise have missed. Brushing the earth away with a grimy hand, or delicately lifting aside a bit of crumbling damp, he would open a view into some other life there, at the grub or chrysalis stage, that in moving through several forms in the one existence was in progress towards miraculous transformation, and whose unfolding history and habits, as he evoked them in his grunting monosyllabic style, moved almost imperceptibly from visible fact into half-humorous, half-sinister fable.

He showed us how to track, to read marks in the softly disturbed earth that told of the passage of some creature whose size and weight you could calculate – sometimes from observation, sometimes from a kind of visionary guesswork – by getting down close to the earth and attending, listening. The place was for him all coded messages; hints, clues, shining particulars that once scanned, and inwardly brooded on, opened the way to another order of understanding and usefulness.

We ate early, before it was dark, Matt choosing what should go into the pot and Jem doing the chopping and seasoning.

Afterwards, bellies full of the cook-up and of the damper Jem had made to soak up the last of the gravy, we sat on as the ghostly late light on the tree trunks faded, and the trees themselves stepped back into impenetrable dark. Slowly the world around us recreated itself as sound. The occasional flapping, off in the distance, of a night bird on the prowl, an owl or nightjar. Low calls. Bush mice crept in, and tumbled with a chittering sound in the undergrowth beyond the fire, lured perhaps by our voices, or by our smell, or the smell of the stew and Jem's damper, the promise of scraps. There was the splash, from close by in the lagoon, of waterfowl, the clicketing of tree frogs or night crickets, a flustering of scrub-turkey or some other shy bush creature that had been drawn to the light, here in the great expanse of surrounding darkness, of our fire.

We sat. Not much was said. Talk out here, at this hour, was not so much an exchange of the usual observations and asides as a momentary reassurance, subdued, unassertive, of presence, of company and speech. The few words, an occasional low laugh, mingled as they were with the hush and tinkle of bush sounds, lulled something in me as I lay stretched on one side on top of my sleeping bag, face to the flames, and led me lazily, happily towards sleep.

The one jarring note was Stuart.

He too said little. But often, when I glanced up, I would find his eyes on me, dark, hostile I thought, in the glow of the fire. His beard had grown. He looked a little mad. Sometimes, when I dropped some word into the conversation, I would hear him grunt, and when I looked up there would be a line of half-humorous disdain to his mouth that in the old days would have been a prelude to one of his outbursts of baffled fury. Braden saw it too. But out here, Stuart kept whatever he was thinking to himself.

I stayed clear of him. Not consciously. But with Braden here it was easy to fall into the old pattern in which Braden and I were a pair and Stuart was on the outer. Perhaps he thought I had told Braden something – I hadn't. That I'd betrayed him in some way, and that we were ganging up on him. Then there was Matt Riley and the things he had to show. It simply happened that for the first two or three days we barely spoke.

It was my job, first thing each morning, to take a couple of billies down to the edge of the lagoon and draw water for our breakfast tea. Usually Braden went with me, but that morning, when I rolled out of the blanket and pulled on my jeans, he was still sleeping. I sat to tie my bootlaces, waiting for him to stir. When he didn't I took the billies from beside the fire and set out. The grass was white with frost. Pale sunlight touched the mist that drifted in thin low banks above the lagoons. Cobwebs rainbowed with light were stretched between the trees, their taut threads beaded with diamond points that flashed and burned gold, then fiery red.

Later, in the heat of the day, the bush smell would be prickly, peppery with sunlight. Now it had the freshness in it of a sky still moist with dew.

I climbed down the weedy bank and trawled the first of the billies through the brownish water, careful not to go too deep. I heard someone behind me, and thought it was Braden, but when I looked up it was Stuart who was swinging his long legs over a fallen branch and glowering down at me.

'Hi, Angus,' he said, 'how's it goin'?' His tone had an edge to it. 'You havin' a good time out here?' He reached down and I passed the first of the two billies up to him, then set myself to filling the second.

'Great,' I said. 'Great!'

'That's nice,' he said. He rested the billy on the log beside him. It sat there, balanced and brimming. 'I been hopin' to catch you an' have a bit of a talk,' he said at last. 'You been avoidin' me?'

I found it easier to ignore this than deny it.

'Aren't you goin' to ask me what about?'

'I suppose it's about Katie,' I said. I was wondering why, after so many weeks, he had broached the subject at last, and so directly. Did being out here make things different, relax the rules? Or was it that he had somehow come to the end of his tether? I emptied the second billy and for a second time drew it slowly across the surface of the lagoon. I had caught the little smile he had given me. Good shot, Angus. You got it in one. Satirical, I thought.

He waited for me to stop fooling with the second billy, then reached down and I handed it up to him.

'So,' he said, holding on to the handle but not yet taking its weight so that I was caught looking up at him, 'what do you know about all this, eh, Angus? What's happening? One minute everything was fine – you saw that. An' the next she's gone cold on me.'

'Honestly, Stuart, I don't *know* what's happened. She wouldn't say anything to me.'

He looked doubtful.

'I'm beat,' he said suddenly, taking the billy at last and hoisting it over to sit beside the other one on the log. I thought there were tears in his eyes. I was shocked.

'I just don't know what she wants out of me.'

'Stuart —'

'Yair, I know,' he said. 'I'm sorry, Angus.' He sniffled and brushed his nose with his knuckled fist. 'If you knew what it was like . . .'

I thought I did, though not from experience.

'The thing is,' he said, sitting on the low branch, his face squared up now, the cheeks under the narrowed eyes wooden, the eyes gazing away into himself, 'if this goes wrong it'll be the finish of me. For me it's all or nothing. If she would just have me – let *me* have *her* – it'd be all right – my life, I mean – hers too. If she won't I'm finished.

She knows that, she must. I told her often enough. So why's she doing it?'

I found I couldn't look at him. We remained poised like that, the question hanging, the open expanse of water like glass in the early light. He got up, took one of the billies, then the other, and set off back to camp.

I sat on at the bank for a moment. Then I crouched down and splashed cold lagoon water over my face, then again, and again.

Stuart's misery scared me. My own adolescent glooms I had learned to enjoy. I liked the sense they gave me of being fully present. Even more the bracing quality I felt in possession of when I told myself sharply to stop play-acting, and strongly, stoically dealt with them. Did I despise Stuart because he was so self-indulgent? Was he too play-acting, but not alert enough to his own nature to know it? I preferred that view of him than the scarier one in which his desperation was real. I didn't want to be responsible for his feelings, and it worried me that out here there was no escape from him.

He tackled me again later in the day.

'You know, Angus,' he said mildly as if he had given the matter some thought and got the better of it, 'you could put in a good word for me. If there was the opportunity.'

We were standing together on a shoot, just far enough from the others not to be heard, even in the late-afternoon stillness.

Braden was with his father and Henry Denkler, a little away to the left. The air was still, the ground, with its coarse short grass, moist underfoot. Steely light glared off the nearby lagoon. The dogs, in their element now, had discovered in themselves, in a way that impressed me, their true nature as bird-dogs, a fine tense quality that made them almost physically different from the rather slow creatures they were at home. They were leaner, more sinewy.

'You could do that much,' he persisted, 'for a mate. We are mates, aren't we?'

I turned, almost angry, and found myself disarmed by the flinching look he gave me, the tightness of flesh around his eyes, the line of his mouth.

I was saved from replying by a clatter of wings, as a flock of ducks rose out of the glare that lay over the surface of the big lagoon and stood out clear against the cloudless blue. But it was too late. I had missed my chance at a shot and so had Stuart. The others let off a volley of gunfire and the dogs went crashing through the broken water to where the big birds were tumbling over in the air and splashing into the shattered stillness of the lake, or dropping noiselessly into the reeds on the other bank.

'Damn,' I shouted. 'Damn. Damn!'

'What happened?' Braden asked, when we stood waiting in a group for the dogs to bring in the last of the birds. 'Why didn't you fire?'

I shook my head, and Braden, taking in Stuart's look, must have seen enough, in his quick way, not to insist. The dogs were still coming in with big plump birds. There were many more of them than would go into the pot.

'Good girl, Tilly,' he called, and the dog, diverted for a moment, gave herself a good shake and ran to his knee. He leaned down, roughly pulled her head to his thigh and ruffled her ears. The strong smell of her wet fur came to me.

I spent the rest of the day stewing over my lost chance, exaggerating my angry disappointment and the number of birds I might have bagged, as a way of being so mad with Stuart that I did not have to ask myself what else I should feel. Braden and I spent the whole of the next morning with Matt Riley and Jem, but in the afternoon I came upon Stuart sitting on a big log a little way off from the camp, with a scrub-turkey at his feet. I stopped at a distance and spent a moment watching him. I thought he had not seen me.

'Hi,' he said. I stepped out into the clearing. 'What are you up to?'

'Nothing much,' I told him.

I settled on the log a little way away from him.

'Listen, Stuart,' I began, after a bit.

'Yair, I know,' he told me. 'I'm sorry.'

'No,' I said, 'it's not about yesterday. You've got to stop all this, that's all. She won't change her mind. I know she won't. Not this time.'

'Did she tell you that?'

'No. Not in so many words. But she won't, I know she won't. Look, Stuart, you should leave me out of it, that's what I wanted to say. I don't know anything so I can't help you. You've got to stop.'

'I see,' he said. 'That's pretty plain. Thanks, Angus. No, I mean it,' he said, 'you're right, I've been foolin' myself. I can see that now.'

'Look, Stuart —'

'No, you're right, it was hopeless from the start. That's what you're telling me, isn't it? That I might as well just bloody cut my throat!'

I leapt to my feet. 'Shut up,' I told him fiercely. 'Just stop all this. Bloody shut up!'

He was so shocked that he laughed outright.

'Well,' he said after a moment, with bitter satisfaction. 'Finally.'

What did *that* mean? He gave me a look that made me see, briefly, something of the means he might have brought to bear on *her*. But she was harder than I was. I knew the contempt she would have for a kind of appeal that she herself would never stoop to.

I stood looking at him for a moment. I did not know what more I could say. I turned and walked away.

'I thought you were on *my* side,' he called after me.

I had heard this before, or an echo of it. I looked back briefly but did not stop.

'I thought we were mates,' he called again. 'Angus?'

I kept walking.

I did know what he was feeling, but he confused me. I wanted to be free of him, of his turmoil. The nakedness with which he paraded his feelings dismayed me. It removed all the grounds, I thought, on which I could react and offer him real sympathy. It violated the only code, as I saw it then, that offered us protection: tight-lipped understatement, endurance. What else could we rely on? What else could *I* rely on?

I walked.

The ground with its rough tussocks was swampy, unsteady underfoot, the foliage on the stunted trees sparse and darkly colourless, their trunks blotched with lichen. I had no idea where I was headed or how far I needed to go to escape my own unsettlement. Little lizards tumbled away from my boots or dropped from branches, dragonflies hung stopped on the air, then switched and darted, blazing out like struck matches where the sun caught their glassy wings.

I walked. And as I moved deeper into the solitude of the land, its expansive stillness – which was not stillness in fact but an interweaving of close but distant voices so dense that they became one, and then mere background, then scarcely there at all – I began to forget my own disruptive presence, receding as naturally into what hummed and shimmered all round me as into a dimension of my own being that it had taken my coming out here, alone, in the slumbrous hour after midday, to uncover. I felt drawn, drawn on.

I had enough bush sense, a good enough eye for recording, unconsciously as I passed, the little oddnesses in the terrain – the elbow of a fallen bough, a particular assembly of glossy-leaved bushes that would serve as signposts on my way back – to feel confident I wouldn't get lost. I let Stuart, seated gloomily back there on his log, hugging his rifle, hugging even closer his dumb grief, fade from my thoughts, and moved deeper into the becalmed early-afternoon light, over spatterings of ancient debris, crumblings of dried-out timber. Slowly, all round and under me, an untidy grey–green world was continuously, visibly in motion. Ti-tree trunks unfurled tattered streamers; around their roots a seepage like long-brewed tea.

I walked, and the great continent of sound I was moving into recorded my presence, the arrival, in its close-woven fabric of light, sound, stilled or moving shadow, of a medium-sized foreign body, displacing the air a moment as it advanced, and confusing, with the smell of its sweat and the shifting of its breath, the tiny signals that were being picked up and translated out there by myriad forms of alien intelligence. I was central to it but I was also nothing, or close to nothing.

In the compacted heat and drowsy afternoon sunlight, I could have kept walking for ever, all the way to the Gulf. It was time, not space, I was moving into. Years it might be. And there was more of it — not just ahead but on all sides — than I could conceive of or measure.

There was no specific point I was heading for. I could stop now, turn back, and it would all still be here. It was myself I was moving into.

One day, far off down the years, I would come stumbling back in my body's last moments of consciousness and here it would be: crumbling into itself and dispersing its particles and voices, reassembling itself cell by cell in a new form that was also the old one remade. I had no need to go on and actually see it, the place where I would lie down in the springy marsh-grass, among the litter and mould, letting the grass take the impression of my weight, the shape of my body's presence, and keep it long after I was gone.

Away back, when I first heard about the Valley and let it form itself in my mind, I had thought that everything I found unsatisfactory in myself, in my life but also in my nature, would come right out here, because that is what I had seen, or thought I had, in others. Kids who had been out here, and whom I had thought of till then as wild and scattered, had come back settled in their own aggregation of muscle, bone and flesh, and in some new accommodation with the world.

Nothing like that had come to me. I was no more settled, no less confused. I would bring nothing back that would be visible to others — to my father, for instance. I had lost something; that was more like it. But happily. As I walked on into this bit of grey–green nondescript wilderness I was happily at home in myself. But in my old self, not a new one.

I don't know how far I had gone before I paused, looked around and realised I was lost. For the last ten minutes I had been walking in my sleep. The landscape of small shrubs and ti-tree I had been moving through was now scrub.

I consulted the sun and turned back the way I had come. Minutes later I looked again and changed tack. It was hot. I had begun to sweat. I took my shirt off, draped it round my neck, and set off again.

Five minutes more and I stopped, told myself sternly not to panic and, standing with my eyes closed and the whole landscape shrilling in my head, took half a dozen slow breaths.

The shot came from closer than I would have expected, and from a direction – to my left – that surprised me. How had I gone so wrong? It was only when I had got over a small rush of relief that it struck me that after the first shot there had been no other. I quickened my pace, then began to run, my boots sinking and at times slipping on the swampy ground. When I arrived back at the clearing Stuart lay awkwardly sprawled, white-lipped and holding his shirt, which was already soaked, to his bloodied thigh.

'Hi, Angus,' he said, his tone somewhere between his old, false jauntiness and a dreamy bemusement at what had occurred and at my being the one who had arrived to find him.

'Better get someone. Quick, eh?'

He glanced down to where blood, a lot of it, I thought, was flooding through the flimsy shirt.

I fell to my knees, gaping.

'No,' he said calmly. 'Just run off as quick as you can, mate, and fetch someone. But be quick, eh? I'll be right for a bit.'

I wasn't sure of that. I felt there was something I should be doing immediately, something I should be saying that would make him feel better and restore things, maybe even cancel them out, and I was still nursing this childish thought as I sprinted towards the camp. Something I would regret for ever if he bled to death before I got back. *Was* he bleeding to death? Could a thing like that just happen, without warning, out of the blue?

In just minutes I had shouted my breathless announcement and we were back.

He was still sitting, awkwardly upright, his back against the log. I took in the rifle this time. It lay on the ground to his right. There was also the heap of dull black feathers that was a scrub-turkey. He was no longer holding the soaked rag to his outflung leg. A pool was spreading under him. He was streaming with sweat. Great drops of it stood on his brow and were making runnels down his chest.

'It's all right, Dad,' he said weakly when the old man and Matt and the others reached him. 'Bugger missed.'

It took me a moment to grasp that it was the bullet he was referring to.

They got his boot off and Matt slashed the leg of the scorched and bloodied jeans all the way to the crotch and worked quickly to apply a tourniquet. 'You'll be right,' he told Stuart. 'Bugger missed the main artery, you're a lucky feller. Bone too.' Blood was seeping out between his hands. There was a smell that made me squeamish. Seared meat. Stuart, bluish-white around the mouth, was raised up on his elbows and staring, fascinated by the throbbing out of the warm life in him. Like a child who has borne a bad fall manfully, but bursts into tears at the first expression of sympathy, he seemed close to breaking.

I was dealing with my own emotions.

I had seen Stuart stripped any number of times, in the changing room at the pool, in the noise and general rough-house of the showers afterwards. A naked body among other naked bodies, with clear water streaming over it and a smell of clean soap in the air, is bracing, functional, presents an image too common to be remarkable or to draw attention to itself. But a single ravaged limb thrust out in the dirt, the soaked denim of the jeans that covered it violently ripped and peeled away, black hairs curling on the hollow of the thigh and growing furlike close to the groin, has a brute particularity that brought me closer to something exposed and shockingly intimate in him, to the bare forked animal, than anything I had seen when he stood fully naked under the shower. I was shaken. His jockeys, where they showed, sagged, and were worn thin and greyish. A trail of blood, still glistening wet, made its way down the long ridge of the shank bone.

Not much more than half an hour ago I had walked out on him. Exasperated. Worn down by the demands he put on me. At the end of my patience with his turmoil, the poses he struck, his callow pretensions to martyrdom. Now I was faced with a shocking reality. It was Stuart McGowan's blood I was staring at. What impressed me, in the brute light of day, was its wetness, how much there was of it, the alarming blatancy of its red.

He caught the look on my face, and something in what he saw

there encouraged him back into a bravado he had very nearly lost the trick of.

'Angus,' he said. He might just have noticed me there in the tense crowd around him and recalled that I was the one who had found him. 'Waddya think then?' He managed a crooked smile, and his voice, though strained, had the same half-jokey, half-defensive tone as when on those early visits to my sleepout he had picked up one of my books and asked, 'So what's this one about?'

As if on this occasion too he were faced with a puzzle on which I might somehow enlighten him, and in the same expectation, I thought, of being given credit for the seriousness of his interest.

A smile touched the corner of his lips.

He was pleased with himself!

At being the undoubted centre of so much drama and concern. At having done something at last that shocked me into really looking at him, into taking him seriously. The wound was worth it, that's what he thought. All it demanded of him was that he should grit his teeth and bear a little pain, physical pain, be a man; he had all the resources in the world for that. And what he gained was what he saw in *me*. Which, when I got back, I would pass on to her, to Katie. When she was presented with the facts – that hole in his naked thigh with its raw and blackened lips, the near miss that had come close to draining him of the eight pints of rude animal life that was in him – she would have to think again and accept what she had denied: the tribute of his extravagant suffering, the real and visible workings of his pure, bull-like heart. He had done this for *her*!

'OK,' Matt Riley was saying. 'That's the best we can do for now.'

He got to his feet, rubbed his hands on the cloth of his thighs and told Jem: 'You – Jem – we'll need some sort of stretcher to get 'im to the truck. See what you can knock up.' Then, quietly, to Wes McGowan: 'The quicker we get 'im back to town now the better. It's not as bad as it looks. Bullet went clean through. Bugger'll need watchin', but.'

It took me a moment to grasp that what was being referred to this time was the wound.

In all the panic and excitement around Stuart, I had lost sight of Braden. He was hunched on the ground a little way off, his back to Stuart and the rest, his head bowed. I thought he was crying. He wasn't, but he was shaking. I squatted beside him.

'You OK?' I asked. I thought he hadn't heard me. 'It's just a flesh wound,' I told him. 'Nothing serious. He's lost a bit of blood, but.'

He gave a snort. Then a brief contemptuous laugh.

Was that what it was? Contempt?

He thought Stuart had done it deliberately! I was astonished. But wasn't that just what I had assumed a moment back, when I told myself 'He's done this for her'?

I touched Braden lightly on the shoulder, then got up and turned again to where Stuart, wrapped in a blanket now and with his eyes closed, but still white-lipped and sweating, lay waiting for the pallet to be brought.

I told myself that it had never occurred to me that he would go so far. It was too excessive, too wide of what was acceptable to the code we lived by. An hysterical girl might do such a thing but not a man, not Stuart McGowan's sort of man. But at the edge of that I was shaken. Maybe what I thought I knew about people – about Stuart, about myself – was unreliable. I looked at Stuart and saw, up ahead, something that had not come to me yet but must come some day. Not a physical shattering but what belongs to the heart and its confusions, the mess of need, desire, hurt pride, and all the sliding versions of himself as lover triumphant, then as lover rejected and achingly bereft, that had led him to force things – had he? – to such lurid and desperate conclusions.

I considered again the nest of coppery hair he sported in the scoop of his underlip.

When it first appeared I had taken it, in a worrying way, as a dandified affectation, out of character with the Stuart I knew. I was less ready now with my glib assumptions. What did I know of Stuart McGowan's 'character' as I called it? Of what might or might not belong to it?

After a moment he opened his eyes, caught me watching, and in an appeal perhaps to some old complicity between us that for a good time now had been under threat, but which the shock of his near miss had re-established, he winked. Only when I failed to respond did it strike him that he might have miscalculated.

He struggled to one elbow, his head tilted, his brow in a furrow, and grinned, but sheepishly, as if I had caught him out in something furtive, unmanly. 'So how's tricks, Angus? How's it goin'?' he enquired. 'You OK?'

This time I did not turn my back on him, but I did walk away, even while I stood watching. Jem and Glen had come up with their makeshift stretcher, and Matt Riley and his father, with Henry Denkler directing, rolled him on to it, all of them quieting his sharp intakes of breath with ritual assurances, most of them wordless. For some reason, what I remember most clearly is the three-day grime on the back of Glen McGowan's neck as he bent to settle Stuart. And through it all, deep in myself, I was walking away fast into a freshening distance in which my own grime was being miraculously washed away.

Walking lightly. The long grass swishing round my boots as the sparse brush drew me on. Into the vastness of small sounds that was a continent. To lose myself among its flutings and flutterings, the glow of its moist air and sun-charged chemical green, its traffic of unnumbered slow ingenious agencies.

An hour later we had loaded up and were on our way home: Stuart well wrapped in an old quilt, laid out in the tray of the McGowans' ute with his father to tend him, Glen driving, and Henry Denkler, who seemed troubled and out of sorts, in the cabin beside him. Braden and I, seated high up on a pile of bedrolls and packs, rode in the back of Matt Riley's beaten-up ute with the guns, a mess of dogs and all our gear.

I sat, my back to the side of the truck, with Tilly between my knees, leaning forward occasionally to hug her to me, and receiving in return a soulful, brown-eyed look of pure affection. How straightforward animals are, I thought. As compared to people, with their left-handed unhappy agendas, their sore places hidden even from themselves.

I thought uneasily of Stuart, bumping about now in the other ute as it wallowed through waist-high grass down the unmarked track; still believing, perhaps, that Katie would be impressed by the badge of a near fatality he would be wearing when we got back.

Would she be? I didn't think so, but I could no longer be sure. She kept eluding my grasp. As Stuart had. And Braden.

I glanced across at him. He had pushed his hat off, though the cord was still tight under his chin, and his eyes were narrowed, his cheeks taut as he grasped the side of the ute with one hand to steady himself against its rolling and stared into space. After a moment, aware of my scrutiny, he turned, and for the first time in a while he smiled his old wry smile, which meant he had returned, more or less, to being relaxed again. Inside his own head. But not in a way that excluded my being in tune with him. I sat back, giving myself up to the air that came streaming over the cabin top as the ute emerged at last on to bitumen, turned north and put on speed.

We were less than thirty miles from home now. The land was growing uneven. Soon there would be canefields on either side of the steeply dipping road, dairy farms smelling of silage, and little smooth-crowned hills that had once been wooded and dark with aerial roots and vines, till the loggers and land-clearers moved in and opened all this country to the sky, letting the light in; creating a landscape lush and green, with only, in the gully breaks between, a remnant of the old darkness and mystery, a cathedral gloom where a smell of damp-rot lingered that was older than the scent of cane flowers or the ammoniac stench of wet cow flop, and where creatures still moved about the forest floor, or hung in rows as in a wardrobe high up in the branches, or glided noiselessly from bough to bough.

I must have nodded off. When I looked up, we were already speeding through settlements I recognised and knew the names of: wooden houses, some of them no more than shacks, set far back and low among isolated forest trees, the open spaces on either side of the bitumen strip narrowing so quickly that what there was of a township – a service station, a Greek milk bar and café – was gone again before you could catch the name on a signpost or register the slightly different smell on the air that signified settled life and neighbourliness.

I loved all this. But Katie was right. I too would leave. As she would, as Braden would.

He met my eye now and then, as the ute swung out to pass a slower vehicle and we had to reach for the side and hang on to steady ourselves, but I was less certain now that I could read his looks. He had already begun to move away.

The difference was, I thought, that he, like Katie, would not come back. But for me there could be no final leaving. This greenish light, full and luminous, always with a heaviness in it that was a reminder of the underlying dark – like the persistent memory, under even the most open of cleared land, of the ancient gloom of rainforests – was for me the light by which all moments of expectation and high feeling would in my mind for ever be touched. This was the country I would go on dreaming in, wherever I lay my head.

We were bounding along now. Sixty miles an hour. From the cabin of the truck, Jem Riley's voice, raw and a little tuneless, came streaming past my ear. 'Goodnight, Irene,' was what he was singing, 'I'll see you in my dreams.'

Braden took it up and grinned at me. I followed. A doleful tune, almost a dirge, full of old hurt, that people were drawn to sing in chorus, as if it were the sad but consoling anthem of some loose republic of the heart, spontaneously established, sustained a moment, then easily let go. Before we were done with the last of it the quick-falling tropical night had come. A blueness that for the last quarter of an hour had been gathering imperceptibly round fence posts and in the depths of trees had swiftly overtaken us, with its ancient smell of the land and its unfolding silence that was never silence. 'Goodnight,' we sang at full belt, foolishly grinning, 'goodnight, goodnight, I'll see you in my dreams.'

JESUS WANTS ME FOR A SUNBEAM

Peter Goldsworthy

'*In us we trust.*' JOHN BERRYMAN

1

RICHARD AND LINDA. Benjamin and Emma. To outsiders, the Pollards seemed more a single indivisible organism than four separate members of a family: a symmetrical unit.

Examined from any angle that unit presented the same number of faces to the world: mirror faces, crystal faces. Two adults, two children. Two females, two males. A father, a mother. A son, a daughter.

Simple statistics, perhaps — unimportant, even trivial, in themselves — but to Rick and Linda, in love with each other and in love with their children, they were an emblem of something larger: of the balance and self-sufficiency of their lives. It seemed to the young parents that not much else was needed, that *any* thing else — a third child, a live-in grandmother, a dog, a cat, even a pet rock — would be somehow excessive, and unbalancing.

'One of each,' friends remarked, enviously, after the birth of their second. 'You're so *lucky*.'

Linda always feigned chagrin at this: 'Credit where credit's due, please — it took years of careful planning.'

She was not entirely joking. If their good fortune was not exactly planned, it was, she felt, at least deserved. It was earned.

More symmetries emerged as the years passed, equally unplanned – or at most half-planned. Often these were merely whimsical: that both adults were Capricorns, both children Sagittarians. Other symmetries seemed more significant, or meaningful. Or even useful: that father and daughter were left-handers, mother and son orthodox, would surely make for exciting family doubles on the tennis court in future years.

The more such harmonious shapes came to light, the more both parents actively sought them out. It became a family game, from which data that didn't fit were excluded, or conveniently ignored: that both children had been dealt their father's mud-brown eyes, for instance.

Their mother's were blue: a pale sky-blue.

Rick and Linda had been happy themselves as children, sheltered in the leafier avenues of the city. They came from solid families, grew up in nice suburbs, attended good schools. Solid, nice, good: these were the specifications of their world, largely interchangeable, universally applicable. They met at a suburban Public Library, as teenagers, studying for final school exams, and felt their way cautiously into love. They discovered sex, equally cautiously, through each other, and only through each other: a slow, almost courtly process of escalating excitements spread over many months. Even after several dozen of those months, Linda would still involuntarily cover her face with her hands at the moment of greatest pleasure, as if shamed by that pleasure, and its sign: the crimson flush that spread across her cheeks and neck.

They married while still at University. It seemed a precipitate step, the first missed beat in a measured rhythm. Both sets of parents were agreed on this – but the young couple, pimple-spotted, barely escaped from their teens, smiled their way past any objections. Strengthened by each other, they had grown immune to parental advice – they could, they found, outlast it. Their constant physical contact – twined fingers, pressed thighs, stolen kisses – seemed to fuse them ever more closely together, amoeba-like, doubling their intelligence and resolve. Both now knew that they were halves of something bigger, that their lives before – their 'previous lives', Rick joked – had been incomplete.

They had married in St Paul's, Linda's parish church. They chose the recently arrived Reverend Cummings as celebrant – a young student-priest, or priest-intern whom Linda had met through the church Youth Group – rather than the older rector whom her parents preferred. John Cummings was their own age; he had permitted a revised set of vows in which both partners promised to love, honour and cherish, but from which the ancient asymmetrical duty of wifely obedience had been removed.

The young couple had salvaged a few dusty, spidery pieces of furniture from the cellars and back sheds of their reluctant families, and rented a small student-flat in the inner city suburbs. To the two families it seemed that their children were still playing at being grown-ups, that their tiny, cramped flat was not far removed from the dolls' houses and backyard cubbies of a few short years before. Both sets of parents offered the support of weekly meals, and a monthly allowance. 'Pocket-money' was the term the two fathers preferred, as if the words might somehow preserve a childlike dependence.

At times, as if bidding against each other in some auction of allegiance, they even offered help with house-cleaning and laundry.

'You won't have *time* with all your studies, dear,' Rick's mother urged her new daughter-in-law. 'Why don't I pick up a laundry basket each week?'

'Rick does the laundry, Mother,' Linda said, a little smugly. 'You'll have to speak to him.'

The older woman was incredulous: '*Rick* does the laundry? But he's never washed a thing in his life.'

'He's a quick learner.'

To Rick and Linda it was the beginning of a shared adventure. Snuggling to sleep each night after love-making, it seemed terrible to both of them to have been forced to sleep all those years apart, alone, in a narrow child's bed. It seemed like something out of Dickens, Linda joked: a cruelty that happened to orphans. Each evening after lectures they took long walks together through their new neighbourhood, holding hands. Each night they shared a steaming, brimming bath. After making love, they often read passages to each other from their favourite books, which were, increasingly, the same books. Over breakfast, they chose items from the newspaper which they also read aloud, as if feeding each other handpicked delicacies. They packed frugal student-lunches which they ate on the library lawns together between lectures. Each Saturday they played mixed doubles in the local Club competition, each Sunday they pedalled their pushbikes – their old school bikes, refurbished – long-distance, visiting families and friends. Their physical resemblance to each other – near-identical height and body-build – seemed to become more pronounced through those first years of marriage, as if eating the same food, and sharing the same exercise caused an even closer convergence of body types. Without exactly planning it, Rick permitted his hair to grow a little longer, Linda cropped hers shorter; they chose, independently, similar gold-rimmed glasses. They often wore each other's T-shirts, and even, at a stretch, before the birth of Ben, each other's jeans.

Their shoe sizes alone refused to converge, although lying together in bed – naked, limb-entwined – they would occasionally compare bare feet, and pretend, playfully, that there had been some shrinkage or enlargement.

'Is that your foot or mine?'

'Wriggle your toes.'

'It must be mine – but it doesn't *look* like mine. Is it my right foot or my left foot?'

'Perhaps you should have them engraved.'

'Left and Right?'

'Love and Hate – like bikies have engraved on their fists.'

'Which is the Love Foot?'

'Let's find out.'

Two years of such bliss followed the wedding – the years before the birth of Ben, their first child – but when they looked back on those two years later, their lives still seemed to be lacking something. Even the memories of those early days of awkward, thrilled sexual discovery faded, even the milestone of their graduation from university, and their first appointments as teachers in the same suburban high school, now also seemed to belong to a previous life: Life Before Ben.

The birth was premature, the labour difficult, the baby undersize. Afterwards, Rick sat on the edge of his wife's bed, holding the tiny, scrawny bundle with great care.

'He's very beautiful,' he said, 'for a frog.'

Linda clutched at her sore stomach, groaning with joy: 'Don't make me laugh, *please*.'

The baby refused to sleep. He sniffled and wheezed. He regurgitated more food than he ate, but still filled an endless procession of nappies at the other end of his sewer, refuting all known laws of the conservation of matter. And, always – and more always at night – he cried. He *screamed*. To Rick and Linda, still surprised to find themselves parents, energised by astonishment and excitement, these trials seemed no more than rites of passage, small sufferings that were more ritualised pleasure than pain: trials half dreaded but also half hoped-for, expected, *imagined*, and therefore surmountable. Once again there was no end of outside help: both pairs of grandparents competed with offers of daily child-minding. Linda's mother, a volunteer worker for Meals-on-Wheels, once even dropped off a spare meal for the young couple at the end of her weekly round among the pensioners and disabled.

'Leftovers from the kitchen,' she explained, defending this small corruption. 'We would only have thrown it out.'

It was thrown out, after she had left, behind her back. The thought counted, Linda declared, even if the food was inedible.

The world that surrounded the young family seemed charmed; every face that turned towards them was smiling, wishing them well, offering help. Their neighbours – Greeks, mostly, in their inner-city suburb – showered them with baby gifts, and honey-cakes, and pastries drenched with icing sugar, and incomprehensible advice.

'He's so ugly!' one black-clad widow peered into the stroller and declared, loudly, to persuade the Evil Eye the baby was not worth troubling with, and the phrase soon became a refrain, and then, after a month or two, a pet name.

'Your turn to bath Ugly.'

'Ugly needs his nappy changed.'

At school, their fellow teachers were benignly tolerant of late arrivals and missed classes. Even the occasional hurried escape from a Church sermon with a howling baby on Sundays was warmed by the glow of a hundred tolerant, knowledgeable faces – and a pause and patient smile from young Reverend Cummings high in the pulpit.

His boyish, slightly podgy smile seemed to bestow on them God's personal, unspoken benediction.

2

Their world was charmed and protected, but not ignorant: news from beyond the municipal limits filtered through. That the lives of others might not be so charmed was clear to them, at least in abstract. They dropped generous donations into the church Christmas Bowl and Easter Appeal each year; they fostered a World Care child in Bangladesh after the birth of Ben, and after Emma's birth fostered another in Ecuador.

Once a year a Christmas card and letter arrived from each child, written with obsessive neatness in Spanish, or the weird extra-terrestrial script of Bengali. Typed, misspelled English translations always accompanied both letters, their tones identically flat and formulaic despite their separate origins, as if written by the same child, or by the same computer. Snapshots were sometimes clipped to the letters, and perhaps these were also of the same child: a small bony waif, dressed in ill-fitting Best Clothes, probably an older sibling's, posed in front of a squalid shanty, half Kim, half Oliver Twist.

They decided not to answer these letters. It seemed demeaning, even humiliating to compel a child to write thank you letters, to report annually to its benefactors — to beg, in essence. It seemed best to keep at some sort of distance. They sought no gratitude. Nor did they seek knowledge. Their quarterly donation was to *prevent* misery, not to learn about it. The payments were debited, automatically, invisibly, against their bank account.

'We do more than most,' Linda argued. 'We shouldn't have to wear a hairshirt as well.'

'You don't think we're sticking our heads in the sand?'

'I can't see the point in torturing ourselves with details. It won't change anything.'

After the birth of Emma she refused, suddenly, to go to movies for similar reasons — disturbed, she explained, by their increasing violence. The announcement, again, caused no argument from her husband — their minds, moving in tandem on most issues, had converged again on this. She had merely put their joint thought into words.

The thought was waiting to be spoken by one of them, its final choice of mouth was unimportant.

To some extent the film boycott was academic: their two infant children permitted no time for movie-going. Ben reverted to his earlier, more demanding state with the birth of his sister: waking at night, refusing food, vomiting at will whenever the baby received too much attention. House-moving added another upheaval to his life. They had outgrown their narrow student house; with help from the four grandparents – a loan for the deposit – they took out a mortgage on a small villa a little further from the city, and a little closer to the golden suburbs of their childhoods.

Linda's boycott of the television news a few months after moving house was not so academic. The decision was reached, or cemented into words, on a late summer Sunday evening. The young couple had arrived home after a long day of tennis, tucked tired children into early beds – *trapped* them in bed, bound beneath tight sheets – and settled themselves in the television nook with shallow silver trays of Chinese take away. Was their mood too tranquil, too pleasantly weary, too resistant to any disturbance? The lead story on the news was surely no more horrific, or blood-spattered, than usual, but Linda shivered – suddenly, involuntarily – and averted her eyes from the screen.

'How horrible,' she said, and turned to her husband. 'Turn it off. Please.'

He hesitated, momentarily: the evening news was a ritual he enjoyed, a warm shower at the end of the day. Its actual content was somehow less important than the comfort of the form: a cathode-ray squirt of images, a steady horizontal stream that washed through his tired mind, beaming him up and away to other places in the world, places so far removed from his world that they might have been other planets. As he wavered, Linda seized the remote control and waved it at the screen; a talking head contracted to a bright pinhead, then vanished, a smooth-shaven genie sucked back inside its bottle.

'Why do they *show* things like that?'

For once he felt the stirring of an argument: 'Because it happens, sweetheart.'

'Why can't they show good news for a change? The million *good* things people do every day? They always choose the one bad thing.'

'Perhaps we should try to understand it.'

'How can you *understand* it? A man who murders his entire family, then himself!'

She shuddered again, as disturbed by her own blunt summary of events as she had been by the original story.

'Maybe he did it out of love,' Rick suggested, weirdly.

She stared at him, incredulous: '*What?*'

He watched the blank screen as if waiting for more information, trying to understand this odd germ of a thought, to *grow* it.

'Misplaced love,' he said, groping. 'If you're depressed, and the world is not worth living in, you want to save your loved ones from it. You want to protect them.'

He paused, caught her astonished eye, and added, hastily: 'Maybe.'

They sat in silence, stunned: Rick even more than his wife, mystified by the origins of these words that had jumped from his mouth, unpremeditated. With his chopsticks he poked a wad of rice into that mouth, and chewed, allowing himself a little thinking time.

Linda saved him from further inspirations; she came up with a more convincing theory: 'I think it's merely selfish. They want someone to go *with* them.'

Rick swallowed his food. 'Like the Egyptian pharaohs,' he said, 'taking their whole households into the pyramids, buried alive.'

Their thoughts were back in harmony.

'Or the rajahs in India,' Linda said, remembering a movie she had seen as a child, 'burning their wives on their own funeral pyres.'

She shuddered, then jerked up out of her chair as if disguising the shudder in a larger, more deliberate movement. Finding herself on her feet, she walked out into the hall, and softly, protectively, closed the doors to the bedrooms where the children slept.

'This is morbid,' she whispered as she returned. 'How did we get onto this?'

'The news.'

'Let's talk about something else.'

Her husband resisted one last time, momentarily; still tantalised, perhaps, by his earlier heresy: 'I know it's unpleasant, but should we turn our backs on the world?'

'If we can't change it, what's the point? I don't want to *know* about those ugly things. I don't see why I should have to.'

She watched him, waiting for agreement.

'We do what we can,' she reassured him. 'We do our bit. Why should we thrust our noses in it?'

She was right, he knew. You had to draw chalk lines, erect barricades. There was so much pain and misery in the world you would drown in it: a great ocean of pain, of which the cathode-ray tube sprayed only a few selected drops in their direction each night. With the zeal of a fresh convert, or a fresh runner in a relay, he took the argument from her and carried it further:

'Maybe we should sell the television. Or give it away. Get rid of it altogether. Especially with the children getting older.'

They watched each other for a few further seconds. At length Rick rose, and wedged open the back door. Without a word he unplugged the television set, carried it outside and heaved it into the back seat of his car. A theatrical gesture, perhaps – the disgraced television would sit there for several days, tamely buckled in a rear seat belt, before being traded in for a new sound system – but both felt somehow cleaner, even purified: a satisfaction akin to the sweet aftermath of spring-cleaning, or the riddance of vermin.

New routines quickly replaced the old. Their evenings were filled with music, with educational games – scrabble, crosswords, Trivial Pursuits – and, above all, with books.

The young couple had inherited a reverence for books, both had brought several tea-chests packed with books to the marriage: an intellectual dowry of children's books, old school texts, gift sets of Shakespeare and Shaw and Jane Austen and assorted Brontës, plus, from Linda's side, everything that Dickens had ever written: a metre-length, at least, of matching volumes, bound in calf, plus assorted school-paperback versions of the same. These had multiplied in the years since: each Christmas they received as gifts almost as many books as they gave. Their shelves – makeshift constructions of plank and brick – were crammed; unread books, many of them, but their presence alone was reassuring, their names were a kind of incantation, like the names of saints or household gods: small geometric household gods of learning and self-improvement and uplift; protectors against ignorance. The books had worn more sacred with time. They were dipped into, like the Bible, as sources of quotations, and poetry, and Trivial Pursuit clues – but seldom read.

Until now. Delivered from television, Linda decided they should read aloud to each other every night, as they had in their first days of marriage, before children.

'And as my father read to me,' she announced over a meal one night, and immediately rose and began tugging books from the shelves before turning to invite Rick to help, or even to agree.

'Where shall we start?' she asked.

'Anywhere but Dickens,' he said, teasing her.

She smiled, and squeezed the book she had already selected back into its narrow slot, and tugged out another.

At first there were frequent interruptions. Emma, placid from birth, slept unbroken from early evening to early morning – but her older brother insisted on staying awake with his parents. The television had often kept him tranquillised in the past, now new routines were needed. A war of attrition followed – a war of tears and nerve and bluff – ending in the parents' capitulation. Weary of running to the child's bedroom every few minutes, it simply seemed easier to have him with them, playing in the lounge, late at night. Listening to, or at least *hearing*, their book-readings also had a soothing, hypnotic effect on the child. His eyes drooped shut, his restless twitching ceased – often, oddly, at the end of a chapter, or on the last page of a book, as if cued by some subtle change in the tone of his mother's voice. Or was it some resolution in the music of the words themselves, words whose meanings were still largely beyond him?

'*The growing good of the world,*' his mother recited, '*is partly dependent on unhistoric acts; and that things are not so ill with you and me as they might have been, is half-owing to the number who have lived faithfully a hidden life, and rest in unvisited tombs.'*

Rick – if he was still awake – would rise and carry the sleeping boy to bed at the end of such passages; this was the sign for a general lights-out.

Isolated from the wider world, their small, shared life contracted even more tightly about their children, their board games and book-readings. Old friends from University, staffroom colleagues from school – many still single – were rarely seen. There seemed so little time. Linda had chosen to stay at home with Ben for the first year; Rick took leave without pay the next year while she went to work. The opposite pattern had continued with the birth of Emma. Rick had spent the year at home, mothering her; Linda went back to school.

'But what of Rick's career?' his mother summoned the courage to inquire one evening as she collected their weekly laundry.

'The family is my career, Mum.'

Linda added: 'In ten years everyone will share work like this, Mother.'

The young couple exchanged satisfied smiles behind the older woman's back. They felt themselves to be pioneers, ahead of their time, and relished their notoriety among less liberated friends. That Rick's mother still did the family laundry, and Linda's mother bestowed a weekly meal, went unacknowledged. The mothers wanted to help; Rick appreciated the extra time this permitted him to spend with his adored baby daughter. Emma was a small, serious child: slow and methodical in her movements, a watcher of games rather than a participant. Her nickname – 'Wol' – came from Rick, amused by his daughter's solemn owl-like appearance, wise beyond her years.

With Ben at kindergarten now for much of each day, Rick's life revolved around his daughter: reading stories, reciting rhymes, singing songs, playing games, finger painting, visiting local playgrounds and paddling pools – and each Wednesday taking her to the neighbourhood playgroup, sole father among a gathering of mildly discomfited mothers.

'It seemed a little . . . awkward,' he reported home to Linda after the first. 'Long silences.'

'They'll get used to you.'

He sat through the weekly coffee and carrot cake and largely ignored the gossip that soon began to fill the silences. The mothers might not have been there, he had eyes and ears only for his precious Wol, studying her interactions with other children, protecting her against their viciousness, excusing her own as over-tiredness – and memorising every detail to report back to Linda. And so within their family geometry a further symmetry, or mirror-reflection, was growing: the father was closer to the daughter, the mother to the son.

3

Emma's sore throat seemed trivial at first: another of the shared communal viruses that were swapped back and forth between the toddlers at playgroup like counters, or dice, in a board game. Ben, at school now, also brought home a regular supply of sniffly noses and sore throats to share with her. He had always been the sickly one; missing one or two days a fortnight of school, his alleged ugliness failing to ward off the mild evil of germs. Emma seemed made of tougher gristle – less complaining, more robust. Rick and Linda paid little attention to her symptoms at first.

But the swollen glands remained swollen; a blood screen hinted at vague abnormalities.

Their local doctor – silver-haired, silver-tongued – was reassuring as he studied the printout.

'I've seen numbers like this before,' he said. 'No cause for concern. Probably just a virus.'

'Could it be serious?'

He shook his head: 'Of course we'll repeat the test in a week or two. Just to make sure everything is back to normal.'

Rick and Linda exchanged glances: 'Then it *could* be serious?'

He smiled reassuringly, but the smile seemed to lack something: 'I can't see any point in worrying about it yet.'

They worried for a week: in small bursts at first, which lengthened and multiplied as the child failed to improve.

The repeat screen was equally ambiguous. The doctor, while conceding the figures on his printout 'might' not be as normal as he first thought, still refused to name any disease, or even nominate a short list of candidates. He filibustered smoothly for some time before Linda interrupted:

'If it might be something, *what* might it be?'

'It would be premature to say. There are many possibilities.'

'Serious?'

'Some serious, some not so serious. But that applies to any illness . . .'

Rick and Linda rose simultaneously, angrily; Rick demanded a copy of both test printouts which were reluctantly provided. From a payphone in the waiting room they made an urgent call, and drove immediately to the rooms of a specialist paediatrician: Eve Harrison, an old school friend of Linda's. Short, compact, quick-talking, Eve had been known for her frankness at school; she showed no hesitation in applying a label to the blood screens at first glance, a word Rick and Linda had already begun to sense, if only from the glare of its previous absence.

Like most parents, they had rehearsed over the years for that moment, emotionally: the moment they might hear the word leukaemia spoken to *them*, spoken *at* them. They had read the true stories, had tears jerked from them by films based on real-life events. They had grieved, vicariously, for other children: small strangers who were nevertheless part of the shared public property of parenthood. News of the illnesses of these others — friends of cousins of friends, or cousins of friends of cousins — spread as rapidly as jokes or gossip through a vast network of waiting, eavesdropping parents, in hushed, horrified tones.

'*Such* a lovely family.'

'Nothing can be done? Surely *these* days — with all the new drugs...'

Beneath the horror of such stories there was also, surely, a deeper half-hidden note of relief: that it wasn't happening to them, and theirs. Perhaps there was even an odd warped gratitude towards the victim, who had somehow — although this dark thought would never be put into words — saved everyone else by being chosen in their place: a statistical scapegoat, a statistical sacrifice.

For Rick and Linda there was also, at the end of that terrible week of worry, a kind of relief that it *had* happened to them, and theirs. Anything was better than uncertainty; the waiting had been intolerable, the fear of the unmentionable had almost come to be a desire for the unmentionable; its certainty, its *mention*, was at least a resolution. To finally hear the word spoken aloud provided a focus for worry, a definite enemy that they could now face, and fight, together, as a family.

A bone marrow biopsy the following morning gave an even clearer view of this enemy.

'Remission is possible,' Eve Harrison told them. 'But everyone who has this type dies of it, eventually.'

The young parents glanced at each other, more composed and prepared: 'How long?'

'The mean survival rate is three years. Fifty per cent of the victims are still alive at three years.'

They felt almost grateful again for these blunt figures: three years was better than, well, three months. They felt, after the initial diagnosis had taken everything away, that they had been given something back.

Emma sat on the thick carpet in Eve's small office, solemnly reading a brightly coloured picture book, ignoring their discussion. Three years was the length of her life to date: she was being offered her entire lifetime, repeated. Her parents sat watching her, breathing a little more easily. For the moment they could fall no further; they could even permit themselves a small ration of hope. A cure might well be found in three years. A marrow donor might even be found, although

Eve was as frank as always on this: odd bloodlines in Rick's family – a Finnish great-grandparent – had left the child with a rare tissue-type, possibly unique.

'Of course we'll type you both,' she said. 'And Ben. And all the grandparents, if they're willing.'

'Of *course* they're willing.'

'You'd be surprised – sometimes family members refuse.'

They were surprised to hear this, very surprised, but the issue was unimportant, and irrelevant to their overriding concern.

'I don't want to raise false hopes,' Eve said. 'I have to warn you that a match is very unlikely.'

Driving home afterwards Linda cried the tears she had been suppressing for days, but softly, to herself and to Rick, maintaining conversation as best she could, trying not to disturb the little girl strapped into the back seat.

'Whassa matter, Mummy?'

'I'm a bit sad, Wol.'

Emma stared out of the window, completely satisfied, as if her question had not required an answer, merely an utterance.

'I want an ice-cream, Daddy.'

'So do I, Wol.'

4

In the months that followed there was much for those wide Wol eyes to take in. The little girl's life now revolved about the hospital. Giant scanners periodically engulfed and disgorged her; sharp needles pricked her tiny thumb pads daily; drug combinations made her ill, or her hair fall out – made her, Rick joked once, bitterly, 'almost ugly'.

Mostly, hospital life was a life of waiting, in bright primary-coloured anterooms filled with picture books and soft toys. Her parents often wondered what she made of it all – what exactly was going on behind those wide solemn owl-eyes. At the age of three, her knowledge of death was limited. A pet goldfish had once been buried in the backyard with due ceremony under a small twig cross, then promptly forgotten. On another occasion, tears filling her eyes, she had chased away a neighbour's cat that was tormenting a spring fledgling on the back lawn. As if choosing to torment *her* instead, the cat had returned overnight and left a pair of tiny, stiff, inedible wings amid a scatter of soft down on the grass: a deliberate and malevolent gift, it seemed, for the little girl to find in the morning. Various species of squashed wildlife that lined the road to a beach holiday one summer had caused less misery – 'road pizza' Benjamin had called it, repeatedly, trying to shock his sister, but only making her giggle.

At four, during her first remission, there was a flurry of bedtime questions. *How old will you be when you die? Will you go to heaven, Mummy?*

The little girl had never appeared concerned by her illness while she was ill, but perhaps – her hair was growing back, and she was gaining weight – she now half-sensed that she was past it, and it was safe to ask such questions. The subject of death would disappear within weeks, Eve Harrison reassured the worried parents.

'It's just a phase. A normal, healthy phase.'

'But what do we *tell* her?'

'Tell her the truth. Tell her what you would like to hear in her place. These are normal four-year-old questions.'

Less normal was an awareness of her own mortality that emerged, obliquely, when signs of the disease returned the following year: a self-awareness that was bent, at first, into an obsession with the health of her grandparents, with the signs of age and deterioration of their bodies.

She burst into tears in the car, without warning, driving home, after a Sunday visit to Rick's parents.

'I don't want Grandma to die,' she blubbered.

Rick turned to face her, alarmed: 'She's not going to die, Wol – not for a long time. She's only fifty years old.'

'But her *hair* is so old.'

The child's own bald head – the scorched earth of chemotherapy – was concealed by a bright, batik scarf. Linda, who was driving, stopped the car; Rick climbed out and into the backseat with Emma, Ben squeezed over the gearshift into the front.

They drove on with the father nursing his daughter.

'No one is going to die, Wol,' he murmured. 'Not Grandma. Not anyone. Not for a long time. In our family everyone lives to be a hundred years old. *Every* one.'

But these were her own anxieties, self-anxieties, removed; they could not be reasoned away.

'Are you going to be cremated or buried, Grandma?' she blurted across the dinner table the following Sunday.

Forewarned, fully briefed, the grandmother – a youthful fifty-five – laughed, lightly: 'It's so far away I haven't thought about it, Wol.'

The small girl watched her solemnly for a time.

'If you're cremated,' she finally said. 'You might not have a body to wear in heaven.'

The adults smiled at each other above her head, allowing themselves to be amused, *willing* themselves to be amused – but breathing a little more easily when Emma pushed herself away from the table and slipped off to play.

The deeper question – the blunt question they had all dreaded – took several more months to find its way through this maze of detours and displacements.

'Am I going to die, Mummy?'

Linda had woken around dawn to find Emma standing at the bedside, gazing down at her. Early birds twittered outside, the first light of morning sneaked between the curtain chinks. She pulled aside the quilt, the little girl clambered up and in. Rick, waking more slowly, rolled to face them; the daughter lay nestled between her parents, her big owl-eyes glistening in the half-dark, gathering what little light there was. Her voice when she spoke was matter-of-fact, unafraid – having finally reached this destination she was far less concerned, it seemed, for herself, than she had been, months earlier, for the health of her grandmother.

'Will I go to heaven?'

'Of course. One day. Not for a long time.'

More questions followed: 'What will I do there? What will I do on my own? Who will look after me?'

She had clearly been preparing a list for some time.

'You won't be on your own, Wol. I'll already be there. Grandma will already be there. We'll all be together.'

'What if I can't find you? What if I'm not allowed to see you?'

'Why wouldn't you find us?'

'Because I've been naughty.'

A catalogue of tiny misdemeanors followed; she was easily reassured that none was unforgivable. Having emptied herself, methodically, of these preoccupations she fell asleep, leaving her parents facing each other, staring at each other in the half-dark, their warm breaths mingling, their thoughts desperately agitating.

5

'Worry achieves nothing,' Eve attempted to reassure the young parents. 'Worry is useless, a total waste of energy.'

There was nothing wasteful about Eve Harrison: her hair cropped short, her face free of make-up. Her clothes – plain smock, sensible flat-heeled shoes – also seemed blunt, functional, to the point. Unadorned.

But the two parents increasingly wanted adornment; they wanted to hear reassuring fibs, or at least half-truths. Their need for bluntness had passed; they now wanted *cosmetics*. Despite Eve's advice, they had also come to depend on worry. Worrying was far from useless, they sensed: the worry process was a restless working through of possibilities and permutations, an exhaustive examination of every path, every fork in the path. Rick, grown accustomed to insomnia over the years of Emma's illness, had come to think of those long hours of tossing and turning and worrying in bed as a search program: a brute search, like a computer chess game he had bought, as a birthday present to himself, some years before. The game had obsessed him. He had glued himself to the video display, fascinated, every night for weeks, as the program checked the consequences of every possible move, counted possibilities, eliminated dead ends in the maze of infinite possible endgames.

Worry was also a kind of fuel, he suspected: a higher-octane fuel, for a higher-temperature furnace. It raised the metabolic rate, it provided the energy that kept them going, that was channelled into *doing* things, into actual physical tasks: the keeping of temperature charts, the counting of bruises, the frequent phone calls to Eve, the trips to the hospital. It got them through the day – through the mundane routines of each day. It also got them through the weeks, and months, and years, powering more optimistic, longer-range tasks: the correspondence that Rick began with tissue banks and bone marrow registers around the world, Linda's volunteer work with the Make-a-Wish Foundation, and the Leukaemia Support Group.

At first resistant to these groups – unwilling to admit that Emma might ever come to need such wishes, or support – Linda was dragged along to an Annual General Meeting by another parent, a mother she had met repeatedly in the same waiting rooms, and found herself nominated onto the support group's fundraising committee. Soon she was immersed completely, finding a real satisfaction, almost a relief, in taking down the minutes, typing the monthly newsletter, Xeroxing and mailing copies. She was, she felt, at last helping her child, expending all that accumulated worry-energy usefully: a small cog in the wheel of Cure.

When the search for paths into the future ended in blind alleys, there was still the past to examine. The feeling was inescapable that they were somehow to blame, that it might even help if they *were* to blame. Had Linda taken some harmful drug during pregnancy? Drunk one glass too many of wine? Had there been something else in Emma's childhood environment – something chemical, or unnatural? Some toxin? If they could not blame themselves, they blamed others. Linda's father – a heavy smoker, two packs a day – came under suspicion briefly.

'It's such a filthy habit, Dad,' Linda berated him one Sunday, over a family meal. 'If you won't think of yourself, think of others. I'm not saying it has anything to do with Wol – but who knows?'

Rick, unwilling to criticise his father-in-law directly, and specifically, told a more general story.

'I was at a curriculum meeting a few weeks ago. In at Head Office. There was only one smoker in the room. Jenny Adams – the chairperson – asked him to put out his cigarette. When he refused, she stood up, leaned across the table and – I kid you not – spat on him.'

His father-in-law was incredulous: 'She *what*?'

'She spat on him.'

'But that's disgusting.'

'Maybe. I don't say I agree with it. But I think we'll see more of it. If he pollutes her, she said, then she was going to pollute him.'

Linda's mother, quiet till that point, but seething with a growing anger, finally spoke up.

'I feel that *you* have spat on your father,' she said to Linda, and through Linda also to Rick. 'Here tonight. You have spat on him in his own house. I don't like smoking any more than you, but to suggest it might have something to do with Wol – well, I think it's the most horrible thing you have ever said.'

Apologies followed, by phone, over several days; normal relations were gradually resumed.

Despite Eve's reassurances, and advice, such obsessions consumed the next few years, and consumed them at speed. If three years was to be their remaining time with their daughter, it was passing far too quickly.

'Remember those interminable Beowulf lectures,' Rick murmured in bed one night. 'I used to think if I had a week left to live I'd spend the entire week in Beowulf lectures. It would make the time last forever.'

'I could read it to you.'

Their older, gentler routines – nightly book-readings, weekend picnics – had become episodic, haphazard. Even church attendance was disrupted. At first, the boyish John Cummings and his ancient congregation had been discreetly supportive as word of Emma's illness spread. Now, when the family did get to church, it was such an event, and such a fuss was made of Emma – so much consolation and pity and even, once, public prayers, were offered – that it became an ordeal.

'Never again,' Linda vowed, as they drove away one Sunday.

Rick defended the young priest: 'He didn't mention her by name.'

'But he was looking directly *at* her. How could he do that? Without even asking us?'

The children sat in the back seat, listening. They had heard the prayers, absorbed the sympathetic smiles of the congregation – there seemed little point in excluding them from the discussion.

'Aren't we going to church anymore?' Ben asked.

'Not for a while.'

'But I want to go. Emma doesn't have to come if she doesn't want to – but I *want* to go.'

'We don't have time, Ben,' his father said, firmly.

Always more difficult than his placid sister, the boy now demanded even more of their attention, as if to keep his share constant, or proportionate. At times he seemed almost jealous of his sister's disease. Over the years he had been the sickly one, the designated patient, now he was forced to compete for the sickbed. Most mornings he complained of aches in the belly or chest or head. He frequently missed school, he insisted on accompanying the family to hospital, he demanded that Doctor Eve examine *his* ears or throat, listen to his chest.

On one memorable visit he even demanded that he, too, be given a needle.

Eve – grown tired of his pestering – was more than happy to oblige. She filled a syringe with saline solution, and attached the largest bore needle she could find. At the sight of that horse-needle, aimed in his direction, the boy changed his mind and fled from the room, amid laughter.

6

At six, approaching the three-year survival milestone, the odds seemed to have altered in Emma's favour.

'To have come this far,' Rick asked Eve, or perhaps begged her, during their weekly visit, 'surely gives her an even greater chance?'

Eve still had no time for false hope: 'It *might* mean she has even less. She has used up her allotted span.'

Her bluntness, which had once seemed an asset – if only because they knew she would never lie to them – on this occasion seemed merely cruel. Rick shivered, a sudden involuntary spasm; Linda reached out and touched the polished wood of Eve's desk.

Neither the protective magic of such gestures, nor the prayers offered up in church, could ward off the greater power of statistics, and the laws of probability. The disease returned a few months later; 'active treatment' was stopped shortly afterwards, after a last failure of response to chemotherapy. The phrase, and its coy replacement – 'palliative treatment' – seemed out of character for Eve Harrison: an evasion, which in itself told the parents of the seriousness of Emma's plight.

'The effects of further treatment would be worse than the disease,' she added, when pressed.

'There must be *something*.'

'We can offer transfusions if her blood count falls too low. We can control bleeding, and infections . . . But no more chemotherapy.'

Eve glanced down at her desk, at a sheaf of blood screens that she had surely checked several times before: another uncharacteristic avoidance.

'The time she has left isn't long,' she said. 'I see no point in making her suffer unnecessarily.'

The parents held each other's gaze, waiting for the other to act as spokesperson, waiting for one of their mouths to speak the thought.

'*How* long?' Linda eventually, reluctantly, asked

'A few weeks. Four. Six. It's difficult to be precise.'

Linda reached out her hand, Rick clasped it tightly.

'I promise that she will be comfortable,' Eve said. 'I promise that she will feel no pain. But that's all I can promise.'

7

There was no time for hysterics, or further recriminations. Even tears seemed a luxury, an indulgence that had to be postponed.

Until.

One question had to be answered rationally, and immediately: how to spend those last few weeks together, how to make them at least halfway happy. The idea of a Last Wish trip to Disneyland or Disney World in America – or even to the cluster of smaller, closer Lands and Worlds on the Queensland Gold Coast – was repellant to both parents: bread and circuses.

What did you do afterwards, they asked each other? After closing time on the last day in Disneyland, pushing through the exit turnstiles in a queue of weary parents and overtired children? Surely that was a kind of death itself, and to pin happiness on one last wish was to die two deaths.

'Imagine the flight home. Like riding a tumbril to the guillotine.

Much better to do nothing special. To spend the last weeks in our ordinary, everyday way.'

By the time they had argued this through – and changed their minds, and decided to override their squeamishness if it was Emma's wish – her weakness and fragility did not permit such long distance trips.

Or so Eve Harrison told them. Eve was still their sole confidante; for the moment they decided to keep all four grandparents in the dark, or half-dark; avoiding constant visits, constant fussing. Above all, they sought normalcy, they sought to restore the family games, the music, the book-readings of an earlier, happier life. Perhaps they also half-believed that a return to these routines might magically transport them back through time, or at least allow them to pretend that they were still back there, that the intervening horror had never occurred.

'You know what I miss most?' Rick whispered in his wife's ear one night.

They lay in bed together, spoon-nestled, having made love for the first time in many weeks, although more as an antidote for insomnia than out of love, or lust. The cure, like all others, had failed.

'What do you miss?'

'The opportunity to be bored. Like when we were first married.'

She almost laughed. 'I used to bore you?'

'Bad choice of words. You know what I mean. Having an empty mind every now and then. Not having this . . . *thing* always there, inside.'

'I miss how we used to read to each other. When Ben was a baby. How just the sound of the words would soothe him.'

'Sedate him, you mean.'

She shrugged in his arms. 'Perhaps we need such sedation ourselves.'

'Beowulf,' he suggested, and she laughed, briefly, then rose and felt her way to the door, and turned on the light. He watched her, naked in the sudden glare, standing at the bedroom bookshelves – every room in the house was filled with bookshelves – head tilted, reading the spines.

'Where shall we start?'

'You had finished *Middlemarch*,' he remembered. 'You were working your way through Dickens – again.'

'It's so long ago I can't remember.'

'*I* remember,' he said, and they both managed another small laugh.

'You're still not a fan?'

'I didn't like his last one,' he said, and they laughed again.

'We never read *A Tale of Two Cities*,' she told him.

'I saw the film when I was a boy. I must have been eight or nine – but I remember it clearly.'

Head still tilted, she searched the close-packed shelves as he talked on.

'My father took me. I was amazed – he never went to the movies. Sorry – the *pictures*. He always said they numbed the mind.'

'A man after my own heart.'

'Even more amazing – it was on a weeknight. We never went *any*where on weeknights. And suddenly he arrived home from work and announced he was taking me to the pictures. Just me. It was an old film – black and white. I can't remember who was in it.'

'Charles Darnay and Sydney Carton.'

'The actors in the film?'

Linda laughed; she had been teasing him: 'The characters in the book.'

He wasn't listening to her; he was back in time, reliving that glowing night: 'I still remember the last scene. The hero climbs the steps, the guillotine waits. He makes a very moving speech – or maybe he only thinks the words. And suddenly he's lifted above it all – the guillotine, the basket of heads, the bloodthirsty mob, it's all a long way away, far *below* him. I had goose bumps all over. I must have been about Ben's age.'

'I wouldn't take Ben,' she said. 'Nine is too young. It would give him nightmares.'

'It's not really violent,' he said. 'Not by today's standards. And it meant a lot to me – I'd forgotten how much. Maybe I'll take him to the movies again when he's older.'

He paused: they both sensed that they were talking about a child with a future. Perhaps they were already talking about him as if he were an only child. They had broken an unspoken rule: that it was unfair to their daughter to make plans that did not include her, that were beyond her.

'I know what the book looks like,' Linda said, as she continued to search the shelves. 'It's not part of the set. Olive-green binding – very old, a little tatty.'

'Maybe it's in the lounge.'

But she tugged the book from some deep recess, blew dust from the pages, then turned immediately to the last page, and began to read:

'*It is a far, far better thing I do than I have ever done; it is a far, far better rest I go to than I have ever had.*'

They sat, silenced, sharing the same thought: that each would willingly, gladly, take the place of their small daughter in the tumbril. And yet they were powerless. They would have donated a kidney or lung to save her – they would have donated both lungs, they would each have sacrificed a still-beating *heart* – but their bone marrow, the only gift she needed, spread plentifully through their bodies, in far, far greater quantities than they would ever require themselves, was useless, even dangerous to her.

8

In the following weeks Emma slowly became aware, again, of the existence of that tumbril in which she was riding, of the fact that it had turned a last corner, and the square ahead, and all it contained, had come into view. Had some developmental threshold been crossed in her growth? A spurt in the imagination, or brain size, which permitted her to clearly see the future, or the absence of future, for the first time? Or had she had come to sense, and be infected by, the desperation of her parents, which they always tried to shield from her? The attentions of her grandparents, fully briefed, finally, on the extent of her predicament, were a further cue. Her stoic, wise-owl manner vanished for longer intervals, and resisted jolting back to equilibrium. When she sat with her books, or paints, or drawing pads, her gaze was often fixed to one side, defocused.

Morbid fascination fuelled her talk at mealtimes: endless questions about bones, dust, ashes, cremation, coffins. She solemnly examined the blue-black bruises that appeared on her body, at times even measured those bruises with her school ruler in a parody of her parents' earlier obsession.

As the end also became clearer to Rick and Linda, they resumed church-going, choosing to look pity in the eye, to stare it down, to spurn it. In part this return to the fold was still a search for the routines of normality, an attempt to travel backwards in time; in part it was a last desperate reaching out – not for miracles, perhaps, but at least for answers. Each Sunday at St Paul's they huddled together in a back pew, in a far corner, wanting only a private, family worship, a communion between them and whatever God might haunt the old church. Privacy was not so easy: once again the Reverend Cummings insisted on intervening, mediating – translating – between them and that God. He asked for shared prayers from the congregation, mentioned their trials in sermons; and after Rick protested – politely, but firmly – began visiting them at home instead, uninvited.

'Don't forget the power of faith,' he exhorted over innumerable cups of tea. 'The power of prayer.'

Linda had reached exasperation point.

'I don't understand,' she said, 'why that would help. And if it did – what kind of God would insist on it? Why should we have to *beg* for favours?'

He sat back in an armchair – Rick's leather armchair, appropriated – and pursed his lips and pressed his fingertips together. More at home in his pulpit lecturing his flock on issues of social justice – poverty, land rights, unemployment – he seemed lost in the world of private, immediate pain. He might have been enacting a role, playing a part meant for someone older: a wise uncle, or grandfather.

'I don't want to sound glib,' he murmured, 'but if we knew all the answers – if knowledge was given to us on a plate – what would be the point of faith?'

'That's fine advice for us,' she said. 'But what do we tell *her*? Jesus wants her for a sunbeam?'

'Perhaps she doesn't want to be told anything,' he said. 'In many ways this is a far more difficult test for you.'

'What you are saying – this is a test? This was given to us as a test of faith? What's the answer? Is it an essay, or multi-choice?'

He paused before answering, shocked by her harshness. He licked his lips, his mouth opened and closed, without speaking, groping for an answer that was not quite ready. His was out of his depth. His avuncular manner had vanished, his eyes reddened, he was close to tears. He mumbled a few words about eternal peace, about Emma going to a better world, but they could plainly hear that his heart wasn't in it. He was of their generation, skeptical of the unknown. His heaven was on earth, and would be man-made, if at all.

'Remember the story of Abraham and Isaac?' he finally said, huskily. 'The Lord tested Abraham's faith by asking him to sacrifice his son?'

Despite his anguish, Linda's face purpled with rage, instantly.

'Fuck you,' she said. 'And fuck any God who would play such horrible games.'

Rick rose from his chair, unastonished by the words she had spoken, even though he had never heard her utter such words before, or even seen such an extreme of anger. The same feelings, if not the same words, were on the tip of his own tongue; there was nothing else that could be felt.

'Perhaps I didn't choose my example well. What I meant to say . . .'

'I think we've talked enough, John,' Rick said. 'We'd like to be alone.'

As they stood at the door, holding each other, watching the Reverend Cummings drive away for the last time, they realised suddenly how much they had aged in the past months, at a much faster rate than their household clocks and calendars had measured out. It seemed that this young priest, approximately their own age, now belonged to a still younger generation.

'It's up to us,' Rick said to his wife. 'No one can help except us.'

9

The priest's words of advice stuck fast in their minds, nevertheless, like a tune heard once in the morning that can't be shaken off, repeating, interminably, through the day. The possibility that it *was* somehow a test, an ordeal, a trial, was difficult to shake loose, if only because of its deeper implication: that therefore there must also be a solution. Their powerlessness was deformed into guilt, which was bent itself into over-attentiveness, into a smothery kind of love that the little girl was forced sometimes to turn away from, to *hide* from. Famine-thin, increasingly fragile, easily bruised, it was as if she sensed that her parents might cuddle her to death, or at least cuddle her back into hospital. She shut herself in her room for long periods, alone, and – it seemed to Rick and Linda, in their worst moments – betrayed.

'It's as if there's a wall there – we're on one side, she's on the other.'

'We can't help her – but I think she thinks we *won't* help her.'

The worry-program had bypassed one possible solution, or pathway, much earlier, but goaded by guilt, and self-blame, returned to it, was dragged back to it, again and again – although for some time neither discussed the path with the other, believing that for the first time in their marriage their thoughts had diverged too widely, that the idea was so outrageous, so *unspeakable*, that no two sane people would ever think it together.

Rick first spoke the unspeakable. They lay talking in bed in the small hours, trying, as always, to talk each other to sleep, to talk themselves empty, to talk out the day's accumulated worries.

'Maybe we should all go together,' he said, inserting the words suddenly, without warning, into a lull in a conversation about household finances.

'What do you mean?'

'Just that. We shouldn't let her go . . . alone.'

'You mean . . . we should go *with* her?'

Linda's tone was surprisingly calm; he peered at her through the half-dark, trying to read her face.

'You don't seem surprised,' he murmured.

'It crossed my mind too. I've thought of it several times. I've tried *not* to think it – it seemed too crazy.'

She shivered in his arms: a convulsion that was more a shudder of disgust. He shivered himself, contagiously.

'It *is* crazy,' he said. 'It's crazy even to talk about it.'

She rolled away from him, but he followed, pressing against her from behind: 'There's Ben to think of, if nothing else,' she murmured. 'What right would we have to take him with us?'

Even now, the idea was only half speakable, couched in the euphemisms of travel and journeys. Of family holidays.

'He would hate to be left out,' Rick said, and they both suddenly laughed, briefly, too-loudly, then lay together for some minutes in silence, their bodies stilled, their hearts pounding, not quite believing that such thoughts had crept out into the open, and were being discussed.

The subject of Ben had opened another door; the worry-program had thrown up another weird solution, only slightly less unspeakable. This time it was Linda who found the words:

'Maybe only *one* of us should go with her. Maybe I should go with her.'

Rick rolled apart from her: 'You want me to lose *both* of you?'

'Is your grief going to be worse?' she said. 'Could it *be* any worse?'

'Of course it would be worse.'

She could hear the doubt in his voice; she knew that he was already there, ahead, or at least abreast of her.

She spoke, as of old, for them both: 'Are two griefs worse than one? How much worse can it be? Can things be worse than *worst*?'

Their hearts pounded on as they lay there at rest, in bed. Sweat broke out across Rick's face, his hands shook, the sheets were damp and clammy against his skin. The darkness, crowding and claustrophobic, surrounded him; it seemed a viscous element, heavy on his senses, preventing clear thought.

'This is absurd,' he said. 'We'll have other children. We can have another baby straight away.'

'It's not us we're talking about,' Linda said.

He lay in silence, rebuked.

'It's Wol,' she continued. 'I can't bear to think of her going away – alone. It's as though we've cast her out into the woods. Abandoned her, like something in a fairytale. And we won't go with her.'

She paused; the idea was growing, taking more definite shape: 'I *want* to go with her,' she announced, more definitely.

'I don't want to hear any more about it,' Rick said. 'It's late – we're both exhausted. In the clear light of day you'll realise how crazy this is.'

'Just think about it,' she urged. 'That's all I ask.'

He rolled away from her, to the far side of the bed.

'No,' he said, angrily. 'I won't. Not ever. I don't want to hear about it again.'

10

As the child's immune system failed, she was fed an exotic salad of antibiotics to prevent infection; these in turn suppressed her appetite, she lost weight steadily over the last weeks. She rapidly came to resemble the snapshots of her forgotten foster siblings in Bangladesh and Ecuador: all skin and bones, her eyes sunk deeply into their dark sockets. Her period of self-isolation had passed, she now preferred to sleep in her parents' bed each night, between them, facing her father – which meant that they often didn't sleep themselves, anxious not to squash her frail bird-bones, or bruise her thin flesh. Often Linda would leave father and daughter together, sneaking off into Emma's room, or into Ben's room, spending the night squeezed even more uncomfortably into the narrow bed of a boy who was as unwilling as ever to be left out.

And as Rick lay there, sleepless, his daughter's small milky breath puffing rhythmically into his face, the realisation grew: that if their lunatic plan was ever followed through, if someone *did* choose to go with her, of course it would be him, not Linda.

Night-thoughts, certainly, bred of insomnia and despair – but he was beginning to suspect that despair was the default state of the human mind, if normally hidden from the mind by lack of imagination, of the balms of warmth and food and love.

This, at least, was clear: the child would want him with her at the end, his presence would most reassure her.

He decided, for the moment, to keep this realisation to himself.

Eve Harrison was visiting the house daily at the time, checking Emma's temperature, listening to her chest, peering into orifices. And pricking her thumb pads, siphoning tiny drops of blood.

'Does she have to go through this?' Linda asked, but the needles seemed to bother her more than her stoical daughter.

Several times Eve urged hospitalisation, but both parents had decided that Emma would die – although they still couldn't bring themselves to utter the blunt word – at home, in a familiar world, believing it would be her own wish.

Home had one other advantage, unspoken: although no decision had yet been made, and their lunatic plan had not been discussed again, both knew that it would be impossible to carry out in hospital.

'How can hospital help her?' Linda demanded of her friend.

'She may need a transfusion. Depending on the blood count.'

'Couldn't she be transfused at home?'

Eve was reluctant to agree, but it was the reluctance of fixed habits: 'I suppose I could arrange a home-care nurse,' she conceded.

This was not enough for Linda: 'I can do whatever needs to be done – I'm sure I can. With your help, of course.'

'It's a 24-hour job. When will you sleep? She will need constant nursing attention.'

'We'll work in shifts. I'll sleep when Rick is awake.'

'A night nurse, then. Someone to watch over overnight.'

Rick, listening to the debate, intervened: 'We don't want to share the remaining time with strangers, Eve. Surely you can understand that?'

Eve, ever practical, quickly realised that to argue with these stubborn parents was a waste of time. A crash course in basic nursing procedures followed, under her supervision. True to her promise, she left a stash of pain-killing liquids and suppositories, and several syringes and ampoules of stronger stuff, with written instructions on dosage schedules. An impromptu lecture on the properties and uses of each drug was followed by a kind of brief oral exam, or viva – delivered with Eve's characteristic efficiency. This in turn was followed by a practical tutorial: she arrived one morning with a bag of big navel oranges, and had her two mature-age students slipping small butterfly needles through the skin of the fruit, getting the 'feel'.

'There should be no need for these,' Eve said. 'But just in case. If she bleeds, I can instruct you by phone on what to give.'

Having passed the orange test, they moved on to human flesh: jabbing needles into each other's veins, repeatedly, under Eve's scrutiny. There was an odd relief in this, a mix of comedy and pain, that provided, temporarily, a release from their preoccupations.

'Stick to the dose I've suggested,' Eve advised, leaving. 'These are powerful drugs. Too much could be fatal.'

Rick wondered for a moment if she were suggesting the exact opposite, subtly: offering them a final pain relief for Emma – a final safety net – although of course Eve had no inkling of the full extent of their hidden agenda.

Still hidden, also, from each other. Their minds were still moving in parallel: along true parallel lines, never touching. Rick, especially, refused to admit that he was still giving the matter thought. At times the plan seemed outrageously stupid – even the simple sums were so wrong. At other times it seemed inevitable, logical – even if it was the logic of despair.

Finally, discussion could be deferred no more: an oblique mention by Linda began a series of escalating arguments. Soon they were debating, whispering heatedly, each night in bed – and thinking up counter arguments in silence all day, with Ben at school, but Emma, too fragile now for school, always hovering at brink of earshot. At first these discussions were in subjunctive mode, preceded by an 'if' or a 'should'; this kept the unspeakable hypothetical, and permitted a discussion of the plan – The Plan – as if it were science fiction, or a kind of algebra which did not deal with real events and things, yet still allowed a plan of action to be fleshed out, and modified, and tested.

'*If* we told her,' Linda said, 'that you were going with her, then we could never change our minds. We could never take it back. We would have to be absolutely certain before we could tell her.'

Behind these abstractions there was a mounting urgency, for time was short. Emma, too, appeared to sense this. She began sleeping poorly, refusing to go to bed, to any bed, even to her parents' bed. She actively resisted sleep. Rick and Linda would wake at night to hear her padding about the house, or softly singing songs in the dark bed between them. Once they were woken by the dazzle of the bed lamp to find her propped up between them, reading.

'I don't feel tired,' she explained.

When pressed to turn out the light and shut her eyes, she burst into tears: 'What if I don't wake up?'

'One day, Wol,' Rick told her, 'you will wake up and you will be in heaven. You will close your eyes, here on earth, and when you open them you will be somewhere else.'

They lay together in bed, the small girl cuddled between her parents. The emotion of the moment stripped bare the cliches he was speaking, freed them from trite associations. They were, simply, the only words that could be uttered.

Rick's heart pounded, he prepared himself to speak again, to force out the next words, knowing that once they were uttered they were a promise, binding and irrevocable. As he opened his mouth, Linda suddenly reached over and gripped his arm.

'Don't,' she said, 'Please. We need more time to think it through.'

11

From that night every light in the house was left burning – even, or especially, Ben's bedroom light, where he demanded equal treatment. But Emma's fear of the dark, also, flushed her parents' discussions out into the open, into the light, from behind the cover of hypothetical ifs and shoulds.

'We need counselling,' Linda suggested. 'That we could even *contemplate* it – don't you think we're a bit mad? That we need some sort of help?'

'No,' he said. 'I mean – yes, maybe we are mad. But no – no counselling. They'd take her away from us. They'd take them *both* from us.'

'But we've lost perspective. We're irrational – so caught up in this we can't see the wood for the trees.'

'Maybe that's the best perspective.'

To some extent the two sides of these debates were interchangeable: pro and con arguments were rotated between them. The deeper disagreement was not between the two parents, but within each of them.

'It's such a weight,' Linda said. 'If we could at least *talk* it over with someone. With friends.'

'Which friends? Who could we possibly burden with this? I wouldn't wish it on my worst enemy.'

In this fashion, passed back and forth, a shared load, too hot or too heavy to handle alone, it was slowly decided. When their daughter next burst into tears, and refused to risk sleep, and Rick opened his mouth, Linda held her peace, allowing him to speak.

The words still took some time to emerge, they seemed stuck to the dry roof of his mouth.

'When you die, Wol,' he said. 'Whenever it is, I will be there with you. I am going to die before you.'

Her tears had vanished; she watched him, curious.

'How do you know that?'

'I can make myself die,' he told her. 'With an injection. I'm going to die first, so I'll be there waiting for you.'

Also so there could be no turning back, no chickening out, abandoning her after she had died. This also had been planned – that she was to see him dead, to *know* him dead, before she died herself.

A calm gravity returned to her face. She asked a few further questions – technical questions – then within minutes her wide Wol-eyes closed, and she was sleeping, snuggled against her father's still-pounding heart. He realised that she took it for granted that he would choose to die with her; it was a wonderful comfort, yes, but his intended sacrifice – a sacrifice of everything – meant nothing else to her. He saw no selfishness in her reaction, not even the normal self-centredness of a child, but an entirely reasonable interpretation of events to an intelligent six-year-old mind: if heaven was such a wonderful place, why wouldn't he choose to come with her?

His own view of the road ahead was a little more terrifying. And yet – at the same time, once the decision had been made, and was locked in place – oddly exciting. A far, far better place? He doubted it. Whatever faith he had once had now seemed shallow: a routine, social faith. He felt he was going nowhere, just ending – but perhaps those last few days, and especially nights, of peace, would make it worthwhile. And perhaps, just *perhaps* . . .

'You know the cemetery's a bit like home to me,' he whispered to his wife, in bed.

She set aside the book she was reading, and looked at him, disturbed, uncertain of his tone: 'Rick – don't be morbid.'

'No – I've been there before. As a boy. I once spent a Saturday night in the local graveyard – camping with a friend.'

She listened, reluctantly. Once such a story would have surprised her, now it seemed little more than tame; she knew that both of them had depths that were darker and weirder than had once seemed possible.

'It was his idea,' Rick was saying. 'We each told our parents we were staying at the other's. We took our sleeping bags, and lay there most of the night, among the gravestones, telling ghost stories, trying to terrify ourselves.'

She shivered: 'You must have been crazy.'

'It was a dare – you had to do it. But it was an anticlimax. Suddenly it was morning – we must have slept – and nothing had happened. Of course we were heroes at school – we made up all kinds of horror stories. But deep down I was disappointed. It was the end of something – the end of the tooth fairy. There just wasn't anything out there – no other dimension. There were no ghosts.'

12

Ben was told of the plan – after further intense discussion – the following night. Both parents were unsure what he would make of it, had even worried that he might demand to go too, jealous to the end of the way his entire world had come to orbit another, different focal point: his younger sister.

To him, their explanation was subjunctive again, peppered with ifs and maybes and even with the outright lie that the decision was not yet made, and what did he, Ben, think?

The boy moved to his mother's side, and held tightly to her, and watched his father for some time, for once silent and undemanding, unable to fully grasp what was being said to him, but sensing its gravity. Rick prattled on, talking far too quickly, telling his son that one day they would be together again, all of them, that until then he would have to look after his mother, that he would be the man of the house.

The boy stared at him, uncomprehending – perhaps, even at eight, disbelieving. Explanations that had sounded profound the night before – talk of journeys, of waking in heaven, of future meetings – now sounded banal, or untrue, or even meaningless. For the first time, panic overwhelmed Rick, a wave of terror of the enormity, and absurdity, of the scheme. For the first time also – as his son watched him, suspiciously, he wondered also at the long-term effects it would surely have on the boy. Agitated, emptied of words, he left the child with Linda, and swallowed a sleeping pill that Eve had prescribed for both of them some months before – knowing that he wouldn't sleep, but that at least he might be calmed. Later, in the silence of the very smallest hours, as the rest of the household slept, he rose from his bed, and spent much of the night writing a series of letters to his son: letters to be opened yearly, posthumously, on each successive birthday. He began with simple declarations of love – messages to a little boy from his father in heaven – then for the later years a gradually more complex mix of explanations and exhortations, and, finally, requests for forgiveness. He tried to recall his own states of mind, his own level of development, at various ages – ten, thirteen, sixteen – and tailor his messages accordingly. This was not as difficult as it first seemed: the chronology of the letters, splashed here and there with tears, followed, simply, the evolving complexity of his own thoughts as the long night progressed. The earlier letters to a younger Ben were drafts for the more subtle and sophisticated versions that the boy would open as he grew older.

You are 18, it's been a year since we last talked, and this is the last time we will talk. I hope these letters have not been a burden to you – hauntings from an old ghost. You are nearly as old as I am now, writing this, and it would seem presumptuous to offer any more guidance . . .

Sometime before dawn he heard Linda rise and begin moving about in the kitchen. He finished the last letter, and joined her outside on the back terrace. She was sitting at the garden table with a pot of coffee and two cups, clearly expecting him.

He seemed to have spent all his agitation of the night before; extruded it, poured it into that pile of letters. The outside world was starkly defined: sharp silhouettes and edges, a world of knife-edge clarity. An early bird glided between trees in a neighbour's backyard; the cool air was so still that Rick imagined he could feel the trace of its passage: a faint stirring of wings, a spreading ripple.

Perhaps the tranquillity of the morning seduced them, lulled them into the belief that their plan was not as difficult or as stupid as it had often seemed. Sitting there, holding hands, sipping coffee as light slowly flooded the eastern sky, they decided, almost matter-of-factly, as if scribbling a dental appointment in a diary, on the date.

13

On the second-to-last evening the four grandparents were invited to dinner. They arrived bearing gifts: big soft toys, chocolates for the children. There were no gifts for Rick; he watched, wistfully, as his parents and parents-in-law spent the evening fussing over Ben and Emma, careful to share their attentions, and their gifts, equably. There was no way of telling them what was planned, or receiving his due share of that attention. There was no proper way of saying goodbye.

Linda brought her father an ashtray as they sat in the family room, sipping pre-dinner drinks, but he declared that he had given up.

'Weeks ago,' his wife added, mildly. 'It's the one good thing to come out of all this.'

The evening ended with offers from both grandmothers to stay in the house 'until the end' – offers that were politely, even gratefully, declined. On the doorstep Rick hugged his mother, and then – impulsively – his father. The older man, surprised to receive any sign of affection beyond the usual handshake – hugged him back.

'Be strong,' he said. 'Our thoughts are with you.'

On the last evening the smaller family ate together at the nearby Pizza Hut, a favourite of the children. Unwilling to carry Emma, increasingly frail, past a hundred staring faces, Rick had rung the manager; they were permitted to arrive and eat early, half an hour before opening time. If this approached the dimensions of a Last Wish, it was never mentioned – and if the ride home would be by tumbril, it would at least be a short trip.

Afterwards the four of them played Monopoly – both children as engrossed as always, both parents unable to concentrate, but doing their best, buying and selling properties on autopilot. Apart from the care with which the fragile Emma had been set down on a sheepskin rug and soft pillows, they might have been one of the idealised families pictured on the boxes of other board games stacked in their shelves, sprawled on carpet in family rooms with a board between them. Reminders of their life together surrounded them: gift books, home videos, souvenirs of family holidays, framed paintings done by the children at school or kindergarten or home, family photographs. If the big open space at the back of the house was more family shrine than family room, these photographs were its icons: small framed group portraits of the four, a smattering of older ancestors, but above all, everywhere, the glowing faces of Ben and Emma, at various ages.

As the game finished, it occurred to Rick that this room had always been their true place of worship – and that these people, these three people, were the core of whatever he believed in.

Later, sitting at his desk, listening to Mozart, he finished a long letter to his parents, asking for forgiveness, hoping for understanding. He also tore open the last letter he had written to Ben, to be read on his eighteenth birthday, and added several more words of love. Perhaps it was the Mozart, perhaps it was the sedative leaching into his veins, but with these tasks completed he found himself facing events if not with equanimity, at least once again with certainty.

Linda appeared in the door, agitated, trembling: 'We can't go through with this. It's absurd.'

He led her into the bedroom; they lay down together on the bed, and held each other tightly. They had planned to make love one last time, but the act suddenly seemed irrelevant, and meaningless. She was still trembling; he rose and fossicked a Bible from the bookshelves, and for a time they read alternately: the poetry of Isaiah, Paul's letters to the Corinthians, St Matthew's version of the Sermon on the Mount, various Psalms. The texts held only a minimal promise for Rick – 'we'll see,' he joked grimly to himself – but some deeper music in the words had a soothing effect on both of them, like the drug he had swallowed, or the Mozart itself: *Yea, though I walk through the valley of the shadow of death, I will fear no evil: for thou art with me* . . .

He might believe little beyond family love, but these words seemed the culmination of all their nights of book-readings, as if those thick books – Dickens, George Eliot, Thackeray – had been a preparation for this moment, this last distillation of the written word.

In the next room someone landed on Mayfair, with hotels; the children abandoned their game and joined them in bed. Linda slipped a small butterfly-needle into Rick's veins, and taped it in place, despite shaking hands; she then repeated the procedure on Emma, finding the task surprisingly easy: the girl's veins were more prominent than her father's, her skin far more delicate than any thick-skinned navel orange. Emma flinched, momentarily, then watched solemnly as two syringes were loaded with morphine. Her wide owl-eyes might have been looking at everything simultaneously, taking everything in. They lay together on the bed, all four of them – just as they had been together at Emma's birth, six years earlier, in the Maternity Suite at the local hospital. Ben seemed finally to grasp the enormity of what was planned, his eyes had reddened, but the seriousness, the methodical ritual of events seemed to keep any terror in check. They had debated allowing him to watch, to participate, but even now, at the point of no return, there was surely something less terrifying, and certainly less bloody, about this occasion for him than there had been at his sister's birth, when her strange alien-being seemed to burst from his mother's innards. Linda felt that for his peace of mind later, as an adult, he should be a participant, he should *be* there. He listened quietly as they explained the last few steps; he kissed his father, and lay on top of him.

And so they lay together, a last few minutes of hand-holding, and tears, before separating. Emma appeared less concerned than her brother. Her clear contentment, lying there, clutching his hand, forced the last doubts from Rick's mind, and induced a parallel contentment in him. His heart pounded, but the flow of his thoughts was suddenly calm and steady. Even Linda felt that her daughter's serenity somehow cancelled out, at least for the moment, whatever misery she and her surviving child would subsequently endure.

When her husband was ready, she nodded, and pressed her face softly onto his, and he squeezed his own syringe, and waited, holding them all, but not for any length of time.

TEN ANECDOTES ABOUT LORD HOWE ISLAND

Louis Nowra

1
Mapping

THEY ARRIVED AT THE HEIGHT of the fever. Captain Denham was anchored in Sydney Harbour for two days, waiting for a customs boat to attend them, but it seemed as though Sydney was in the grip of a plague. Through his telescope Denham could see a few people walking through the streets and the occasional workman on the docks, but it was nothing like the bustling metropolis he was led to believe the city had become since its founding such a short time ago.

It was February 1853 and gold fever had possessed Sydney. Shops were shut, banks opened odd hours, vessels rotted away in the harbour because their crews had jumped ship, and the horse manure stayed uncollected on the streets. It was a ghost town, with thousands of men having rushed off to distant Bathurst to dig for their fortunes. Only the women, a handful of sensible men and the feeble-minded were left.

Denham's ship, the ten-gun sloop HMS *Herald*, was at the beginning of a remarkable feat of map-making. The voyage would take some eight years and its aim was to chart the land and waters of the south-west Pacific. Denham was under secret orders from the British government to make a thorough examination of Lord Howe Island as a potential penal colony, now that New South Wales had stopped taking convicts from the Mother Country.

Captain Denham was one of the most notable hydrographers of his time but was frequently torn between a love of his family and a love of the sea. Some years earlier he had been demoted – he had disobeyed naval regulations by having his wife on board while surveying the Bristol Channel. But this time he had received special permission to take on board his son, Fleetwood, who was thirteen years old at the beginning of the epic journey. Although considered an intelligent boy Fleetwood was severely crippled, with little use of his legs. If a crewman wasn't available to help, he would creep along the deck, pulling himself along with callused hands, like, in the words of the ship's naturalist MacGillivray, some *dung beetle*. MacGillivray scribbled his comment next to a small sketch of the Captain's son, in the margin of a large page of delicate drawings of African lilies he had studied on the way to Australia.

Next to the drawing of the boy is a pair of brown feet, belonging to Sing Pear, the Fijian who accompanied Denham from London with the job of translator, and the additional task of carrying Fleetwood and caring for him. But not long after leaving Cape Town, Sing Pear died of tuberculosis. The other civilian who could have looked after the boy was MacGillivray, but he was a coarse drunkard who grew a wild beard in spite of the Captain's desire that everyone be clean-shaven on the voyage as a conscious act of daily self-discipline. Believing the naturalist would not be a good influence on his son, Denham kept them apart as much as possible.

Eventually, Denham and his crew were allowed on shore. Even

TEN ANECDOTES ABOUT LORD HOWE ISLAND

though Sydney was a shell of its former self Fleetwood was desperate to see it. The task of stocking their ship was so tediously slow and expensive, however, that his father didn't have time to show it to him. One morning, as Denham was returning to the storehouses in the Rocks from Admiralty House (where the Admiral was more concerned to talk about gold than the feasibility of Lord Howe Island as a penal settlement), he came upon a giant of a man wearing a threadbare marines uniform. The man was the tallest person Denham had ever seen – over seven feet on the old scale. He stood on the pier spitting on the brass buttons of his uniform and methodically polishing them with the cuffs of his jacket. His trousers barely reached his ankles and his scruffy, unpolished shoes seemed as large as two dugout canoes. He looked both comical in his uncoordination and ferocious in his unsmiling demeanor. It was said, however, that he was a gentle man, perhaps intelligent, but it was hard to know. For most of the time he seemed inward looking, as if caught up in his own thoughts about his dismal fate. Having resigned from the marines to search for gold, all he had found was debt and doubt. Denham made him an offer, and as this meant money, the giant man – Mr Lock – quickly agreed.

Captain Denham was relieved that Fleetwood had someone to care for him. Mr Lock and Fleetwood seemed to get on extremely well and became familiar figures in the streets of Sydney for the ten days the HMS *Herald* was docked. Sitting on the giant's back, the boy would direct Lock where he wanted to go, whether it was the shops or tramping through the overgrown Botanical Gardens (most of the gardeners had absconded to the diggings). Every day, the giant man carried Fleetwood to church. Apart from the uncomfortable fact that Mr Lock was a papist, Denham was pleased that Fleetwood was with a religious man, a believer in God, unlike the blasphemous MacGillivray. But even so there was something disturbingly earnest and raw about Mr Lock's intense prayers, as if the giant were attempting to find redemption for some horrible wrong he had committed.

The boy grew so close to Mr Lock that when it came time to continue the voyage, Fleetwood realised that his new friend would be left behind. He howled and pleaded with his father to allow his companion to come with him, but Denham had no room for an extra man on his already crowded ship. The crying boy pulled himself up onto the ship's railing and, as they pulled away from the pier, he watched the giant slowly vanish, his huge arm waving like a broken windmill in a mild breeze. But as the *Herald* was about to sail out through the Heads some rigging broke and it had to return to the docks where Mr Lock was still waiting, as if he had expected the boy to come back.

Realising Fate had determined that his son and Mr Lock were destined to be companions, Denham finally allowed the giant man aboard. The next day, perched on Lock's shoulders, Fleetwood gazed back at the Sydney that slowly disappeared into a summer haze and the malaise of animated suspension, as it patiently waited for the delirious dreamers to return to their senses and the city.

The voyage to Lord Howe took only four days, but on the final night a wild thunderstorm burst around the ship. Mr Lock, who slept on the floor beside Fleetwood's hammock, noticed that the boy was missing and went looking for him. He found him in a supine position on the deck, gazing in awe at the lightning branding the sky. It was as if the electric power of God had short-circuited. The ship rocked in the heavy swell and Fleetwood dug his nails into the deck so he wouldn't roll with it.

Is anything the matter? cried out Denham, who was at the wheel with his First Officer. Mr Lock shook his head and, as he picked up the boy, now laughing at the sheer dangerous beauty of it all, a glowing, shimmering ball of phosphorescent light ran towards them and engulfed them both. This was the rare phenomenon of St Elmo's fire. From his position behind the wheel Denham could see his son in the giant's arms surrounded by a glorious incandescence. The St Elmo's fire left the boy and man, danced along the deck and then leapt at them, absorbing them in its light once more. Then, it vanished as suddenly as it had appeared. It left the rapt Fleetwood and Mr Lock unable to move, as if paralysed by their amazement at the beauty of what had consumed them. *It's a sign, it's a sign*, the giant muttered to MacGillivray, who had come up on deck to see what all the commotion was about. *It's a sign that you're mad as a March hare*, crowed the naturalist.

Lord Howe, which is about 700 kilometres from Sydney, had been discovered in 1788 by the HMS *Supply*, the crew of which were probably the first humans to have ever set eyes on it. By the time Denham's ship arrived, there were three families on the island, living in slab-built cottages roofed with palm leaves. It reminded MacGillivray of a Malayan hamlet. Lord Howe is a small island, eleven kilometres by one and a half kilometres at its widest. It has two peaks: Mount Gower, the taller, and Mount Lidgbird (named after the Captain of the HMS *Supply*). There are coral reefs and a lagoon on the western side and precipitous cliffs on the easten beaches. The vegetation is sub-tropical;

banyan figs, palms, ferns – nearly sixty unique species of plants and over one hundred species of birds. It was always considered to be an Eden from the time of its first settlers in 1834, who believed they could make money by selling the produce of their market gardens, especially the abundant onions, to passing whaling ships.

While Denham spent weeks mapping the waters and reefs around Lord Howe, MacGillivray and his team investigated its unique nature and also produced a topographical map of the island, which the naturalist J. Etheridge blasted as *completely useless* in 1887. There is a common theory that after a long, exhausting day examining fauna and flora, and after the naturalist had downed a few cups of the local brew, he deliberately concocted a coarse map as part of his continuing battle with the prim and humourless Denham. (The tension between Denham and his naturalist would eventually escalate to the point at which MacGillivray would not be allowed back on board the ship after it docked in New Zealand the following year.)

As his father and the bad tempered MacGillivray surveyed Lord Howe, Fleetwood spent all his time with Mr Lock, whose experience with the St Elmo's fire fed the flames of his religious enthusiasm. As an act of atonement for whatever crime he had committed, Mr Lock decided to create a monument to Jesus. He thought of building a church for the sixteen people who lived on Lord Howe but soon realised that the pagan residents would not appreciate the gift. Then, one day as he and the boy sat on the lagoon beach listening to the distant cannon fire (the *Herald* was firing her guns to enable the surveyors' boats to check their relative positions by timing the interval between the flash and the sound), Mr Lock had an idea.

Next day, leaving Fleetwood back at the base camp, Mr Lock set off to Mount Lidgbird with the equipment and food he would need on his broad back. He climbed up the severe eastern side and, near the top, had to clamber across the branches of a pandanus to reach the apex. Fleetwood, enthralled, watched all of his journey though a telescope. Using a rope, the giant let himself down the rock face and began to hack away at the lichen and moss. When drunk, MacGillivray would tell Fleetwood that the giant had gone crazy, but the boy thought that what his friend was doing was as beautiful as the St Elmo's fire.

For a week, from dawn to dusk, Mr Lock stayed on Mount Lidgbird, working on his act of atonement. Gradually, the shape he was carving out became visible to those on the island. First there was a long, vertical line, about three meters wide and fifty meters long. Then, towards the end of the week, he started on the cross-beam. Against the dark green rock face, his cross resembled the gigantic shadow of a crucifix.

Denham returned after two weeks of mapping, and prepared to continue the long voyage. The cross was finished but the giant man had not come back. Fleetwood was frantic and Denham sent the irritated MacGillivray to search for him along with some of the sailors. In his pack the naturalist carried a large bottle of the local brew. By the time he reached the slopes of Mount Lidgbird he was thoroughly drunk. In order to test the mettle of any naturalist who came to the island in the future, he scattered the seeds of the Madagascar Lily he had collected, an act of tampering with the ecosystem he thought hilarious. Just when the sailors thought they might have to carry the drunken naturalist back to base, one of them came upon the body of Mr Lock and his broken rope. It was said that the expression on his face was not one of anguish but of peace and contentment. Later, examining the rope, Denham realised the giant man had deliberately cut it.

When MacGillivray tried on the dead man's shoes as a joke he discovered that inside each heel was a hollow carved out in the shape of a flask. Both heels were hiding places for drink. As Denham had never seen Mr Lock drunk or tipsy, he surmised that the giant must have once had a drinking problem and that renouncing alcohol must have been part of his atonement. Whatever had happened to Mr Lock back in Bathurst or Sydney, no one ever found out, but it must have been something grave for Mr Lock to seek atonement in hacking out the enormous cross and finding release in suicide.

Fleetwood wept for days and did not recover from the loss of his friend. He grew sick and remained bedridden on the *Herald* for months as it continued its voyage. He died not long after the ship left Auckland and was buried on Raoul Island, between New Zealand and Fiji. His gravestone reads: *Fleetwood James Denham died aboard the* Herald *at this island on the 8th day of July, 1854, aged 16 years, leaving an afflicted parent to mourn his loss here, and many at home who dearly loved him.* The cross on Mount Lidgbird faded with time as the lichen and moss returned. Only a keen-eyed local (on days when the light shines at the most opportune angle) can see its shadowy form. Just as the cross faded away, so did Mr Lock's grave vanish with time.

Denham recommended Lord Howe as the perfect place for a penal settlement but London decided that a place described by so many as Eden was no place to send convicts.

2
Drink

From the beginning of settlement, the people of Lord Howe had their own particular food and drink. A staple food is the *pilleye*, made by mixing a bucketful of sweet potato with a saucer of flour and a handful of fat, then baking it like a loaf of bread. The residents are famous for their drink, especially the strongly alcoholic brew nicknamed the *Howie*, made from fermented bananas and wild figs. Potent as absinthe and just as dangerous, the Howie can be compared to an hallucinogenic drug. In fact, so attractive and potent was it that some whaling captains and crew refused to leave the island, preferring to get drunk and dream away their lives under the shade of the kentia palms.

It was the Howie that caused the New South Wales government to intervene in the affairs of the island. During the winter of 1877 the island schooner *Mary Peverley* arrived to salvage the remains of a wrecked collier. For a week, Captain Amora rowed ashore daily to negotiate with the settlers for a supply of labourers to help him and his crew. Every night he returned saying negotiations were still continuing. The crew grew impatient and then they discovered the reason for their captain's long absences. It was the Howie. Under its influence he was content to let the negotiations drift on indefinitely. The crew then undertook one of the more unusual mutinies. They arrived on the island, kidnapped their drunken captain and sailed back to Sydney.

Enough was enough. Although technically citizens of New

South Wales, Lord Howe's residents had title to no land, paid no taxes and obeyed no laws. It was thought that their way of life was a disgrace – especially their disgusting indulgence in such things as the Howie. The New South Wales government appointed former Royal Navy Captain Richard Armstrong to govern the island. A stern believer in authority and strict discipline, he was genuinely horrified at their primitive way of life. He brought to the island a respect for New South Wales law, developed the kentia palm industry, and proved himself extremely brave when he swam through huge waves to rescue the drowning crewmen of a sinking ship.

But the benefits the Governor brought to Lord Howe were nothing compared to the residents' sense of lost freedom. Armstrong suppressed the manufacture of the Howie, claiming it was for the sake of the islanders' welfare. As a substitute he sold them his own liquor at inflated prices. But the residents presented a petition to the New South Wales authorities and Armstrong was convicted of selling sly-grog. His position was terminated.

Free of government interference, even though much of it had been to the good, the residents again lived in the freedom they were accustomed to until 1913, when a Board was established to run the island. This benevolent oligarchy tried unsuccessfully to ban the Howie. The Board's revenge for their failure was to make it law that no one on Lord Howe was allowed to buy alcohol on credit.

3
The man with fire in his eyes

In the late 1840s a man called Moss – no one knew his first name – deserted his whaler and went to live on Lord Howe. Angry and extremely aggressive, he found disagreement with each and every member of the small settlement, including its children. He retreated from the humans to the slopes of Mount Lidgbird where he lived on fish, woodhens and feral goats. After a time his clothes rotted away and he took to wearing a filthy piece of goat skin. He was considered mad by the locals and, in turn, decided to avenge himself on them. He rolled boulders down the slopes of the mountain, hoping they would crush the houses and their occupants below, but the boulders missed the settlement and fell harmlessly into the sea. Next he lit a fire in the kentia palm forest, which burned for a day and a half. The inhabitants retreated from their settlement to the beach but, luckily, the rains came and doused the fire before it touched their palm-thatched homes.

Every night for a week the disappointed Moss came down from the mountain and threatened the settlement, yelling, *I'm gonna burn you all into Hell.*

Former sailor Captain Poole took upon himself the leadership of the settlement. Knowing that Moss would carry out his threat, Poole surrounded the vulnerable settlement with casks and butts filled with water. At night he heard Moss call out his name and abuse him and even laugh at the flimsy defences he had set up. Poole organised the men in watches throughout the night and, a month or so after the original fire, he was woken by one of the men on watch. He had seen a spark skipping down the slopes of Mount Lidgbird – and it was heading in their direction. Poole quickly organised a handful of men to hide in the Valley of the Shadow of Death, the name given a huge area of the island that was filled with banyan trees, a tree that could be as large as three acres. The tree started as a seed that settled on another tree and sent roots down to the ground, gradually strangling the host tree. The roots then formed trunks and trailed out more roots, until there were arches twenty meters from the ground. After decades of prodigious growth, they formed a grand combination of natural arches. Amidst the banyan trees thatch palms grew some thirty meters high, forming a canopy and creating a ghostly twilight, below which nothing else grew. The arches, aerial roots, palms and gloom had the stillness and atmosphere of a graveyard.

Whistling and muttering curses to himself Moss came into the tangle of darkness and moonlight carrying a thick piece of burning wood. Before he knew what was happening Poole and his men had jumped him, nearly splitting his head open with an axe handle. They stripped him of his stinking goat skin, tied his arms and legs and carried him back to the settlement where they placed him in wooden stocks they had specially built for his capture.

Unanimously, the islanders decided to send Moss to Sydney on a passing ship but, after a week, there was still no sign of one and several women were worried the stocks might cripple him. So Poole drained water from one of the casks, cut a small hole in the side as a trap door and, with the help of the men, placed the struggling, obscene-mouthed Moss inside it and nailed on the lid. Each dusk the cask was laid on its side so Moss could sleep and each morning it was lifted into an upright position so he could stand. It was so cramped he couldn't even sit and despite cursing and protesting he was forced to remain standing until nightfall. Mrs Poole would shove food through the trap hole and leave Moss to eat in the fetid darkness of his prison. If ever the residents glanced at the cask they would see a pair of fiery eyes glaring back at them.

Finally, after two months, a ship arrived. Cranes lifted the cask onto the deck and Poole accompanied his prisoner to Port Jackson. What happened in Sydney will always be ingrained in the folk memory of Lord Howe and has produced in every generation a hatred of the *nonnies'* (non-islanders') system. In court Moss admitted that he had wanted to burn the settlement and kill all its inhabitants but he got off scot-free because of the inhumane treatment to which he had been subjected. The horrible irony was that Poole was judged the criminal and just managed to avoid being sent to jail himself by paying a fine of 50 pounds – a huge sum in those days.

From the moment Captain Poole arrived back on the island, bankrupted by the New South Wales judicial system, the people of Lord Howe opposed the numerous attempts to inflict the mainland's jails on them. In 1891, Sydney delivered a portable jail to the island. It soon saw use as a cricket shed. In 1933, another jail was shipped to the island and was immediately returned to Sydney. In 1989, determined that this part of New South Wales (as it had officially become) should have a prison, authorities sent over a jail kit to be assembled and erected near the local hall. A year later authorities came to Lord

Howe to inspect the new jail only to discover it had not been built. It seems the builders had sold off sections of the kit to various families. The builders were tried and fined and the locals were offered an amnesty if they returned the stolen property. Not one ever did.

This paradise on earth, however, decided on the cruellest punishment of all for its residents, a punishment that no *nonnie* could have ever conceived of. A punishment so severe, that on the five occasions it has been issued all who have suffered it have died of grief before being able to return. Exile.

4

Flotsam and jetsam

Although Lord Howe may be only a speck in the South Pacific Ocean, its beaches seem to attract flotsam and jetsam from across the world; wrecks, masts, booms, planking, clothing, life jackets and the remains of monstrous fish thrown up from the depths. There have been many wrecks on its reefs. Perhaps the most dramatic occured in 1909, when the barque *Errol*, bound for Peru, broke into three on hitting a reef. The captain's wife, who was on board with her four children, saw her husband tumble over the side in a desperate attempt to help a crewman. As he tried to clamber back on board sharks devoured him. The sight of her husband screaming as he was eaten alive sent her mad and, believing she had nothing to live for, she attempted to kill her children, only to be physically restrained by the crew.

In 1911 two adolescents, Mary and Jimmy Perkins, had just

finished collecting mutton bird eggs and were about to return home when they spotted something yellow emerging from the sea. It was a young woman in a yellow dress. She was about sixteen or seventeen and could not speak. Whether she had never spoken or had lost her voice through terror, no one ever found out. There was no ship on the horizon and it seemed to the two children that this woman, who had come from the bottom of the sea, was a mermaid.

They took her home. She was a peculiar creature – and creature she seemed to be, because she seemed a bundle of animal instincts rather than a human being conscious of what she was doing. She refused to wear any dress but the yellow one and, while it was being washed, she would remain naked and scream if anyone tried to cover her up. She urinated when she felt like it and didn't care where she did it or who was watching. If she wanted something – a ribbon, piece of food or bright object – she would snatch it out of the hands of whoever held it. She didn't seem to sleep at night and was often found sitting on the floor (she refused to lie in a bed), wide-eyed and humming tunelessly. Sometimes of a day she'd curl up in a warm spot on the verandah that overlooked the lagoon. And like some cat or dog she'd sleep, occasionally whimpering as if experiencing a bad dream.

Mary and Jimmy thought there was something special – even magical – about her. The adults believed she may have fallen overboard from a passing ship. But on questioning the crews of the many ships that stopped at Lord Howe, none had heard of such an incident. A captain or curious crewman might come and stare at the woman in the yellow dress in the hope they might recognise her, but none did.

The woman would follow Mary and Jimmy about as they played on the beach or killed mutton birds. When the settlement had a picnic or a party she would attempt to join the singing or dancing, but she had a squeaky voice and danced like a marionette whose strings were operated by an epileptic.

If it wasn't for Jimmy and Mary's love for her, the residents would have shipped her to Sydney. But in her humming, the two children heard a language more strange and beautiful than human talk and in her distant eyes they saw someone who could see other, more exotic worlds; especially the one she had come from.

She had been on the island for a month when one morning she emerged from the bakery at the rear of the general store covered in white powder. Apparently, she had poured the island's whole stock of flour onto the floor, rolled in it and urinated on it. For five days Lord Howe went without bread. She was scolded by the adults but didn't appear to understand. Then, one day, while Mrs Perkins was riding along the beach on one of the island's few horses, she saw Mary and Jimmy staring at the woman. She was lying on the sand in the sun with her yellow dress lifted up around her thighs. Riding closer, Mrs Perkins was appalled to see what the woman was doing to herself.

A meeting of adults was called and it was decided to send the unfortunate mad woman to Sydney. When Mary and Jimmy heard what was going to happen they pleaded with their parents to allow her to stay, but the adults were unmoved. A few hours later, Lowell Andrews saw the two children leading the woman in the yellow dress into the Valley of the Shadow of Death. Obviously the children were running away with her. A search party went out but couldn't find the trio. Night was coming and the adults were hoarse with yelling out the childrens' names. It was Mrs Wilson who finally saw them, far from the dark world of the banyan trees. The boy and girl were standing on the beach, watching the woman slowly walk into the waves. Mrs Wilson ran down through the hills pitted with mutton bird holes, crying out their names, but the wind was blowing in off the sea and they couldn't hear her. By the time she reached the beach, only the woman's head was visible. Mrs Wilson ran past the surprised children into the water but it was too late. The woman in the yellow dress had vanished from view.

According to the children the woman knew she was going to be sent away and had led them from the Valley of the Shadow of Death down to the beach because, as they put it, she wanted to return to the sea. Far from being upset, Mary and Jimmy were pleased. They'd been in no doubt that, like a mermaid, the woman usually lived in the sea and that one day she would return there.

Her body was never found and the mystery of how she had arrived seemed never to be solved. Years later, long-term resident of the island and its self-appointed historian Bob Cockburn studied newspapers and shipping movements of the time and surmised that the woman had jumped from a ship that was probably making for Norfolk Island.

Whatever the truth is, it has always seemed to the residents that the humans who arrived on the island, either as tourists or as accidents, were strange people. Or perhaps it was the island that changed them. In the 1930s, Francis Chichester (later to achieve fame as the first solo around-the-world yachtsman, for which he was given a knighthood) arrived at Lord Howe from the sky in his seaplane. It had been damaged by a storm and during the many weeks it took to repair it, his previously repressed sexually voracious nature flourished. Many of the women remember his invitation to go fishing on the other side of Rabbit Island where, as one bemused old woman once said to Cockburn, *A line was never cast.*

Seven Russians were also stranded on the island. They were hired as architects and builders by a French firm to construct a five-star lodge where Poole's Lodge had been but, as if to confirm the bad luck of the site, the firm went broke. The Russians were never paid. Their relatives back in Russia couldn't afford to pay for their return, so the men spent their days doing odd jobs around the island for a pittance or lying on the beach sunbaking. Their English was woeful. They tried to tell the residents and tourists about their plight but, after a time, misery in paradise becomes boring. They were human wrecks, sun-browned castaways who feared they would never see their homeland again. Bob Cockburn approached a former Premier of New South Wales, one of several from the southern States who holiday on Lord Howe, and asked him to help the Russians. *Hell, no*, he said. When Cockburn reminded him that he had recently given a character reference for a local clergyman who had been caught sexually assaulting a teenage girl, the former Premier said that was different. *Dave voted for me. No Russian ever voted for my party, so why should I help them?*

5
Chooks

It all began with the smallest of the domestic fowls – a bantam.

Abe Station had come from the mainland to construct a lodge of serviced apartments and to rebuild his life. There were only a few lodges on the island as the Board had decided early in the 1950s that, as a World Heritage site, Lord Howe could only sustain four hundred tourists at a time.

Abe was middle-aged. He and his wife had no children. After a moderately successful career as a builder he looked to his lodge to supply him with a constant and reasonable income in his retirement. He also thought that a change of lifestyle might reinvigorate a marriage gone stale with habit and the silence of boredom. With the help of several locals, he built a lodge of twenty serviced apartments, one of which was for him and his wife. He called it *Poole's Lodge*, after the early settler. Around the apartments he planted kentia palms, frangipani and hibiscus.

It was an immediate success. Soon it became obvious that he and his wife would need help to run it. She recommended a cousin of hers who came over from Perth and lived in one of the apartments, working for her board. Gayle was an attractive but abrasive woman, a hard worker who, most importantly, got on well with Abe's finicky wife. The Lodge was working like clockwork when, as Abe later put it at the trial, *There came a fly in the ointment*. The next-door neighbour decided to add a rooster to her flock of bantam hens. Every morning, just after dawn, the rooster crowed and kept on crowing for hours, waking the guests. Naturally they complained about their broken sleep and, as word spread that it was impossible to get a decent night's sleep at Poole's Lodge, the business began to lose bookings.

Abe approached the neighbour, a widow called Mrs Johnson, who denied that it was her rooster making the noise. Frustrated, Abe made a tape recording of the crowing but Mrs Johnson was adamant. *How do I know that thing on your machine is my bantam?* she argued, her comment also recorded by the tape recorder and played at the trial. Desperate, Abe went to see Sergeant Pettersson, the only policeman on the island. Everyone thought his job was the easiest on Lord Howe. Because there was no crime, he spent much of his time fishing or down at the bowling club, drinking with the locals. If his superiors on the mainland queried his arrest record he would spend a few days booking cyclists (the main form of transport on the island) for not wearing helmets and giving speeding tickets to those motorcyclists who exceeded the twenty-kilometre limit. Pettersson loved westerns; he wore his policeman's badge on his breast pocket like a sheriff and practised twirling a gun around his finger like the cowboys in his favourite movies.

After Abe told the sergeant about his predicament, Pettersson visited Mrs Johnson. She annoyed him by laughing off the complaint and telling him to *Get back to Tombstone*. The policeman instructed Abe to keep a diary of the bantam's crowing because he was going to charge Mrs Johnson for disturbing the peace and destroying the livelihood of the owners of Poole's Lodge.

Mrs Johnson was duly arrested and the trial was set for the following month. The drinkers down at the bowling club teased Pettersson but he saw the case as one of principle. Even though he knew both he and Abe would be laughed at because they were *nonnies*, he hoped that winning the case would put a stop to the locals not paying their speeding fines and would force them to wear bicycle helmets. This was to be a turning point in his relations with the locals, whether they knew it or not. They would see that he was serious about what they wrongly considered to be comical. He also hoped that winning the case against the bantam owner would put a stop to the dreadful abuse from the Watkins boys, who kept calling him *Wild Bill Swede* and *Buffalo Turnip*. A great consolation for him was that Bob Cockburn, the wealthiest man on the island and the owner of the most glamorous resort, was on their side. Tourism was the major industry now that kentia palm seeds were not selling and, as he said, anything that hurt tourism would have a deleterious effect on Lord Howe.

Abe spent a week in Sydney before the trial, arranging for new, expensive brochures for his lodge and helping his sick brother, who had been hospitalised for bowel cancer. While he was away his wife and Gayle kept their own diaries detailing the dates and times when the bantam crowed.

The trial was one of the biggest events to happen on Lord Howe. A stipendiary magistrate flew from Sydney, as did a clerk of courts, a police prosecutor and a defence lawyer. The trial was held in the local hall. The magistrate sat behind a desk on the stage, which was half a metre high. The prosecutor, defence lawyer and clerk of courts sat below, around an oval table fixed with wheels. The prime exhibit, the bantam, was in a cage in the corner of the stage, looking small, sleepy and seemingly incapable of any ferocious crowing.

The magistrate arrived at the hall just in time to see an example of the local humour. Tied up next to the cage was an enormous rooster with a sign pinned to the curtain above it that read *Not me!* A sign was placed on the cage that held the bantam that said *Evil Doer!* Like Sgt Pettersson the magistrate realised the time had come to make the locals understand that justice doesn't have a sense of humour. He lectured the full hall about the fact that courts were not places of levity and ordered the clerk of courts to remove the extra rooster. But after the clerk untied him, the previously lethargic rooster suddenly burst into a hysteria of crowing and hurtled off the stage. He attempted to fly, causing mayhem as the spectators jumped out of his way. The men abandoned the oval table, which rolled away and crashed into the wall. The clerk sprained his ankle trying to capture him, though eventually, with the help of Pettersson, he cornered the chook and took it outside. They tied him up at the rear of the toilets in the hope that the practical joker who owned the rooster would claim him. No one did and at the afternoon recess, those who had gone out on to the back lawn for a smoke were horrified to see that the rooster had been ripped apart, its guts and feathers scattered across the couch grass. It was thought that one of the few cats or dogs allowed on the island had done the deed.

The court case was supposed to be over within a day but by the end of the first two sessions, the magistrate was still listening to evidence. He heard from Sgt Pettersson, from Abe and his tape recording, Abe's wife and part of Gayle's evidence. The defence lawyer was so slow and tedious in his questioning that some of the spectators fell asleep. Abe, like Sgt Pettersson, was confident of victory. The evidence given by both he and his wife had been faultless and thorough. By the end of the first day the defence lawyer was sullen and his questions rambled as if he were trying to discover flaws by accident rather than design.

But when Abe sat down in the front row that second morning he noticed that the lawyer seemed smug, even pleased with himself. The previous day he seemed impatient for the case to be over but now he was taut and expectant, as if he could hardly wait for it to resume.

While Gayle was reminded by the clerk of the court that she was still under oath, the defence lawyer absent-mindedly tapped Abe's wife's exercise book and Gayle's notebook in a jaunty, military-type rhythm. Once the clerk of courts sat down the lawyer jumped up and began to interrogate Gayle with a relentless series of questions.

Is it true that while Mr Station was in Sydney, you and Mrs Station would immediately write down the date and time on being woken by the alleged crowing?

Yes, that is true, answered Gayle.

So, asked the lawyer, *there was no collusion between both of you women?*

Not at all, said Gayle in that haughty voice of hers, as if addressing a particularly stupid shop assistant.

Every morning you and Mrs Station, in your separate apartments at opposite ends of Poole's Lodge would wake up at the exact same time and write the time the rooster crowed in your separate diaries?

Abe laughed out loud – did the city slicker think that the chook crowed at different times for each woman? As if reading her employer's mind Gayle replied in almost exactly the same words.

And you both used a purple ballpoint pen?

I suppose we did, said Gayle, glancing at the two diaries the lawyer held up in his hand.

An unusual colour, he remarked with great deliberation.

Maybe Abe bought a whole lot of cheap purple biros, sniggered Gayle. This irritated Abe a little, as she always seemed to be making cracks about his parsimonious habits.

Did you and Mrs Station use the same ballpoint pen? he asked in a quiet voice that seemed so ominous in its implications that everyone in the hall stopped fidgeting and paid full attention.

Well, I don't know, murmured a suddenly unconfident Gayle who glanced uneasily at Abe's wife, who in turn looked away guiltily. At that moment Abe realised his whole life was about to be destroyed.

I only ask, the lawyer went on, *because you'll notice that the purple ink is fading in Mrs Station's diary entry which details a rooster crowing at 4.35 a.m. and yours begins with the same faded pen making an entry at the same time and then runs out of ink before you continue with a black ink pen and the next day you are both using black ink. You say you were in separate apartments and yet you seem to be using the same pen. Did you rush to her bedroom early in the morning or were you there all night? Remember, you are under oath . . .*

The lawyer made a liar out of the rattled Gayle and he finished his cross-examination with the rhetorical, *Where do the lies end?* The question should be, thought Abe, where did the lies begin? The rest of the day in court was a nightmare, a miasma of Abe silently recalling life with his wife as witnesses came and went. He reinterpreted his wife's close friendship with her women friends and, on reflection, she seemed to have so many. He wondered why he had been so stupid as to not draw the obvious conclusions from such close female companions. What was obvious was that his marriage had been a sham and the happiness he had found on Lord Howe was based on a lie.

And worst of all, not only did he know now, so did the whole island. For the rest of the day, and probably for the rest of his life, he could not look anyone in the eye for fear that they would be laughing at him. He did not dare glance at his duplicitous wife, so he spent the day staring at the caged bantam, finding some sort of empathy with that miserable, dozing bird. He barely heard Mrs Johnson's testimony and there were no surprises when she denied that her bantam was the offender.

Look at it, she said, melodramatically pointing at the sluggish bird. *Do you think it would cause all that noise?* And everyone in the hall inwardly agreed with her.

After hearing all the evidence the magistrate decided to establish conclusively if the bantam was the culprit by getting up the next morning at dawn and, from a position in the garden of Poole's Lodge, listening for the crowing. The only other people to be involved were Pettersson, the clerk of courts and the lawyer. The magistrate ordered everybody else to stay away from the scene.

Abe didn't care what happened anymore. He returned to the Lodge and, avoiding his wife and her lover, shifted into one of the many empty apartments. After drinking a whole bottle of whiskey he slept through the morning, unlike the locals who disobeyed the magistrate and rose before dawn, hiding themselves in the trees and kentia palms surrounding Abe's lodge. The magistrate, his clerk,

Pettersson and the lawyer sat in the garden of Poole's Lodge and waited for the coming of dawn and when it came, in beautiful yellow light, reflected off the clear green water of the lagoon, so did the crowing of distant roosters greeting the rising sun. There were so many roosters it seemed as if every household on the island had one, but at Poole's Lodge there was an eerie silence and no noise escaped from the bantam next door.

Shamed and shattered, Abe didn't react to the news that he had lost his case. His wife and Gayle flew to Sydney with the magistrate, clerk and lawyer. He closed down the Lodge. For a week he seemed intent on drinking himself to death. One time he glanced out the window and saw the larrikin Watkins twins, returning from having again secretly rearranged all the plant and tree label stickers Ephraim used to instruct tourists on the island's natural beauty during his popular rambles. They stopped outside Abe's lodge and repainted the sign out front so it read *Sappho's Lodge*. Before, he would have been angry but now Abe was so detached that life outside the window of his apartment seemed like a dream and the sign merely confirmed his humiliation. On the eighth day of his binge, hungover and unshaven, he pedalled unsteadily to the liquor store, which the Board ran. Bob Cockburn, walking to the post office, waved to him but the depressed man either refused to acknowledge him or pretended he didn't see him.

Later that same afternoon, Cockburn was walking to his house when he saw an alert Abe talking to Rhino, an adolescent thug. Even though he was only eleven years old, he scared everyone. Rhino was listening intently to Abe and then both began to laugh as if at some dirty joke. Abe patted Rhino on the back and both walked off into the shade of the palms together. The sight of Rhino with Abe, a disturbing and unlikely pairing, made Cockburn uneasy. His feeling of apprehension increased when he returned home. As his wife was opening a bottle of wine to celebrate their twenty-eighth wedding anniversary, she told him about a curious incident at the liquor shop earlier in the day.

She was trying to choose a good wine from the Board's limited stock while the shop manager and two Board employees laughed about the rumour that Mrs Johnson had ground up valium tablets with the grain for her bantam before its court room appearance. She had also stuffed so many valium tablets down its throat on the morning the magistrate came to hear the rooster that the bird almost died. Mrs Cockburn found herself laughing too, and, like the three men, suddenly stopped when a shadow seemed to creep in on them. It was Abe, standing in the liquor shop doorway. In all probability he had heard everything. But instead of getting upset he merely smiled and asked for his daily bottle of whiskey. *How curious that smile was*, said Mrs Cockburn, pulling out the cork with a lovely plump sound. Bob Cockburn remembered that phrase when he heard the news next morning. Mrs Johnson's bantam rooster had been savagely ripped apart, as if by a wild animal. She blamed Abe but he had the perfect alibi; he was out fishing with Pettersson at the time. But Cockburn knew the culprit and his suspicions were confirmed when, the following day, he saw Rhino and Abe, both with sledgehammers in their hands, standing outside the first apartment of Poole's Lodge.

It took Abe and the boy two weeks to demolish the Lodge. It was done with a concentrated fury that resulted in every single brick being pulverised so they could never be reused. Once the apartments were in ruins Abe gave Rhino several hundred dollars, and with a broad grin on his face, pedalled to the airport. Before boarding the plane to Sydney on a one-way ticket, he asked to borrow a van in the car park and repeatedly ran over his bicycle so none of the locals could use it.

6
The Queen of Rat Tails

In the winter of 1918, during a wild storm, the supply ship *Makambo* left Lord Howe. Despite having made the voyage between the island and Sydney many times before, the Captain ran aground on a local reef. Mrs Dunne, the wife of the island's storekeeper, was for some reason on the deck and the moment *Makambo* hit the reef she fell over the side and was never seen again. The Captain, who it was rumoured had been drinking Howies when he'd made the fatal decision to depart during a storm, gave the order to throw crates of fruit and copra over the side. The crew tossed hundreds of crates overboard until the ship was light enough to be refloated. Once the *Makambo* was free of the reef it sailed on to Sydney. Many of the crates floated onto the Lord Howe beaches and with them, as reluctant passengers, came the rats.

Within the year there was a rodent plague. They devoured the kentia palm seeds and were in danger of destroying the industry. They ate the eggs of the many species of birds and, after only eighteen months, had exterminated the Robust Silver-eye, *Zosterops strenua*. Something had to be done or else the rats would obliterate all bird life and reduce the settlement to poverty. The New South Wales government decided to offer a bounty of sixpence – quite a lot of money in those days – for every rat killed. As proof, a rat tail would be enough. The locals caught over twenty thousand rats a year and, as the Board only paid the bounty every six months, for the rest of the year the rat tails were used as the local currency. Even in church the tails were substituted for cash on the collection plates and the general store accepted rat tails as payment for goods.

Some of the men made a very good living by hunting rats through the palm forests and thick undergrowth of the slopes of Mount Lidgbird and Mount Gower. They would be out killing them for up to a week. But what puzzled the men was that when they returned, Mrs Digham, without great effort or ranging widely, would have more rat tails than they could ever gather. With her contribution and her husband's they grew wealthy, especially in comparison with other Lord Howe inhabitants.

Willie Thompson, who was a second-generation islander, after his father Nathan had sailed all the way from Nantucket in the 1850s to escape the pernicious rejection of Jefferson's ideals of American democracy, would shake his head whenever he talked about the Queen of Rat Tails. It seemed odd that he would spent days hunting the rodents and would return home to the settlement covered in scratches, bruises and bite marks and there'd be Mrs Digham, not a hair out of place, her shoes shiny and her dress ironed and clean, returning from what seemed just a stroll, with a large leather bag filled with rat tails. At church services she'd make whoever was holding the collection plate wait while she grabbed handful after handful of rat tails and ostentatiously piled them up on the plate, until it resembled a huge mound of black spaghetti. The Dighams renovated their house and bought a large fishing boat. Even when it seemed that the rat population was in decline, so much so that the bounty on a tail was reduced to threepence, Mrs Digham still was able to find an unlimited supply of rats.

The women of the settlement laughed at Willie's envy of the woman rat catcher and teased him endlessly, making odious comparisons between her skill and his lack of manhood. If that wasn't bad enough, after a year or so the rest of the island's women also seemed to get lucky. Without any apparent effort they returned from their gambols – for that is what they seemed, so little effort did they appear to make in their search for rats – with hundreds of tails. Their success bred contempt for the men of the island, or so Willie thought. It seemed as if the women were ganging up on the men; even his own wife seemed to treat him like some sort of infant as her pin money grew at an alarming pace. With what she earned from catching rats, she bought new clothes and lace curtains for the house with no thought of his opinion, as if it didn't matter anymore. It was like that Greek play *Lysistrata* where all the women ganged up on the men for some stupid reason and denied them their conjugal rights. Willie feared that this might happen. As patriarch of the island, this was extremely galling.

One Sunday, as he watched the happy women try to outdo each other by stacking as many rat tails on the collection plate as possible, Willie began to think mighty hard. Not about God but about the devil in women. There had to be a reason why they were more successful than the men. Later that day Willie secretly followed Mrs

Digham as she went about her rat catching. Things had come to such a pretty pass that she was out slaughtering rats even on the Sabbath. He followed at a distance and watched her vanish into the Valley of the Shadow of Death.

Mrs Digham walked with great purpose through the penumbra, up and down the soft grey mounds and between the smooth arches of the banyan trees. Then, before he knew what had happened, Willie lost her. She had vanished as she walked across a deep, dry creek bed, as if the grey loam had swallowed her up. He retraced his steps but still couldn't see her. He listened intently for her footfalls but heard nothing and was going to return home when he heard shrill cries, which abruptly stopped before starting up again. This went on for some twenty minutes. Just as Willie realised the sounds were coming from the gully he saw a figure appear, walking purposefully along the dry creek bed, her leather bag so plump with rat tails that some dropped out. Willie hid behind a tree and watched Mrs Digham return to the settlement, a smile of satisfied greed on her face.

So that's how she had caught so many rats so quickly, thought Willie. He slid down the bank of the creek and walked along its bed. The sun was setting and it was getting dark. He could find nothing and then he heard that familiar squeal. They were close. He looked around and heard the noise coming from the side of the creek bed under a banyan tree, the roots of which had eaten into the side of the bank. He leant forward and saw an opening, somewhat bigger than a space a man could crawl into. He peered into the hole and smelt the musty stink of rats and their high-pitched squeals grew louder. It was too dark to see so he pushed himself half way into the hole and lit a match. It hissed into life and he was stunned at what appeared briefly before his eyes. Inside was a cavern the size of his living room and rows upon rows of wooden crates with wire-mesh fronts. In each crate that had once held fruit were now hundreds of rats. All told there must have been thousands upon thousands. The strange, monstrous vision vanished as the match burnt out and Willie lay in the hole, lost in thought. Although he now had the answer to how the women caught their rats, he brooded about what he would do with this information.

He returned home without coming to a solution. Next morning he followed another woman to the creek and watched her slip out of her dress and, wearing only undergarments, squeeze through the hole. He sat on the bank of the creek listening to the slaughter of rats and then hid when the woman came out, clutching her bag of tails. He watched her dress and return to the settlement. He was left with several options. He could reveal what he had found, but that wouldn't give him the satisfaction he was after. He could kill all the rats by dousing them with petrol after he had set aside several thousand tails for himself, but his newly acquired wealth would be a dead giveaway and the burning of the rats would indicate that a man had found out about the rodents' hiding place. No, he had to be more subtle. The more he thought about it, the more he realised that one of the other women had followed Mrs Digham to her hiding place like he had, and blackmailed her into being part of the chilling set-up. Then, before long, other women had found out, but not one of them had told their husbands or lovers. They had deliberately excluded the men. This knowledge gnawed away at Willie for some days until he decided what he should do.

One night while his wife was asleep he grabbed a torch and went to the Valley of the Shadow of Death. Once he was inside the cave he opened all the doors of the breeding crates and freed the thousands of rats. They escaped through the cave entrance into the night. There would be a plague of rats but it had been contained once before and the men would contain it again. What he had hoped would happen, did. The women began to mistrust each other, thinking the culprit was in their midst because none of the men had taken credit for the freeing of the rats and, of course, they couldn't talk to their men about it because of their hypocrisy. Mrs Digham tried to re-establish the breeding crates but Willie released the young rats and she gave up.

The men were puzzled at the sudden increase in the rat population and bewildered as to why the women were no longer catching them, especially now that they were needed to keep the rat population under control. After a long day of rat-catching in the undergrowth, the men, now making a small fortune, would gather together to smoke and drink. After a tumbler of Howie, Willie would start talking in that thick New England accent of his, with its strange nineteenth-century dialect, which was a product of his father's teaching. He'd say, *Yes, yes sirrie, 'tis strange about women, isn't it? When you need them they going missin' because they can't stand pressure as we can. Now jus' suppose, for supposin' sake, that our women, and I could be sailin' with dry sails and a broken rudder here, that the women had a secret breedin' cave for rats, but unlike men who stick together through thick and thin, they began to mistrust one another. So one, in order to spite the others – for the nature of women is to destroy another woman rather than help all women – so one of these women let all the rats go free, and the end result is these women no longer trust or talk to one another and we men are back in favour, if you get me drift...* And on Willie would talk, just shooting the breeze as the saying goes. The men thought he was just making up a cock-and-bull story, without realising he was partly telling the truth. And the full bags of rat tails that each man had was the result of Willie's revenge on the women who had once been so disparaging of mankind.

7
A land of giants

In 1935, the worst cyclone in recorded history struck the island. It pummelled the palms, destroyed homes and savaged the two mountains. During the clean-up a skeleton was found, having been washed free of its dwelling place. The amazing thing about it was that, on the old scale, it was over seven feet tall.

The find excited everyone and the *Sydney Morning Herald* reported speculation that perhaps the first inhabitants of the island were giants. Archeologists and a naturalist visited the island. They patiently examined the creek and its source and in the hard, dried mud found several buttons belonging to a uniform of the colonial marines, circa 1850.

The archeologists were disappointed but the naturalist wasn't. He was visiting the home of a resident when he spotted the 1918 wedding photograph of Perry Johnson, who married his companion of fifty years after it was discovered that the priest who had originally married them had been an impostor. Perry Johnson had struggled so hard to find a bride that he was sickened that he and the woman he loved for so long might have never been really married. Johnson was a black American who had come to Lord Howe to find a freedom that was impossible for men of his colour in the United States. Once he had decided on marriage he sailed to Sydney and, after being unable to find a black woman he desired, waited at Circular Quay for two years, visiting every vessel that docked until he spotted a beautiful black woman on the deck of an American schooner. The woman worked as a maid for a wealthy Mississippi plantation owner. Johnson wooed her and took her back to Lord Howe where a priest, who was a passenger on a passing ship, married them in a simple ceremony; a marriage that had turned out to be a sin in the eyes of God for half a century.

It was the bouquet of the old bride that attracted the naturalist's attention. It was made of lilies, which grew in a spot near Mount Lidgbird. Because it was a species not native to Australia, the naturalist had a mystery on his hand. The lilies only grew in Madagascar. How did they get to Lord Howe? Perhaps, like the flotsam and jetsam, the seeds arrived on the waters, but unlike the humans who were also accidentally thrown up on the beaches only to succumb to their inner demons, the seeds took root and flourished.

Somewhere, the ghost of MacGillivray laughed.

8
Expulsion

As has been pointed out, the greatest punishment that one can administer to a native of Lord Howe is exile. And so it came about that the residents had to expel Rhino from his Eden, although the world 'expel' was never used.

Rhino was a thin, wiry boy who from an early age seemed incapable of knowing good from bad; or if he did, always chose the latter. His real name was Alan but he was nicknamed Rhino because of his large nose, which had developed a prominent bump after his father, frustrated at having such a badly behaved child, hit him with a cricket stump, and also because of his skin, which was so impervious to pain it seemed as thick as a rhinoceros hide. You could hit him and he didn't seem to feel it. As a child Rhino would put his arm in a fire and, long after an adult would have screamed in pain, he stoically keep it in the flames. If he was angry with you he would attack you, regardless of your age. Even as a six-year-old he would throw himself at an adult he didn't like, kicking and biting him. The adult would pry the ferocious little boy loose and throw him away but after landing the boy would bounce back, eager for more violence.

If he didn't like a dog or a cat, he killed it. The endangered woodhen became even more so when Rhino killed several because he didn't like the noise they made. He would leave his excrement on the front doorsteps of people he didn't like and would urinate on you as soon as talk to you. Many called him the original bad seed. Knowing he was detested – even hated – made him even more resentful. His father had left his mother because of him and his mother dealt with the problem of her monstrous son by existing on drugs the island's doctor gave her freely, realising that she needed the refuge of an illusory existence.

After Abe had destroyed his lodge and given Rhino several hundred dollars, the boy's behavior grew worse. Rhino bought a spear-gun with which he would threaten adults if they didn't give him what he wanted. He practised his aim by spearing mutton birds and the few remaining woodhens. Bob Cockburn knew that Rhino had slaughtered the two chooks that had been part of the famous bantam rooster case, probably with his own hands and teeth, but what could he do?

Cockburn always held to the theory that no one really changed during their lifetime; the bad remained bad and the good remained good, even if they made some dreadful decisions. There was no such thing as redemption. To Cockburn, Rhino would always remain bad, if not evil. But Cockburn's wife a had a more benign view of humans and believed they could be transformed into better people. She was very persuasive and persistent. Eventually, her husband gave in and came up with an idea that might solve the island's problem. He visited Rhino's mother, who lived in a sort of genteel poverty that was not as bad on the island as it would be in a major city and, despite her drug haze, she acquiesced to Cockburn's plan. Cockburn then visited several important Lord Howe families. Everyone wanted Rhino to leave the island, but none wanted to expel him forever.

Cockburn had an answer for their dilemma. If these people provided money he would send Rhino to a strict boarding school on the mainland, to learn discipline and gain an education. The only stipulation would be that he was not allowed to come back – except during summer holidays – and was only allowed to return permanently when he reached the age of twenty-one. The families who gave money for Rhino's schooling were to remain anonymous for fear of Rhino's reprisals if he didn't reform. All Cockburn would say to Rhino was that there were nine other families who contributed the money. If Rhino didn't agree to this plan then he would be sent to a borstal and never allowed to return for the term of his natural life.

Rhino was furious at the ultimatum and vowed to kill those who contributed money towards his expulsion. But, given the choice between never returning to the island and perhaps returning permanently, he decided on the latter. He departed, escorted by Sgt Pettersson, who was himself soon to leave Lord Howe reluctantly now his tour of duty was finished, and by his outwardly dazed but inwardly joyous mother. Rhino remained true to himself right to the end. Before getting onto the plane Rhino gave the policeman a quick, hard blow to the stomach that caused Pettersson to double up in pain.

I know you're too much of a miser to pay for my boarding school, he said, *but that's for the fact you won't be here when I come back for my revenge.*

9

History as a snake devouring itself

Rhino returned to Lord Howe for his first summer vacation. He seemed happy. Not that anyone tried to provoke him; most stayed their distance. They could not believe their luck, that when they inadvertently found themselves in his company, his first reaction was not to lash out with his fists but to smile and address the surprised resident in the formal manner of a well-behaved Christian child.

For the first few years of his semi-exile his new-found behaviour unnerved people. Although at first his behaviour seemed false (as if beneath that carapace of pleasant talk and manners, there was the bad seed of old), locals began to believe he had changed, inside and out. Only once did he show a glimpse of his former self – during a visit he assaulted his mother, who refused to lay charges. She blamed herself, saying he was trying to stop her from drinking and taking drugs.

His transformation seemed so genuine and profound that a mainland newspaper ran a story on him. In the article, he told of his previously terrible behaviour and his desire to reform. He sounded contrite and had a desperate need to show the people of Lord Howe that he was a new man. *Eventually,* he was reported as saying, *I want to live permanently on Lord Howe and personally thank all those anonymous donors who put up the money to send me to boarding school. I do not think of it as exile but as a chance to redeem and prove myself.*

And so it seemed. Every summer he returned to assist his mother and other residents. He helped build and renovate houses and accompanied the scientists in their eventually successful attempt to save the woodhen. He also took part in the annual sports carnival, organising the cricket teams, the treasure hunts and the Lord Howe marathon, a strenuous race that went three times around the island. Not content with just participating, Rhino would carry something heavy in each race. One year it might be a goat, the next year an aeroplane tyre. He seemed to have no desire to win, only to punish himself in order to show that he wanted to reform. Even the last of the doubters, Bob Cockburn, had to agree that Rhino had gone much of the way towards self-reformation. Watching the scrawny but strong, sweat-soaked Rhino staggering towards the marathon finishing line with the hefty chef of Pine Trees Lodge clinging to his shoulders convinced Cockburn that only a man determined to reform would put himself through so much pain. Obviously the plan had been successful way beyond his most fanciful expectations.

So pleased were some of his anonymous benefactors that they announced to Rhino their true identities and he shook them by the hand, effusively telling them how much he appreciated what they had done for him. One year, while he was back in Sydney, his mother died but even that did not disturb the upward curve of his changed demeanor. He returned to Lord Howe for the funeral and gave a moving eulogy and asked for her forgiveness. He could have gone to university but he said he was impatient to succeed in the outside world. He started a scrap metal business in Parramatta and in only three years it began to turn a profit. He sold it on his twenty-first birthday because he wanted to return permanently to Lord Howe.

You don't know what it's like to be exiled from the only thing you love, said Rhino when he was greeted by dozens of Lord Howe residents at the airport. And all of them, even the *nonnies*, could understand that. For Bob Cockburn, there were plaudits from everyone for a job well done. Rhino knocked on his door the night after returning from exile and held out his hand.

Thank you, said Rhino, *for all you did. And you too, Mrs Cockburn,* he added, spotting her over her husband's shoulder, standing in the living room. *If you ever need any help, Mr Cockburn, then just ask me.*

At that time Rhino was exactly the man Cockburn had been seeking. Cockburn was organising the most extravagant entertainment Lord Howe had ever seen. It was the one hundred and fiftieth anniversary of Poole's miscarriage of justice and Cockburn was going to produce an historical pageant based on Lord Howe history. He needed someone to help design and build theatre sets. Rhino did more than help. He became Cockburn's right-hand man. Many times before the gala night, Cockburn would tell people how dependent he had become on Rhino and how much effort the young man was putting into every aspect of the production. Rhino became fascinated by the history of Lord Howe and would pump Cockburn for every fact and anecdote. He was particularly intrigued by the cave of rats story because he'd never known such a cave existed. *I thought I knew this place backwards,* he said. But, as Cockburn explained, much of Lord Howe's history had been forgotten, which was why he was putting on the pageant.

It seemed to the older man that the energy that Rhino had once invested in hurting people he now put into helping them. The more Rhino learnt about the past the happier he became, as if he had put himself into some sort of historical context. He co-wrote with Cockburn some of the revue skits for the show and even volunteered to play Moss in the re-enactment of Poole's martyrdom at the hands of Sydney's biased judicial system. No one else wanted to be huddled up in the large cask. Cockburn suggested having a larger one so that the person playing Moss wouldn't feel so claustrophobic but Rhino would hear nothing of it. *We have to make it real,* he said. Cockburn tried to dissuade him from playing Moss because Rhino's tall frame could barely fit upright into the cask unless he twisted his body like a contortionist. But nothing could stop Rhino from performing a role he said he was destined to play, a statement that Cockburn paid no attention to at the time as it seemed just another example of his masochistic behaviour, like those heavy objects and people he carried on his shoulders in the marathons. It also seemed to be part of his general desire to atone for past misdeeds, not unlike those men who flagellate themselves for Christ.

The hall was filled for the one and only night of the anniversary pageant. To the Russians standing in the rear of the hall (all the seats having been taken) the history of Lord Howe passed in a feverish chronicle of women in yellow dresses, crowing roosters, the slaughter of rats, shipwrecks, drunken sea captains and a hatred of prisons and the law that culminated in the strange spectacle of the tall young man they knew as Rhino being locked into a cask, much too small for him, and a man called Captain Poole being treated as a maligned hero, a victim of a judicial system that was as partisan as that during Stalin's reign of terror.

The night was a huge success. Wine, beer and Howie flowed. As a present for his invaluable assistance Cockburn gave Rhino a Polaroid camera and he took many photographs of the opening night party. Not a man who liked carousing, Cockburn left the celebrations early with his wife. They lived over a kilometre away from the hall but they could still hear the sounds of shrieks and laughter. Cockburn was tired but pleased. His research into Lord Howe's history had proved successful and for most of the residents illuminating – and surely

Ephraim would stop criticising him behind his back now. He went to sleep with a satisfied sigh but suddenly woke several hours later from a nightmare. In this horrible dream he saw Rhino staring at him through the trap door of the cask with eyes that were bright with hatred. As if in slow motion, the eyes turned and focused on an individual in the audience with the same reptilian hunger.

Cockburn rose from his bed quietly so as not to wake his wife and sat in the living room, trying to decide if he had dreamt of Rhino's coruscating, fierce eyes – or was it merely Rhino pretending to be the character? But even if he were in character, it was disturbing how much he seemed to have identified with the lunatic Moss. Unable to go back to sleep, Cockburn dressed and returned to the hall. The party was still going, with about a dozen drunks dancing and singing to hideous pop songs. No one remembered seeing Rhino leave the party. Cockburn went to Rhino's shack, but he wasn't there.

Walking home through the kentia palms Cockburn tried to tell himself he was stupid to be so uneasy but the memory of Rhino's eyes kept piercing his veil of resolute calm. He recalled Rhino's behaviour during the rehearsals. He seemed normal and helpful – only his stubborn determination to play Moss was anything out of the ordinary. Then something occurred to Cockburn that made him stop in midstep. With a retrospective vividness he remembered Rhino taking Polaroids of people at the party and seeking out specific individuals amidst the milling crowd of happy well-wishers. At the time there seemed to have been no reason why he should be taking pictures of those particular people and not others. Then he recalled Rhino's eyes as he stared out of the cask as it sat on stage; those bright savage eyes took in each person whom he was later to photograph.

Cockburn felt cold with apprehension; the last photograph Rhino had taken was of him. Where could Rhino be and what was he going to do with those instant photographs? He racked his brain, trying to connect all Rhino had done, in order to ascertain a pattern, an objective or even a plan. What else had fascinated Rhino, besides Moss? Then, like a thunderbolt, Cockburn knew where he would be. He ran home, grabbed a torch from his shed, and hurried on to the Valley of the Shadow of Death.

He hadn't exerted himself this much in years, but he pushed his lithe, middle-aged body and strode into that dark underworld. Guided by the narrow, sharp beam of his torch he ran along the dry creek bed to the cave behind the banyan tree roots. He paused, panting, and softly called out Rhino's name, but there was no answer. Then he crawled into the cave through the dank hole, smelling the pungent stink of petrol. Once inside, the beam of light from his torch landed on a collection of shiny four-litre tins. And then, much to his horror, Cockburn saw something else. There was a long row of sticks, each about half a metre high, stuck in the soft earth of the cave floor. On each of the ten sticks was pinned a Polaroid, like a needle stuck in a voodoo doll. On the bottom of each white border was written, in careful script, the word *Rat* and next to it was a number ranging from one to ten. The first picture was of Joe Barrett and the last one showed his own face. All ten photographs were of the people who had funded Rhino's expulsion.

Cockburn sat on the damp loam of the cave floor wondering what to do. He knew he didn't have much time. But who would he have to warn first? It seemed as if the row of photographs was in order. And that probably made sense because, if Rhino were going to retrace the steps of Moss, his hero, then he would begin at Mount Lidgbird and then move on to each of his victims one at a time, until he reached the farthest part of the island, where the man who'd thought up the plan to expel him still lived.

Jolted into action, Cockburn crawled out of the hole and headed towards Mount Lidgbird. Once he was out from under the banyan trees he ran towards the Barrett house where Joe lived with his aged mother and a dozen or so woodhens they had successfully saved from extinction. Hurrying towards the dark silhouette of the mountain he stopped when he saw a brilliant orange begin to flicker at the base of it. His heart sank. It was Joe's house. He rushed forward and, upon reaching it, found it in flames. Joe's mother was wandering back and forth in a daze outside the gate, cradling several of the woodhens in her arms. Joe was throwing buckets of water on the fire.

Did you see who did it? Cockburn cried out. But Joe and his mother had been asleep at the time and had heard and seen no one. They had no telephone, there was no fire brigade, and the house was certain to burn to the ground.

Cockburn ran back the way he'd come. He had to reach the cave first. No doubt Rhino would pick up more of the petrol cans so as to continue his rampage. As he ran, his lungs feeling as if they were burning and his heart near bursting, Cockburn cursed himself. He had been blind. It was so obvious now. Rhino's behaviour had been mimicry, nothing more than that, except he was cleverer than anyone had ever believed. His transformation hadn't been one of someone evil becoming good, but of someone who had always enjoyed the pleasure of hurting others, and had come to the decision that the greatest pleasure was in revenge served cold. How he must have hated those who had exiled him! How delighted he must have been to gradually discover who his benefactors were and to thank them. Yes, to thank them must have been so delicious when they didn't suspect a thing. And, as he sat squashed up in that cask, how he must have quivered with excited anticipation with what he was about to do after all those years of pretending goodness.

Even a great cynic like Cockburn had been conned. As he hurried through the long grass and palms, Cockburn imagined Rhino in bed at night in the mainland boarding school, unable to contain the pleasure of the insidious way he had convinced Lord Howe he'd become a different person. And Cockburn not only knew he was to blame for Rhino's revenge but also that Rhino's love of history was going to destroy nine others as well as himself, as if history were a snake devouring itself.

Cockburn ran into the darkness of the Valley of the Shadow of Death and switched on his torch. If Rhino had already retrieved the petrol then he should make for the third victim, because in all likelihood Rhino would reach his so-called Rat Number Two before Cockburn did. But would he make it? Cockburn felt like his heart was giving out. He was struggling for breath and his torch beam seemed to dance around the towering banyan roots like some hysterical firefly. His legs felt rubbery and they grew uncoordinated. History was a snake devouring him. He was a rubber snake with no muscles. Suddenly an aerial root loomed up in front of him. He tried to side-step it but instead fell forward. The last thing he remembered was that the root hitting him on the head felt like a bag of wet cement.

He awoke groggy and with a sore forehead. Dawn light was filtering through the banyan trees. For a few moments he wondered where he was. A phrase kept wheeling through his head like raucous seagulls in the sky, *History is a snake*... Then, with a shock, he realised where he was and why. He was stunned. He must have been out cold for hours. How many houses and lives had Rhino destroyed? It was all his fault. He heard his name being called. It was a woman's voice. It was his wife. She sounded distraught. An image of a devastated settlement filled his mind. Thank goodness his wife was still alive. He stood up and found himself face to face with a pair of dangling shoes.

His eyes slowly moved from the shoes, up the trousers, up the torso to the neck, which had a rope around it. This is what he had run into. It was Rhino. There was no noise; only the gentle squeak of the rope on a banyan bough protesting the weight it bore. Cockburn stared at the face. Rhino seemed grim and preoccupied, as if he had forgotten something.

Of course the residents tried to guess why Rhino had not gone on to burn down the houses of his other nine benefactors. But only Cockburn knew the reason. Burning Joe's house hadn't been enough and Rhino had known that to burn those other nine houses and even kill those ten rats wouldn't be enough. As Joe's house burnt he had understood that his greatest pleasure had been all the years he had maliciously fooled everyone. It had been a profound, almost overwhelming gratification that had kept him going all through the years of his exile, continually stoking the fire of his thoughts of revenge, giving him an inner warmth no real fire could provide. A final act of revenge was no good at all. Revenge had to be constant, duplicitous and secret for it to stoke the hunger but never satisfy it. Satisfaction is never enough.

10
The Valley of the Shadow of Death

Ephraim's rambles are very popular with tourists. For a reasonable price (made even more reasonable by the fact that he doesn't pay tax) Ephraim takes people on a tour throughout the island, instructing them on its botany. (He had been forced to learn by heart the names of the plants and trees after being tormented for years by the Watkins twins constantly switching the name tags around.) He points out interesting geological facts about the island (it is basically a sunken volcano) and tells anecdotes about its history. Sometimes a tourist might contradict Ephraim's version of history and it always turns out that Bob Cockburn, who regards himself as Lord Howe's historian, will have been the source down at the Bowling Club. And with a chuckle Ephraim will reply, *Old Bob couldn't lie straight in bed.* Yet Ephraim is no paragon of truth himself, telling his credulous tour groups that he is in his middle forties when everyone knows for a fact that he wept for days when he turned fifty, and also telling them that his wife has a PhD in botany, when in fact on the mainland she had been a hairdresser.

I must say that if I had to choose whose stories about Lord Howe were true, I would lean towards Bob Cockburn's versions every time. And it's interesting that when a tour group reaches the Valley of the Shadow of Death, Ephraim will point out the infamous cave and tell the stories almost word for word the way Bob Cockburn tells them. And in the gloom the tourists are amazed to think they are standing on the spot Moss passed on his way to burn down the settlement, just as one hundred and fifty years later Rhino took the same journey to avenge himself on the ten families who had exiled him from this paradise.

Standing at the rear of the enthralled group is Andrei, a plump, courteous Russian Ephraim employs to lug the bags and knapsacks of middle-aged tourists who have overestimated the weight they can carry on the sometimes arduous walk. Andrei isn't paid much, but it is a job and he is determined never to resign himself to failure like his fellow Russians. He has accepted that, like many of his compatriots, he is part of the flotsam and jetsam of Russians stranded in their own country and across the world in a no-man's-land of poverty because of the high tide of capitalism. He likes the Valley of the Shadow of Death because as he learns more English he realises this saturnine cathedral of nature is a very Russian sort of place and is the source of many marvellous stories. Sometimes he wishes he had learnt English instead of becoming a Latin professor because, once the Soviet Union collapsed he was, as the Americans say, *downsized* from his university. He went broke driving taxis in Kiev and foolishly agreed to follow his best friend, Vladimir, Down Under to earn a fortune building a five-star lodge.

Vladimir thinks that Lord Howe is merely the flipside of a Siberian gulag. Both are prisons; only one is tropical and the other is snow and ice. Musing about his fate Andrei will be woken from his reveries by Ephraim's catch cry of *Come on, you commie bugger* and Andrei will bring up the rear of the group, in order to help the stragglers as they move sluggishly across the grey loam. And, as they emerge from the tangled darkness into the bright sunshine, Andrei stuffs cotton wool into his ears. For it is in the next section of the ramble that Ephraim names the majority of plants on the island and his pronunciation of the Latin nomenclature is so excruciating that the Russian needs to deafen himself and grit his teeth; the babble Ephraim utters sounds to Andrei's ears like someone gargling stones. While Ephraim mangles that exquisite ancient language Andrei looks up at the nearby Mount Lidgbird. If it is not obscured by mist he can make out the faint silhouette of a gigantic cross on its rock face. He has been told that if he can see it, he is no longer a *nonnie*, but is on his way to becoming a local.

HONOUR

Helen Garner

ON SUMMER NIGHTS THEY walked through city gardens.

The air stood thick in their nostrils, a damp warmth lay upon their shoulders. Water dripped somewhere, randomly, without rhythm. On the other side of the banked plants people were murmuring idly in a foreign language. Jenny's head swam in the heat: her pores opened for the sweat to break. She saw his face floating by the fleshy flowers, eager, sharp and gentle. She wanted to take him in through her skin.

'What is that tree? What is that plant?' he asked her, and she told him the names. He did not try to remember them much, asked merely to hear her say the words in her English accent.

'How is it you know their names?'

'Oh, my father. And there are days,' she said, 'when the only things that don't look sad to me are plants.'

'Why are women so sad?' said Frank.

'I don't know,' she said. 'I don't think it's catching. Is that what you're worried about?' She stopped walking and looked him in the eyes. Behind her an iron fence with spikes rose up against the sky, which was deep blue with points of yellow light.

'Maybe,' he said after a moment. She was looking at him. One of her eyes was set very slightly higher than the other, as in some Cubist painting he may have once seen. He stepped off the path and cartwheeled lightly away over the springy grass. Once he had seen his daughter, on a sandbank in a desert, do fifty cartwheels in a row under moonlight.

*

When Kathleen answered the phone, Frank's sharp voice said,

'Hullo. It's me.'

Kathleen laughed out loud. Only a husband would announce himself thus.

'What?' he said.

'Nothing,' she said, sobering up.

'Listen. Can you come over tonight? I'd like to have a talk.'

'Anything wrong?'

'No. Just some stuff I'd like to clear up.'

The front door of the long house was left open for her and Frank was writing something in his violent, swooping hand at the kitchen table.

'Time one of you swept the hall,' she said from the doorway.

'Well, I won't be here much longer.' His cackling laugh rang out among the teacups hanging from their shelf. He sprang up nervously, took two big steps around the table and leaned against the stove with his bare arms crossed. He stared down at his feet with an assumed air of perplexity.

'Listen, Kathleen!' He leaped forward, gripped the table edge with both hands and leaned over it, but kept his face turned up to where she stood on the step. She noticed with a small shock that his hair was quite thickly grey at the sides. He narrowed his greenish eyes and stretched his thin mouth sideways like a man at the start of a hundred yard dash. The familiar drama caused her stomach to start trembling with the desire to laugh.

'Things have got to change! They can't remain the same!' he cried.

She laughed in confusion. 'What, Frank?'

'Sit down. Do you want a cuppa?' He would bounce wildly to the ceiling.

'You'd burn yourself. Spit it out.'

He gathered himself into a bunch and threw it at her. 'There's something I want. I want a divorce.'

He propped in front of the cupboard door, staring round at her to watch her cop it. She remembered suddenly how a dog they had once used to catch a thrown stick in his mouth – it stopped him dead at the moment of impact, *whack* between his black and pink jaws, but fitted: he regained his stride and ran on.

'See?' he burst out, pacing up and down with one forefinger laid against his cheek. 'It won't be any different between us. Just on paper.'

'But – what's put this into your head?'

She felt blankly curious, looking down at the bandy curves of his legs, brown and stringy in baggy khaki shorts.

'It wasn't *my* idea.' He spun round as if accused. 'Jenny wants me to – sort of – clean up my past.' His laugh was high-pitched, almost a giggle. He pulled his mouth down at the corners.

Kathleen turned blind with rage for two seconds. This time it took her a good moment to swallow it, spit from the caught stick. Frank squinted at her and suddenly the speed went out of him. He sat down at the table.

'That was a bit undiplomatic,' he remarked quietly, as if to an invisible audience.

She stared, blank as blotting paper.

'Come and sit down, Kath.'

She needed to, and obeyed.

There was a pile of papers, written on, between them on the table. Frank shifted his feet on the matting. A meek breeze came down the hall from the open front door, slid loosely across the papers and confounded itself with the warm air in which husband and wife sat. The top sheet of paper lifted as if to move sideways. Frank dumped the sugar bowl heavily on to the stack. In the fluorescent light the grains glittered.

'You see,' he began in a gentler voice, with his head on one side, 'I've always thought I'd go on being related to you, for the rest of my life.'

Normal existence began to tick steadily again. Someone had cleaned the louvre windows over the sink, and the panes gleamed darkly. In fact, the kitchen was full of shining surfaces. Frank was a great cleaner. When she was sick, even years after they had separated, he would burst into her room with broom, dust-pan and brush and whirl about like a winnowing wind, setting all to rights, placing objects in piles and at right-angles to each other.

'We will be, won't we? Related, I mean. Because Flo will relate us.'

'Yes.' His face turned soft at the name. 'But Jenny – well . . . she hasn't lived like we have all these years. "Smashing monogamy."' He laughed bitterly. 'She wants things to be resolved. "Resolved" is a word she uses a lot.'

'You don't mean you want to get *married* again?'

'If I do, it'll only be to get European work papers,' he said hastily.

'I thought one reason why we never got a divorce before was so we wouldn't make the same mistake again! Remember what you always used to say? "Getting married isn't something you do – it's something that happens to you."'

'That's true. The first time, anyway.'

She hung dangerously, as if the other half of a high-wire act had failed to show up for work. He looked down at his hands.

'You know one thing she's done for me – she's made me cut right back on my drinking.'

'How'd she do it? She must have something I haven't got.'

'I've been living like a maniac for five years, Kath. Not just when you shot through with Perfect-Features – but afterwards – doing nothing but work, drink and fuck – look at my hair!' Getting back into his stride, he indicated his grey temples with a gun-like gesture. 'Look at me! Thirty-two years old and grey as a church mouse!'

She laughed with a twist of the mouth.

'I've been bullshitting myself all these years,' he went on. 'I want a *real* place to live, with a back yard where I can plant vegies, and a couple of walls to paint, and a dog – not a bloody room in a sort of railway station!' Breathless with rhetoric, he sat smiling shyly at her, one arm resting on the tabletop.

'Does Jenny want that too?'

'Yes.' He might have blushed.

She would have to be mingy indeed to stay hard-faced against his hopefulness. 'What about Flo?'

'Jenny loves her. Can she come and live with us for a while? For a month or so? It would be a home. I'll drive her to school.' He looked eager, leaning over his arm.

'Does she want to go?' It was only a formality.

'Oh yes. I think so.'

Some half-gagged splinter-self in the depths was twisting in protest: what about *me*? but Kathleen kicked the door shut on it. There were no demands or protests she might rightfully make. He had always treated her honourably. In five years she had never given it one moment's conscious thought, but had lounged upon the unspoken assumption that she was still somebody's, even when she was most alone.

She looked up and saw a tiny liquid twinkling in the inner corner of Frank's left eye.

'Look!' he shouted, pointing to it. 'A tear! It is! I can still squeeze one out!'

*

Kathleen ran in from the glaring street. Through the screen door she perceived dim shapes moving at the other end of the passage. The wire smelled coldly of rust as she pressed her nose to it and rattled her fist against the wood. Jenny was calling back over her shoulder as she approached the door.

'So I told her I considered my contract fulfilled,' she was saying in a tone of such dry resoluteness that Kathleen envied her a firm life: orderliness, self-esteem. She saw Kathleen and said, 'Oh!' They had never met, but stared at each other through the clotted wire with suddenly quailing hearts.

'I've just come for Flo,' said Kathleen.

'Would you like to come in? We're watching the news.'

Frank was hunched forward, elbows on knees. 'Come to check up on me, have you,' he said, not taking his eyes off the screen where a man's face opened and closed its mouth.

'Who's this clown?' said Kathleen, ignoring the jibe.

'Lang Hancock.'

'What's he on about?'

'Sssh!' said Frank. 'Watch and find out.'

'He claims,' said Jenny tactfully, 'that he flew through a radio-active cloud thirty years ago and that it didn't do him any harm – thus, that it's all right to mine uranium. A fine piece of Australian political reasoning.'

'But who's the woman?'

'His daughter. He's brought her along to show that his genes didn't suffer.'

'What! He reckons he didn't suffer genetic damage, and that's his *daughter*, with that huge polka dot *bow* round her neck?' Kathleen started to giggle.

Frank turned round crossly and said, 'Sssh, will you? This is serious!'

Kathleen put her beach towel over her mouth and pulled a

chastised face. She picked up a newspaper and flipped through it.

'My God,' she said. 'It says here that a lady went into hospital in France to have a baby, and when she came out of the anaesthetic they'd cut one of her *hands* off.'

Frank switched off the television. 'Do you ever read the actual news, Kath? Apart from Odd Spots, death notices and so on?'

'Of course,' said Kathleen, obviously bluffing.

Jenny stared at her, and thought in a vague blur of fear, 'Is it being a mother that makes her head racket round like that? Will this happen to me?'

The two women sat in similar poses, limbs arranged so as to appear casual. They did not perceive their striking similarity; they both made emphatic hand gestures and grimaces in speech, stressed certain words ironically, cast their eyes aside in mid-sentence as if a sustained gaze might burn the listener. Around each of them quivered an aura of terrific restraint. If they both let go at once, they might blow each other out of the room.

'This is a nice house,' said Kathleen recklessly. 'Why doesn't Frank just move in here, instead of both of you having to look for another place?'

The air bristled.

'Because then he would be living at my place,' enunciated Jenny carefully, 'and we would like to start off on equal terms.'

'We've found a place, anyway,' said Frank.

'I'll give you a hand to move then, whenever you like,' Kathleen charged on. There was a short hush.

'Will you have a beer, Kathleen?' said Jenny.

'No thanks. I was going to take Flo for a swim.'

'It's a scorcher, all right,' said Frank, shifting in his chair.

Light filtered through drawn curtains, the three characters floated in watery dimness. Pale objects burned: cotton trousers, a dress faded as a flour bag, a flash of eye-white in a turned head. There was a faint smell of lemon.

Flo ran in, dragging a white dog by its collar.

'I heard you talking, Kath. See? This is Jenny's dog. She *loves* me.'

'I bet she does. Come on – we'll go to the baths.'

'Come into my room and get your things, Flo,' said Jenny.

Flo took Kathleen's hand. 'Come and look at Jenny's things. She's got jewels, and a special thing like scissors for your eyelashes.'

The brown floor in the passage creaked under them. Jenny snapped on a lamp in the front room and the heavy double bed sprang into the light. Flo edged her way round its obtrusive foot to reach the treasure box by the empty fireplace. The two women stood awkwardly, embarrassed by the meaning of the bed, but Flo turned round with a tweezer-like object in her hand and applied it brusquely to her eyelashes.

'Careful!'

'See? They make your eyelashes *curly*.'

Jenny laughed and flicked a glance at Kathleen to see if she disapproved. Kathleen did, but was also curious, and looked to see if Jenny had used the tool on her own eyes, which were brown and unevenly set.

'When are you coming here to spend the night, Flo?' said Jenny.

Flo looked shyly at her mother, not wanting to make her jealous. 'Can I, one day?'

'Of course.'

'I'll phone you,' said Jenny.

Jenny and Flo took a step towards one another and Flo raised her arms as if to kiss her goodbye. They both stopped at the same instant and looked at Kathleen with identical expressions: waiting for dispensation. Kathleen smiled and nodded, they were released and kissed smackingly.

Outside the front door the hot afternoon enfolded them in its dry blanket. The gate disturbed vegetation and set free a dizzying wave of privet smell and the peppery scent of pink climbing roses.

Halfway down the lane Frank caught up with them and took hold of Flo's other hand.

'Hang on, Kath! I've got something to ask you. Don't you ever walk slowly?'

'No. Do you?'

'No.' He fell into step beside Flo. 'I'd like to be able to saunter. I read that in a book of aphorisms: "It is a great art to saunter." Anyway I have to go down to Mum and Dad's.'

'Is anything wrong down there?'

'Mum's a bit under the weather.'

'What? Why didn't you tell me?'

'I only found out last night. Dad rang up. Poor old blighter can hardly see to dial the number.'

'What's actually wrong with Shirl?'

'I don't know. Some sort of nervous complaint. Quite painful. She's had the doctor.' He lashed savagely at a hedge. 'I don't think Dad can manage by himself. He's never asked me for help before.'

They walked along in silence.

'Do you want me to come down with you?' said Kathleen. 'Unless you're taking Jenny, of course.'

'Would you? It'd get the load off me a bit. They haven't met Jenny yet. Mightn't be the moment to break that one to them.'

'Can I come?' Flo inserted the request purely for form's sake.

'No,' said Kathleen. 'You can't miss school. You can stay home with the others.'

'Well, can I go and live with Frank and Jenny in their new house, then?' She was only flying a kite, barely listening for the answer, lining up her sandal toes with the cracks of the footpath so that the end of each fence fell upon an even number.

'Yes. If you want to.' Kathleen was trying to smile.

Flo seized her round the waist with her wiry arms. 'But what if you miss me too much? You won't cry or anything, will you?'

Her teeth were uneven and her forehead at this anxious moment displayed five horizontal lines of wrinkles so exactly like Frank's that Kathleen was all at sea.

'I can come and visit you,' she said. 'You can invite me over for dinner and we can both cook.'

Kathleen looked up from this bony embrace and saw Frank leaning against the fence with a strange smile on his face. 'He must be happy,' she thought. Flo pranced about. The parents' faces were stiff and their expressions inappropriate. Kathleen felt old, and perhaps bitter, but not against these two creatures whose separateness from herself, no matter how many times it had been demonstrated, she could never really bring herself to believe in.

Frank and Kathleen stood side by side like children in the doorway. Shirley was asleep, her head turned sharply to one side on the pillow, her mouth open as if she had just cried out.

'The doctor says it's called psoriasis,' offered Jack in the kitchen. 'She sleeps most of the time.' He smiled helplessly at them, bewildered, wanting to be appeased and approved of. Age had shrunk him, and he hardly reached Frank's shoulder.

'What's the doctor giving her? I mean – she shouldn't be knocked out like that, should she?' Frank moved agitatedly about the room, pulling open cupboard doors and slamming them again without looking inside.

'Blowed if I know, Frankie,' said the old man. His knotty hands were resting on the back of a chair. 'The doctor's a young chap, 'bout your age. I s'pose he knows what he's talking about.'

'I wouldn't be so bloody sure. They're drug-happy, those blokes – eh, Kath?'

She nodded, watching.

'I was just going to wake her up and give her something to eat, when you two arrived,' said Jack. 'I had a snack a little while ago.' On the sink were a plate, a knife and a fork, rinsed.

'I'll do it, Dad,' said Frank. 'You sit down there and take a break. What'll we give her, Kath?'

They cobbled together a dish of yoghurt and fruit, and Frank took it into the bedroom. Jack, legs crossed in his favourite corner chair, deerstalker cap pulled down over his bristly eyebrows and transistor whining faintly on his lap, began a soft tuneless whistle, tapping his fingertips on the armrests and looking out the window with elaborate casualness.

'Tum te tum te tum. Well . . .' he murmured. He sneaked a look at Kathleen and returned to his contemplation of a bush outside the glass.

'Think I'll pop out the back for a sec and have a look at the garden before it gets too dark,' said Kathleen at last, to put him out of his misery.

'Mmmm . . . there's quite a show out there. Pick some to take home.' One foot in its gleaming brogue beat rhythmically on air.

She made her escape and stood in mild air on the sloping lawn. A wind moved in the garden, very gentle and sweet: it shifted pleasantly among the leaves of small gums and roses past their season. The sky blurred upward, pearly as the inside of a shell, and in this delicate firmament there floated a perfect moon, its valleys and mountains lightly etched.

Shirley's voice rose sharply from the bedroom, and Frank's answered. Their words were indistinct. Then footsteps thumped, and Frank burst out the back door and stood staring desperately into the massed hydrangeas. Kathleen stepped up beside him.

'I had to feed her with a spoon,' he said, grinding his teeth and sniffing. 'She didn't want me to. She only wants Dad.'

'She's probably ashamed.'

'What? What of?'

'Being weak in front of you. And she's probably worried about being ugly.'

'Ugly! I don't give a damn about that! I just want to know what drugs those bastards have got her on. I've never seen her as dopey as this!' He clenched his fists and let out a sob. Kathleen slipped one arm round his waist and tried to hug him unobtrusively. He was rigid and very thin.

'Does she know I'm here?'

'Yes. Go and say hullo. I think she might want a drink. I'll stay out here and calm down.'

The old woman struggled to sit up. 'No, don't kiss me,' she said in distress, moving her head from side to side as Kathleen approached. 'I'm all –' She pulled her night-dress together at the neck to hide the scaly patches of skin on her chest. Jack smiled vaguely and felt his way along the wardrobe and out of the room.

'I've brought you a drink, Shirl.' Kathleen was all solidity and hearty tone, sticking her hand out with the fizzing glass in it. After two sips of dry ginger, great runs of air rumbled up from Shirley's stomach, and she turned her face away, blushing feebly and covering her mouth with her hand.

'I'm sorry,' she whispered.

'Makes you burp, does it,' said Kathleen. 'That's what fizzy drinks are for.'

'I hate it,' cried Shirley passionately, still with her shoulder turned.

'Do you? I love it,' said Kathleen without a shadow of a lie but full of motive. 'It's good for you.'

The bedclothes were all skew-whiff, the sheets out of alignment with the blankets, the whole lot dragging on the floor.

'Will I tidy up a bit for you, Shirl?'

'Oh, it's too much trouble, love.' She fretted among the pillows, turning her head in abrupt movements like a bird.

'No it's not. I'll call Frank.'

Frank settled his mother on a chair while Kathleen took hold of the bedclothes and yanked them away. A shower of silvery dead skin flakes flew out and fell in drifts on the polished wood floor.

'It's awful,' moaned Shirley, humiliated in her dressing-gown.

'Don't be silly, Mum,' said Frank. 'It's *not* awful, and you *must* accept being looked after.'

Kathleen worked away efficiently with clean linen, shoving her hands between mattress and base and plumping up pillows. She remembered sitting thinly on a chair with her feet dangling while her mother 'made her bed nice'.

'There you are. Hop in here. I'll run the old sheets through the machine.' She gathered them up in her arms and forged out the door.

Shirley's splintery voice trailed after her. 'The second cycle, lovey – don't forget to open both the taps, and not too much soap powder . . .'

'She knows how to *do* it, Mum,' snapped Frank. Kathleen almost laughed. When Frank and his mother talked like that, things were getting back to normal. She blundered round in the laundry, unused to machines that worked without the introduction of coins, and got the thing going at last. She was standing there thinking in the cloth-muffled room when Frank slipped in and shut the door behind him.

'What's Jack up to?' said Kathleen.

'Fumbling round in the study trying to find Mum's prescription.'

Frank picked up a basket full of pegs and rattled it fiercely. 'I think this is probably the beginning of the . . . race to the end.' He grimaced, pointed one finger heavenwards and then down to the earth, and mimed sleep as children do, eyes closed and palms together under one cheek. They both laughed painfully.

In Shirley's kitchen the autumn sunlight was oblique and very bright. Kathleen squinted and moved constantly from one part of the room to another in search of an area of shade for her face. There was a blinding sheen on the table-boards, shafts of light sprang from cutlery, Frank's hair stood out like an aureole. The plastic cover of the photo album dazzled relentlessly.

'Look,' said Frank.

'I can't see.'

'It's my dog, a foxy I had when I was a kid.'

Shuffling footsteps came along the passage, and Shirley stood in the doorway with a mustard-coloured shawl wrapped round her.

'What are you doing out of bed, Mum?'

'Oh . . . I'm all right,' she insisted in her cracked voice, pushing past him and sitting down at the table. 'I'd rather be up and about.'

Frank clicked his tongue, but passed her the album. 'Look, Mum. Remember when Auntie Hazel used to stay in her caravan in our back yard?'

Shirley seized the album and shielded her eyes over it. 'Oohoo, that Hazel,' she crooned with a note of malice.

'Look at that dress she's got on! We said at the time, Brocade's as dead as a dodo, we said. We all knew what she was after when she latched on to Keith. There was the house in Kyneton, all his mother's things, you never saw such lace – and the furniture, a cheval glass she'd had made up for her by an old Chinaman up Ballarat way . . . Hazel hung on like grim death, but she only got hold of it a clock here, a chair there.' She turned the pages with a sigh, and they sat listening, half-hypnotised as she murmured. 'Ah, there's Jack as a younger man. He had a finely turned ankle in those days. It was the first thing I noticed about him. Why should I tell you all this? Dear God, it's life, I suppose.'

'I've got something to tell *you*, Mum,' said Frank suddenly. Kathleen looked up startled and saw him take the deep breath before the plunge.

'What, love.' Shirley hovered over the grey snaps like a map-reader.

'Kath and I are getting a divorce.'

The plastic page flopped loosely under her idle hand, as if she had not heard.

'Now, we don't want you to get *upset* about this, Mum,' he said, his voice sharpening into the old warning note.

'What, lovey?' She turned the book sideways and bent over it the better to scrutinise.

'I might be getting *married* again, Mum. I'm going to *live* with someone.'

Shirley looked up from the picture book and spoke very clearly, with a note of world-weariness that they had never heard before. 'Oh, I don't give a damn. She can come down here. That couch turns into a double bed. I only ever wanted you, Kath, and Flo, but it's no use growling. I can't be worried about it now. Bring her down.'

Frank was shocked. Not only had he expected her to be outraged, but he needed her to be, so that he might define himself against her protest. It was perhaps the moment of his growing up. Before Kathleen's eyes the knot dissolved, and she watched him float free, feet groping, full of alarm.

Kathleen and Frank went walking down by the shore, under the avenues of huge cypresses rooted deep in the sandy ground. Perhaps they would have liked to walk arm in arm: there were historical reasons for the fact that they did not.

'I love it here,' said Frank. 'It seems so old. I bet Yalta on the Black Sea must be like this – flat and mournful. When I read *The Lady with the Dog* I imagined it happening here.'

On the pier their footsteps rang hollow and water slapped way below. Long ships, business-like, slid past on their way to the heads: some quality of absence in the air brought them unnaturally close. It was late afternoon, and a strange metal light intensified most vividly the dark greens and greys of the shore, and of the sad water that seemed to stream past them oceanwards. Frank, absorbed in his Chekhovian fantasy, planted himself squarely at the very end of the pier, slitting his eyes and loosening his coat to let it flap in the wind.

'There's going to be a storm,' remarked Kathleen in a neutral tone, absent-mindedly brushing dandruff off his shoulders.

'Have you no eyes, Kathleen?' trumpeted Frank. He fronted the brisk wind with a histrionic gesture. 'Look about you! Is there no poetry left in your soul?'

'Oh, I think there might be a bit left,' she said drily. She stared past him.

The water was lashing at the encrusted supports of the pier, and the big lifeboat groaned on its pulleys. Their hair streamed back off their skulls and rain began to sprinkle sharply on to their up-turned faces.

'Let's go, Frankie.'

'OK,' he grumbled good-naturedly, 'you old prune. I wish Floss was here. *She'd* play with me.'

They turned up their collars and let the wind hurry them back towards the car. On the dashboard Frank had sticky-taped a type-written notice which read, *This car should last another ten years.* He drove with nervous efficiency. As he drove he sang, accompanying himself with sharp taps of the left foot:

There's a trade we all know well
It's bringing cattle over
On every track to the Gulf and back
Men know the Queensland drover

and she joined in the chorus because she knew it would give him pleasure:

Pass the billy round boys
Don't let the pintpot stand there
For tonight we drink the health
Of every Overlander

Loudly and in harmony they sang, sneaking each other embarrassed, happy smiles, then laughed and avoided each other's eyes.

'I'm scared Dad'll go before I can get his story out of him,' said Frank.

'Didn't you start taping it?'

'Yes. But it's so hard to get him going. He's shy, and he gets mixed up.'

'Did you get the one about the carrot?'

Frank knitted his brows and mimicked his father's slow, musing voice: 'I was sitting on the verandah after work when Reggie Blainey came down the road dragging over his shoulder what looked like a *young sapling*. He got closer and I saw it was actually the fronds of a *giant carrot*. I says, Well, Reggie, that's the biggest carrot *I've* ever seen! And he looks up at me and he says, Listen, you reckon this is big? I dug for three hours – and the bloomin' thing forked at twenty foot.'

Under the rain, the lights of Geelong were coming on as they sped down the Leopold Hill.

*

Kathleen's brother-in-law opened the door to them in a flustered moment. An invisible child was throwing a tantrum in the kitchen, and from the stereo in the living room a string quartet was straining away loudly.

'Hul-lo!' he cried in amazement. 'What a treat! Come in! Pin was whizzed into hospital straight after lunch – the baby's overdue. We're just waiting for news.'

They followed him into the kitchen, where the benches and tables were covered in bright blue formica and the small window looked out over fruit trees and a chook pen. At their appearance the child on the floor ceased to beat his fists and sat up to stare, his cheeks puce and tear-stained.

'My goodness!' said Charlie. 'I haven't seen you two together for – must be five years! There's not a reconciliation, is there?' He clapped his hand over his mouth as if he had made a gaffe. Kathleen and Frank, whose lack of interest in divorce had given them a certain bohemian status in both their families, remained collected. Kathleen swept a mass of blocks off a chair and sat down. The two men stood about, Charlie flipping a teatowel, Frank grinning at the floor. The older boy appeared in the doorway as the string quartet reached its climax and resolved itself into one drawn-out, quivering harmony. Silence. Charlie sighed voluptuously.

'Wonderful, isn't it,' he said.

'When's mummy coming home. I want mummy to come home.'

'Yes dar-ling,' sang Charlie irrelevantly on two notes, his mind on something else but not soon enough, for a covered saucepan erupted on the stove and milk went everywhere. 'Damn. Blast it.'

Kathleen spoke up without forethought. 'I could stay for a few days, if you like, and give you a hand with the kids.'

'Oh, would you?' He spun round with the inadequate wettex dripping on his shoes.

'Am I neurotic?' thought Kathleen, already aware of a trickle of regret behind the smile.

She hurried the trolley along the bright shelves of the supermarket, Ben trotting at her side and Tom lording it in the seat above the merchandise. No matter how fast she moved, something horrible kept pace with her, ran smoothly along behind the ranged and perfect shining objects: something to do with memory, with time past she thought she had escaped, as long ago as childhood when she had striven to imagine her mother's life and her own future: meals, meals, meals: the meal as duty, as short leash, as unit of time inexorable into everlastingness. She dared not glance at other women passing lest she see confirmation of it in their faces. There was no word for this sickness in her, running alongside her, but *void*.

In the checkout queue she realised she had forgotten fruit.

'Will you stay here and mind the shopping while I run back?' Ben gripped her hand convulsively.

'I won't be long,' she pleaded. 'There's nothing to worry about – we'll go home and have some lunch.'

She wrenched herself free and bolted along the slick alleyways, frantic to be by herself even for sixty seconds. She glanced back at them as she skidded round the great cabinets steaming with frost and saw Ben's pale face eyeing her and Tom's mouth opening to let out one of his leisurely roars. *I can't stand it, can't stand it*, a whining chipmunk voice began up in the back of her skull, it chattered at her, jibbered, she dived both hands into the pile of netted oranges, flipped them this way and that, mould whiffed at her, *the skull beneath the skin* pipped the voice, *shit shit shit*, two bags at sixty-five cents, she counted on her fingers a dollar thirty something, now where are those two little buggers? God help them, God send me back to Flo, how did I stand it when she was only two? Only three more days and I'll be on that train.

Outside, she trundled the pusher up the hill. It was quicker to carry Tom in it than to round him up on foot, but he was fat and the heavy shopping bags, one in each hand against the handle of the flimsy pusher, bumped clumsily against her legs and the wheels as she progressed. Ben gripped the handle, continually swinging the triple load out of line. She fought herself for patience. The sky was thick, big drops started, they had no coats. Tom began to bellow,

'Wet! Wet! Wet! Wanna det out!'

'Oh shut up Tom!' she raged, wrenching hard to get the pusher wheel out of a crack in the pavement. Ben slid her a sly look.

'Will I shove a jelly bean into him?' he hissed.

They began to laugh conspiratorially.

'Where did you get 'em?'

'While you were paying the lady.'

The pathetic cavalcade struggled up the hill.

She sat on the back verandah cutting slice after slice off a rubbery ginger cake she had found in a tin and stuffing it into her mouth. The boys played in their sandpit. The sand was dark yellow but the rain had stopped. She remembered reading somewhere: only if you have been a child in a certain town can you know its sadness, bone sadness, sadness of the blood. *Every day the clouds come over.* She went and stood by the sandpit. The little shovels made a damp grating sound as the children sank them into the sand.

At teatime when Charlie came home from work, she served up for dessert a kind of pudding. Everyone but Tom ate it enthusiastically. Enthroned in his high chair, holding his spoon like a sceptre, he scowled into his bowl.

'Eat up, Tom,' said his father. He glanced at Kathleen and poked the pudding into a more attractive shape in the bowl. 'It's cake.'

Tom withered him with a look. 'That is *not cake*.' His aunt and his father lowered their lying heads on to the table among the plates and laughed in weak paroxysms.

The baby came, a girl. Kathleen sniffed the head of the creature rolled tightly in its cotton blanket. Looking at her sister had always been like looking into a mirror: large forehead, eyes that drooped at the outer corners, pointed chin, small mouth. Kathleen laughed.

'What's funny?' said Pin, shifting uncomfortably in the hospital bed.

'I was looking at your mouth. It's exactly the same as mine.'

'Small and mean,' said Pin, whose devotion to the church did not damp her vulgar sense of humour. 'Wanna see a cat's bum?' She pursed her lips into a tight bunch. They snickered in the quiet ward.

'You'll never go to heaven,' said Kathleen. 'You're rude.'

'Don't be a dill. Sit down here and tell me what you've been doing. The only way I can get away from the kids long enough to have a good talk with someone is by having another one.'

'Oh . . . I muck round. Read, you know. Clean up.'

'Charlie says Frank was down. You're not getting together again, are you?'

'Hardly. Too late for that, even if we wanted to.'

'What a shame. I always liked Frank.'

'So did I. Still do. I think he's the ant's pants. What've *you* been up to, apart from having babies?'

'Praying.' At Kathleen's polite attempt to conceal her disgust, Pin burst out laughing. 'I have – but I only said it to provoke.'

'How was the birth?'

'Oh, lovely. I mean – it would have been, if they'd left me alone. I was managing quite well, being a bit of an old hand, but I was probably making a lot of noise, because one of the doctors came in and mumbled something to the nurse, and next thing I know she's approaching with a big cheesy smile and one hand behind her back. Righto, Mrs Hassett! she says. I want you to curl up on the table with your bottom right out on the edge, just like a little bunny rabbit. No you don't! I said. No one's giving *me* a spinal – I was a nurse before I got like this. I *know* that bunny rabbit line – just get away from me, thanks very much. And I battled on, and voila!' She indicated with a flourish the sausage-shaped bundle in the cot beside the bed. 'Anyway, Kath – 'scuse me for a sec. I'm going to stagger to the toilet.'

When Pin came back she was as white as a sheet.

'Is anything wrong?'

'I'm not sure. Here, help me back into bed, will you? I think I'd better call the doctor.'

'What, Pin?'

'I was wiping myself just now, and I felt something hard, right down in my vagina. I put my head between my knees and had a look. I think it's my cervix.'

They stared at each other. Pin tried to laugh. 'It's probably nothing.'

A nurse came. She slipped her hand under the bedclothes.

Kathleen wandered over to the window and looked out over the grey bay with its stumpy palm trees and, further away towards Melbourne on the endless volcanic plain, the two dead mountains, rounded as worn-down molars.

The nurse said, 'I'll go and call doctor.' Her expression was respectful as she padded away on her soft white shoes. Pin grimaced and shrugged.

'Oh Pin. What a drag.' Kathleen sat down on the bed and took hold of her sister's hand with its heavy silver engagement and wedding rings. 'Are you still playing the piano?'

'Yes, and I'm getting better too.' Pin grinned defiantly. 'My teacher said, "For a thirty-five-year-old with a rotten memory, you're not doing too badly."'

Across her mouth flitted a stoicism, a setting of the lips, still well this side of martyrdom.

*

The house was at the bottom of a dead-end road with narrow yellowing nature strips, and a railway line running across its very end like stitches closing a bag. It was twelve o'clock and there was no one around.

Jenny came out the front door and saw Kathleen dawdling by her car, arm along brow against the strong sun. She looked small, dwarfed by the big blue day, and unusually hesitant, leaning there looking this way and that, squinting up her face so that her top teeth showed. Jenny felt a throb of almost sexual tenderness towards her: a hard spasm of the heart, a weakening in the pelvis. She darted out the gate and stopped in front of Kathleen, seized her wrist. With force of will she kept the other woman's hand, studied with a peculiar flux of love her sun-wrinkled eyes, the marks of her shrewd expressions. They could even smell each other: flower, oil, coffee, soap: and under these, warmed flesh, dotted tongue, glass of eye, glossy membrane, rope of hair, nail roughly clipped.

'Welcome,' said Jenny.

Perhaps they would never dare again. They stepped out of each other, frightened.

'There's nothing here to drink,' called out Frank on the verandah. 'I'm going to find a pub.'

Jenny turned away from Kathleen, distracted. 'I'll come with you.'

Kathleen waited, still leaning against her car, until they were out of sight, walking slowly in the heat with their arms round each other. Two ragged nectarine trees fidgeted their leaves in the scarcely-moving air. Her head was faint in the dryness. She heaved herself up and turned to tackle the house.

Its facade, a triangle on top of a square, was slightly awry and painted the aqua colour favoured by Greek landlords. She ducked under an orange and green blind rolled up on rotted ropes at the outer edge of the verandah, and turned the key in the handle-less front door. In the tilting hallway she walked quickly past two or three small rooms with brown blinds half-drawn and opened the door into the kitchen, in which a combustion stove, painted white to indicate its decorative status, crouched in the chimney place, superseded by a gas cooker, itself forty years old, standing in a nearby corner alcove. Someone had slung a blanket across the window on two nails to keep the hot day out: its woollen folds muffled all movement of air and absorbed the knock of her footsteps.

She stood still in the bare centre of the room, on boards, in dimness. The heat was breathless. A drop of water bulged and quivered under the tap.

The back door was shut. It was made of four vertical strips of timber, also painted white, and closed with a loose brass knob. The timber had worn thin top and bottom, like the business end of front teeth, so that the dry brightness off the concrete outside was felt in the room as two insistent, serrated presences of light.

She opened the door, stepped down into the dazzling yard, and walked along by the grey wooden fence and through the green, dried-out trellis door into the wash-house with its squat copper and pair of troughs under the window never meant to open. She placed her palms lightly on the edge of the troughs. They were grey, forever damp and cool, clotted of surface and rimmed lead-smooth in paler grey; she had been bathed when very small in troughs such as these, and her mother had let her play with the wooden stick that she used to stir the copper, a stick with a face on the knob. The wash-house smelled of wet cloth and blue bags, and she could not climb out of the high trough by herself, so she was obliged to sit there nipple-deep in cooling water waiting for her mother, gazing blankly out the blurred window panes to the corner next to the dunny where the tank stood on its wooden stand, up to its ankles in grass even in summer, and if you tapped its wavy sides it would not give out a note for it was full to a level higher than you could reach, and its water was clear and swirly with wrigglers, baby mosquitoes that would not hurt you if you guzzled fast enough, and she sang out, 'Mu – um! I've fi – nished!' but her mother did not hear, for she was outside in the yard at the clothes line putting a shirt to her mouth to see if it was dry enough to be unpegged and taken in for ironing.

A bike clattered against the front fence.

'Kath – leen!' shouted Flo.

Kathleen slipped out of the wash-house and halfway down the yard came upon a rotary clothes line rusting away on an angle, a skivvy faded to sand-colour hanging by one wrist from its lowest quadrant, like a flag left tattered and forgotten after a rout. She took hold of the body of the shirt and, without thinking, raised it to her lips in that gesture of mothers, breathed in its sweet dry weathered cotton soapy perfume; and at that moment saw a to-and-fro movement behind the wash-house window panes. It was Flo waving to her.

She dropped the skivvy and plunged on towards the back fence, beyond which dizzy cicadas raved endlessly in trees bordering the railway line. The faint voices of Flo and Frank, a little duet for piccolo and banjo, were still behind her in the back of the house. She stood at the end of the yard, almost off the property. A door banged somewhere else, water ran loudly into a metal container, fat hissed in another kitchen. The sky, without impurity, went up for miles.

It was the house of her childhood. She knew its impermanent, camp-like feeling. When front and back doors were open, the house would be no more than a tunnel of moving air. Under rain, its roof would thunder and its downpipes rustle as you turned in your sleep. Heat in winter would have to be generated inside and cunningly trapped, in summer repulsed by crafty arrangements, early in the morning, of curtains and blinds. Unlike stone or brick, its weatherboard walls would not absorb the essence of its inhabitants' existence: they were as insubstantial as Japanese screens: disappointment and anxiety, hope and contentment would pass through them with equal ease and rapidity. The house laid no claim to beauty. It was humble, and would mind its own business.

The last piece of furniture to be persuaded through the narrow front door was an oval table missing all four castors. They worried it into the kitchen, pulled up chairs and sat around it.

'Didn't this used to be our dining-room table back at Sutherland Street, Frank?' said Kathleen.

'Yep. Four dollars at the Anchorage, remember? That was when I cornered the market in cane chairs, too.'

'Come off it! We only had three.'

'Yes, but the price had doubled by the following Saturday.'

The fridge was already whirring behind the door. Jenny passed out cans of beer and sat down next to Frank. He smiled at her, but Kathleen's opening line had launched him on a tide of domestic memory and he was away.

The impromptu performances that Frank and Kathleen put on at kitchen tables and other public places were the crudest manifestation of the force-field that hummed between them: an infinity of tiny signals – warning, comfort, rebuke – flashed from one to the other ceaselessly and for the most part unconsciously. In its most highly coded form it passed unobserved in a general conversation; in public garb it called others to witness, embraced them as audience or participants in embroidered tales of a common past. It was hatred, regret, pity; it was respect and the fiercest loyalty. They could no more have turned it off than turned back time.

Jenny was left striving for grace, for a courteous arrangement of features while they recited, delighted in the ring of names without meaning for her. Frank put his arm round her bare shoulders, but she kept looking at her beer can and fiddling it round and round, letting her curly hair fall across her face to shield her. There was a short silence in the room, during which Flo could be heard splattering the hose against the side wall of the house. They had opened the door and taken down the blanket as the afternoon drew on and the sun shifted off the concrete outside the kitchen, but the heat was still intense.

'Give the concrete out here a bit of a sprinkle, love,' Frank shouted. Flo did not answer, but a great silvery rope of water flew past the open door and whacked against the bedroom window.

'Down a bit! Down! Don't wet all our stuff!'

The dog, saturated and hysterical, darted into the kitchen and ran about in a frenzy. At the same instant they heard the first signs of life from next door, a rat-tat-tat of voices in a language they did not understand.

'Is that Greek?' said Jenny.

'Might be.' Frank was absent-mindedly stroking her neck. His dreamy smile sharpened into a cackle of laughter. 'Hey Kath – remember Joe and Slavica?'

'Oh God.' She turned to Jenny. 'They were a Yugoslavian couple who lived next door to us when we were first married.'

'We got on fine with them for a while. They used to ask us in for dinner and force us to drink till we were falling off the chairs. We'd sing all night, it was great.'

'Yes, but poor Slavica,' said Kathleen. 'She didn't even score a place at the table. We'd arrive and there'd be three places set. Slavica would be out in the kitchen like a servant.'

'You mean – she actually *ate* out there?'

'Standing up. We used to have to drag her in and make her sit down.'

The two women exchanged their first straight look of solidarity. Frank galloped onwards, heading for the drama of it.

'Anyway, Joe got crazier. He used to come home from work with half a dozen bottles and drink the lot all by himself in front of the TV.'

'About ten o'clock one night we heard him start to curse and smash things —'

'Their little boy nicked over our back fence to hide.'

'He couldn't speak English. He let me cuddle him.'

'And then we heard the back door crash, and Slavica was locked out in the yard. She called out to us very softly, and we passed the kid back over the fence.'

'He didn't want to go back.'

'And straight away we heard Joe rush out into the yard and abuse her —'

'He *thumped* her!'

'And he dragged the kid inside and left her in the yard all night, she told us later. She slept in a corner near the chook pen.'

'Didn't you *do* anything?' said Jenny, horrified.

'*We* were scared of him, too!' said Frank. 'He was big! He was a maniac! We rang the police, but they didn't want to know about it – a domestic.'

Frank was on his feet now, his narrow eyes alight with story-teller's fervour. 'But one night Kath was driving home and she caught this ghostly figure in the headlights. It was Slavica running across the road with no shoes on. He'd kicked her out in the street. So Kath brought her into our place and she slept on the couch.' He made two stabbing motions with his fore-finger towards the living room. 'That couch in there, the white one. She said he was crazy because he suspected her of having an affair with the lodger. How corny can you get?'

'The lodger was a classic. A real lounge lizard. He gambled all his money away and couldn't pay the rent. He had a pencil moustache, slicked back hair, the lot.'

'Well, next morning we waited till Joe went to work and then sneaked out to see if the coast was clear. It was raining, and there were all the lodger's pathetic belongings chucked out on the footpath – a tattered suitcase, a pair of pointy two-tone shoes, a couple of lairy shirts —'

'Slavica dashed in and got the kid,' said Kathleen. 'I took them down to the People's Palace.'

'The Salvation Army?'

'We didn't know where to take them, and it wasn't safe at our place.'

'But wasn't there a Halfway House or something?'

'Not back then!' said Kathleen. 'This is Australia, mate!'

'Oh.'

Frank was poised to continue, bouncing on the balls of his feet. 'Anyway, Kath found her a room in a house in Northcote run by an older Yugoslavian who said she'd been through the same story, and on Saturday morning Kath drove Slavica home to pick up some kitchen things.'

'I pulled up out the front in this old VW we had at the time, and Slavica ran in and came out with an armful of pots and pans. She was too scared to go back for her clothes. Joe was on the front verandah with this terrible smile on his face, his arms were folded and he'd laugh – God it was awful, a sort of mad, bitter cackle – I said, Get in, Slavica, we have to get out of here. She jumps in, I'm trying to start the flaming car, the kid in the back with eyes as big as mill-wheels – and at the last minute Joe comes tearing out with a long piece of string and a saucepan, and ties it on the back bumper bar, like people do at weddings.'

'My God.'

'I get the car into gear, he's raving and shrieking and half the street's hanging over their front gates watching – and just as we take off he gives the back of the car an almighty kick, and away we go with the saucepan rattling behind us. Talk about an undignified retreat! I stopped about four blocks away and tore it off.'

Kathleen, out of breath, laughed nervously and glanced at Frank, who took up the tale. 'Well, so Slavica was OK, but from then on we got no rest at night. He'd drink himself off the map after work, then at ten o'clock he'd start this awful yelling.'

'Not yelling, exactly,' said Kathleen. 'Worse. More like loud whispering. Right under our bedroom window, which fortunately was on the first floor.'

'What did he say?'

She mimicked it slowly and dreadfully. ' "Australian – bitch – cunt. I make you trouble. I burn. I kill." And so on.'

There was a silence.

'Was I born then, Kath?' said Flo from the door. She was holding the dripping hose in her hand, and the dirt round her mouth made her look as if she were grinning.

'You were born all right,' said Kathleen. 'You slept in a basket, and we were so scared of him that we kept you in our room all night, just in case. Point the hose the other way.'

'In fact,' said Frank, 'we were so scared of him that *I* started drinking too.'

'Is *that* why you started?' said Jenny dryly.

'I kept a sort of wooden club thing on the shelf above the front door.'

'And you used to prowl around the house brandishing it and saying —'

' "*He's strong, but I'm clever!*" ' The ex-couple chorused it and burst into a roar of laughter.

'Why doesn't Jenny tell a story now?' said Flo, carefully directing the dribbling hose down her leg and off her ankle on to the concrete.

Faces relaxed, a softer laugh ran round the table, Jenny let her shoulder lean against Frank's and turned up her face towards Kathleen. They were, after all, people of good will.

Soon Frank and Flo wandered outside to inspect the site of the vegetable garden and the two women sat shyly at the table, touching the same boards with their bare soles, the same table-top with their forearms, but clumsy, a thousand miles from the moment of blessing which had united them that morning.

Jenny spoke. 'I was —'

'Frank's mother gave us those willow pattern plates,' gabbled Kathleen, without hearing her. 'You haven't met Shirley, have you? I'm glad you've got my old kitchen cupboard. It used to belong to my best friend when *she* was married. And those knives, see where they're engraved JF? Those are my grandfather's initials.'

Jenny, sick of it and too polite, fell back. What hope was there? Tongues were wagging stumps before such entanglement, such opaqueness of desire.

Out the back, in the long sun of late afternoon, Frank and Flo saw a bird hop extravagantly off the concrete, with a worm in its beak. They laughed, and with one accord folded their arms wing-like behind their backs and mimicked its irresistible self-satisfaction.

Flo in baby's bonnet and mosquito bites; Frank bearded like a Russian and wearing a sheepskin coat; Kathleen looking embarrassingly plain, her hair pulled back harshly off her forehead, her mouth drooping ill-temperedly; Frank chest-deep in a swimming pool with Flo perched on his shoulder; Kathleen squinting suspiciously, walking away from the camera with a huffy turn of the shoulder, standing awkwardly against bare asphalt in a silly mini-skirt. Then Frank and Kathleen grinning carelessly, open-faced and confident, audacious almost, shoulder to shoulder as if nothing would ever trouble the effortless significance of their being a couple.

Jenny shuffled the photos back into their box and knelt there among the cartons. Which was worse? Her utter non-existence at that moment when they had been happy, or her twinge of pleasure at Kathleen's plainness? She was disgusted with herself. She slid out the painful photo again and indulged the pang, like a child shoving its tongue against a loose tooth. She turned the photo over and read *Perth February 1970* in a round slanting hand. In February 1970 she had had no meaning to them, neither flesh nor spirit, no voice, no form. She was nebulous. She wrestled with her anonymity, tried to force herself into premature, retrospective existence. Serenely there on the glossy sheet they laughed up at her, brown-faced. Their being flowed oblivious beyond her. It was as outrageous to her spirit as if she had tried to imagine life continuing after her own death.

'Snoopers never find out anything nice,' said Frank behind her.

She jumped and shoved the picture away as if it had burned her.

'I used to snoop on Kath's diary, years ago,' he said. 'Know what the worst thing about it was? I never even got a mention.' He laughed out loud, cheerfully. 'Look. I brought you something.'

He held out his closed hand to her. Inside it something whirred loudly. She shrank back, dreading a prank, but he shook his head and kept proffering it to her.

'No. Look. It's a cicada.'

'Will it bite?'

'No. They sing!'

He opened his hand cautiously and took hold of the insect with thumb and forefinger. It goggled at her.

'*La* cigale et *la* fourmi! Par Jean de la Fontaine!' chanted Frank.

He was charming her, and she laughed. 'Let it go, Frankie. It might have a tiny heart attack.'

Lost in a dreamy curiosity, Frank wandered off down the hall to the back door, holding the dry creature up to his face and murmuring to it. He said out loud, 'Take this message to the Queen of the Cicadas!' and opened his hand: away it soared into the blue evening. He had forgotten Jenny, imagining that she had gone back to her unpacking, but when he turned he saw that she had followed him softly into the kitchen and was watching him. He laughed uncertainly, caught out in his game, afraid of being thought foolish. He stood poised in the doorway waiting for judgement. She did not know if she could speak.

'I love you,' she whispered.

'Do you?' The light was behind him and she could not see his face. 'I hope so. I want you to.'

At the moment where day passed into night, the house and yard were still.

'You remind me of a lizard,' she said, blushing. 'You remind me of a lizard on a tree trunk.'

He laughed. 'Pommy. I bet you've never even seen a lizard, let alone one on a tree trunk.'

'I have so. I saw it on television.'

'Come here,' he said.

They sat on the step and she put her head on his knee.

'Let me smell your neck,' he said. 'Mmmm. Sweet as a nut. A nut-brown maiden.'

'Do you think we should make a meal?'

'Sooner or later. Hey. Kath and I were a bit hard to take today, weren't we. Talking about old times.'

'It was worse when you were outside and she formally surrendered the crockery and furniture to me. She reminded me of the mother of a bloke I used to live with in England. "Jen – nee! You *do* know how to defrost a fridge, don't you?" She was the closest I ever came to having a real Jewish mother-in-law. She was so generous I kept thinking, "Look out – there's something else going on here."'

They laughed.

'Well,' said Jenny, 'maybe I'll be able to talk with Kath one day, just the two of us.'

'What for? You'll find out what's wrong with me soon enough.'

'No. Not for that.' She sat up and pushed her back into his shoulder. There was still a faint slick of sweat between their skins. 'It's risky, isn't it, what we're doing.'

'Yes. Very.'

'And not very fashionable, either.'

'No. There are quite a few people around who wouldn't mind seeing me slip on a banana peel.'

'Not Kathleen.'

'No. I mean the opinion-makers. The anti-marriage lobby. Of which I remain one of the founding members, as if anyone needed another contradiction.' He let out his sharp, cackling laugh. 'I'm game, if you are.'

She thought she was probably game. She twisted herself round to smile at him. Her teeth were white and good, with a gap between the front two.

'Your teeth are like Terry Thomas's,' he said. 'I saw him once, walking along Exhibition Street. He was wearing a loud check suit. And he said to me, "Hel – lo! Would you laike to go for a raide in mai spawts car?"'

'He did *not*!'

'Actually it was Kath who saw him, not me. Is there any beer left?'

They stepped up into the kitchen and began rummaging for food.

*

They were waiting for Frank.

Flo's half of the children's room was quite bare, once they had put things in piles and packed up her belongings to go. She had few clothes but dozens of books. The room echoed. They stood by the stripped bed, not sure what to do next.

'Want to draw?' said Flo.

They settled down at the table with the box of Derwents between them and coloured away companionably, discussing patterns and the condition of the pencils.

'Gee I'll miss you,' said Kathleen. 'I'll miss that awful piercing voice going "Kath? Kath!"'

'And I'll miss you going "Psst – psst – hurry up!"' said Flo.

They smiled at each other and got on with their work.

'Kathleen,' said Flo after a while. 'Have I got perfect teeth?'

'Who has.'

'Some people do.'

'Mmmm.'

'Kath. Is there anything . . . sort of . . . *special* about me?'

'Yes. You've got a wart on your elbow.'

'No! Really.'

'I don't know, Floss. Lots of things, probably.'

'Will you tell me the true answer, if I ask you a serious question?'

'Sure.'

'Am I adopted?'

'Not exactly. I found you under a cabbage.'

Flo drummed her feet, trying not to laugh. 'You said you'd be serious. Am I?'

'No, sweetheart.'

'How can I be sure?'

'*I'm* sure, for God's sake! I lugged you round inside me for nine months, and I had you in the Queen Victoria Hospital, with several witnesses present.'

'Did I hurt, coming out?'

'Yes . . . but it's not like ordinary pain. You got a bit stuck, after trying to come out for about twenty-six hours. The doctor had to help you out with a thing called forceps, like big tweezers.'

'Yow.' Flo had heard this story at least fifteen times before, and never tired of it. 'What did I look like? Was I cute?'

'It was hard to tell. You were a bit bloody.'

'*Bloody?*'

'There was blood on you.'

'*How come?*'

'Inside the uterus there's lots of spongy stuff partly made out of blood, which you lived in for nine months. And they had to make a little cut in the back of my cunt, to make it bigger and let you out.'

'*Poor Kath,*' said Flo luxuriously.

'Oh no – that part didn't hurt, because they gave me an injection. And then they cut the cord and washed you and wrapped you up in a cotton blanket and let me hold you.'

'Aaaah,' said Flo with her head on one side.

'And then I cried with happiness.'

'Aaaah.' Flo dropped her pencil and came round the table. She backed up to Kathleen and sat on her knee. 'I love that story. It's my favourite story.'

'I'm pretty keen on it too.'

'Guess what – Jenny might be going to have a baby.'

'What?'

'Hey – I can hear a car.' She sprang off her mother's knee and went racing out into the hall. Very carefully, Kathleen began to slide the pencils back into their right places.

Kathleen stood outside the front gate with a forgotten jumper in her hands. In the oblong back window of the diminishing car she saw a brown blob become white: Flo turning to look back. A child would be born to which Frank would be father, Flo half-sister, and Kathleen nothing at all. With a sharp gesture she shoved her hands down the little knitted sleeves.

*

Jenny and Frank hardly slept, for days, in their house. He lay with his arm under her neck and round her chest so she was folded neatly with her back against his wiry flank, her right cheek resting on his upper arm.

'Tell me, tell me,' he said.

Stumbling at first, finding a pace, she talked to him about her childhood. He asked and asked for details: what sorts of trees? what did you look like? what was on the table? and while she talked he saw again, richly, his own small town, Drought Street, the oval behind the house, the white tank on its stand beside the school, the dusty road, the dry bare leafy dirt of the track home.

'In our marsh there were snipe,' she said.

'We ate monkey nuts,' he replied.

'I sat under a tree, in a striped dress of silky material.'

'A boy had his mouth washed out with soap for swearing.'

'My father had the best garden in the village: people passing in buses admired it over the hedge.'

'I ran a sharp pencil down the big river systems on a plastic template of Australia.'

'My grandmother took me to London for tea. A long white curtain puffed in the wind on to our table: when it fell back there was jam and cream on it.'

'On the first day of school it was so hot that the door of the general store was shut because of the north wind and the dust. I went to buy an exercise book off Mrs Skinner and I sat on the doorstep waiting.'

'My father did his accounts at night, and light came through a hole in the wall up near the ceiling, into my room.'

'On the track between the ti-tree the air ticked, and there was a smell like pepper.'

'Were you happy?'

'I don't remember.'

'I don't remember.'

Sleep, what was it? Sometimes Flo stirred or cried out. Someone next door was awake, a white night; they heard soft footsteps, a door closing quietly, a restless person moving. There were hours, it seemed, of lying perfectly still, wide awake, flooded into stillness by the melting of their skins. Secretly, each of them dreamed that Flo was their common child, that they were lying close to each other in some inexpressible dark intimacy of bodies and of history.

After dinner Jenny set herself up with her exercise books at the kitchen table. Flo edged in with a red tartan shirt in her hand.

'Jenny. Is it you who mends my stuff now?'

'Me or Frank. I expect. What is it?'

'I ripped it on the equipment at school. I could ring up Kathleen,' said Flo.

'Um – no, don't do that. Go and hop into bed. You can read till nine o'clock.' How briskly should she speak? Her voice rang falsely in her ears.

'Kath always lets me read till about ten o'clock. Five to ten,' said Flo, speaking rapidly and keeping her eyes on the ground.

'*Flo.*'

'Well, she did! Sometimes!' Flo turned up her face defiantly and went very red; her gaze sheered somewhere to the right of Jenny's. Jenny blushed too.

'Give me the shirt, Flo.'

Flo shoved it at her, darted into her room and sprang into bed. She began to read immediately so as not to think of her failed manoeuvre. Jenny was not sure whether she should go in and kiss her goodnight. She dropped the shirt on to the kitchen table and started twisting a handful of her hair, flicking the springy ends between her fingers and letting her eyes blur. Frank would never notice the tear in the shirt. She could do it quickly now without saying anything, thus adding a drop to the subterranean reservoir of resentment that all women bear towards the men they live with, particularly the ones they love; or she could point it out to him in a *pleasant tone* and they could discuss it like *civilised people*. Why did they always have to be bloody trained? She stuck a piece of hair in the corner of her mouth. She heard the front door slam, and sat down quickly at the table. He came in whistling with eyes bright from the street.

'Frank. There's a problem.'

'What?' He stopped.

'There's a tear in your daughter's shirt.' She pointed at the red garment on the table.

'Oh!' He picked it up by its collar. 'Is it my job, then?'

'I think so.' She was solemn as a judge at the head of the table. 'Also, I've got some other work to do.'

'I can do buttons,' he said doubtfully, 'but I've never been too hot on actual tears.'

She said nothing, hooked her bare feet on the chair rung and fought the treacherous womanly urge. He darted her a quick sideways glance.

'Well!' he said with a rush of his determined cheerfulness. 'I'll see what sort of a fist I can make of it.' He hurried out of the room and returned with an old tea-tin which disgorged a tangled mass of cotton, buttons, coins and drawing pins. Jenny turned back to her books and began to mark them, looking at him every now and then. Frank leaped to the task. He spread the patch over the rip, fidgeted it this way and that, clicked his tongue at his clumsy fingers.

'There! Got the bugger covered. Now for the pins. Heh heh. Just a matter of applying my university education, in the final analysis.'

He looked up. Pen poised, she was gazing at him in that state of voluptuous contemplation with which we watch others at work. With joy he sank the needle into the cloth.

'At the school I went to,' said Jenny in a little while, 'we had an hour of sewing every day. One person read out loud, and the others sewed. We even had to use thimbles.'

'Sounds like *Little Women*,' said Frank, negotiating a corner with his tongue between his teeth. He was sewing away quite competently now. 'Didn't kids muck around?'

'No. It was very peaceful, actually. We all wanted to be nuns for that hour.' She laughed.

'I'm glad it was only an hour a day, then. Otherwise we might never have met. Well – aren't you going to read to me?'

'What shall I read?'

'I'm not fussy.' He was round the corner and on to the home stretch.

She opened a book at random and read, '*Her Anxiety*. Earth in beauty dressed / Awaits returning spring / All true love must die / Alter at the best / Into some lesser thing / Prove that I lie.'

Frank, paying no attention, was holding out the small garment to show her. He was as pleased as Punch.

*

In her room, for days, Kathleen found traces of Flo everywhere: half-filled exercise books, a slice of canteloupe skin with teeth marks along its edges, a skipping rope with wooden handles. She picked up her nightdress and Flo's little flowery one dropped out of its folds.

She wandered out to the kitchen and sat at the table cutting her fingernails. She sat sideways on her chair looking out the windows at the very clear air. A gum tree over the fence flashed its metallic leaf-backs in the wind. A bird flew across the yard in patchy sunshine, its wings gathered as it coasted on air; it disappeared behind the bamboo which was being jostled by the wind. Kathleen's eyes filled with tears.

'I feel unstable,' she said. 'Not *bad* – just —' She made her flat hand roll like a boat. The other woman at the table looked up over her glasses and nodded, saying nothing.

She worked, throwing away page after page and plugging on, sharpening the pencil every five minutes. The floor around her was sprinkled with shavings. At three thirty she knew it was no good. For four years she had been programmed to stop thinking at school home-time, and will was powerless against this habit. She got under the eiderdown with the most boring book she could find and tried to read herself into a doze so she could get through the moment when Flo would not push open the door and stand there grinning with her school-bag askew upon her back. In a little while she got up and sat at the table again and kept forcing.

She went for a walk up to the top of the street to the old people's settlement. There were yellow leaves everywhere. She leaned against a gate-post, dull, feeling nothing in particular. An old woman came out her back door to empty a rubbish bin and saw her standing there.

'Hullo dear,' she called. She had a silver perm and knobbly black shoes and an apron which lifted a little in the wind.

'Hullo.'

The woman moved closer. 'Anything wrong?'

'Not really. I'm missing my little girl.'

'Oh.' The old woman knew what she was talking about. Kathleen wanted to ask her the imponderables: what do you understand that I don't? Does it get easier or harder? If she had dared she would have asked something simpler: will you invite me into your kitchen and let me watch you make a cup of tea?

'Do you do any gardening, dear?'

'No.'

'I've found that a great help,' said the old lady. 'My gardens have got me through two nervous breakdowns.'

The old woman was small and wrinkled, and her large ear-lobes had become floppy with the weight of the gold rings that hung from them. Her skin looked waxy, and on her cheek-bones were several enormous blackheads. Her dark blue crêpe dress, unlike Kathleen's, had probably been owned by the same person ever since it was bought. She was not looking at Kathleen, perhaps so as to spare her from social duty, but simply stood beside her, following her gaze to the turbulence of coloured clouds behind the trees in their fullness, the upper sky veiled with pale grey, the parsley trembling in thin rows, the worn-out tea towels showing their warp and woof on the line. In a little while she heaved a sigh, and gave Kathleen a quick look from her bright eyes. 'Well. Back to work, I s'pose. It'll be teatime d'rectly. Ta ta!'

'Bye,' said Kathleen, and walked on.

Flo's voice sounded very high-pitched and childish on the phone.

'How's everything over there, Flo?'

'Oh, great! We have roast pork, and Jenny makes these *great* noodles.'

'Are you getting to school OK?'

'Well . . .' She gave an adventurous giggle. 'Frank said not to *say* but most mornings I'm late, because Frank and Jenny don't wake up as early as you do.'

What mean satisfaction she derived from this. 'I bet you drag the chain, do you?'

'A bit.'

A pause fell. Flo was making crunching noises.

'What are you eating?'

'A carrot.'

Kathleen felt shy and importunate. She had no small talk.

'Kath? Know what I wish?'

'What.'

'I wish we could all live together.'

'Who?'

'You, and me, and Jenny, and Frank.'

'Hmm. I'm afraid that's almost certainly never going to happen.'

'But *why*?'

'There's not a room for me over there, for a start.'

'You could sleep in my room, with me.'

'I don't think so. I don't think I'd be very . . . welcome.'

'I *wish* you could!' cried Flo urgently, as if mere force of desire might change a hostile destiny.

'I could come and live in the broom cupboard, and every time Jenny or Frank opened it I'd pop out and sing that song that goes, "Ullo! I'm a reject / Does one arm 'ang down longer?"'

'Don't talk like that, Kath.' Flo's voice was heavy with disapproval. 'You're trying to make me not like Jenny.'

'Excuse me,' said Kathleen, mortified at her own grossness. 'What a nasty thing to say. And not even historically correct.'

'Never mind. I didn't think you really meant it. When are you coming to visit? So you and I can cook, and have the meal ready to surprise Frank and Jenny?'

'I could come on Tuesday. You go and ask Frank now if that's all right.'

Flo muffled the phone with her hand. Tuesday was all right. There was nothing else to say so they hung up.

*

Before Tuesday could come, the old man died. He stepped out of the bath and his heart simply stopped.

The ground they stood on was untended, unlawned, littered untidily with fallen gum leaves and unruly twigs. The trees gave no sign of autumn in the bush cemetery, but it was in the light, its doubtful angle, its mildness on the skin. Shirley's eye rolled on that strange warm day but she gave Flo a thick bunch of roses to hold in her two fists beside the grave. Beside the grave in order stood: Shirley, trembling and smiling into space like a vague hostess; Frank, frowning and clearing his throat and standing with his heels together and daylight between his knees; Flo, wishing the coffin lid might open a crack so she could see a dead body; Kathleen, folding herself, putting herself away now, decorous as a spectre; Jenny, almost wife but fighting it, singed from behind by the inquisitiveness of Frank's cousins and (to Frank, who saw how her brown smooth skin made her lips seem pinker) suddenly resembling Flo, as all people we love at moments resemble each other.

At the house people laughed more than they had thought they would, or ought to. Against a clock stood a very old photograph of Jack as a boy in a striped suit with short pants and lace-up boots; his face bore the good-natured, musing expression he had never lost.

'It's a beautiful photo, Mrs Maxwell,' said Jenny.

'I'll bet he hated that suit!' cried Shirley with the shrill laugh of someone right on the edge.

'Poor Papa,' agonised Flo, who wanted there to be more tragedy in the occasion. 'He was a good man, wasn't he, Nanna. He led a good life.'

'He certainly did, sweetheart. Oh, he was the kindest of men.'

Shirley seized Flo in her skinny arms and they hugged eagerly, their eyes full of tears. 'The first time he asked me out,' she went on in a conspiratorial tone, glancing around her as she spoke, 'we drove out into the country. There we sat among the bush irises – flags, we used to call them – white and blue – and Jack asked me if I wanted a drink!' Her laugh cracked in the middle. 'He must've thought I drank! Well, I did, I suppose – and he said he had a bottle of beer in the car. I thought, Oh good, this is nice. And he got the bottle out of the car but he didn't have an opener because *he* didn't drink! So he knocked the top off the bottle against a tree. And I've often thought, later, we could've died. One piece of broken glass.'

Over by the window, behind the couch on which the three women and the child were sitting, one of the cousins was hissing to Frank,

'Who's the new one, Frankie? Got any legal advice?'

Frank tossed his empty glass from palm to palm, smiling furiously and whistling through his teeth. 'We're all *reasonable people*, Brian,' he replied in a light, tense voice.

'Ah yeah . . . that's what they all say.' The cousin laughed loosely and looked away. He planted his feet wide apart and tightened his thighs like a footballer. 'You'll end up paying a packet in alimony, mate,' he predicted comfortably, draining his glass.

Shirley, Jenny and Kathleen walked down to the beach in their funeral clothes. Their heels sank and they sat down in the sand, Shirley in the middle, and watched the water, the oceanward rushing of the tide, the tiny waves crisping helplessly towards the leftover line of dried seaweed that ran crookedly all along the water's edge. The younger women, set about the older one like a pair of brackets, did not know each other, did not know what they were protecting the mother-in-law from, but felt their positions to be proper.

'What am I going to do now?' asked Shirley.

Nobody answered. The sea ran by. The day seemed very long to them all.

*

Flo dangled maddeningly over into the front seat and whistled and called to the dog. 'Come! Come! Come in the back with me!'

'Don't treat the dog like a toy, Flo,' said Jenny, irritated. 'She wants to stay in the front with me.'

'It's all right for you two!' burst out Flo, flinging herself back into her seat. 'There's plenty of love in the front seat, but none in the back.'

'Are you jealous?' said Frank. He winked at her over his shoulder.

'*I am not jealous*,' cried Flo in a fury. She slouched in her corner and stared out at the trees. 'I haven't got anything to *do*.'

'We told you if you came away with us there'd be no whingeing,' said Frank.

'I am *not whingeing*.'

'Look out the window, then.'

'There's nothing to *see*.'

Jenny glanced back over her shoulder and caught an odd cast to Flo's scowling face: a snubbing of nose, a stretching of eyes, a rising of top lip. She looked sinister. The word passed instantly and was forgotten.

The wind tore steadily past the house, racing off the sea and over the sandhills and up the gravelly drive and through the scraggy hedge. All day the house groaned and shook in the wind, which relented a little at nightfall, leaving pinkish clouds looped neatly above the drab green humps of ti-tree. They were all sunburned in such a way that the sides of their fingers looked silvery-white, as if they were underwater.

On the clifftop the wind still blustered fitfully. On the ocean beach they made a fire, and Frank and Flo ran half a mile beside the cold white and green surf, still clear to Jenny's eyes no matter how far they ran, so empty was the air. She wrapped herself in a sleeping bag and waited for stars, roasting her face and chilling her back; before it was dark the others came panting back to her through the soft sand. The first planet swung for them, burned pink and green like a prism, spinning idly in the firmament.

The wind blew itself right out in the dark, and next morning sun was flooding quietly into the beach house when they awoke.

Five in the afternoon was the appointed hour, but when Kathleen crossed the creaking verandah and knocked at the front door, the house was silent. No dog barked. She tried the side gate, but it was locked from the inside and had no hand-hole by which she might have climbed it and gone down to the back door. It was quite shocking to her to be locked out of the house of people she knew. She was aggrieved and hurt and cross. It was hot. She sat bad-temperedly on the verandah and swore to herself. Surely they couldn't have forgotten her.

After ten minutes she got up and tried the front window. It slid up obediently. Jubilant, she crawled in, closed it behind her and ran down to the kitchen where she filled the kettle and set about making herself a drink and a snack, the ingredients for which she found in abundance in the fridge. She opened the back door and sat contentedly on the step, chewing and swallowing.

Half an hour later a key rattled in the front door and they were upon her: the dog yapping dutifully, Flo leaping on her back with cries of welcome, Frank looking preoccupied, Jenny frozen-faced and very sharp-footed. At the sight of Jenny, whose eyes avoided hers after the first obligatory greeting, Kathleen realised that something was badly wrong. She scrambled to her feet, noticing that her shirt was covered with crumbs. Jenny opened the fridge and began to forage in the lower shelves.

'There's a fresh pot of tea made,' said Kathleen, performing a dance of appeasement behind Jenny's back. Flo was dragging at her, and she followed into the girl's bedroom.

'What will we make for dinner?' Flo was saying, sitting up importantly at her table. 'We could have a tomato salad, and ice-cream.'

Kathleen knew that everything she said would be overheard in the kitchen, where the silence was being broken only by the movement of feet and chair legs on the wooden floor. She felt miserable, superfluous, and would have disappeared as impolitely as she had come had it not been for oblivious Flo with her pencil and paper, waiting eagerly for her reply.

'Hold your horses, Flo,' she said quietly. 'I don't think we're going to be able to make the dinner after all.'

'But why?'

'Because . . .' She heard Jenny's heels go out of the kitchen in the other direction. 'Because maybe Jenny or Frank would rather do the cooking here. I'm a guest – guests aren't supposed to act as if they owned the place.'

Flo could see her plans slipping out of her grasp again, sliding away for reasons that would be carefully explained to her in words of one syllable, adding to the load of childish trouble not of her making that she must lug about with her. She let out the eternal cry of childhood, prelude to resignation: 'It's not fair!'

At that moment Frank stepped into the room. He was smiling awkwardly. 'Kath – look, don't get excited – I want to talk to you for a minute. There's a crisis on here.'

Kathleen's face was burning with resentment. She knew what was coming, and stuck out her chin to cop it.

'Now listen —' He was unconsciously making calming movements with his flat hands. 'Jenny's feeling extremely . . . *uncomfortable* that you're here.'

'But I was invited!' she cried, knowing that by climbing in the window she had effectively dispensed Jenny from the hostly obligations that would have otherwise been due. She sat there on the edge of the bed, spine erect, hands under thighs, feet dangling.

'Yes, yes, I know. But – you didn't – *wait*. You —'

'I know. I came in the window. Well, what am I going to do now? I came to see Flo. That's why I *came*.' Although this was true, she had a nasty feeling that it was not the whole story. She saw that Frank was floundering out of his depth, did not know what was the right thing to do, hated carrying the bad news between the two women who were too cowardly to face each other. She was full of disgust, and pity, for all of them.

'We're going to have to talk about a few things,' said Frank urgently. 'Can you meet me and Flo at the school in the morning? Eight thirty?'

'OK.' She got off the bed.

'You're not going *home*, are you, Kath?' Flo too was in over her head.

'Let's go out in the back yard, Flo, just you and me,' said Kathleen desperately. 'And we'll think what to do.'

They shuffled outside past Frank who nodded anxiously at them, and squatted against the fence at the very bottom of the yard. The little dog nosed about them, and Flo scratched its woolly coat and squinted up at her mother, waiting for enlightenment.

'I made a mistake, Floss. I shouldn't have climbed in the window when there was nobody home.'

'But there's nothing wrong with climbing in someone's window. We used to always get in the window at Sutherland Street, if we forgot the key, and so did everyone else.' There was a moral in here somewhere, Flo knew, and she wrestled to get at it.

'Yes, but Jenny's never lived like us, in big open houses where groups of people live and anyone can come in and out in the daytime and the night. She doesn't agree with that sort of way of living. Most people would be mad if they invited someone to dinner and came home and found them already making themselves a snack in the kitchen.' She felt quite giddy and disorientated, trying to remember ordinary social formalities. 'Also,' she went on, forcing herself, 'there are sometimes funny feelings between an old wife and a new one.'

'Jenny isn't Frank's wife. You are.'

'That's true in one way. But Jenny lives with Frank now, and I don't any more, so it's sort of the same, really.'

The little girl squeezed the struggling dog in her arms. 'I don't like this,' she said stubbornly. 'I asked you to come and visit, and nothing's working out like I want it. It's not fair. I don't think grown-ups should fight when children want to have a visitor.'

The back door banged and Jenny, who had taken off her shoes, was coming down the yard towards them with a glass of wine in her hand. She crouched down three feet in front of Kathleen and offered her the glass. The two women looked each other steadily in the eyes, and their mouths curved in identical grimaces of embarrassment which they could neither conceal nor metamorphose into smiles. It was the best they could manage.

Kathleen leaned against the school gate from eight thirty till nine o'clock when the siren cleared the yard of children and only a few papers blew about in the dust. She was wondering whether it was time to panic when she spotted Frank and Flo, walking hand in hand and uncharacteristically slowly, coming round the building from the other side. She rushed up to them.

'Where were you! I've been waiting for half an hour.'

'We said at the *gate*,' said Flo, her face straining against tears. 'We've been at the *gate*, we got there at half past and you weren't *there*.'

'Oh Floss! We were at different gates.' She dropped to her haunches, but the child stood stiffly holding her father's hand, unapproachable.

Frank was darting agitated looks about him. 'Let's get out of here. We could go to the espresso bar.'

Kathleen took Flo's other hand and they crossed the road and sat at the window table of the café, Flo in the middle, one parent at each end. Kathleen began.

'I know I shouldn't have climbed in the window. I'm not in the habit of climbing in windows.' Her voice sounded huffy, and Frank let out an impatient laugh.

'Windows, windows! What we should really be talking about is getting this bloody divorce.'

'*Divorce?*' Flo burst out sobbing. 'Oh no! I don't *want* you to get a divorce!'

'Come and sit on my knee, Floss,' said Kathleen wretchedly.

'No!' She fought them both off and sobbed desperately in the exact middle of her side of the table, refusing to touch either of them, battling for honour.

'But Flo!' said Frank. 'Divorce is no different from how me and Kath have already been living for years!'

'I don't care! Oh, I want us *all* to live together, in the same house. Can't we all go back to Sutherland Street? I *know* it would work! Oh, can't we?'

She wept bitterly, in floods of grief: she did not touch her face, for she was sitting on her hands so that neither of her parents might seize one and sway her into partiality. The tears, unwiped, splashed off her cheeks and on to the table. The Italian waiter behind the espresso machine turned his face away in distress, his hands still clinging to the upright handles.

'It's just – it's just *life*, Flo,' stammered Frank, the tears standing in his eyes. 'We have to make the best we can of it.'

They sat helplessly at the table, survivors of an attempt at a family, while the little girl wept aloud for the three of them, for things that had gone wrong before she was born and when she was only a baby, for the hard truth which they had thought to escape by running parallel with it instead of tackling it head on.

*

By nightfall there was nowhere else to go.

Jenny opened the door in a night-dress, red pencil in hand, curly hair pinned back off her forehead. With her shoes off she was the same height as Kathleen.

'Oh. I was working. Frank's out.'

'It was to see you. Excuse me for coming without being invited.'

'Oh Kathleen. I'm not a monster, you know.'

'Neither am I.'

'Come in.' She stood aside. Flo was curled up on the floor. The book had slipped sideways from her hand, and her mouth was open. A little trail of dribble had wet the cushion. The women sat down on two hard chairs.

'I came because, because things are a bit much for me, right now. I'm a mess, in fact.'

'You, a mess?'

'Do I have to break plates?'

'No. I shall try to see for myself.'

'All this is very painful for me. I can't get used to living without Flo.'

'I thought Frank said you wanted to work.'

'I *do*. But it's so long now that I've had to make my life fit around her – it doesn't make sense without her.' She twisted her face, trying to make a joke. 'I'm bored. I don't get any laughs.'

'I have the impression that you judge the whole tenor of your life by whether or not you're laughing enough.'

'You could say that.'

'I don't know if that's a good criterion.'

'Know any better ones?'

'Why is it so important, laughing?'

'Look. I've got this sign stuck on my bedroom wall. It's by Cocteau. It says, *What would become of me without laughter? It purges me of my disgust.*'

'What disgusts you?'

'Oh, my whole life, sometimes. Things I've done. Things I haven't done. My big mouth. My tone of voice. The gap between theory and practice. The fact that I can't stand to read the paper.'

They looked down uncomfortably.

'Sometimes the only person I can stand is Floss here. For years I've thought I'd be glad to see the back of her. Now I don't know what to do with myself. I roam around. Try to work. Think about falling in love. I can't help thinking of all the horrible things I've done to Flo and Frank.'

'What things?'

There was a long pause.

'I've never told anyone about this.'

'You don't have to.'

'Once, a long time ago, I ran away with another bloke. I was crazy about him. I didn't care about anything else. I felt as if I'd just been born.' She blushed and pushed her clasped hands between her thighs. 'One night, walking along the street, I told him I loved him more than I loved Flo.' She laughed. 'I even thought it was true. Pathetic, isn't it.'

'No.'

'Anyway. I wanted to go away with him. Frank, Frank cried, he got drunk and broke all the windows upstairs, kicked them in. I was so scared I fainted and fell down the stairs. It was the middle of the night. One of the girls downstairs picked me up and dusted me off. Frank was out in the street by that time chucking empty milk bottles around. She said, Frank's being ridiculous. But he wasn't.' She breathed out sharply through her nose. 'I went away with the other bloke. Flo was only about two, at the time. One morning I came back, on my way to work. I walked in the front door and in the lounge room I saw Flo sitting up in front of the television. She must have just woken up. She was all blurry and confused. She didn't see me. She was sitting in an armchair with her feet sticking out, all by herself in the room. It was Sesame Street. And Frank came into the room with a bowl of Corn Flakes for her breakfast. He had this look – his face was – I can't talk about this.' Kathleen put her face on her arms on the back of the chair, lifted it up again, and went on. 'He was trying to get ready for work and feed her and do everything. He was *running*.'

Neither of them spoke.

'I suppose it doesn't sound like much,' said Kathleen.

'Go on. I'm listening.'

'Of course, I was absolutely miserable with this other bloke. I used to type his fucking essays for him. Jesus. He had this way of looking at my clothes. I couldn't do anything right. He told me I was like a bull in the china shop. Of his heart.' Again she tried to laugh. 'I don't know why I'm telling *you* this. There are some things I'll never forgive myself for. That morning I was talking about. Never. I don't know if you . . .'

Jenny leaned forward and spoke very clearly. 'Listen, Kathleen. I'm nuts about Frank. *Nuts* about him.'

Flo, who had turned over on to her back with her knees splayed like a frog, drew herself together with a start and sat up.

'Oh! I dreamed! Hullo Kath! Did I go to sleep? When are we going?'

'Going where?' said Jenny.

'Down to the park to play on the swings, like you said at tea-time.'

'That was hours ago, Floss. It's nearly ten o'clock. And I'm only in my nightie.'

'What if we all went down,' said Kathleen. 'Just for quarter of an hour.'

'I only said that because I thought mothers were supposed to,' said Jenny. 'If I put a belt on, it will look like a dress.'

Outside the gate Flo galloped ahead with the dog. The two women came along slowly in the almost-dark. The sky, which was indigo, had withdrawn to the heights as if to make room for a sliver of moon, dark dusky yellow, rocked on its back like a cradle.

'Kathleen? I don't feel disgusted. Kath? When I met Frank, I knew he liked me, because he kept his body turned towards me all the time, wherever I was in the room. We were in a room with some other people. I didn't know him.'

'Frank and I had a dog, once. But he got a disease. He was going to die. I carried him to the vet wrapped up in an old blue coat. I put him on the table and they were going to give him an injection. We went walking in the Botanic Gardens, after we left him. We were both crying. Then we saw a bird hop in a bush.'

'I dreamed about you and me becoming friends. I've been in Australia two years now, and I haven't got a good girlfriend.'

'But I was unbearable, the day we moved the furniture, and climbing in the window.'

'You were always barging on to my territory.'

In the park, beside the concrete wall of the football ground, the women sat down close together on the shaven grass. There was a strong scent of gums, and earth.

'Are you having a baby? Flo told me you might be.'

'I thought I was pregnant, but not yet. I'm going to. I want to.'

Flo and the dog were tearing about in the thickening darkness, over by the swings and slides. They saw her leap up and grab the high end of the see-saw.

'Hey! Come over here! Jenny? Kath? Come over!' She was beckoning enthusiastically.

They got up and picked their way barefoot off the grass and across the lumpy gravel.

'It's a game,' said Flo. 'You two get on.'

They hesitated, glanced at each other and away again. Flo was nodding and smiling and raising her eyebrows, one hand holding the ridged wooden plank horizontal. They separated and walked away from each other, one to each end. They swung their legs over and placed themselves gingerly, easing their weight this way and that on the meandering board.

'Let go, Floss.'

The child stepped back. Jenny, who was nearer the ground, gave a firm shove with one foot to send the plank into motion. It responded. It rose without haste, sweetly, to the level, steadied, and stopped.

They hung in the dark, airily balancing, motionless.

BONER McPHARLIN'S MOLL

Tim Winton

TO SAY THAT I went to school with Boner McPharlin is stretching things a bit because he was expelled halfway through my first year at high school. That would make it 1970, I suppose. I doubt that I saw him more than five times in his grotty hybrid uniform but I was awestruck when I did. We'd all heard about him back in primary school. The local bad boy, a legendary figure. And suddenly, there he was, fifteen and feral-looking, with grey eyes and dirty-blond hair past his shoulders. In his Levi's and thongs he had that truckin stride, like a skater's wade, swaying hip to hip with his elbows flung and his chest out. He had fuzz on his chin and an enigmatic smirk. His whole body gave off a current of sexy insouciance. To me, a girl barely thirteen, he was the embodiment of rebellion. I wanted that – yes, right from the first glance I wanted it. I wanted him. I wanted to be his.

I watched him swing by, right along the lower-school verandah with a bunch of boys in his wake – kids who seemed more enthralled by him than attached to him – and I must have been pretty obvious about it because my best friend, Erin, stood beside me with her hands on her hips and gave me a withering look.

No way, she said. Jackie, no way.

Erin and I went back forever. We were at a cruel age when we clung fiercely to girlhood yet yearned to be women, and everything excited and disgusted us in equal measure. Sophistication was out of reach yet we could no longer remember how to be children. So we faked it. Everything we did was imitation and play-acting. We lived in a state of barely suppressed panic.

I was only looking, I said.

Don't even look, said Erin.

But I did look. I was appalled and enchanted.

Boner McPharlin was the solitary rough boy that country towns produce, or perhaps require. The sullen, smouldering kid at the back of the class. The boy too brave or stupid to fear punishment, whose feats become folklore. When he strutted by that day I knew nothing about him, really. Only the legend. He was just a posture, an attitude, a type. He represented everything a girl like me was supposed to avoid. He posed some unspecified moral hazard. And I sensed from Erin that he was a peril to friendship as well, so I said nothing about him. I went on being thirteen – practised shaving my legs with the old man's bladeless razor, threw myself into netball, tore down my Johnny Farnham posters and put David Bowie in his place. I had a best friend – I shared secrets with her – yet they felt inconsequential once I saw Boner. Boner was my new secret and I did not share him.

I don't know what it was that finally got Boner expelled from school. He did set off pipe bombs in the nearby quarry. And there was, of course, the teacher's Volkswagen left on blocks in the staff carpark and the condoms full of pig blood that strafed the quadrangle in the lead-up to Easter, but there were plenty of atrocities he didn't commit, incidents he may have only inspired by example, yet he took the rap for all of it. With hindsight, when you consider what happened later in the seventies when drugs ripped through our town, Boner's hijinks seem rather innocent. But teachers were afraid of him. They despised his swagger, his silence. When he was hauled in he confessed nothing, denied nothing. He wore his smirk like a battlemask. And then one Monday he was gone.

The rest of us heard it all at a great remove. Everybody embellished the stories they were told and the less we saw of Boner the more we talked. Much later, when there was a fire at the school, he was taken in for questioning but never charged. I heard he went to the meatworks where his old man worked in the boning room. That was where the name came from, how it was passed from father to son. On Saturdays Boner lurked in the lee of the town hall or sometimes you'd see his mangy lumberjacket wending through cars parked around the boundary at the football.

At fourteen Erin and I began to be dogged by boys, ordinary farmboys whose fringes were plastered across their brows by built-up grease and a licked finger, and townies in Adidas and checked shirts whose hair didn't touch their collars. They were lumpy creatures whose voices squawked and their Brut 33 made your eyes water. We were more alert to their brothers who drove Monaros and Chargers. But we weren't even sure we were interested in boys. We were caught in a nasty dance in which we lured them only to send them packing.

The drive-in was the social hub of the town. My parents never went but they let me walk there with Erin and we sat in the rank old deckchairs beside the kiosk to watch *Airport* and *M*A*S*H* and *The Poseidon Adventure*. We wore Levi cords, Dr Scholls and 4711 ice cologne. Neither of us would admit it, but in our chaste luring and repelling of boys, Erin and I were locked in competition. There was a tacit score being kept and because she was so pretty, in an Ali McGraw kind of way, I was doomed to trail in her wake. I kept an eye out for Boner McPharlin and was always thrilled to see him truckin up toward the kiosk with a rolly paper on his lip. I kept my enthusiasm to myself, though there were times on the long walk home when I thought aloud about him. I was careful not to sound breathless. I did my best to be wry. I aped the new women teachers we had and adopted the cool, contemptuous tone they reserved for the discussion of males. I was ironic, tried to sound bemused, and while I waxed sociological, Erin lapsed into wary silence.

At about fourteen and a half Erin started letting a few boys through the net. Then they became a steady stream. Our friendship seemed to survive them. I tagged along as though I was required for distance, contrast and the passing of messages. She made it clear she wasn't easy. Nothing below the waist. Friendship rings were acceptable. No Italians. And she did not climb into vehicles.

I must have been fifteen when Boner McPharlin got his driver's licence. Suddenly he was everywhere. He wheeled around town in an HT van with spoked fats and a half-finished sprayjob in metallic blue. That kind of car was trouble. It was a sin-bin, a shaggin-wagon, a slut-hut, and as he did bog-laps of the main drag – from the memorial roundabout to the railway tracks at the harbour's-edge – the rumble of his V8 was menacing and hypnotic. Sometimes he cruised by the school, his arm down the door, stereo thumping.

Erin and I walked everywhere. Outside of school there was nothing else to do but traipse to the wharf or the beach or down the drab strip of shops where the unchanging window displays and familiar faces made me feel desperate.

I wish something would happen, I often said.

Things are happening all around us, said Erin.

I didn't mean photosynthesis, I muttered.

By the time anything's happened, it's over.

Well, I said. I look forward to having something to remember.

We were in the midst of one of these ritual discussions when Boner pulled up beside us. It was a Saturday morning. We stood outside the Wildflower Café. I had just bought a Led Zeppelin record. In the rack it had been slotted between Lanza and Liberace. Over at Reece's Fleeces people were buying ugg boots and sheepskin jackets. The passenger side window of Boner's van was down.

Jackie, said Erin.

Nothing wrong with saying hello, I said.

Even as I turned toward the mud-spattered car growling and gulping at the kerb, Erin was walking away. I saw the black flag of her hair as she disappeared into Chalky's hardware. Then I stepped over and leaned in. Boner's smirk was visible behind a haze of cigarette smoke. I felt a pulse in the roof of my mouth.

Ride? he said, just audible over the motor.

I shook my head but he wasn't even looking my way. He squinted into the distance like a stunted version of Clint Eastwood. Yet he must have felt something because he was already putting the car into gear and looking into his side mirror when I opened the door and slid in. He seemed completely unsurprised. He peeled out. Heads turned. I clutched the LP to my chest.

Boner and I drove a lap of town in silence. We idled past the pubs on the waterfront, the cannery, the meatworks, the silos. We passed grain ships on the wharf, the whalers on the town jetty and eased up by the convict-built churches on the ridge where the road wound down again toward the main beach.

I tried to seem cool, to make him be the one to break the silence, but he seemed disinclined to speak. The van was everything you'd expect, from the mattress and esky in the back to the empty Bacardi bottle rolling about my feet. Feathers and fish bones hung from the rear-view mirror. Between us on the bench seat was a nest of cassettes, tools, and packets of Drum tobacco. I knew I'd done something reckless by climbing in beside Boner McPharlin. I'd made something happen. What frightened me was that I didn't know what it was.

We didn't stay at the beach – didn't even pull into its infamous carpark – but wheeled around beneath the Norfolk Island pines and headed back to the main street of town. We slid into a space outside the Wildflower and a dozen faces lifted in the window. The big tricked-up Chevy motor idled away, drumming through the soles of my denim sneakers.

So, I said. How's things at the meatworks?

He shrugged and looked up the street. Erin stood in the door of the café, her hair ensnared by a rainbow of flystrips. Her face was clouded with rage. I wanted to prolong the moment with Boner but could think of nothing to say.

Well, I chirped. Thanks for the ride.

Boner said nothing. He eased in the clutch and scoped his mirror, so I got out and hesitated a moment before shoving the door to. Then he took off with a howl of rubber and I stood there hugging my record in the cold southern wind with a jury of my peers staring out upon me from the café.

In the doorway Erin did not step aside to let me in. She tucked her hair behind her ear and stared into my face.

I can't believe you.

Don't be wet, I said.

Jackie, what did you do?

I took a breath and was about to tell her just how little had happened when a jab of anger held me back. The crossly-folded arms, the solemn look – it wasn't concern but a fit of pique. I'd ignored her warnings. I'd let her walk away without giving chase. And now, worst of all, I'd upstaged her. The realization was like a slap. She was jealous. And this very public interrogation, the telegraphed expressions to everybody inside – it was all a performance. We weren't friends at all.

All I gave her was a sly smile.

Oh my God, she murmured with a barely-concealed thrill.

What? I asked.

You didn't!

I shrugged and smirked. The power of it was so delicious that I didn't yet understand what I'd done. With little more than a mute expression I'd just garnered myself a reputation. I was already Boner McPharlin's moll.

It was a small town. We were all bored out of our minds. I should have known better, should have admitted the unglamorous truth, but I didn't. I discovered how stubborn I could be. The stories at school were wild. I wasn't ashamed – I felt strong. I found a curious pleasure in notoriety. The rumour wasn't true but I owned it. For once it was about me. But it was lonely, too, lonelier for having to pretend to still be friends with Erin. To everybody else her protestations about my purity looked like misguided loyalty, friendship stretched to the point of martyrdom, though from the chill between us I knew otherwise, for the more she said in my defence the worse I looked, and the further my stocks fell the faster hers rose. By the end of that week I wanted the rumours to be true. Because if I was Boner's jailbait then at least I had somebody.

After school I stayed indoors. I went nowhere until the next Saturday when, in a mood of bleak resignation, I went walking alone. I was at the memorial roundabout when Boner saw me. He hesitated, then pulled over. I will never know why he did, whether it was boredom or an act of mercy.

He pushed the door open and I got in and through the sweep of the roundabout I had the weirdest sense of having been rescued. I didn't care what it took. I would do anything at all. I was his.

Within five minutes we were out of town altogether. We cruised down along the coast past peppermint thickets and spud farms to long white beaches and rocky coves where the water was so turquoise-clear that, cold or not, you had the urge to jump in fully clothed. Wind raked through our hair from the open windows. The tape deck trilled and boomed Jethro Tull. We didn't speak. I ached with happiness.

Boner drove in a kind of slouch with an arm on the doorsill and one hand on the wheel. The knob on the gearstick was an eightball. When his hand rested on it I saw his bitten nails and yellow calluses. He wore a flannel shirt and a battered sheepskin jacket. His Levi's were dark and stiff-looking. He wore Johnny Reb boots whose heels were ground off at angles.

The longer we drove the stranger his silence seemed to me. I couldn't admit to myself that I was becoming rattled. We drove for thirty miles while I clung to my youthful belief that I could handle anything that came my way. Slumped down like that, he looked small and not particularly athletic. I knew that while he had those boots on I could easily outrun him.

We drove all the rest of that day, a hundred and fifty miles or more, but no beach, no creek nor forest was enough to get him out from behind the wheel. Now and then, at a tiny rail siding or roadhouse, he slid me a fiver so I could buy pies and Coke.

At four he dropped me at the Esso station around the corner from my house. There were no parting speeches, no mutual understandings arrived at, no arrangements made. Boner left the motor running. He ran a hand through his hair. The ride was over. I got out; he pulled away. It was only after he'd gone that I wondered how he knew this would be the best place to drop me. I hadn't even told him where I lived. I didn't expect him to be discreet. It didn't fit the image of the wild boy. I was as irritated as I was flattered. It made me feel like a kid who needed looking after.

But that's how it continued. Boner collected me and dropped me at the Esso so regularly that there arose between me and the mechanics a knowing and unfriendly intimacy. They knew whose daughter I was, that I was only fifteen. Like everyone else who saw me riding around with Boner after school and on weekends, their fear and dislike of my father were enough to keep them quiet. Perhaps they felt a certain satisfaction.

My father was the council building inspector. It wasn't a job for a man who needed to be popular. Dour, punctilious and completely without tact, he seemed to have no use for people at all, except in their role as applicants, and then he was, without exception, unforgiving. For him, the building code was a branch of Calvinism perfected by the omission of divine mercy. His life was a quest to reveal flaws, disguised contraventions, greed and human failure. Apart from dinner time and at the end-of-term delivery of school reports, he barely registered my presence. My mother was passive and serene. She liked to pat my hair when I went to bed. I always thought she was a bit simple until I discovered, quite late in the piece, that she was addicted to Valium.

My parents were lonely, they were insular and preoccupied, yet I still find it hard to believe that they knew nothing at all about Boner and me that year. If they weren't simply ignoring what I was up to then they truly didn't notice a thing about me.

I loved everything about Boner, his silence, his incuriosity, the way he evaded body contact, how he smelled of pine resin and tobacco smoke. I liked his sleepy-narrow eyes and his far-off stares. The bruises on his arms and neck intrigued me, they made me think of men and knives and cold carcasses, his mysterious world. Sometimes he'd vanish for days and I'd be left standing abject at the Esso until dark. And then he'd turn up again, arm down the door with nothing to say.

He never told me anything about himself, never asked about me. We drove to football games in other towns, to rodeos and tiny fairs. When there were reports of snow we travelled every road in the ranges to get a glimpse but never saw any. Out on the highway, on the lowland stretch, he opened the throttle and we hit the ton with the windows down and Pink Floyd wailing.

It's not that he said absolutely nothing, but he spoke infrequently and in monosyllables. By and large I was content to do all the talking. I told him the sad story of my parents. I filled him in on the army of bitches I went to school with and the things they said about us. Now and then I tried to engage him in hot conjecture – about whether David Bowie was really a poof or if Marc Bolan (who *had* to be a poof) was taller than he looked – but I never got far.

We drove out to the whaling station where the waters of the bay were lit with oily prisms and the air putrid with the steam of boiling blubber. I puked before I even saw anything. At the guardrail above the flensing deck, I tried to avoid splashing my granny sandals. Boner brought me a long, grimy bar towel to clean myself up with. He was grinning. He pointed out the threshing shadows in the water, the streaking fins, the eruptions on the surface.

Horrible, I said.

He shrugged and drove me back to town.

Although everyone at school assumed that Boner and I were doing the deed every time I climbed into his van, there was neither sex nor romance between us. Erin and the others could not imagine the peculiarity of our arrangement. There was, of course, some longing on my part. I yearned to kiss him, be held by him. After the reputation I'd earned it seemed only fair to have had that much, but Boner did not like to be touched. There was no holding of hands. If I cornered him, wheedling and vamping for a kiss, his head reared back on his neck until his Adam's apple looked fit to bust free.

The closest I ever got to him was when I pierced his ears. I campaigned for a week before he consented. It began with me pleading with him and ended up as a challenge to his manhood. One Sunday I climbed in with ice, Band-Aids, and a selection of needles from my mother's dusty sewing box. We parked out off the lowlands road where I straddled him on the seat and held his head steady. A few cars blew by with their horns trailing off into the distance. The paddocks were still. I pressed ice to Boner's earlobes and noticed that he'd come out in a sweat. He smelled of lanolin and smokes and that piney scent. When he closed his eyes, the lids trembled. I revelled in the luxury of holding him against the seat. I lingered over him with a bogus air of competence. Like a rider on a horse I simply imposed my will. At the moment I drove the needle through his lobe I clamped him between my thighs and pressed my lips to his clammy forehead.

He was so tense, so completely shut down in anticipation of contact, that I doubt he felt a thing.

For a few weeks my riding with Boner brought me more glamour than disgrace. The new hippy teachers gave me credit for pushing social boundaries, for my sense of adventure and lack of snobbery. To them my little rebellion was refreshing, spirited, charming. They preferred it to my being the dutiful daughter of the council inspector. I knew what they thought of homes like ours with the red-painted paths and plaster swans. Their new smiles said it all. But when my experiment proved more than momentary their Aquarian indulgence withered. They despised boys like Boner as much as my parents would have, had they known him, and after a while my feisty rebellion seemed little more than slumming. Boner was no winsome Woodstock boy. He was a toughie from the abattoir. My young teachers' sisterly hugs gave way to stilted homilies. Free love was cool but a girl didn't want to spread her favours too thin, did she. I grimaced and smirked until they left me alone.

The gossip at school was brutal. In the talk, the passed notes, the toilet scrawl, I sucked Boner McPharlin, I sucked other boys, I sucked anybody. And more. At the drives Boner hired me out, car to car, Jackie Martin meatworker. Slack Jackie. The slander hurt but I bore it as the price of love. Because I did love him. And anyway, I thought, let them talk, the ignoramuses. Part of me enjoyed the status, the bitter satisfaction of being solitary but notable. I was, in this regard, my father's daughter.

I could bear the vile talk behind my back, but all the icy silence on the surface wore me down. I had enough remoteness at home. And Boner himself barely said a word. I craved some human contact. The only people who would speak to me were the opportunists and the outcasts, boys newly-emboldened to try their luck and hard-faced sluts with peroxided fringes who wanted to know how big Boner's bone was. The boys I sent packing but the rough chicks I was stuck with. They were a dim and desperate lot with which to spend a lunch hour.

At first they were as suspicious of me as they were curious. I was a cardigan-wearing interloper, a slumming dilettante. Their disbelief at Boner's having chosen *me* was assuaged in time by the incontrovertible fact of it, for there I was every afternoon cruising by in the van. I didn't challenge the legend. On the contrary, I nurtured it. By nods and winks at first and later with outright lies. I told them what they wanted to hear, what I read in *Cleo* and *Forum*, the stuff I knew nothing about. It seemed harmless enough. We were just girls, I thought, fakers, kids making ourselves up as we went along. But the things I was lying through my teeth about were the very things these girls were doing. That and much more. And they had the polaroids to prove it.

Only when I saw those photos did I begin to understand how stupid my playacting had been. One lunchtime five of us crammed into a smoky toilet stall, our earrings jangling with suppressed laughter. The little prints were square, felt gummy in my hands, and it took me several moments to register what I was looking at. God knows what I was expecting, which fantasy world I'd been living in, but I can still feel the horrible fake grin that I hid behind while my stomach rolled and my mind raced. So this was what being Slack Jackie really meant. Not just that kids thought you were doing things like this with Boner McPharlin; they believed you did them with anybody, everybody, two and three at a time, reducing yourself to this, a grimacing, pink blur, a trophy to be passed around in toilets and toolsheds all over town. All the gossip had been safely abstract but the polaroids were galvanizing. With all my nodding and winking I'd let these *creatures* believe that I was low enough to have mementoes like this myself, conquests that would bind us to one another. I'd never felt so young, so isolated, so ill. Those girls had already lived another life, moved in a different economy. They understood that they had something men and boys wanted. For them sex was not so much pleasure or even adventure but currency. And I was just a romantic schoolgirl. Maybe they suspected it all along.

I didn't go to pieces there in the fug of the cubicle but afterwards I subsided into a misery I couldn't disguise. I had always believed I could endure what people thought of me. If it wasn't true, I thought, how could it matter? But I'd gone from letting people think what they would to actually lying about myself. I'd fallen in with people whose view of life was more miserable and brutish than anything I'd ever imagined. It was as though I'd extinguished myself.

I went to class in a daze. The teacher took one look at me and sent me to the sick room.

Are you late with your period? asked the nurse.

I could only stare in horror.

You can imagine how the news travelled. I'm sure the nurse was discreet. The talk probably started the moment I left the class. Jackie went to the sick room. Jackie was sick at school. Jackie was bawling her eyes out. Jackie's got a bun in the oven.

It wasn't that I refused to answer the nurse's question. I was simply trying so hard not to cry that I couldn't speak. And saying nothing was no help at all.

During the final term of that year I went back to being a schoolyard solitary. I spent hours in the library to avoid scrutiny and to stave off panic, and the renewed study brought about a late rally in my marks. I heard the rumours about my 'condition' and did my best to ignore them. The only thing more surprising than my good marks was the new pleasure they gave me. It was all that kept me from despair.

I still felt a bubble of joy rise to my throat when Boner burbled up but it didn't always last out the ride. On weekends, as spring brought on the uncertain promise of the southern summer, I took to wearing a bikini beneath my clothes and I badgered Boner to let me out at the beaches we drove to. I couldn't sit in the car anymore. I wanted to bodysurf, to strike out beyond the breakers and lie back with the sun pressing pink on my eyelids. I wanted him there, too, to hold his hand in the water, for him to feel me splashing against him. But there wasn't a chance of it happening. He let me out but I had to swim alone. The beaches were mostly empty. There was nobody to see my flat belly. The water was cold and forceful and after swimming I lay sleepy-warm on a towel. The best Boner could do was to squat beside me in his Johnny Reb boots with a rolly cupped in his palm.

I began to demand more of Boner. Perhaps it was a renewed

confidence from good marks and maybe it was a symptom of a deeper bleakness, a sense of having nothing left to lose. Either way I peppered him with questions about himself, things I hadn't dared ask before. I wanted to know about his family, the details of his job, his honest opinions, where he wanted to be in ten years' time, and his only responses were shrugs and grins and puckerings and far-off looks. When I asked what he thought of me he murmured, You're Jackie. You're me navigator.

I didn't find it charming; I was irritated. Even though it dawned on me that Boner was lonely – lonelier than I'd ever been, lonely enough to hang out with a fifteen-year-old – I felt a gradual loss of sympathy. I could sense myself tiring of him, and I was guilty about it, but his silence began to seem idiotic and the aimless driving bored me. With no one else to speak to, I'd worn myself out prattling on at him. I'd told him so much, yearned so girlishly, and gotten so little in return.

The weather warmed up. The van was hot to ride in. The upholstery began to give off a stink of sweat and meat. I found shotgun shells in the glovebox. Boner wouldn't discuss their presence. I found that a whole day with him left me depleted. I missed being a girl on foot, I wanted the antic talk of other girls, even their silly, fragile confidences. Boner wouldn't speak. He couldn't converse. He couldn't leave the van. He wouldn't even swim.

I tried to find a kind way to tell him that it wasn't fun anymore but I didn't have the courage. One Saturday I simply didn't go to the Esso. On Sunday I helped my startled mother make Christmas puddings. The next week I stayed in and read *Papillon*. I watched 'Aunty Jack'. When I did venture out I avoided places where Boner might see me.

It was only a few days before he found me. I heard him ease in beside me on the road home from school. I felt others watching. I leant in to the open window.

Ride, Jack? he murmured.

Nah, I said. Not anymore. But thanks.

He shrugged and dragged on his rolly. For a moment I thought he'd say something but he just chewed his lip. I knew I'd hurt him and it felt like a betrayal, yet I walked away without another word.

Every summer my parents took me to the city for a few weeks. I was always intimidated and self-conscious, certain that the three of us were instantly identifiable as bumpkins, though I loved the cinemas and shops, the liberating unfamiliarity of everybody and everything in my path. That year, after the usual excursions, we walked through the grounds of the university by the river's edge. The genteel buildings were surrounded by palms and lemon-scented gums and here and there, in cloisters or against limestone walls, were wedding parties and photographers and knots of overdressed and screaming children.

I sensed a sermon in the wings, a parable about application to schoolwork, but my father was silent. As we walked the verandahs he seemed to drink in every detail. There was a softness, a sadness to his expression that I'd never seen before. He rubbed his moustache, wiped his brow on the towelling hat he wore on these trips, and sauntered off alone.

What's with Dad? I asked. Did you guys have your wedding pictures taken here, or something?

My mother sat on a step in her boxy frock. Sweat had soaked through her polka dots to give her a strangely riddled look.

No, dear, she said. He wanted to be an architect, you know. Thirty years is a long time to have regrets.

I stood by her a while. Despite the languor of her tone I sensed that we'd come to the edge of something important together. I could feel the ghosts of their marriage hovering within reach, the story behind their terrible quiet almost at hand, and I hesitated, wanting and not wanting to hear more. But she snapped open her bag and pulled out her compact and the moment was gone, a flickering light gone out.

On the long hot drive home that summer I thought about the university and the palpable disappointment of my parents' lives. I wondered if the excursion to the campus had been an effort on their part to plant a few thoughts in my head. Consciously or not they'd shown me a means of escape.

In the new school year I more or less reinvented myself. Until that point, except for my connection with Boner, I had believed that I was average; in addition to being physically unremarkable I assumed I wasn't particularly smart either. The business with Boner was, I decided, an aberration, an episode. For the bulk of my school life I'd embraced the safety of the median. And now, effectively friendless, with the image of the university and its shady cloisters as a goad, I became a scowling bookworm, a girl so serious, so fixed upon a goal, as to be unapproachable. I never did return to the realm of girly confidences. Friends, had I found them, would have been a hindrance.

In an academic sense I began to flourish. I saw myself surrounded by dolts. Contempt was addictive. In a few months I left everyone and everything else in my wake.

Of course no matter what I did my louche reputation endured. These things are set in stone. Baby booties and condoms were folded into my textbooks. The story went that Boner had dropped me for not having his child, that he was out to get me somehow, that my summer trip to Perth had involved a clinic. Last year's polaroid tarts were all gone now to Woolworths and the cannery, there was nobody to share the opprobrium with. Yet I felt it less. My new resolve and confidence made me haughty. I was fierce in a way that endeared me to neither students nor staff. I was sarcastic and abrupt, neither eager to please nor easy to best. I was reconciled to being lonely. I saw myself in Rio, Bombay, New York; being met at airports, ordering room service, solving problems on the run. I'd already moved on from these people, this town. I was enjoying myself. I imagined an entire life beyond being Boner McPharlin's moll.

Boner was still around of course. He wasn't as easy to spot because he drove an assortment of vehicles. Apart from the van there was a white Valiant, a flatbed truck and a Land Rover that looked like something out of *Born Free*. Our eyes met, we waved, but nothing more. There was something unresolved between us that I didn't expect to deal with. Word was that the meatworks had sacked him over some missing cartons of beef. There were stories about him and his father duffing cattle out east and butchering them with chainsaws in valley bottoms. There was talk of stolen car parts, electrical goods, two-day drives to the South Australian border, meetings on tuna boats. If these whispers were true – and I knew enough by now to have my doubts – then the police were slow in catching them. There were stories of Boner and other girls, but I never saw any riding with him.

Town seemed uglier the year I turned sixteen. There was something feverish in the air. At first I thought it was just me, my new persona and the fresh perspective I had on things, but even my father came home with talk of break-ins, hold-ups, bashings.

The first overdose didn't really register. I wasn't at the school social – I was no longer the dancing sort – so I didn't see the ambulancemen wheel the dead girl out of the toilets. I didn't believe the talk in the quad. I knew better than to listen to the bullshit that blew along the corridors, all the sudden talk about heroin. But that overdose was only the first of many. Smack became a fact of life in Angelus. The stuff was everywhere and nobody seemed able or inclined to do a thing about it.

It was winter when Boner McPharlin was found out at Thunder Beach with his legs broken and his face like an aubergine. They made me wait two days before I could see him. At the hospital there were plainclothes cops in the corridor and one in uniform outside the door. The scrawny constable let me in without a word. Boner was conscious by then, though out of his tree on morphine. He didn't speak. His eyes were swollen shut. I'm not even sure he knew who I was. With his legs full of bolts and pins he looked like a ruined bit of farm machinery.

I stayed for an hour, and when I left a detective fell into step beside me. He was tall with pale red hair. He offered me a lift. I told him no thanks, I was fine. He called me Jackie. I was still rocked by the sight of Boner. The cop came downstairs with me. He seemed friendly enough, though in the lobby he asked to see my arms. I rolled up my sleeves and he nodded and thanked me. He asked about Boner's enemies. I told him I didn't know of any. He said to leave it with him; it was all in hand. I plunged out into the rain.

I visited Boner every day after school but he wouldn't speak. I was chatty for a while but after a day or so I took my homework with me, a biology text or *The Catcher in the Rye*. For a few days there were cops on the ward or out in the carpark, but then they stopped coming. The nurses were kind. They slipped me cups of tea and hovered at my shoulder for a peek at what I was reading. When the swelling went down and his eyes opened properly, Boner watched me take notes and mark pages and suck my knuckles. Late in the week he began to writhe around and shake. The hardware in his legs rattled horribly.

Open the door, he croaked.

Boner, I said. Are you alright? You want me to call a nurse?

Open the door. Don't ever close the door.

I got up and pulled the door wide. There was a cop in the corridor, a constable I didn't recognize. He spun his cap in his hands. He was grey in the face. He tried to smile.

You okay, Boner? I said over my shoulder.

Gotta have it open.

I went back and sat by the bed. I caught myself reaching for his hand.

Least you can talk, I murmured. That's something.

Not me, he said.

You can talk to *me*, can't you?

He shook his battered head slowly, with care. I sucked at a switch of hair, watched him tremble.

What happened?

Don't remember, he whispered. Gone.

Talk to me, I said in a wheedling little voice. Why do you want the door open?

Can't read, you know. Not properly. Can't swim neither.

I sat there and licked my lips nervously. I was sixteen years old and all at sea. I didn't know how to respond. There were questions I was trying to find words for but before I could ask him anything he began to talk.

My mother, he murmured, my mother was like a picture, kinda, real pretty. Our place was all spuds, only spuds. She had big hands all hard and black from grubbin spuds. I remember. When I was little, when I was sick, when she rubbed me back, in bed, and her hands, you know, all rough and gentle like a cat's tongue, rough and gentle. Fuck. Spuds. Always bent down over spuds, arms in the muck, rain runnin off em, him and her. Sky like an army blanket.

She's . . . gone, your mum?

I come in and he's bent down over her, hands in her, blanket across her throat, eyes round, veins screamin in her neck and she sees me not a word sees me and I'm not sayin a word, just lookin at the sweat shine on his back and his hands in the muck and she's dead now anyway. Doesn't matter, doesn't matter, does it.

Boner gave off an acid stink. Sweat stood out on his forehead. I couldn't make out much of what he was saying.

Sharks know, he said, they know. You see em flash? Twist into whalemeat? Jesus, they saw away. It's in the blood, he had it, twistin all day into hot meat. And never sleep, not really.

Boner —

Sacked me for catchin bronzies off the meatworks jetty. Fuck, I didn't steal nothin, just drove one round on the forklift for a laugh, to put the shits up em. Live shark, still kickin! They went spastic, said I'm nuts, said I'm irresponsible, unreliable.

The bedrails jingled as he shook.

But I'm solid, he said. Solid as a brick shithouse. Unreliable be fucked. Why they keep callin me unreliable? I drive and drive. I don't say a word. They know, they know. Don't say a fuckin word. Don't leave me out, don't let me go, I'm solid. I'm solid!

He began to cry then. A nurse came in and said maybe I should go.

Boner never said so much again in one spate — not to me, anyway. I couldn't make head nor tail of it, assumed it was delayed shock or infection or all the painkillers they had him on. When I returned next day he was calmer but he seemed displeased to see me. He watched TV, was unresponsive, surly, and that's how he remained. I had study to keep up with. The TV ruined my concentration, so my visits grew fewer, until some weeks I hardly went at all. Then one day, after quite a gap, I arrived to find that he'd been discharged.

I didn't see him for weeks, months. The school year ground on and I sat my exams with a war-like determination. As spring became summer I kept an eye out for Boner in town. I half expected to hear him rumble up behind me at any moment, but there was no sign of him.

I was walking home from the library one afternoon when a van eased in to the kerb. I looked up and it wasn't him. It was a paddy wagon. A solitary cop. He beckoned me over. I hesitated but what could I do – I was a schoolgirl – I went.

You're young McPharlin's girlfriend, he said.

I recognized him. He was the nervous-looking constable from the hospital, the one who'd started hanging around after the others left. I'd seen him that winter in the local rag. He was a hero for a while, brought an injured climber down off a peak in the ranges. But he looked ill. His eyes were bloodshot, his skin was blotchy. There was a patch of stubble on his neck that he'd missed when shaving, and even from where I stood leaning into the window he smelt bad, a mixture of sweat and something syrupy. When I first saw him I felt safe but now I was afraid of him.

Just his friend, I murmured.

Not from what I've heard.

I pressed my lips together and felt the heat in my face. I didn't like him, didn't trust him.

How's his memory?

I don't know, I said. Not too good, I think.

If he remembers, said the cop. If he wants to remember, will you tell me?

I licked my lips and glanced up the street.

I haven't seen him, I said.

I go there and he just clams up. He doesn't need to be afraid of me, he said. Not me. Tell him to give me the names.

I stepped away from the car.

I only need the other two, Jackie, he called. Just the two from out of town.

I walked away, kept on going. I felt him watching me all the way up the street.

Next day I hitched a ride out along the lowlands road to Boner's place. I hadn't been before and he'd never spoken of it directly though I'd pieced details together over the years as to where it was. I rode over in a pig truck whose driver seemed more interested in my bare legs than the road ahead. Out amongst the swampy coastal paddocks I got him to set me down where a doorless fridge marked a driveway.

I know you, he said, grinding the truck back into gear.

I don't think so, I said climbing down.

I glanced up from the roadside and saw him sprawled across the wheel, chewing the inside of his cheek as he looked at me. The two-lane was empty. There wasn't a farmhouse or human figure in sight. My heart began to jump. I did not walk away. I remembered how vulnerable I felt the day before in town in a street of passing cars and pedestrians while the cop watched my progress all the way uphill. I didn't know what else to do but stand there. He looked in his mirror a moment and I stood there. He pulled away slowly and when he was a mile away I set off down the track.

A peppermint thicket obscured the house from the road. It was a weatherboard place set a long way back in the paddocks, surrounded by sheets of tin and lumber and ruined machinery. I saw a rooster but no dogs. I knew I had the right farm because I recognized the vehicles.

As I approached, an old man came out onto the sagging verandah in a singlet. He stood on the top step and scowled when I greeted him.

I was looking for Boner? I chirped.

Then you found him, he said, looking past me down the drive.

Oh, I stammered. I meant your son?

His name's Gordon.

Um, is he home?

The old man jabbed a thumb sideways and went inside. I looked at the junkyard of vehicles and noticed a muddy path which took me uphill a way past open sheds stacked with spud crates and drums. Back at the edge of the paddock, where fences gave way to peppy scrub and dunes, there was a corrugated iron hut with a rough cement porch.

Boner was startled by my arrival at his open door. He got up from his chair and limped to the threshold. Behind him the single room was squalid and chaotic. There was an oxy set on the strewn floor and tools on the single bed. He seemed anxious about letting me in. I stepped back so he could hobble out onto the porch. In his hands was a long piece of steel with a bronzed spike at one end.

What're you making? I said.

This, he said.

But what is it?

Shark-sticker.

You, you spear sharks?

He shrugged.

So how are you?

Orright.

Haven't seen you for ages, I said.

Boner turned the spear in his hands.

I hitched out, I said.

He was barefoot. It was the first time I'd seen him without his Johnny Rebs. He had hammer toes. Against the frayed hems of his jeans his feet were pasty white. We stood there a long while until he leant the spear against the tin wall.

Wanna go fishin?

I didn't know what to say. I lived in a harbour town all my life but I'd never had the slightest interest in fishing.

Okay, I said. Sure.

We drove out in the Valiant with two rods and a lard bucket full of tackle and bait. Boner had his boots on and a beanie pulled down over his ears. It took me a moment to see why he'd chosen the Valiant. He didn't say so but it was obvious that, for the moment, driving anything with a clutch was beyond him.

Out on Thunder Beach we cast for salmon and even caught a few. We stood a few yards apart with the waves clumping up and back into the deep swirling gutters in a quiet that didn't require talk. I watched and learnt and found to my surprise that I enjoyed the whole business. Nobody came by to disturb us. The white beach shimmered at our backs and the companionable silence between us lasted the whole drive back into town. I didn't tell him about the cop. Nor did I ask him again about who bashed him. I didn't want him to shut down again. I was content just to be there with him. It was as though we'd found new ground, a comfortable way of spending time together.

We saw each other off and on after that, mostly on weekends. These were always fishing trips; the aimless drives were behind us. We lit fires on the beach and fried whiting in a skillet. When his legs were good enough we'd climb around the headland at Massacre Point and float crab baits off the rocks for groper. If he got a big fish on, Boner capered about precariously in his slant-heeled boots, laughing like a troll. He never regained the truckin strut that caught my eye on the school verandah years before. Some days he could barely walk and there were times when he simply never showed up. I knew he was persecuted by headaches. His mood could swing wildly. But there were plenty of good times when I can picture him gimping along the beach with a bucket full of fish seeming almost blissful. No one was ever arrested over the beating. It didn't seem to bother him and he didn't want to talk about it.

I didn't notice what people said about us in those days. I wasn't even aware of the talk. I was absorbed in my own thoughts, caught up in the books I read, the plans I was making.

During the Christmas holiday in the city, I met a boy at the movies who walked me back the long way to the dreary motel my parents favoured, and kissed me there on the steps in the street. He came by the next morning and we took a bus to Scarborough Beach and when I got back that evening, sunburnt and salt-streaked, my parents were in a total funk.

The boy's name was Charlie. He had shaggy blond surfer hair and puppy eyes and my father disliked him immediately. But I thought he was funny. Neither of us had cared much for *The Great Gatsby*. Charlie had a wicked line in Mia Farrow impersonations. He could get those eyes to widen and bulge and flap until he had me in stitches. In Kings Park I let him hold my breast in his hand and in the dark his smile was luminous.

The first time I saw Boner in the new year he was parked beside the steam cleaner at the Esso. The one-tonner's tray was dripping and he sat low in his seat, the bill of his cap down on his nose. I knew he'd seen me coming but he seemed anxious and reluctant to greet me. A sedan pulled up beside him – just eased in between us – and the way Boner came to attention made me veer away across the tarmac and keep going.

The last year of school just blew by. I became a school prefect, won a History prize, featured as a vicious caricature in the lower school drama production (Mae West in a mortar board, more or less).

Boner taught me to drive on the backroads. We fished occasionally and he showed me the gamefishing chair he'd bolted to the tray of the Land Rover so he could cast for sharks at night. His hands shook sometimes and I wondered what pills they were that he had in those film canisters on the seat. I smoked a little dope with him and then didn't see him for weeks at a time.

At second-term break Charlie arrived with some surfer mates in a Kombi. My mother watched me leave through the nylon lace curtains.

As I showed Charlie and his two friends around town I sensed their contempt for the place. I apologized for it, smoked their weed and directed them out along the coast road. We cruised the beaches and got stoned and ended up at Boner's place on the lowlands road. But nobody came out to meet us. In front of the main house stood the bloodstained one-tonner, its tray a sticky mess of spent rifle shells and flyblown hanks of bracken. When Charlie's mates saw the gore-slick chainsaw they wanted out. We bounced back up the drive giggling with paranoia.

In my last term I lived on coffee and Tim-Tams and worked until I felt fat and old and crazy. Charlie didn't write or call. I remembered how short of passion I'd been with him. When he kissed me or held my breast I was more curious than excited. I wanted more but I wouldn't let him. I wasn't scared or ashamed or guilty – I just wasn't interested. There was none of the electricity I'd once felt with Boner squeezed between my thighs as a fifteen-year-old. I felt annoyed, if anything, and Charlie's puzzlement curdled into irritation. I didn't consciously compare him to Boner. Even Boner was someone I could sense in my wake. There was something shambling and hopeless about him now, something mildly embarrassing. I had got myself a driver's licence. I hardly saw him at all.

The final exams arrived. The school gym buzzed with flies. The papers made sense, the questions were answerable. I was prepared. The only exam where I came unstuck was French. I knew I'd done well at the Oral but the paper seemed mischievous, the questions arch and tricksy. It shouldn't have mattered but it made me angry and I tried way too hard to coat my answers with a sarcasm that I didn't have the vocab for. I wrote gobbledy-gook, made a mess of it. I came out reeling, relieved to have it all behind me, and there in the shade was Boner parked illegally at the kerb beneath the trees.

Ride? he murmured.

Thanks, but I'm going home to bed. That was my last exam.

Good?

All except French. I was in *beaucoup* shit today.

Bo-what?

Beaucoup. It's French. Means lots of.

I pressed my forehead against the warm sill of his door.

Made you somethin, he murmured.

I looked up and he passed me a piece of polished steel, a shark that was smooth and heavy in my hand.

Hey, it's lovely.

Friday, he said. I'm havin a bomfire. Massacre Point. Plenty piss. Bo-coo piss. Tell ya mates.

Sure, I said. But what mates did I have?

A teacher came striding down the path.

You better go, I said.

He waited until the teacher was all but upon us before he cranked the Chev into life.

I didn't tell anybody about Boner's party. I felt awkward and disloyal about it but there wasn't anybody I cared to ask. It was so unlike him to organize something like this. He was probably doing it for me and I hated to think of him disappointed.

When I got out to Massacre Point in the old man's precious Datsun, Boner's fire was as big as a house. The dirt turnaround above the beach was jammed with cars and there must have been a hundred people down there, a blur of bodies silhouetted by flames. As I made my way down in my kimono and silly gilt sandals the shadows of classmates spilled from the fire to wobble madly across the trodden sand. I thought of the shitty things these kids had said about us. They were the same people. Fuck the lot of you, I thought. I'm his friend. His only friend. And only his friend.

All of Boner's vehicles were there. At the ready was a pile of fuel – pine pallets, marri logs, tea chests, driftwood, furniture, milepegs and fence posts. Stuck in the sand in the firelight was the school sign itself with the daft motto – SEE FAR, AIM HIGH – emblazoned on it. More like FAR OUT, GET HIGH tonight, I thought.

Beyond the fire was a trailer full of ice and meat. On old doors between drums were beer kegs, bottles, cooking gear and cassettes. There were cut-down forty-fours to barbecue in and a full roasting spit with a beast on it.

Boner's Land Rover was backed down near the water and the tray of the nearby one-tonner was crammed with tubs of blood and offal that boys were ladling into the surf to chum for sharks. Boner had a line out already. I saw a yellow kero drum adrift beyond the breakers and his marlin gear racked at the foot of the game chair on the Landy. Pink Floyd was blasting across the beach. Everybody was pissed and laughing and talking all at once and I was remote from it, just watching while Boner moved from the fire to the water's edge trailing crowds like a guru. When he finally saw me he grinned.

Jesus, he said. You told everyone!

I found a bottle of rum and followed him down to the shorebreak to wait for sharks. While we stood there kids burnt kites above us and fireworks fizzed across the sand. The air was full of smoke and of the smells of scorching meat. It was the beach at Ithaca, it was Gatsby's place, Golding's island. My head spun.

About midnight the beef on the spit was ready and we hacked at it, passed it around and ate with our hands. Everyone's eyes shone. Our teeth glistened. Our every word was funny.

Then the big reel on the back of the Landy began to scream. While Boner gimped up onto the tray, a boy from the Catholic school started the engine. Boner's earrings glittered in the firelight as he took up the rod, clamped on the drag and set the hook with a heave. Line squirted out into the dark. The drum set up a spray and a wake and Boner leaned back and let it run. After a while he banged on the tray and the St Joe's boy reversed down to the water so that Boner could bullock back some line. It went on like that for hours – backing and filling, pumping and winding – until the Land Rover's clutch began to stink and the radiator threatened to boil over. The first driver was relieved by another boy whose girlfriend sprawled across the bonnet to pour beer down his neck through the drop-down windscreen. Now and then he backed up so far that there were waves crashing on the tailgate and I half expected the shark to come surfing out into Boner's lap.

He looked beautiful in the firelight, as glossy and sculpted as the steel carving he'd given me. When the shark bellied up into the shallow wash, Boner limped into the water with his inch-thick spear and drove it through the creature's head and a kind of exhausted sigh went up along the beach.

The fire burnt down. We drank and dozed until sun-up.

Within two days I was gone and it was a long time before I looked back.

During my years at university, I met my parents every Christmas in the dreary motel in the city. We had our strained little festivities, the walks through the campus and down along the foreshore. They told me stories of home but it didn't feel like home anymore. I saw a few old faces from down there but never let them think that I remembered them. I liked the expressions of hurt and confusion that came upon them. I got satisfaction from it. I heard that Erin began teacher's college, but dropped out, married young and had children. One summer afternoon she pestered me on a bus the entire length of Stirling Highway. She was fat. She wanted to catch up, to show me her brood. I got off two stops early just to be rid of her.

When I finished my Honours I drove south just the once to please my parents. The whaling station was defunct. The harbour stank of choking algae. I saw Boner parked in an F-100 outside a pub the tuna men liked. He blinked when he saw me. He was jowly and smelled nasty. He looked a wreck. His teeth were bad and his gut was bloated.

Jackie, he said.

What *are* you doing? I asked, forgetting myself enough to lay hands on his sleeve along the window sill.

Quiet life's the good life, he mumbled, detaching himself from me. Wanna ride? Go fishin?

Gotta meet my oldies in five minutes, I said. Why don't I drive out tomorrow?

I'll get you.

No, I'll drive out.

He shrugged.

When I drove out the next day the McPharlin place was even more of a shambles than I remembered. The old man sat on the verandah, frail but still fierce. I waved and went on up to Boner's shack and found him on his cot with a pipe on his chest and the ropey smell of pot in the air. He was asleep. On the walls were sets of shark jaws. The floor was strewn with oily engine parts. I almost stepped away but he sat up, startled. The little pipe hit the floor.

Me, I said.

He looked confused.

Jackie, I said.

He got off the bed in stages, like an old man.

One day I'll kill him, he said. Take me sticker down there and jam it through his fuckin head.

It's Jackie, I said.

I don't care. You think I care?

I went east for postgrad work and then left the country altogether. I did the things I dreamt of, some diplomatic stints, the UN, some teaching, a think-tank. I took a year off and lived in Mexico, tried to write a book but it didn't work out; it was like *trying* to fall in love. I was lonely and restless.

Then my father died and my mother went to pieces. I was almost grateful for the excuse to fly home to escape failure. I came back, sold their house and set my mother up in an apartment in the city. For a while I even lived with her and that's when I discovered that she was an addict. We didn't get close. We'd got a little too far along for that but we had our companionable moments. She died in a clinic of pneumonia the first winter I was back.

For several months I was lost. I didn't want to return to being a glorified bureaucrat. I had no more interest in the academy. I had an affair with a svelte Irishwoman who imported antiquities and ethnographic material for collectors. As with all my entanglements there was more curiosity from my side of it than passion. Her name was Ethna. She must have sensed that my heart wasn't in it; it was over in a matter of weeks but we remained friends and, in time, I became her partner in business.

It was 1991 when I got the call from the police to say that they had Gordon McPharlin in custody. They asked whether I could come down to help them clear up some matters relating to the death of Lawrence McPharlin.

I flew to Angelus expecting Boner to be up on a murder charge, but when I arrived I found that he was not in the lock-up but in the district hospital under heavy sedation. The old man had died in his sleep at least ten days previous and an unnamed person had discovered Boner cowering in a spud crate behind the shed. He was suffering from exposure and completely incoherent.

There's no next of kin, said a smooth-looking detective who met me at the hospital. We found you from letters he had. And we know that you went to school with him, that there'd been . . . well, a long-standing relationship.

I knew him, yes, I said as evenly as I could.

He was in quite a state, said the detective. He was naked when he was found. He had a set of shark jaws around his neck and his head and face were badly cut. His shack was full of weapons and ammunition and . . . well, some disturbing pornography. There was also a cache of drugs.

What kind of drugs? I asked.

I'm sorry, I'm not at liberty to say. Ah, there was also some injury to his genitals.

And is he being charged with an offence?

No, said the cop. He's undergone a psychiatric evaluation and he's being committed for his own good. We need to know if there's anyone else, family members we don't know about, who we might contact.

You needed me to fly here to ask me that?

I'm sorry, he murmured. I thought you were his friend.

I am his friend, I said. His oldest friend.

Good, he said. Good. We thought you could accompany him, travel with him up to the city when he goes. You know, a familiar face to smooth the way.

Jesus, I muttered, overcome at the misery and the suddenness of it. I was determined not to cry, or be shrill.

When?

Ah, tomorrow morning.

BONER McPHARLIN'S MOLL

Fine, I said. Can I see him now?

The cop and a nurse took me in to see Boner. He was in a private room. There were restraints on the bed. He was sleeping. His lungs sounded spongy. His face was a mess of scabs and bruises. I cried.

That afternoon I hired a car and drove out along the lowlands road to the old McPharlin place. The main house gave off a stink I did not want to investigate. All the old cars were still there, plus a few that had come after my time. The HT van was up on blocks, the engine gone. I looked around the sheds and found broken crates, some bloodstains.

Boner's hut looked like a cyclone had been through it. The floor was a tangle of tools and spare parts, of broken plates and thrown food, as though he'd gone on a rampage, emptying drawers and boxes, throwing bottles and yanking tapes from cassette spools. His mattress was hacked open and the shark sticker had been driven into it. They were right, he'd lost his mind. A squarish set of shark jaws lay on the pillow. It took me a moment to register the neat pile of magazines beside it. On impulse I reached down to pick one off the pile but froze when I saw it. This was the porn they'd told me about. The cover featured the body of a woman spread across the bonnet of a big American car, her knees wide. There were little holes burnt in the paper where the woman's anus and vagina had been, as though someone had touched the glossy paper with a precisely aimed cigarette. On the model's shoulders, boxed in with stickytape, was my face, my head. A black and white image of me at sixteen. Unaware of the camera, laughing. I felt a rush of nausea and rage. The fucking creep! The miserable, sick bastard.

I didn't even touch it. I went outside and sucked in some air. I felt robbed, undone. The ground was unstable underfoot. I had to sit down while something collapsed within me.

When I left I hadn't really got myself into good enough shape to drive but I couldn't stay there any longer. I was halfway down the rutted drive when another car eased in from the highway. At least it was twilight. At least I wasn't crying. As the car got close I recognized the cop from earlier that day. There was another detective with him, a taller man. They pulled up beside me.

Everything alright? the cop asked.

Just wonderful, I said, wanting only for him to get out of my way so I could get the hell off the place and find a stiff drink in town.

You need to talk about it?

No, I don't need any talk. I'll be there in the morning. Let's get it over with.

The cop nodded, satisfied. His mate, the tall redhead, didn't even look my way. I wound up my window and they crept past.

Next day I sat beside Boner in the back of an ordinary-looking mini-van with another woman who I could only assume was a nurse. We didn't speak. What I'd seen in Boner's cabin made it difficult for me to sit there at all, let alone make conversation. During the five hours, Boner mostly slept. Sometimes he muttered beneath his breath and once, for about half an hour without pause, he sobbed in a way that seemed almost mechanical. The only thing he said all day was a single sentence. *Eat though young.* Perhaps it was *thy* young or even *their* young. I couldn't make it out. His mouth seemed unable to shape the words. I couldn't bear to listen. I dug the

Walkman from my bag and listened to a lecture on Buddhism.

Boner was never released. He didn't recover. Even though I drove past the private hospital almost every day I only ever visited at New Year. I went because I conceded that he was sick. He hadn't been responsible for his actions. I didn't go any more frequently than that because my disgust overrode everything else. When I went I wheeled him out into the garden where he liked to watch the wattlebirds catch moths. He had an almost vicious fascination for the Moreton Bay fig. He said it looked like a screaming neck.

Over the years there were visits when he was hostile, when he refused to acknowledge me, and occasions when I thought he was faking mental illness altogether. He had been lame for some time but after years of shunting himself about the ward in a wheelchair he became so disabled by arthritis that he relied on others to push him. His hands were claw-like, his knees horribly distorted. When I realized how bad it had become, I sent along supplies of chondroitin in the hope that it might give him some small relief. I don't know that it ever helped but he seemed to enjoy the fact that the nasty-tasting powder was made from shark cartilage. It brought on his troll-laugh. He'd launch into a monologue that made no sense at all.

The visits were always difficult. The place itself was quiet and orderly but Boner was a wild, twisted little man; an ancient child, fat and revolting. And of course I was busy. The import business had become my own when I bought Ethna out. I travelled a lot. I sold my house and the weekender at Eagle Bay and bought a Kharmann

Ghia and an old pearling lugger. I lived on the boat in the marina and told myself that I could cast off at a moment's notice. I would not be cowed by middle age; I was my own woman. And I valued my equilibrium. I didn't need the turmoil of seeing Boner McPharlin more than once a year.

This year, on New Year's Day, I wheeled Boner out among the roses and he slumped in the chair, slit-eyed and watchful, and before we got to the tree that provoked his usual spiel about his mother's screaming neck, he began to whisper.

Santa's helpers came early for Christmas.

What's that? I said distractedly. I was hungover and going through the motions.

Four of the cunts. Same four, same cunts.

Boner, I said. Don't be gross.

Cunts are scared. Came by all scared. Big red, he's lost his hair. Frightened I'll dog him. Fuckin cunts, every one of em. Come in here like that. Fuckin think they are?

Someone visited? I asked.

Santa's helpers.

Did you know them?

Wouldn't *they* like to know? he said with a wheezy giggle.

I stopped pushing him a moment. The light was blinding. Already his hair hung in sweaty strings on his neck. The sunlight caused him to squint and he licked his cracked lips in a repulsive involuntary cycle. There were scars in his earlobes where he'd torn his earrings out years before. Despite the heat he insisted on a blanket for his legs.

So, did you? I asked. Know them, I mean.

You put me here, he said.

I'm your friend.

Friend be fucked.

Your only friend, Boner.

You see that tree? You see that tree? That tree? That's my mother's screamin neck.

Yes, you've told me.

Screamin neck, not a sound. You can hang me from that tree, I don't care, you and them can hang me, I don't care.

Stop it.

Let em do it, let em see, the pack a cunts. Never know when I might bite, eh. Even when I'm dead. Shark'll still go you when you think he's dead.

Happy New Year, Boner.

Get me out, Jack. Let's piss off.

You are out. See, we're in the courtyard.

Out! *Out*, you stupid bitch.

I'm going now.

You're old, he said mildly. You used to be pretty.

That's enough.

They said it, not me.

I have to go.

See if I fuckin care.

I really have to leave.

Well it's not fuckin right. I never said a word. Never once.

Boner, I can't stay.

Just drivin, that's all I did. Never touched anythin, anybody, and never said a word – Jesus!

I'll turn you around.

Please, Jackie. Let's ride, let's just arc it up and go.

Both of us were crying when I wheeled him into the darkness of the ward. He slumped in the chair. I left him there.

A week later he was dead. The hospital told me it was a massive heart attack. I didn't press for details. Looking back I see that I never did, not once.

There were six of us at the cremation – a nurse, four men and me. Nobody spoke but the priest. I didn't hear a word that was said. I was too busy staring at those men. They were older of course, but I knew they were the cops from back home. There was the neat one in the good suit who'd called me about Boner's breakdown. Two others whose faces were familiar. And the tall redhead who'd asked to see my arms when I was sixteen years old. His hair was faded, receding, his eyes still watchful.

I began to weep. I thought of Boner's fire, his twisted bones, his terrible silence. I got a hold of myself but during the committal, as the coffin sank, the sigh I let out was almost a moan. The sound of recognition, the sound of too late.

I walked out. The redheaded detective intercepted me on the steps. The others hung back in the shade of the crematorium.

My condolences, Jackie, he purred. I know you were his only friend.

He didn't have any friends, I said, stepping round him. You should know that, you bastard – you made sure of it.

I'm retired now, he said.

Congratulations, I said as I pushed away.

I drove around the river past my office and showrooms and went on down to the harbour. I cruised along the wharf a way and then along the mole to where the river surged out into the sea. I parked. The summer sun drove down but I was shivery.

The talk on the radio was all about the endless Royal Commission. I snapped it off and laid my cheek against the hot window.

I didn't see it whole yet – it was too early for the paranoia and second-guessing to set in – but I could feel things change shape around me. My life, my history, the sense I had of my self, were no longer solid.

All I knew was this, that I hadn't been Boner's friend at all. Hadn't been for years. A friend paid attention, showed a modicum of curiosity, made a bit of an effort. A friend didn't believe the worst without checking. A friend didn't keep her eyes shut and walk away. Just the outline now, but I was beginning to see.

They'd turned me. They played with me, set me against him to isolate him completely. Boner was their creature. All that driving, the silence, the leeway, it had to be drugs. He was driving their smack. Or something. Whatever it was he was their creature and they broke him.

I sat in the car beneath the lighthouse and thought of how I'd looked on and seen nothing. I was no different to my parents. Yet I always believed I'd come so far, surpassed so much. At fifteen I would have annihilated myself for love, but over the years something had happened, something I hadn't bothered to notice, as though in all that leaving, in the rush to outgrow the small-town girl I was, I'd left more of myself behind than the journey required.

GRASSHOPPERS

Elizabeth Jolley

Also when they shall be afraid of that which is high, and the fears shall be in the way, and the almond tree shall flourish, and the grasshopper shall be a burden, and desire shall fail because man goeth to his long home, and the mourners go about the streets.

Ecclesiastes 12:5

*Jetzt wird mein Elend voll, und namenlos
erfüllt es mich...*

*Jetzt liegst du quer durch meinen Schoss,
jetzt kann ich dich nicht mehr
gebären.*

*Now is my alienation full, and without name
it floods me...*

*Now you lie hard across my lap,
now can I no longer
carry you.*

'Pietà'. Rainer Maria Rilke.

The long hot afternoon was coming to an end, the only sound in the stillness was from the endless energetic imagination of the grasshoppers. Their sound was so monotonous it was possible not to notice it unless some persisting thought or sorrow caused the noise to become an intrusion, a nuisance. The old woman, surprised to hear a car turning slowly on the gravel peered through the window to see who was coming.

'Mother, this is Bettina,' Peg said as she stepped into the neat kitchen.

'Pleased to meet you,' the old woman said to Peg's friend. 'I wasn't expecting you for another week Peg,' she said with the nervous little laugh which belongs to people who live alone.

Outside there was a noise, the geese and the ducks had taken fright and the hens were cackling and squawking, the strident voices of the children could be heard as they ran, making the most of the chase, scattering the disturbed poultry.

'Kerry! Kerry!' Peg shrilled from the porch, 'Kerree – come along and see Grandma,' she laughed. 'They've been right down the paddock, here they come, they're like grasshoppers in that long grass. Oh Mother, your grass is high this year, and dry!'

As the two small girls came indoors, the old woman bent to kiss her grandchild but Kerry drew back staring at her with cold blue eyes,

'I don't like you,' she said. She had never said that before.

The old woman tried again,

'Let me see,' she said. 'How old are you now dearie?'

'I'm not dearie,' Kerry said. 'I'm five,' she said. 'And Miranda's five and her Billy's gone away like our Lucien's gone.' Both the children raced off through the living room onto the verandah, banging the door and the fly-screen door.

The old woman noticed that they had little bunches of feathers tight in their hands. She had always had the feeling that the discarded poultry feathers were dirty things, that they might even carry some sort of illness or disease. She would have liked to tell the children to throw the feathers away, that they were not clean and that they must wash their hands now because they might have picked up something nasty.

'Billy's my little girl's father,' Bettina said. 'He's an ex, he's left me.'

'Oh, I'm sorry,' the old woman said.

'There's no need to be sorry,' Bettina said. 'I'm better off without him, eh Peg?' And it seemed to the old woman that the two young women smiled at each other in an intimate way which was more than a little sly.

'It's very quiet and lonely here,' the old woman said. 'I hope you'll be comfortable. I expect you both need a rest and it'll be a change for the children.' She was wondering if she was saying the right things. She noticed her daughter's friend was restlessly taking stock of the cottage; her hair was cut long over her greedy eyes and the skirt she wore, instead of being tied round the waist, was tied high under her armpits and looked as if it would slip down any minute. She felt she must do her best but, straight away, she had not taken to Peg's friend; for one thing, why didn't the girl wear a blouse like other people. She had been looking forward to having her daughter and little granddaughter come to stay. Nothing had been said about this, what was her name, Betty, Bettina and this Miranda coming too.

'I've never seen such a small house with so many beds in it,' Bettina said hitching up her garment. The old woman felt sure she had nothing on under it.

The old woman laughed her nervous laugh, 'Oh we were quite a big family once upon a time,' she said. Peg brought in a case from the car.

'We'll have tea directly,' the old woman said. 'And I'll make up the beds when you've made up your minds where you want to sleep.'

The children rushed through the cottage again banging the doors and shrieking. Peg said comfortably, 'They slept all the long way up here. They get on so very well together, Mother, they react with each other perfectly.'

As they drank their tea the old woman tried to make conversation with the silent young women.

'Are you a teacher too?' she asked Bettina.

'Lord no!' Bettina said, and she laughed with Peg as if over some private joke. 'I've just been overseas,' she explained.

'Bettina is a faith healer,' said Peg.

'Oh, I see,' said her mother. 'Kerry! Kerry!' She poked her head out of the door, she had a little parcel all ready. 'Kerry!' she called. 'Come and see what Grandma's got for you! Come and see what I made for you!'

'Not now I'm busy,' came the childish voice from the lean-to shed which was the bathroom.

'Perhaps they're playing medicals,' Peg said.

'I think they're having a bath,' Bettina said and laughed. 'I could do with one myself. I might just get under the cold hose,' she added. 'It's killingly hot!'

'Oh, you can have a nice shower later,' the old woman said. 'I'm not all that short of water.'

'I'm afraid we shan't have time,' Peg said. The old woman was surprised, she hesitated, her thin arms hugging folded sheets.

'Not have time?' she said. 'You going out then? Tonight?' she asked. 'You've only just got here, won't you be too tired?'

'No, we'll be all right Mother,' Peg said slowly and deliberately. 'We were wondering if you would watch the children for us.'

'You are going out then,' the old woman said. 'Of course I'll look after the children if you want me to. But where can you go tonight from here?'

'Well mother,' Peg said. 'It's not just for tonight, it's for a week. Bettina and I want to go away for a few days.'

'Oh, I see,' the old woman tried to hide her disappointment. 'It's a little holiday you're having?' She thought Peg was looking very worn and tired; she had a lot to do with her school work and housekeeping in the flat and looking after Kerry with no one to help her. It was lonely being a woman on your own, she had known that herself for a good many years.

The two young women stood smiling at each other. 'We'll have to leave at once, more or less, to get to the airport in time,' Peg said to her mother.

'And not have a meal?' the old woman cried out. She wanted to say, 'Airport, so you're going somewhere far away.' But she did not say it. She tried not to show that she had had a shock.

'I'm afraid so Mother,' Peg said. 'But we'll be sure to get something on the way. I'm sure the children will be good,' she added.

While Bettina went to get the children to come and say goodbye to their mothers, Peg said in a low voice, 'You know Mother, Bettina's very brave, she had Miranda on purpose, all on her own, because she felt she ought to experience motherhood to be a more complete person.'

'I'd say that was very foolish, not brave,' her mother replied.

'There's some clothes and things in that case, Mother, and here's some money.'

'Oh, there's no need . . .' the old woman started to say, but Peg pushed some notes into her hand.

It was dusk and the large moon climbed quickly. The old woman, standing on the gravel clutching a child on either side, watched her daughter's car turn slowly and drive off. In the moonlight she saw that Bettina sat right up close to Peg and that Peg was driving with one hand on the steering wheel and one arm round the bare shoulders of her friend. For a moment she remembered Lucien and his handsome fair face and how he had come rather late into their quiet lives with his poetry and his songs, and with such tenderness. He had turned the car and driven up the track with his arm just like that, round Peg's shoulders. Then, not all that long ago, they had driven off after a visit and the next time Peg had come alone, paler and thinner but brave, even seeming not to care. The old woman often wondered how much Peg cared. She would have liked to ask her how she really was, and she would have liked to help her.

She was not sure that having these two children for a week would be a help.

Back inside the cottage the little girls took off all their clothes and tickled each other with the feathers they had picked up in the yard.

'I'm Bettina,' Miranda explained giggling and squirming. 'She's Peg. In a minute we're going to have a cuddle.'

'I see,' said the old woman. She finished making the beds and then could not find the children. The cottage was so small it did not take long to look in the corners and under the beds.

The old woman called to the little girls. She was suddenly frightened. She never thought that they would go outside alone in the dark. She knew they could not be far away, but when she went outside it was so quiet. The moonlight lay in silent patches over her land and sheds. Her almond trees stood dark and indifferent. There were shadows moving over the long dry grass in the paddock and a sweet smell came up as the night air touched the grass. Softly she called their names, trying not to frighten them, and trying not to be afraid herself. It was hardly half an hour since Peg and Bettina had driven off and she had lost their children. She thought of the dam, steep clay, slippery down to the summer lowered water and, in spite of the warm night, she shivered.

Close by in the yard the geese were talking softly to one another, helping each other with the burden of their lives, softly comforting each other in the dark. To and fro they talked first one and then the other. They would talk like this for hours and only cry out in alarm if something startled them. Sometimes during the day they whispered at the back door, standing, stretching first one leg and then the other, their long necks outstretched and their feathers preened and softly ruffling like the frills of petticoats put on to attract. It seemed to the old woman then that they forgot that they were widowed geese as they paraded and danced, pirouetting, and eyeing her and all the time, singing their little whispering song of flirtation. A young rooster, cheated by the moon, flapped his wings and crowed close by and the old woman, in the shock, trembled as if she had never heard a cock crow before. And, as if she had forgotten that they crow at odd times, she was sure it was unlucky.

Stumbling, she twisted and hurt her foot and it was painful. Not able to see what it was that had caused her to fall she limped back into the house. Both the children were there dressed up now in different clothes taken from the case. They must have come in at the other door while she was across the yard, searching the sheds in the dark. Somehow, noiselessly, they had managed to pull the flyscreen door off its hinges so that it would not open properly or close. It was incredible that two such small girls could break something as strong as the door. Later on in the evening they did the same thing to the other door swinging out across the porch on it chasing each other with pretend spiders and screaming with a terrified joy.

They ate steadily from a supply of jelly babies and chewing gum.

The old woman felt they should not have taken fresh clothes without asking, and she said so, but Miranda said that Bettina let her wear what she liked, and that Peg said Kerry could wear what she liked too. With tiny capable hands she folded and unfolded clothes, she shared the clothes into two heaps and then put them away again. The old woman was sure that all the clothes belonged to Kerry really, she saw things she had sewn and knitted herself for her little granddaughter.

Miranda shared the sweets in the same way, restlessly dividing them into little portions and then, with hot sticky fingers, gathering them in again.

'These are for you Kerry to eat in the morning and these are for me and these are for you Kerry not to eat now.' She hopped from one foot to the other.

'If you need the toilet, Miranda, don't put off going,' the old woman, in her pain, was irritable. Something spoiled children. The spoiling seemed in some way connected with cheap frilly nylon underclothes, and the ugly colours of toffee papers, and the crunching of boiled sweets, and the unnatural green and yellow of the different lemonades. The children smelled of the things they were chewing, she would have liked to say something about it.

The children were sucking their thumbs, hardly able to keep their eyes open, and the old woman told them to go to bed. She wanted to lie down herself, her foot was bleeding and painful. She needed to see to it.

'We don't go to bed yet,' Miranda said, but she lay down and tucked her little hand between her little thighs. Before the old woman had time to feel relief, Miranda was up again.

'Mrs Mercer, I want something to eat and drink,' she said. 'Kerry wants icing sugar, have you got icing sugar?' and, unable to open the cupboard, she pulled at the knob till it broke. The children took turns dipping their fingers in the sugar and licking them. The old woman hovered with a sponge and a cloth trying to clear up the mess they made.

While the children coloured in each other's finger and toe nails with green and purple crayons, the old woman took off her stocking and bathed the blood off the hurt foot. She was afraid she had broken open a vein where there was a discoloured patch on her ankle. Something had spiked into her when she fell. It was very painful and she tied it up with clean rag.

The children had a new game. They were dancing on the beds with cushions on their heads.

'We're widows,' they told the old woman. 'This is how you have to be a widow,' they said. The old woman told them she did not need to be told how to be a widow. She thought how pale and tired they looked. She longed to put them to bed. They had such dark rings round their eyes. She said she thought children should not dance on beds.

'Oh, we won't fall,' Miranda said and, overbalancing, she broke the lamp.

The old woman did her best to clear up the broken glass but she was hardly able to put her foot to the floor. She thought a bit of rusty metal must have gone in under the skin. Her eyesight was not good, in daylight it would be easier to see.

'Mrs Mercer, Kerry wants a paper hat, will you make paper hats for us. Kerry wants a nurse's hat, Mrs Mercer make us hats!'

The children said the paper hats were no good and they tore them up.

'Let's dance,' Miranda said. 'Let's have some music.' So the old woman sang for them. Perhaps they would sleep if she sang. She chose a hymn,

All things bright and beautiful,
All creatures great and small,

All things wise and wonderful,
The Lord God made them all.

She liked the hymn she said, she told them to look out for the mountain and the river,

The purple headed mountain,
The river running by,
The sunset, and the morning
That brightens up the sky.

'Do you know any Disco Mrs Mercer?' Miranda called. 'Kerry wants Disco.' The old woman said she did not know what Disco was. So the little girls danced to the hymn. They danced across the room and back, they danced with their mouths open, they rolled their eyes and their hips and they nodded their heads and shook their shoulders, they swayed and kicked and wriggled.

The old woman could not understand the children. In spite of the long soak in the bath, they seemed grimy as if they were soiled in some way which she did not know about. Suddenly she knew she could not trust them at all. It was dreadful, horrible to know this. She searched crazily along the mantelpiece.

'Miranda! Kerry! Where are the matches! Where's my purse and my keys!' The children looked up at her with clear blue eyes.

'Mrs Mercer, perhaps they've fallen in the dam.'

'Yes Grandma, we saw them fall in the dam.'

The old woman would not believe them. Tomorrow she told

them they would find the things. She told them she would have to slap them both. It was a long time she said since she had slapped anyone.

Sometime after midnight Miranda was sick and the old woman, badly in pain, had to change all the bed covers and wash the child's long hair. As she sat by the child she longed to go to sleep herself. The pain in her foot and leg was worse. However would she manage the whole week. Peg should never have done this. Her other daughters would never have done something like this.

'Oh Peg,' she moaned softly. 'What's happened.'

There seemed to be someone in the kitchen, there was the noise of teaspoons being put on cups and saucers. The old woman was pleased.

'Are you there Mary? If you're making tea I'd love some it's such a hot night is that you Mary thank God you've come my good girl my foot's so painful it's not really I just fell in the yard really silly of me it's just a nuisance that's all I'll be better directly but oh Mary I'm so glad you're here silly of me to cry,' the old woman woke with tears on her cheeks. The child was asleep and she lay down on her own bed. She was thirsty. Of course Mary was not there, how could she be, she'd gone to Canada years ago.

'Oh Mary I wish you were here.' The old woman was surprised at her easy tears, she must try to sleep.

'Mary it's lovely to see your kind face like this I remember when I was so ill after Peg was born and you stayed off from school and looked after me and then later on when poor Dora died I was thinking Dora would be home for Christmas but of course I was forgetting it's my silly leg and it was only a little fall out there by the shed Mary I'm so glad . . .'

A plate broke in the kitchen. It was bright daylight. The old woman heard the children, some more crockery was dropped and broken. She must have overslept. She could not get up, her leg was swollen and stiff.

'Kerry! Come to Grandma, Grandma wants you Kerry!' It was Miranda who came, her hair was knotted and sour in spite of being washed.

'Where's Kerry?' the old woman asked. 'Tell Kerry I want her to find my keys and my money purse.' It was hard to talk, her mouth was so dry.

'I've got a pain Mrs Mercer and I feel sick can I come in bed with you?' The little girl scrambled up on to the bed beside the old woman.

'Why you naughty girl, there's clay all over your feet,' the old woman tried to move away from the clumsy child, 'Mind my leg,' she moaned. She struggled off the bed.

In the kitchen there was a pool of milk on the table and the water jug was broken. Kerry was not there.

'The matches!' the old woman suddenly remembered. She thought of her paddock, neglected, and the children like grasshoppers hidden in the long grass; they were like grasshoppers coming up through the dry grass.

'Mrs Mercer! Mrs Mercer! I'm going to be sick again!'

'Wait if you can, dearie, while I find the pail.' The old woman could hardly cross the small kitchen. It was strange that she minded the children so much, she had always loved children. She supposed it was because she was old now, and that made looking after the children such a burden.

'I'll find the matches and put them away,' she muttered. 'I'll get some water. I need some water.'

The children must have turned on the tap and left it on all night. She never thought to look, she was unaccustomed now to children. Her own children, and other children she had known, would never have let the water tank run out.

She knew she might faint and she struggled back to the bed and lay down gratefully. If Kerry would come she could remind her about the other tank.

'Miranda,' she said to the sleeping child beside her. 'Fetch Kerry, tell her Grandma needs a drink of water. Please go and fetch Kerry.'

The old woman and the child slept.

'Miranda!' the old woman tried to rouse the child. 'Tell Kerry not to go down to the dam, it's dangerous down there, there's water by the fowls, Miranda, please find Kerry and tell her, there's a good girl.'

In spite of the severe pain it seemed to the old woman that she was having refreshing little sleeps and that she would be better soon.

It was better to sleep as she had no real wish to wake up.

Peg was on her way home. She could hardly wait to be back with her mother and her little girl. The tedious journey would have been unbearable if she had not raced ahead in her thoughts to the peaceful farm. She kept thinking, with pleasure, how she would have time at last to play with Kerry. She always went home to her mother's for holidays and it was a relief to be going there after all in spite of the other arrangements she had made. She longed to feel the soft cool flesh of her little girl and she longed to hear her voice.

There was something about Bettina, during the short time she had known her, that made her not notice Kerry. Perhaps it was something in herself, not just in Bettina, which made her find Kerry a nuisance at those times when she so urgently wanted to be alone with her new friend.

It was easier just now not to think about Bettina.

She wanted to be with her mother too. Her mother could comfort without appearing to be doing anything other than the work in hand. Looking forward to going home, she was even able to smile to herself during the long journey back.

'What's Miss Moles been up to this term?' Her mother liked to hear what was going on at the school. Deep in her comfortable seat Peg thought of her mother's question.

The Head Mistress, Miss Moles, though concerning herself chiefly with the necessary ugliness of the girls' summer uniforms, repeatedly made opportunities for calling Peg into her office, or she would wait at staff tea time to be alone with Peg at the end of the afternoon. She liked to talk with Peg, she regarded her as one of her more mature and senior mistresses. She liked to talk, among other things, about poetry, and how poems should be introduced in the class room.

'You know Pegeen,' she was always breathless over poetry. 'Before I left England I had the kids in the East End absolutely bonkers over Keats. They lapped him up! Ectually.' She had an accent which put an affectation into everything she said. Peg knew this haughtiness was not intentional. 'Ectually,' Miss Moles was in earnest. 'You can get the kids to love Keats. We've got to get through to the little morons,' she said. 'And Pegeen, I know you can do it!'

It was a strange thing to think, but Miss Moles and Bettina, though so completely different, had a similarity. Peg felt vague about this and let the thought go. If worthwhile it would be sure to return. She smiled comfortably, that was what her mother would have said.

Miss Moles wanted the students to be encouraged to write, especially the seniors. The Muse had, she admitted with the gleam of inspiration in her eyes, visited her. Gazing towards further inspiration somewhere beyond the top of Peg's head, she confessed,

'I'm afraid Peglette, I do suffer from literary pretensions, it's unavoidable. I belong to the minority of the literati, I am myself a compulsive poet!'

In an embarrassed way she pushed some sheets of paper into Peg's unwilling hands.

'The Children of my Muse. He visits me frequently,' she breathed and left the staff tea room quickly, saying awkwardly over her shoulder, 'you can keep them, I have other copies.'

Unable to say to Miss Moles that she did not look upon the children in her classes as morons, she was equally unable to say one word about the poems to the writer of them who, it was clear, from quick nervous looks and raised eyebrows, was waiting from day to day for appreciation and comment.

A few days later Miss Moles, recovering herself, continued with her request. Writing she said was cultivated all too easily in the young who had no difficulty in self expression. It was the older ones who were locked away, she said, and these senior students were to be encouraged to unlock themselves, and made to hand in three or four complete stories in a term.

Peg, burdened with so much extra reading, most of it in illegible handwriting, took the manuscripts home when she visited her mother. With mounting despair she sat with the exercise books in her lap making shy comments here and there in pencil. Her mother, with pursed lips, folded clothes and ironed them on the other side of the table. All the students were handing in writing which contained characters, plots, themes and adequate symbolism, perhaps too many symbols really. They achieved a suitable balance between narrative and dialogue, in fact the stories contained all the qualities of the art and were incredibly dull. It seemed as though, in the effort of contrivance, the real art was lost or destroyed. Not one writer seemed able to present a living character. Peg said something about it to her mother.

'Well Peg,' her mother replied. 'I look at it this way, it's like a percentage of the harvest, if one out of the twenty five achieves something then all your work isn't wasted. And as for the other twenty four, who's to know what they'll make out of it later. Nothing's ever a waste unless you look at it as a waste,' she said.

Peg had known all along that her mother counted only the survivors among the chickens and that she took pleasure in picking whole fruit and did not pine over bird pecked peaches. She dismissed failure of any kind, it was a waste of time to think about it. She was able to ignore completely the little piles of peach and nectarine stones left by the midnight feasting possums. It was her mother's way to reckon on the sound thing, anything else was of no account.

Peg, on her return journey, would have liked to regard Bettina like this, but it was not so easy. It would be better not to think about Bettina till she was safely home and comforted, and then perhaps there would be some sort of perspective.

Peg had lived on the farm for quite a lot of her life and, whenever she could, she went back there even though it was really too far for an ordinary weekend visit.

When she was staying there, there were times of the day which she knew without any clock. It was the constantly changing light as the day wore on. And it was the changing movement and noise of the poultry, the sheep and the calves. Towards the end of the afternoon a transfiguration of the trees took place as the sun, dropping down, sent a last golden light up into the highest branches. Long shadows began to reach up the slope and there were sharper contrasts in the light and shade of the varying greens. The sun sinking lower and lower wrapped glowing colour round bark and, softening the outlines of rocks and old tin cans, made the rubbish heap mysterious and beautiful. At that time the few sheep and calves came up into the yard filling the silence with their noise. They even came into the porch if her mother was slow in coming out. The poultry gathered too and even the cockatoos, in their enchanted flocks, had some knowledge of the farm routine, for, when the old woman appeared in her blue overall, these birds came flying low, screaming, over the long paddock.

It was her custom to cross to the shed followed by her subjects and she would fling several measures of oats at them and stand watching their trust with reverence.

'I'm always so touched at their dependence and their faith,' she would say to Peg. 'It doesn't always do for humans like it does for them.'

It often comforted Peg in her life away from home to know that this ritual continued, especially at times when her own life, for inexplicable reasons, seemed to have no shape, or when it began to take an unexpected turn.

Sitting with Lucien on their last evening together while he read aloud a poem which had turned out not to be for her, she remembered clearly the bewildered expressions on the soft, but strong faces of the calves when they looked up at her and stared, with the oats stuck all round their gently moving black mouths. She had laughed with her mother at their perplexed expressions, but while Lucien read she began to cry.

'Darling!' he said in his tender way. He had just explained very gently and kindly about the change that was to be a part of their lives, and that the poem, with the little rhyming refrain repeated in the middle of every stanza, would help them both to understand the change. He said she would know from the poem who it was he had loved and who it was he loved now. He said she could keep the copy of the poem. He thought the tears were for him so she never explained about the calves.

As she helped him to pack, the dark blue silkiness of his body shirts seemed to slip quickly through her fingers into the new case. Carefully she folded the white trousers he always wore, a bit like a sailor, she thought, who wears the right clothes but never goes to sea. His love poems resembled this sailor. Handling his fresh clean clothes made her aware, perhaps for the first time, that it was possible that she did not mind that he was leaving, that she might manage to live without him. The thought, like the seriousness of the poem, made her smile while the calf tears were still wet on her cheeks.

They shared a chicken and a bottle of Moselle, and Lucien put on a record and moved towards her.

'Lucien must dance,' he said somewhere down in his throat. 'Lucien feels like dancing.' Slowly he turned round and round, he seemed to move without lifting his feet from the floor.

'Dance Maria,' his name for her. 'Dance!' He raised his long fingered hands above his fair head and smiled at her. Bewitchingly and gracefully he tilted his head and looked at her over one shoulder as he turned. He twitched his hips, first the left one and then wickedly, though she knew without any feeling for her, the right.

'One last dance Maria,' he said. When he smiled like this it was impossible to imagine that his jaw could exchange the smile for an obstinate, cold, cruel look.

Clumsily, because she was unwilling as well as big, Peg danced and caught her hip on the edge of the table. Long after he was gone she still felt the ache, there was quite a bruise, as if the last thing he had done was to hit her.

'Where's my daddy gone?' Kerry asked the next morning.

'Daddy's gone to America to find a nice house for Kerry and mommy,' Peg said.

'Are we going there?'

'Some time. But not for ages yet.'

'When we go can Doossa come too?'

'Of course.'

'Doossa's got white lacy stockings, can I have some like Doossa's, can I?'

'Yes of course.'

'This week, can I? can I? can I?'

'No, next week.'

A few days later she moved with Kerry into a much smaller flat very close to the school. This closeness she supposed would make up for the ugliness.

With Bettina's last words she had almost cried but at the time there were people on all sides enjoying their curry.

She was not absolutely sure, at the time, that Bettina's little phrase was final, though it was Bettina's way to make sure that whatever she wanted could never be misunderstood. In the crowded restaurant she made an effort to return, in her thoughts, to that time of the transfiguration, when the long afternoon began to change to the evening. This gathering and noise of the animals belonged to the times when her mother had been out and was returning. She drove an old and battered car, and when this car, covered in dust, rattled into the yard it did not matter what time of day it was, all the life of the farm responded as if the return signified that special time of serenity with the setting sun, the long shadows, the extra light on leaves and bark, and the contrast of deepening spreading shade, together with the hospitable scattering of oats from a tin basin. It would be the same for anyone returning.

On these occasions, when the creatures discovered their mistake, which they did quite soon, they would disperse shyly as hotel guests do when they have mistaken the time for dinner and arrived at the dining room while it is still locked.

Peg understood on the return journey that Bettina had not confided in her to protect her but it was simply in desperation.

'I must get to a cold tub,' Bettina burdened Peg suddenly with the mysterious pain. 'I can't stick it any longer.' Her pain intruded so much that Peg, already tired with travelling, was worn out for her friend. Bettina kept longing for a cold bath to sit in, even though it was cold in India. She was quite unable to stand the discomfort of her very unpleasant condition.

'All you have to do is to open the door and clap your hands, and someone will come.' She was restless and irritable. Peg longed for her to lie down and rest, she wanted to sleep herself.

'Up all those terrible stairs at this time of night?'

'Yes, why not, the hotel offers room service, it says so here on the back of the door, but there's no 'phone and Indians clap their hands for things. They'll expect other people to do the same. Go on!' Bettina's hoarse voice was persistent, she looked at Peg with her head lowered so that her eyes seemed to threaten from under the long fringe. The first time Bettina had looked at Peg, in the flat on the first evening, like this, both of them had laughed aloud. And for Peg, who had some time before stopped laughing, this laughter brought deep refreshment.

In the hotel bedroom neither of them laughed. They were both exhausted with the long journey. The covers on the beds were not clean and the light bulb, without any shade round it, was fly specked and mournfully dim.

'Perhaps they'll give us a better light tomorrow,' Peg said.

'They'd better give us a better room,' Bettina said. 'And we want something now.' Peg had to agree they were cold and hungry and it was that dreadful hour of arrival in the night when it seems impossible to get anything, though they could have had a dozen taxi drivers, there were so many of them falling over each other to take passengers.

Peg opened the door to the cold draught which rushed up the stairwell. The hotel was built round a narrow courtyard, they had crossed the cracked cement to reach the stairs. Beyond the banister, immediately outside their door, it was all blackness.

Peg clapped her hands. Unaccustomed to clapping she made a soft sound. She waited with uneasy wretchedness.

'Is there a bell anywhere, by the beds or by that little table?' She re-entered the room closing the door quickly as if to shut out her feeling on the landing.

'No of course there isn't, Dilly!' Bettina said. Together they inspected their bathroom, the towels looked thick and seemed clean. Somehow, for a moment, Peg was reminded of her mother. It was the towels; she knew how her mother would take Kerry laughing from her bath and put her, wrapped in the soft towel, on the kitchen table and pat her dry. Her old capable hands would have everything ready, clean nightgown, bread and butter and warmed milk.

'The bath looks all right,' Bettina said. The brass taps, well polished, were reassuring. She turned on the taps, they hardly trickled.

'Oh dam and blast! Shit!' Bettina said. 'Bloody hell!'

'We'll have to go all the way back down if we want anything, even water,' Peg said. So they went groping down the dark stairs. Peg, who was so much older, felt responsible. And she loved Bettina, this made her all the more responsible. She loved Bettina. That was why they had made the journey.

Back in the flat they had talked about it.

'I'd do anything in the world for you,' Peg said to Bettina. She had cried a little when she said it. It was a silly thing to do, to cry, she had said laughing through the tears. It was a rare thing in her lonely world to have found someone to love she told Bettina.

'You've got Kerry, you love her,' Bettina said in her hoarse whisper. They had to be quiet because of the children.

'Yes, I know dearest Bettina, of course I love Kerry,' Peg replied. 'But loving a child and loving an adult are two different things. Thank you for letting me love you.'

'What I want to do in this world,' Bettina said stretching and yawning in Peg's bed, 'is to be able to cure people.'

'Why that's wonderful!' Peg was pleased. 'Oh little Bettina, that's wonderful.'

'I've got quite a reputation,' Bettina said yawning again. 'Overseas,' she stretched. 'For the laying on of hands.'

'I don't quite know what that is,' Peg said, feeling that she ought to know.

'Faith healing, Silly Dilly!' Bettina said. 'Faith healing, I want to be a faith healer. I want a mission in my life, the only trouble is I haven't any money, not a bean.' She frowned and looked up at Peg from under her long fringe. 'I'm flat broke! I'm on the rocks!'

Bettina, naked in Peg's dreary flat transformed the small rooms. Even the light seemed different when she was there. Sometimes Bettina seemed smooth and radiant and her body glowed. At other times her restless vitality made every word and movement urgent and mysterious, and it was like being in the presence of a fierce unpredictable little animal. An unnamed one.

She had an entirely unselfconscious way of being naked while she fried an egg or read a magazine. As people often kick off their shoes when they come home Bettina shed her few clothes. Peg, on the edge of this liberation, could not help telling Bettina,

'I think you're beautiful Bettina, really I do, you're really beautiful.'

'Aw, there's spare tyres all over me!' Bettina laughed. 'I'm fat and skinny in all the wrong places.' Peg could tell that, though she laughed, Bettina was pleased to be admired.

Peg had not known Bettina very long. It was strange, she reflected, that it seemed as if Bettina and Miranda had been a part of their lives for a long time. Before Bettina had come there, the flat was a place where she looked after Kerry and prepared her school work. It was a place she left every day when she went to school, and then came back to try to recover from her work, and once more prepare for it.

In her loneliness she attempted to recapture the days of her childhood and she chose poems which carried, in their words, the sounds of the earth and the countryside. She described the grasshoppers and she read to her class,

The poetry of earth is never dead:
When all the birds are faint with the hot sun,
And hide in cooling trees, a voice will run
From hedge to hedge about the new-mown mead,
That is the grasshopper's . . .

She avoided poems which reminded her of the pain of loneliness; and she avoided the obscure. Obscurity was a form of loneliness, or so it seemed to her when she remembered Lucien and his friends. Instead, she reminded her pupils of the sound of a baby crying and of a baby laughing. She read to them,

My baby has a mottled fist,
My baby has a neck in creases
My baby kisses and is kissed
For she's the very thing for kisses.

She suggested that they might like to write poems about grasshoppers and babies, perhaps even to write a poem to a baby.

There were times when she longed to give up school work. Every day it was the effort required and the draining of her energy. Often she tried to avoid Miss Moles who, with bright new ideas, lay in waiting for her at the end of the afternoon. Just when Peg was trying to slip away from school Miss Moles would come out of the staff tea room holding out a cup of tea to her.

'Pegeen! I've saved you a cake bravely rescued from the jaws of the Crimp, here you are, pink icing! Miss Crimp, dear, you shall have two cakes on the morrow.'

Sometimes Peg felt quite unfit to be teaching and, because she needed to have work, she hoped Miss Moles would not notice.

Miss Moles often put her head round the classroom door. 'May I come in?' She was coy. 'The word of the day is creative,' she would say, smiling at Peg and at the class. Once she stayed sitting at one of the empty desks. 'Take absolutely no notice of the fact that I am here,' she said.

Uncomfortably Peg continued to read, '... "trees, rocks and flowers send back the echo man desires." It's from Beethoven,' she told the girls. 'Beethoven wrote it in his diary when he was composing the symphony number six, the *Pastoral Symphony*.'

Miss Moles interrupted, 'Peg, didn't you know that Beethoven was not the gentle creature you are making him out to be, he didn't love the country and he used to beat his wife!'

A sigh of soft laughter went through the girls.

'Beethoven never married,' Peg said quickly and, too late, understood her mistake. She should have waited. The roomful of girls saw Miss Moles blush painfully all down her neck. And in the open front of her white blouse the red colour spread, giving more than a hint of embarrassment. Peg ached with the knowledge of what must have seemed like unkindness, the ache lasted for some days.

She was tired all the time. Some days she seemed only able to think about the end of the afternoon when she could leave and fetch Kerry from the kindergarten, and get home as quickly as possible.

For some reason, however much the sun might be shining, no sun came into the flat. The opposite wall came towards her as soon as she opened the front door. Because of the way the flats were built, there was no view from the window. Though the sea was so close, its sighing could be heard all night, it was not possible to look out across the sea. The windows of the flats faced each other. Often she tried to recall the pleasure of looking at the narrow paddock directly outside her mother's window. It was possible to sit in the small living room there and look right down the long slope to the willow trees overhanging the dam. Sitting in that room was almost the same as being out in the paddock. Because of the grass and the trees and the water there were birds. So near to these it was impossible to feel alone.

All the tiredness and the depression of the day, and of the days following one another, fell on her as soon as she was inside the tiny flat. Any food she prepared tasted of the flat. Kerry was discontented and white faced and always wanting things she could not have.

Often they went, the two of them, down in the lift and out on to the grass at the side of the flats. The tall buildings blocked out the sun. Kerry, too near her mother, pretended to play with a ball, talking in a silly voice to Doossa, while Peg tried to mark compositions and read the forced stories handed in by the seniors. The wind, bringing dust and grit, caught at the pages.

'Tell Doossa it's my turn,' Kerry insisted.

'Doossa it's Kerry's turn.'

'Tell her again, she didn't listen. Go on tell her, tell Doossa again.'

'Oh Kerry I must get my marking done.'

'Doosa's going to wear her second party dress tomorrow, can I wear my second party dress, can I? Can I? like Doossa?'

GRASSHOPPERS

'Yes, yes but be quiet just now, play with your ball, there's a good girl.'

'Doossa's good too, tell Doossa she's good.'

'Yes, yes two good girls, now be quiet do!'

And Kerry skipped and chattered and stared shamelessly at anyone who went by.

It was all different when Bettina came. Everything changed when she came. She came by mistake. She said she was looking for someone, Peg could not now even remember the name she had said. It turned out to be the wrong address. She had a little girl with her.

'What's your name?' Kerry asked her, from Peg's side, at the door.

'Miranda,' said the other child.

'Mommy, can Miranda have tea with us?' Kerry asked, her voice rising with excitement.

'Oh well, I'm afraid not . . .' Peg began, and then she hesitated, she had just told the young woman that she must have made a mistake with the address.

'Oh please!' Kerry said.

Peg looked awkwardly at Bettina who appeared to be clothed from head to foot in sunshine though there was no sun on the concrete stairways and landings. So often she had explained to Kerry that little girls did not ask people to tea like this, not in front of them, but only privately so that mothers would not be forced to invite. Her blue and white frock was like a uniform confronted in this way.

Bettina, audacious, smiled at Peg.

'Would you like to come in?' Peg asked Bettina shyly.

The two little girls rushed through the flat shrieking and banging the doors. The two women followed slowly, smiling slowly at one another.

With some makeshift arrangements Bettina and Miranda stayed the night.

The place was full of sunlight with Bettina there. She had ideas, and she had ways of moving things so that with four people instead of two, the flat actually seemed to have more space. She pulled the rug from Peg's bed and flung it over the shabby settee. Peg had never imagined such a transformation possible.

The next day at school she thought all the time, with pleasure, of going home to Bettina. Towards the end of the afternoon two girls in the music room were practising the duet from Orpheus, the young voices carried the pleading and the refusal along the empty corridors. Peg, hurrying to her poetry class, was moved by the two voices singing with so much feeling. She had never noticed before how the perfection of the harmony enhanced the feeling. To accompany her poetry reading she chose music with drums and a song with a throbbing beat. In the class room suddenly there seemed a sharing of anticipation and pleasure. She told her girls how to find the pulse which was the heart beat.

'Put your right forefinger on your left wrist, inside, in line with the thumb and feel your own hearts beating,' she said. And, feeling the steady beat of her own heart, she thought of Bettina and read

But hark my pulse
like a soft drum

Beats my approach
tells thee I come.

'Now listen again to the music,' she said. 'Listen to the music of the drums and listen to the beating of the heart in the poem,

But Hark my pulse
like a soft drum
Beats my approach
tells thee I come.'

The little flat was so close to the school, it would take only a few minutes to be back there with Bettina.

Downstairs in the hotel the young English man was still at the reception desk. He was pale with bluish rings round his eyes. He could not do anything for them he said. 'No food is served during the night,' he said.

'That's no way to treat hotel guests!' Peg was angry. For herself it did not really matter, but there was Bettina. 'My friend is very tired,' she said. She was tall, taller than the young man. In her awkwardness and anger she was more unkind in her voice than she meant to be. They were both extremely tired after their journey.

'Tomorrow I shall see the hotel manager. I shall report you and we shall move somewhere else.'

A deep colour spread over the young man's haggard face. As if it hurt him to blush, his eyes looked as if they would burst in tears out of his face. Looking down at his feet he said, 'Just a minute, I'll see what I can do.' He slipped away through a small door curtained off behind the desk.

At once Peg felt incredibly unhappy. She had made an unbearable mistake in speaking to him as she had. His pale eyes looked at her in disbelief as the little veins and capillaries, misplaced on his crooked boyish face, slowly reddened. She had not imagined that she could strip him of covering and dignity. It was as if she had peeled him and left him raw without his skin. It wasn't his fault she thought.

'What a perfect drip!' Bettina said. She walked restlessly in the poorly lit foyer. The hotel was not one which reminded of better or more glorious days. It seemed as if it had never known much of anything.

'What I need,' Bettina said, 'is a nice bath, now!'

It was not possible to put on the hot water during the night the young man explained when he came back.

'It will be on at six o'clock sharp,' he promised them, almost sharing the tones of an Indian as though, having discussed with the person in charge, he had taken on the voice. Peg had for a moment, in her mind, a picture of the Indian proprietoress, glossy and fat, propping herself on her elbow in bed to speak to the young man, uneasy at disturbing her, half in the doorway of her stuffy room. She imagined the voice,

'Tell them it will be on at six o'clock sharp.'

The young man brought with him a handsome little tray of beaten metal with cracker biscuits, some sort of sweets in silver foil, a banana and an orange, two small glasses and a small bottle of soda water.

The young women, not pleased, carried their supper upstairs, looking up anxiously to the square of yellow light which came from their open door.

'I should have chosen a better hotel, dearest,' Peg apologised while they examined the sweets. The bath water trickling made Bettina very impatient.

'It's going to take ages to fill that great big bath,' she complained.

'It will be cold,' Peg said, and shivered.

'I must get to a cold tub.' It seemed to Peg that Bettina was obsessed in some way, or ill. Peg longed to comfort Bettina but felt awkward and foolish in the strange surroundings, and Bettina had lost her happy carelessness in her present trouble. Peg, on her own, could not achieve carelessness.

Though Bettina had borrowed five hundred dollars from Peg, it was Peg who paid their fares. She was the one earning money. Because of this she carried money and she paid. As many generous people do, Peg suffered from moments of knowing that she was behaving stupidly with her hard-earned money. She disliked, not Bettina, she loved her, she found herself disliking the moments when she knew how foolish she was over the money and the giving of presents. The money was not lent to Bettina, it was given because Peg could never, and did not, expect it to be returned. Thinking of this made her feel huge and stupid. She disliked, if it was possible to dislike, and perhaps it was just possible, more so in India, to hear Bettina's ways of asking for money, the particular note in her voice, the false half swallowed words in her special language when describing her moneyless plight.

'It's terrible to be without money darling,' Peg agreed and soothed. 'But you've no need to worry, honestly, there's no need.'

'That's just where you're so wrong,' Bettina said, her hoarse voice, which normally attracted, becoming rough. 'I'm right down on the rocks, though I hate to talk about it I simply don't know how I'll manage. Everything costs so much. I don't like saying this, but it's . . . it's all very well for you, you've got it, but when you haven't it's serious. You see I haven't a soul in the world I can ask, no one at all to help me.'

Peg was touched deeply. She kissed Bettina on her wet hair.

'Come out of that miserable bath,' she said softly. 'We ought to get to bed, d'you know it's nearly three and we'll have to get up quite early.'

'I really need money badly,' Bettina said. 'I hate asking favours of anyone, specially you.'

Peg, even more touched, put her arms round Bettina. She did not allow herself even a moment's thought about the five hundred dollars and its apparent disappearance.

'You're sweet, really sweet,' she said tenderly. 'Come on, let's try to forget all the sad things, it's so sweet to be alone together,' she said. 'Come to bed.'

Peg tried and Bettina tried.

'How can I set up as a faith healer when I'm scratching myself to ribbons,' Bettina complained. She sat bouncing angrily away to the side of the bed, her eyes red rimmed and sore with lack of sleep and infection.

'Bettina, darling, you must not scratch!' Peg, appalled, tried to comfort her. 'And really you shouldn't rub your eyes, you'll make them much worse.'

'Oh, what's the use!' Bettina said. 'I feel every minute as if I could bring it off but I can't. I just can't get there!'

She got up and moved restlessly all round the room, she picked up Peg's hair brush. 'Perhaps this'd do the trick.' She put it down. 'Oh! I could scream,' she almost screamed.

'Perhaps you should see a doctor,' Peg suggested gently. She felt the disappointment too, with the failure of their first night really alone together; the disappointment of being sleepless and having to understand that sensations from disease can easily be confused with other sensations, but do not respond and bring about the desired relief and satisfaction.

'Perhaps you should see a doctor,' Peg suggested again, just as gently as before.

'Me see one of the crummy doctors here!' Bettina was scornful. 'I can handle this myself,' she went into their bathroom and, as there was now water in plenty, she mixed herself another bath.

'Some Indian doctors are very good,' Peg said from the doorway. Bettina lay back in the water.

'Good at fleecing,' Bettina said. 'I'd have to pay through the nose,' she said. 'Who'd pay,' she said. 'You know I haven't got a bean.'

'I'll pay,' Peg said quietly.

'If they're so good why don't you go!'

'Me?' Peg said. 'Why should I go?'

'Because,' Bettina said, 'Because you're sure to need to soon.'

*

Before setting out for the house in the hills where the faith healer was known to give classes in his art, Peg and Bettina went together to shops in Madras and bought scented lotions and medicinal oils. Bettina would try them all she said.

The two hundred dollar taxi ride was frightening, partly because of the loneliness and wildness of the countryside, but mainly because of Bettina's frantic need for another bath, and her inability to be comfortable sitting still. She was not comfortable walking either, and when the driver stopped the car on the particularly steep and nasty little road, Peg suffered severe misgivings for Bettina.

'Here we have to walk only this last part,' their driver said. 'Follow me, is not in the least difficult to walk, but for car is not possible!' He set off rapidly.

The two young women, Peg with raised eyebrows, and carrying a case, and Bettina with her tiny picturesque bundle slung over her shoulder, slowly followed.

It was soon clear why the car had to remain so dangerously parked on the steep bend. The rains had washed deep gullies across and into the road. These gullies gaped so horribly Peg did not trust herself to step or jump from one crumbling edge to the other. The first one was so deep it was not possible to see to the bottom of it; it was wide enough for a man to fall down, and narrow enough to make it impossible to rescue him. Peg felt dizzy on the edge of it. The road too made her feel dizzy. On one side the hill went up solidly like a wall and on the other side there was nothing; the slope fell away so steeply she could not bear to look over. A long way down this steep hillside were dark ugly scars of earth and rock, where the water, during the rains, like an infection taking the line of least resistance, found a way out from these bottomless holes.

The driver, as if aware of their fear, for they were afraid, straddled the first gully, his thin feet, in the unsuitable patent leather shoes, hardly planted in either edge. His undernourished body swayed backwards, dangerously, but quite faithfully unconcerned that death was certain with one clumsy movement. He held out his hand to Peg.

'Trust me,' he said simply. She thought his hand too small and too incompetent but she was wrong. As she made her first jump she knew he felt safe because it simply did not matter to him whether he stood there helping the ladies or whether he fell like a little cloth doll, head over heels, all the way down to the bottom of the hill. His life and their lives, so it seemed to Peg as she made her landing, were all to him as only a small part of something much greater. His own life was of little consequence to him. She wondered perhaps if she would ever be able to cultivate and keep this thought for herself, and living on it, give this same impression.

The last day of the term came into her mind, the last tea time in the staff room where Miss Moles was waiting for her when the other teachers had gone. Peg had been anxious to slip off quickly to Bettina. Miss Moles had saved a cream cake for her.

'Pegeen!' Miss Moles was excited. 'In so far as being head mistress is concerned I am at last joining the ranks of the liberated! For the first time in my life, and not too soon either.' She paused. 'Pegeen, I am at last a whole complete woman, fulfilled at last! I am myself pregnant!'

Peg was shocked, though she did not say so. She would have liked to say how lonely it was being a mother on your own. She said nothing, even though she knew Miss Moles would regard what she said as being important. Miss Moles discussed all kinds of things with her. They were usually the last for afternoon tea and the time was suitable for conversation, or so Miss Moles thought.

'Let me see.' Miss Moles hurried on as if to cover up the unexpected silence from Peg. 'We don't seem to have one pregnant girl in the school,' she said sounding disappointed. 'When I was teaching in the East End some years ago a number of the school girls were preggers. Some were already mothers, their babies were in the school creche. The girls, you know Peg, were encouraged to feed and bath their babies there, and to attend their lessons as usual.' Miss Moles paused thoughtfully, her keen eyes searching Peg's. 'Some of the boys went to the nursery quite unselfconsciously, you know, and nursed the babies or watched the young mothers. Really quite touching and lovely,' Miss Moles sighed. 'It doesn't seem to happen like that now,' she said and then, squaring her shoulders, she said, 'I shall of course remain at the school as long as possible, and later I hope to . . . or should I say, we hope to come back. We shall come back. Who was it who said, "The value of education is the knowledge of its worth".' Miss Moles took a deep breath and looked hard at Peg, it was a moment of deep emotion for her, 'Well Peg,' she said. 'Have a splendid holiday. Ad astra per arduam and all the rest of it.'

Peg had very little imagination, and so her thoughts hardly ever intruded but, in the moment of relief at being on firm ground, she laughed. Suddenly she was wondering about the moment of conception. Miss Moles in charge of all those girls was herself an eternal school girl. Peg laughed again, Miss Moles awkwardly undressing? Or had someone undressed her?

'Miss Moles!' she said aloud.

Bettina, making her jump with the little Indian did not notice Peg laughing and talking to herself. Bettina would never be interested in Miss Moles, but Peg's mother would be sure to ask, 'What's Miss Moles been up to now?'

Bettina cleared the gully safely. And slowly, gully by gully, they made their way up to the house, which was almost hidden by the steepness of the hill and an overgrown garden which had been planned for the kind of leisure enjoyed by those who do not have to work.

Even when they could see the house they still had a long way to walk to it. The secluded garden hinted at secret meetings. Voluptuous, but broken curves of marble and fragmented white balustrade, moss covered and hidden by leaves and branches, achieved a desolation which seemed to come towards them as they approached. It was impossible not to notice the dirty arms and legs of once admired statues, and they turned back quickly from a flight of steps which led down through the damp earth to broken marble baths of enormous size and filled with rubbish. Clearly, the garden held all the fallen down summer hiding places of lovers long since forgotten.

No one came out to meet them.

The house was double storeyed with balconies. It was white, stained and crusted from the weather and from birds. All the windows were boarded and no sound of any kind came from within.

Peg felt very cold and she was frightened too.

'The front door's open,' Bettina cried in triumph. 'It's wedged, it only needs a shove.' She kicked off her shoes. 'Come on Peg!' Together they pushed the door open a little way.

'I don't think we ought to just barge in,' Peg said. 'Perhaps we should knock.' She wondered what sort of person would answer the door.

'I'm so hot and thirsty Peg. Ring the bell Peg. Can you see a bell Peg?' Bettina was excited. 'Thank God we're here at last!'

Peg shivered. She wondered again about Bettina being so hot, and her ever present thirst. It was as if she burned inside and could not cool this burning. She wished she could persuade Bettina to go to a doctor.

'You know Bettina, dear,' Peg had renewed her attempts at persuasion during the taxi ride. 'I always go to the doctor if I think I've got something wrong with me.'

'Oh yes, sure!' Bettina had scoffed. 'I can just see you taking every blemish on your body to show to the doctor; doctor,' she mimicked. 'See here doctor, I've got a freckle on my bum, is it dangerous?'

As Peg looked at the house, and thought of the need for a doctor when there was no hope of finding one, she felt more and more hopeless. How stupid she'd been to come.

'Come on Peg, don't be so wet!' Bettina was impatient.

'Is a very nice house,' the driver said. 'But is empty, quite empty.'

'It can't be!' Bettina's voice was high pitched and sharp.

'Oh yes,' he said simply. 'I can see at once it is empty,' he shrugged. 'It has all the signs of an empty house, do you not see for yourselves, it has not people.'

'But the faith healer wrote that he lived here,' Peg explained gently and firmly as if her explanation could place him at once in the house and cause him to come out to welcome them.

'Madam,' the driver said. 'I should think no longer.' And there was no reply to this.

They did not walk far into the deserted house. The once noble staircase was melancholy. Their footsteps and voices made too much noise so they crept rather than walked, and they talked in whispers.

'It's a lovely house,' Bettina's hoarse voice reached Peg. 'But just look at the dreadful plastic lampshades, and here's a packet of custard powder!' Disappointment in her laugh made Peg sorrier than ever. Restlessly Bettina peered into rooms.

'There's only a few dirty old mats,' she complained. 'It's such a shame! I love the stairs. The house could be so lovely, it is lovely!'

'Yes, very nice house, but is quite empty,' their driver insisted.

Bettina stood by the partly open door, 'I love it here,' she said, 'I think it's glorious here, look at the view. I shall sleep in one of the rooms looking out this way, a room with a window looking out down there. Think of waking up every morning to see that view.'

But Peg could not see any beauty, she could not look for any mountain, purple in the distance, and she had no idea if any river was close by. She could not look at beauty there however much it may have been at her feet.

'Bettina dearest, we can't stay,' she said.

'He may come back at any moment.' Bettina did not seem worried at all by the isolation or the deserted appearance of the house. 'He's sure to come soon,' she said.

'But where on earth could he come from?' Peg asked uneasily.

Bettina, she thought, did not seem to notice that it would be dark soon.

'Wonnerful ride back, for you, very cheap.' The taxi driver had the immediate solution for his own problem.

How comfortable an aeroplane was Peg thought on her return journey. It was better to travel alone. Most of her present exhaustion had come from Bettina's ambition and the trouble of her sudden symptoms. This illness she was sure had not come about from dirtiness. Bettina looked dirty, especially when she went round the supermarket dressed in an old towel knotted high up under her armpits, but she was really very clean and very fresh in her youth and her wish for life. It was something in life which had spoiled her. It was an infection from living. A little extra tenderness for Bettina welled up in Peg. She was fifteen years older, that in itself was an indication; the fifteen years, or some of them, should bear the responsibility. Mixed with the tenderness was envy too, not for the illness which was too horrible, but because she had to admit to herself that she had none of Bettina's ability to turn experience into moments of pure happiness.

Though she longed for Kerry it was a relief to be travelling without her. Kerry was ambitious and wanted things, so that there was never any real rest in her company either, or with the imaginary Doossa who was always even more in need than Kerry of every dress, every toy, every sweet, and all the other unnameable never ending wants. Doossa had, through the years of being Kerry's ever present companion, been an equal destroyer of rest.

There were similarities between Miranda and Doossa. Miranda perhaps more explicit in her needs and, of course, since her arrival Doossa had disappeared.

It really was better to travel alone. To travel with Lucien, Peg discovered at once that she needed tremendous energy, and personal discipline, to keep up with his cleanliness.

'Your young man looks so clean,' her mother said after seeing him for the first time. 'He looks as if you could safely eat your dinner off him! If you marry him, Peg my girl, you'll spend your days in the laundry tub.'

Peg told her mother, 'He's got such a terrible landlady, Mother, at the place where he lives. Every time he uses the toilet she rushes in straight after and cleans it with a brush.'

'Well,' her mother replied, 'I suppose if he'd seen to it himself she wouldn't have needed to.'

Peg never discussed Lucien with her mother after that except once, at the beginning, when they read his first poems together, *Come live with me and be my love/And we will all the pleasures prove*, and there the discussion really only took the form of a pause at the two lines. Knowing that they were not the young poet's but, as if by an unspoken agreement about the possibilities for the future, neither of the women said anything. Though later Peg's mother said to Peg, when they were alone, 'I like those two lines, Peg, and what's said in them. All Lucy's got to do is put a couple of inverted commas and it doesn't matter then who's written them.'

'His name's Lucien, Mother, not Lucy.'

'Of course, Lucien,' her mother said.

Peg knew too that Lucien's cleanliness and freshness was more an appearance of both these qualities. This was a shock. But even so, keeping up appearance was a lot of work. She guessed too that with other people there were appearances and shocks, and that the other people managed to live in spite of them. It did not occur to her then that Lucien may have experienced some sort of shock too, but was either too well mannered or too unconcerned to mention it.

There was nothing of shock in his final poem. But by then he had passed on to other experience.

Bettina slept most of the way back on the ride down from the hills. She slept sweetly and Peg, feeling her body so innocently and so trustingly against her own as the car swung and jolted, experienced fresh tenderness and desire for her friend. Perhaps she would be better soon. Peg felt she must get Bettina cured quickly. Perhaps they would find another faith healer anxious to pass on his art to those with the gift in their finger tips, or wherever it was the gift concealed itself. Faith healing, Peg told herself in the dark car, could do so much for mankind. Lovingly she steadied the sleeping Bettina. She pictured her walking lightly between rows of sufferers putting her soft hands on a stomach here and on a stomach there and, for a moment, she smiled as she saw the tortured faces of those who had been in such pain looking up at their little healer with gratitude.

But pain was pain and came from a cause, toothache, appendicitis, gall stones, any kind of pain had to be regarded with truth and Peg, in her heart, knew she had to put aside Bettina's skill. Bettina, she thought, should be encouraged to sit at a desk and study, she should give up the idea of the feet of the faith healer. Rattling along in the taxi Peg acknowledged the necessity of having doctors and nurses and dentists. In the morning she would gently and firmly tell Bettina,

'Bettina darling, listen to me, if something is bad and has to be removed from the body then nothing will do but to remove it. It's no use, Bettina, to cover a splinter of wood, or glass, or metal with a clean rag or a bandage. Bettina, however much a person might care for another person, love them and observe them, if something needs to be taken out from the body, it has to be taken out. If there is an infection in the body it has to be identified and treated. Bettina, faith and belief are good but by themselves they are not enough.'

Peg fidgeted in the car and smoothed her knee length blue and white dress. Sometimes the good quality of her clothes worried her, she felt she was not casual enough about them.

Straight away on that first evening Bettina had examined Peg's wardrobe. She needed to wash out her skirt, she said, and laughing she thought Peg might have something she could borrow. She had not been in the flat an hour,

'Why ever don't you get some long things, dresses or skirts – instead of these, I never saw such boring colours!' she said, tossing through Peg's dresses and suits.

'I've never worn anything long,' Peg said shyly.

'There's always a first time,' Bettina said.

Bettina was probably right about her clothes. She was so used to dressing suitably for school.

'I feel absolutely huge in this,' Peg said to Bettina in the hotel bedroom. They had needed to rest after the long drive down from the house in the hills. She turned round slowly in the cramped space. 'It's just not me!' she said plaintively. Awkwardly she peeled off the prickly cotton caftan bought hastily during the early morning hunt for the scented and medicinal oils for Bettina. 'It's such a gorgeous colour, this orange,' she sighed. 'You try it on.' She passed the garment to Bettina. 'Perhaps we could make it smaller for you, it's your colour.' She patted herself, regretting her height and the size of her creamy thighs. Carefully she shook out her dress and hung it up. The heavy silky material would endure. The blobs of blue and white reassured her, the pattern was so meaningless and safe.

'I'm starving!' Bettina ignored Peg's clothes. 'Let's go out to an expensive restaurant and have some really good food.' She was feeling a lot better she said. Peg laughed and quickly tucked her nightdress back under the pillow. She kissed her friend's round wet head.

'Of course, darling,' she said. 'That's a wonderful idea.'

In the busy restaurant in Madras, Peg started to think of her homecoming. She ate the large and expensive meal alone. On the table were dishes of curried meat and fish and vegetables. There were small dishes among the larger ones which looked as if children, playing, had arranged fragments of fruit and ginger, generously covered with shredded coconut. There were platters of rice patted into balls. Some balls were coloured and stuffed with prunes and sultanas. On a side table were a dozen tiny plates, as if put there for a dolls' tea party. The little plates were filled with various Indian sweets and puddings which shivered when they were moved. She hardly noticed the food. She thought she would cry. But to cry in a place where people have come to enjoy themselves, and particularly to enjoy food, is hardly acceptable, so Peg did not cry. She ate the unwanted food quickly glancing shyly from time to time at all the different people and their different ways of eating. The restaurant was crowded.

Bettina, as soon as they had chosen their meal and ordered it, thought she saw someone she knew sitting at a table on the far side of the room.

'I must just go over,' she said. 'See you around Peg.'

Thinking about going home while she ate alone in the restaurant was just the right thing for Peg to do. She needed to be comforted and looked after, and the best place for these needs was the farm, so far away but so close in her thoughts.

Her holiday time was all before her. She would take her mother and Kerry to the sea. They could manage a trip in one day so that the animals need not be left uncared for. Peg remembered going with her mother years ago. Her mother drove the car, a crazy carload of girls, a neighbour had once described them, with beach towels and food to the sea. They always went to the same place, to an estuary where the river widened till the banks were hardly visible. On one side there was a wooden structure known as the baths. There it was possible to swim safely protected from waves, hidden currents and sharks, inside grey splitboard fences supported by enormous grey weathered piles. The lively water lapped to and fro through the spaces between the boards. Only small harmless things moved with the freedom of the water, in and out of the boards.

Out of their depths Peg and her sisters clung to the piles and peered at the expanse of swelling river through the wide cracks. The water, outside the fence, shone and rippled and the swell, as it came and went, lifted them up and dragged them down so that their screams and laughter were a mixture of high pitched joy, and a choking and gasping for breath. Sometimes one of them pretended to sink, crying for help, one arm raised high, and then disappearing with only thin white fingers above the water.

'Hep! Hep! I'm drowning. Hep! Hep!' And the others, splashing and kicking, pretended to rescue.

The angry old man, the attendant, said no one should ever pretend to drown. He gave swimming lessons to the children of the well-to-do. He stood up to his chest in water, hour after hour, giving private tuition to individual children. Their rich mothers sat nearby on the solid boards round the baths to make sure their children were having their money's worth. He said he taught every child separately, but it was clear he was shouting to at least twenty children at once.

Peg and her sisters threw jelly fish at one another and the old man said they must move away, and keep away from the serious swimmers. Peg's mother told him to hold his tongue or else she'd report him and his open pan lavatories. Peg smiled as she remembered the days in the river and she smiled even more as she thought how she would take Kerry and her mother there as soon as possible.

There was no doubt that air travel was very comfortable, quite mindless in a sense, because it was not possible to do anything about anything, however much you might want to.

She suspected she had been dozing instead of reading, she had a book open on her lap, like an old woman, she thought, but the last few days had been too much. Among other things, Bettina had a sore on her lip. It was not there one day and then the next day there it was broken and painful.

'You should eat fresh fruit,' Peg was gentle and quick with advice. 'Bettina dear, fresh oranges. I'll get you some.'

'I'll hit the roof with them,' Bettina said and refused the fruit. Peg had the extra sorrow of knowing that Bettina was in more pain, the sight of the dry cracked painful lip was more than Peg could stand. She suffered dreadfully for every one of Bettina's symptoms. She admitted, for she was always honest with herself, silently, that more than a small part of her suffering was intense disappointment for, in knowing Bettina, Peg had come to know passion and desire for the first time in her life.

She had never imagined that travelling could be so dream like. It was strange to be purring like a cat through the sky, with clouds on either side looking like soft mountains which could be walked on quite easily.

Soon it would get dark, and be dark before she could reach home.

Perhaps because of the sense of being not responsible during the journey, Peg remembered the times of mounting and heightened feeling between Lucien and his friend, a pretty young man with prematurely white hair and clean childish clothes. Taking no part in her aeroplane journey was like being on the edge of the rising laughter of the two young men. She took no part in that either but moved on in her life, rather as if on a quiet journey. She was not discontented.

'Sit! Sit for me Maria, Marienchen,' Jaffa would say to Peg. He imitated Lucien in saying she was Mary, Maria the Madonna. 'You are a nice plain one,' he said. 'With your smooth face, it is an oval! And your smooth neat hair and this – your big big belly. Let me feel,' he said, placing his delicate hand where he thought the baby's feet would kick. Peg smiled.

'Ah!' Jaffa said. 'You must sit for me, just like this, you must sit,' and he described circles in the air with an imaginary camel hair brush. And then he ran back a little and, after a little pause, ran forward in a nimble little dance squinting at her, his head on one side, screwing up his eyes, measuring the proportions of her body, seeing where her shadows lay, noticing her stillness.

'One day I am going to paint you,' he said every time he went through this amusing little ritual. 'I'll paint you with your baby at your fine breast,' he promised. 'You will be the Madonna del Jaffa!'

But by the time Kerry was born Jaffa did not come to visit them any more and Lucien had a new friend. It happened that one night Jaffa and Lucien had a quarrel. Peg heard them from where she lay in the next room reading herself to sleep. Jaffa stabbed Lucien with Peg's embroidery scissors, it was not serious in itself.

'But it's the idea!' Lucien sobbed his startled grief and pain onto Peg's big stomach and she stroked his soft fair hair, and comforted him. When Jaffa called the next day to say he was sorry Peg answered the door and, towering over the frightened young man, she sent him away.

'I'll come back and paint you when you know your misery,' Jaffa said over his shoulder. 'I'll paint you when your lap is full, I'll paint you in a Pieta!' It was a threat. Peg felt it then, in spite of it being uttered chokingly through rising tears. She never forgot how he looked at her, though in her comfortable way, she did not spend much time later wondering about his words.

Lucien and his friends laughed and laughed, and often spent hours teasing and sulking in turns. When they were melancholy it was impossible to rouse them. Peg knew better than to try. She did not laugh with them, but neither did she waste time sharing in any of their unhappiness.

When Peg sat holding Bettina close between her strong naked thighs they did not speak. It was serious and they did not laugh. Peg thought it was sweet and tender to cherish this young Bettina, so very sweet and special. She would have liked to say more to Bettina about her happiness; perhaps to say that all the time she was at school she was looking forward to the times when they could forget everything except the excitement of their kisses and the pleasure of caressing each other. She would have liked to ask Bettina exactly how she felt, perhaps to ask too if Bettina loved her as she loved Bettina. There was not much use in thinking about any of it since it had come to an end.

Years ago at the baths a little girl pushed her foot through the split fence and then was unable to pull it out. Peg's older sister tried to help the child. The water, slapping and tossing came up too high, and Peg saw them struggling, almost fighting in the water. As she watched, trying to keep herself afloat, she felt herself choking. The water seemed to rise in a tower, there was nothing under her feet, and she had to struggle up, up in the tower of water.

From the bank and the entrance to the baths the water always looked smooth and peaceful. It had a vigorous life of its own, which did not show from the bank. Perhaps all water was secretive.

In spite of praise and comfort from the people, Peg's sister cried and cried in the car on the way home.

'Hold your noise or you'll get something to cry about.' It was not often their mother slapped anyone, but sometimes she said there were times when she needed to slap someone.

Lucien's new friend, the one in the final poem was called Helen. Peg had never seen her.

'I really ought to have married a gynaecologist,' Lucien used to say at parties.

'Why Lucien darling,' people laughed, their elegant fingers clutching their drinks, their beads and each other.

'Because,' Lucien said with his arm resting lightly round Peg's thick shoulder, 'they earn so much more than teachers, eh Peg?'

Peg did not mind, it was one of Lucien's little party jokes. Perhaps Helen was the longed for gynaecologist. Because she was on her way home it did not seem to matter.

It was dark when Peg at last reached the little farm. There were no lights on in the house. She had difficulty getting in because both doors were hanging broken and wedged.

'Mother!' she called in a frightened voice. It seemed as if she was returning after being away for years instead of a few days. There was a different smell about the house. She thought it might be because of all the strange smells of India she had forgotten the smell of home. Perhaps too, it was the severe change from excitement and anticipation, as well as the very long journeys, which helped to give this impression of being away for such a long time.

'Mother! Mother! What's happened? Mother are you there?' She stood quite still in the dark. All the anxiety of the last few hours seemed gathered in this one spot. She had waited and waited for Bettina in the hotel room. The night seemed impossibly long and lonely as she, half sleeping, waited for Bettina to come.

Bettina did not return that night nor the next day, and Peg, afraid of being all alone in the strange city, and with no reason to go on staying there, packed her few things, paid the bill, and set off for home. Now here she was at home at last. Standing in the dark kitchen; without really wanting to, she found herself thinking of Lucien, and she remembered the first time she had brought him to the farm. It was after one of Miss Moles' poetry evenings. She quite often had small performances as she called them, intimate evenings of music and poetry at her own house. Miss Moles unselfishly never read her own poems, but simply invited others to read, while she busied herself even more unselfishly in the kitchen bringing out sandwiches and cups of coffee at the right moments.

Peg first met Lucien at Miss Moles' house. Lucien was so fair, his hair was cream coloured like Peg's. He was young and tender like a sapling. While the other poets read he sat with his eyes closed, deep in concentration and, when it was his turn to read, he repeatedly looked up from the pages, looking straight at Peg till it seemed he was reading only for her. When the others applauded, they clapped for them both, as though Peg was a part of the poetry. She felt she was.

Lucien sat down gracefully beside her. He was grateful to her, for some reason he thanked her. Peg was touched. She was going home that night to the farm she told him, and Lucien said how wonderful to be going out to the country on a summer night.

'You can come with me,' Peg said to him quite simply.

'Oh could I,' the young man said. 'Oh could I!'

'Yes, of course, but it's a long drive.' She was laughing.

'But would it be all right if I came?' he asked.

'Oh yes, of course, Mother would love to have you come.'

They arrived during the hay filled night, the moonlight lay in silent patches over the land and the sheds. A sweet smell came up as the night air touched the grass. Peg took Lucien by the hand to lead him into the dark kitchen.

'Mother!' she called. 'Mother it's me, Peg, are you awake?'

The old woman roused herself and welcomed the young poet and made up a bed for him in the living room. The next morning he sat up in his bed and saw the long narrow paddock which came right up to the window. He looked down the slope to the willow trees overhanging the dam.

'It's enchanting,' he said to Peg later that day, and he asked her to marry him, and he wrote a poem about it.

'Mother!' Peg, alone in the dark kitchen, called softly. 'Mother it's me, Peg, are you awake?' In the dark she was unable to find any matches on the mantelpiece.

'Mother? Kerry? it's me Peg, I've come home.' She thought she heard a moaning from the bedroom and then a slight rustling.

'Here's matches,' Miranda burrowed in the case. Peg lit the lamp. The kitchen smelled of sour milk. The children must have been playing with the dishes and saucepans, they were all over the table with spoons in them and bits of bread and broken up biscuits. Some dishes were broken on the floor. Miranda, very sleepy, rubbed her eyes.

'Where's Bettina? Where's my mommy?' She began to cry.

'She's coming later, pet, now hush your crying.' Peg took the lamp into the disordered bedroom.

'Mother!'

The old woman moved slightly, she moaned and she did not know her daughter. Peg could smell the infection and, when she saw the swollen angry leg, she knew she must do something quickly.

'Where's Kerry?' she asked Miranda. 'Is she asleep?'

Together they went down through the sweet smelling dry grass and stood at the edge of the ugly dam. The willow trees were dark and motionless at the edge of the secretive water. Something moved lightly on the water, a shadow crossing that light which water holds in the night.

Peg called, 'Kerry?' knowing it was stupid. 'Kerry?' she called softly.

'It's the gooses,' Miranda, clutching Peg's skirt, explained. The geese slowly floated from the black shadows of the willows and circled slowly in the shining unmoving water. They made no noise and they were without blame. The only sound in the stillness was from the grasshoppers. They kept up their monotonous sound all night, it was not possible not to notice it.

In the narrow space at the side of her mother's bed Peg crouched and cried and cried as she had never cried before. It did not need imagination to know this grief would be there for the rest of her life.

'These sweets are for you Kerry and these sweets are for me Kerry these are for you to eat now and these are for you to eat later . . . Peg tell Kerry not to eat her sweets the ones for later I mean Peg tell Kerry it's my turn to wear the party dress . . . these are my clothes Kerry and these clothes are yours Kerry . . .'

Peg heard the weary voice of the child somewhere behind and inside her own weariness. Miranda, too near to Peg, pretended to play, talking in a silly voice almost falling asleep and then waking in an endless energetic imagination. Peg at last stopped crying and set about what she had to do. Because of what she already carried there, she knew it would be some time before she would be able to take this other child on her lap.

THE CHANCE

Peter Carey

1

IT WAS THREE SUMMERS since the Fastalogians had arrived to set up the Genetic Lottery, but it had got so no one gave a damn about what season it was. It was hot. It was steamy. I spent my days in furies and tempers, half-drunk. A six-pack of beer got me to sleep. I didn't have the money for more fanciful drugs and I should have been saving for a Chance. But to save the dollars for a Chance meant six months without grog or any other solace.

There were nights, bitter and lonely, when I felt beyond the Fastalogian alternative, and ready for the other one, to join the Leapers in their suicidal drops from the roofs of buildings and the girders of bridges. I had witnessed a dozen or more. They fell like over-ripe fruit from the rotten trees of a forgotten orchard.

I was overwhelmed by a feeling of great loss. I yearned for lost time, lost childhoods, seasons for Chrissake, the time when peaches are ripe, the time when the river drops after the snow has all melted and it's just low enough to wade and the water freezes your balls and you can walk for miles with little pale crayfish scuttling backwards away from your black-booted feet. Also you can use a dragonfly larva as live bait, casting it out gently and letting it drift downstream to where big old brown trout, their lower jaws grown long and hooked upwards, lie waiting.

The days get hot and clear then and the land is like a tinder box. Old men lighting cigarettes are careful to put the burnt matches back into the matchbox, a habit one sometimes sees carried on into the city by younger people who don't know why they're doing it, messengers carrying notes written in a foreign language.

But all this was once common knowledge, in the days when things were always the same and newness was something as delightful and strange as the little boiled sweets we would be given on Sunday morning.

Those were the days before the Americans came, and before the Fastalogians who succeeded them, descending in their space ships from god knows what unimaginable worlds. And at first we thought them preferable to the Americans. But what the Americans did to us with their yearly car models and two-weekly cigarette lighters was nothing compared to the Fastalogians who introduced concepts so dazzling that we fell prey to them wholesale like South Sea Islanders exposed to the common cold.

The Fastalogians were the universe's bush-mechanics, charlatans, gypsies: raggle-taggle collections of equipment always going wrong. Their Lottery Rooms were always a mess of wires, the floors always littered with dead printed circuits like cigarette ends.

It was difficult to have complete faith in them, yet they could be persuasive enough. Their attitude was eager, frenetic almost, as they attempted to please in the most childish way imaginable. (In confrontation they became much less pleasant, turning curiously evasive while their voices assumed a high-pitched, nasal, wheedling characteristic.)

In appearance they were so much less threatening than the Americans. Their clothes were worn badly, ill-fitting, often with childish mistakes, like buttoning the third button through the fourth buttonhole. They seemed to us to be lonely and puzzled and even while they controlled us we managed to feel a smiling superiority to them. Their music was not the music of an inhuman oppressor. It had surprising fervour, like Hungarian rhapsodies. One was reminded of Bartok, and wondered about the feelings of beings so many light years from home.

Their business was the Genetic Lottery or The Chance, whatever you cared to call it. It was, of course, a trick, but we had nothing to question them with. We had only accusations, suspicions, fears that things were not as they were described. If they told us that we could buy a second or third Chance in the lottery most of us took it, even if we didn't know how it worked, or if it worked the way they said it did.

We were used to not understanding. It had become a habit with the Americans who had left us with a technology we could neither control nor understand. So our failure to grasp the technicalities or even the principles of the Genetic Lottery in no way prevented us from embracing it enthusiastically. After all, we had never grasped the technicalities of the television sets the Americans sold us. Our curiosity about how things worked had atrophied to such an extent that few of us bothered with understanding such things as how the tides worked and why some trees lost their leaves in autumn. It was enough that someone somewhere understood these things. Thus we had no interest in the table of elements that make up all matter, nor in the names of the atomic sub-particles our very bodies were built from. Such was the way we were prepared, like South Sea Islanders, like yearning gnostics waiting to be pointed in the direction of the first tin shed called 'God'.

So now for two thousand inter-galactic dollars (IG$2000) we could go in the Lottery and come out with a different age, a different body, a different voice and still carry our memories (allowing for a little leakage) more or less intact.

It proved the last straw. The total embrace of a cancerous philosophy of change. The populace became like mercury in each other's minds and arms. Institutions that had proved the very basis of our society (the family, the neighbourhood, marriage) cracked and split apart in the face of a new shrill current of desperate selfishness. The city itself stood like an external endorsement to this internal collapse and recalled the most exotic places (Calcutta, for instance) where the rich had once journeyed to experience the thrilling stink of poverty, the smell of danger, and the just-contained threat of violence born of envy.

Here also were the signs of fragmentation, of religious confusion, of sects decadent and strict. Wild-haired holymen in loincloths, palm-readers, seers, revolutionaries without followings (the Hups, the Namers, the L.A.K.). Gurus in helicopters flew through the air, whilst bandits roamed the countryside in search of travellers who were no longer intent on adventure and the beauty of nature, but were forced to travel by necessity and who moved in nervous groups, well-armed and thankful to be alive when they returned.

It was an edgy and distrustful group of people that made up our society, motivated by nothing but their self-preservation and their blind belief in their next Chance. To the Fastalogians they were nothing but cattle. Their sole function was to provide a highly favourable inter-galactic balance of payments.

It was through these streets that I strode, muttering, continually on the verge of either anger or tears. I was cut adrift, unconnected. My face in the mirror at morning was not the face that my mind had started living with. It was a battered, red, broken-nosed face, marked by great quizzical eyebrows, intense black eyes, and tangled wiry hair. I had been through the lottery and lost. I had got myself the body of an ageing street-fighter. It was a body built to contain furies. It suited me. The arrogant Gurus and the ugly Hups stepped aside when I stormed down their streets on my daily course between the boarding house where I lived to the Department of Parks where I was employed as a gardener. I didn't work much. I played cards with the others. The botanical gardens were slowly being choked by 'Burning Glory', a prickly crimson flowering bush the Fastalogians had imported either by accident or design. It was our job to remove it. Instead, we used it as cover for our cheating card games. Behind its red blazing hedges we lied and fought and, on occasion, fornicated. We were not a pretty sight.

It was from here that I walked back to the boarding house with my beer under my arm, and it was on a Tuesday afternoon that I saw her, just beyond the gardens and a block down from the Chance

Centre in Grove Street. She was sitting on the footpath with a body beside her, an old man, his hair white and wispy, his face brown and wrinkled like a walnut. He was dressed very formally in a three-piece grey suit and had an old-fashioned watch chain across the waistcoat. I assumed that the corpse was her grandfather. Since the puppet government had dropped its funeral assistance plan this was how poor people raised money for funerals. It was a common sight to see dead bodies in rented suits being displayed on the footpaths. So it was not the old man who attracted my attention but the young woman who sat beside him.

'Money,' she said, 'money for an old man to lie in peace.'

I stopped willingly. She had her dark hair cut quite short and rather badly. Her eyebrows were full, but perfectly arched, her features were saved from being too regular by a mouth that was wider than average. She wore a khaki shirt, a navy blue jacket, filthy trousers and a small gold earring in her right ear.

'I've only got beer,' I said, 'I've spent all my money on beer.'

She grinned a broad and beautiful grin which illuminated her face and made me echo it.

'I'd settle for a beer.' And I was surprised to hear shyness.

I sat down on the footpath and we opened the six-pack. Am I being sentimental when I say I shared my beer without calculation? That I sought nothing? It seems unlikely for I had some grasping habits as you'll see soon enough. But I remember nothing of the sort, only that I liked the way she opened the beer bottle. Her hands were large, a bit messed-up. She hooked a broken-nailed finger into the ring-pull and had it off without even looking at what she was doing.

She took a big swallow, wiped her mouth with the back of her hand and said: 'Shit, I needed that.'

I muttered something about her grandfather, trying to make polite conversation. I was out of the habit.

She shrugged and put the cold bottle on her cheek. 'I got him from the morgue.'

I didn't understand.

'I bought him for three IGs.' She grinned, tapping her head with her middle finger. 'Best investment I've ever made.'

It was this, more than anything, that got me. I admired cunning in those days, smart moves, cards off the bottom of the deck, anything that tricked the bastards – and 'the bastards' were everyone who wasn't me.

So I laughed. A loud deep joyful laugh that made passers-by stare at me. I gave them the fingers-up and they looked away.

She sat on her hands, rocking back and forth on them as she spoke. She had a pleasantly nasal, idiosyncratic voice, slangy and relaxed. 'They really go for white hair and tanned faces.' She nodded towards a paint tin full of coins and notes. 'It's pathetic isn't it? I wouldn't have gotten half this much for my real grandfather. He's too dark. Also, they don't like women much. Men do much better than women.'

She had the slightly exaggerated toughness of the very young. I wondered if she'd taken a Chance. It didn't look like it.

We sat and drank the beer. It started to get dark. She lit a mosquito coil and we stayed there in the gloom till we drank the whole lot.

When the last bottle was gone, the small talk that had sustained us went away and left us in an uneasy area of silence. Now suspicion hit me with its fire-hot pinpricks. I had been conned for my beer. I would go home and lie awake without its benefits. It would be a hot sleepless night and I would curse myself for my gullibility. I, who was shrewd and untrickable, had been tricked.

But she stood and stretched and said, 'Come on, now I've drunk your beer, I'll buy you a meal.'

We walked away and left the body for whoever wanted it. I never saw the old man again.

The next day he was gone.

2

I cannot explain what it was like to sit in a restaurant with a woman. I felt embarrassed, awkward, and so pleased that I couldn't put one foot straight in front of the other.

I fancy I was graciously old-fashioned.

I pulled out her chair for her, I remember, and saw the look she shot me, both pleased and alarmed. It was a shocked, fast flick of the eyes. Possibly she sensed the powerful fantasies that lonely men create, steel columns of passion appended with leather straps and tiny mirrors.

It was nearly a year since I'd talked to a woman, and that one stole my money and even managed to lift two blankets from my sleeping body. Twelve dull stupid drugged and drunken months had passed, dissolving from the dregs of one day into the sink of the next.

The restaurant was one of those Fasta Cafeterias that had sprung up, noisy, messy, with harsh lighting and long rows of bright white tables that were never ever filled. The service was bad and in the end we went to the kitchen where we helped ourselves from the long trays of food, Fastalogian salads with their dried intoxicating mushrooms, and that strange milky pap they are so fond of. She piled her plate high with everything and I envied the calm that allowed her such an appetite. On any other night I would have done the same, guzzling and gorging myself on my free meal.

Finally, tripping over each other, we returned to our table. She bought two more beers and I thanked her for that silently.

Here I was. With a woman. Like real people.

I smiled broadly at the thought. She caught me and was, I think, pleased to have something to hang on to. So we got hold of that smile and wrung it for all it was worth.

Being desperate, impatient, I told her the truth about the smile. The directness was pleasing to her. I watched how she leant into my words without fear or reservation, displaying none of the shiftiness that danced through most social intercourse in those days. But I was as calculating and cunning as only the very lonely learn how to be. Estimating her interest, I selected the things which would be most pleasing for her. I steered the course of what I told, telling her things about me which fascinated her most. She was pleased by my confessions. I gave her many. She was strong and young and confident. She couldn't see my deviousness and, no matter what I told her of loneliness, she couldn't taste the stale self-hating afternoons or suspect the callousness they engendered.

And I bathed in her beauty, delighting in the confidence it brought her, the certainty of small mannerisms, the chop of that beautiful rough-fingered hand when making a point. But also, this: the tentative question marks she hooked on to the ends of her most definite assertions. So I was impressed by her strength and charmed by her vulnerability all at once.

One could not have asked for more.

And this also I confessed to her, for it pleased her to be talked about and it gave me an intoxicating pleasure to be on such intimate terms.

And I confessed why I had confessed.

My conversation was mirrors within mirrors, onion skin behind onion skin. I revealed motives behind motives. I was amazing. I felt myself to be both saint and pirate, as beautiful and gnarled as an ancient olive. I talked with intensity. I devoured her, not like some poor beggar (which I was) but like a prince, a stylish master of the most elegant dissertations.

She ate ravenously, but in no way neglected to listen. She talked impulsively with her mouth full. With mushrooms dropping from her mouth, she made a point. It made her beautiful, not ugly.

I have always enjoyed women who, whilst being conventionally feminine enough in their appearance, have exhibited certain behavioural traits more commonly associated with men. A bare-breasted woman working on a tractor is the fastest, crudest approximation I can provide. An image, incidentally, guaranteed to give me an aching erection, which it has, on many lonely nights.

But to come back to my new friend who rolled a cigarette with hands which might have been the hands of an apprentice bricklayer, hands which were connected to breasts which were connected to other parts doubtless female in gender, who had such grace and beauty in her form and manner and yet had had her hair shorn in such a manner as to deny her beauty.

She was tall, my height. Across the table I noted that her hands were as large as mine. They matched. The excitement was exquisite. I anticipated nothing, vibrating in the crystal of the moment.

We talked, finally, as everyone must, about the Lottery, for the Lottery was life in those days and all of us, or most of us, were saving for another Chance.

'I'm taking a Chance next week,' she said.

'Good luck,' I said. It was automatic. That's how life had got.

'You look like you haven't.'

'Thank you,' I said. It was a compliment, like saying that my shirt suited me. 'But I've had four.'

'You move nicely,' she smiled. 'I was watching you in the kitchen. You're not awkward at all.'

'You move nicely too,' I grinned. 'I was watching you too. You're crazy to take a Chance, what do you want?'

'A people's body.' She said it fast, briskly, and stared at me challengingly.

'A what?'

'A people's body.' She picked up a knife, examined it and put it down.

It dawned on me. 'Oh, you're a Hup.'

Thinking back, I'm surprised I knew anything about the Hups. They were one of a hundred or more revolutionary crackpots. I didn't give a damn about politics and I thought every little group was more insane than the next.

And here, goddamn it, I was having dinner with a Hup, a rich crazy who thought the way to fight the revolution was to have a body as grotesque and ill-formed as my friends at the Parks and Gardens.

'My parents took the Chance last week.'

'How did it go?'

'I didn't see them. They've gone to . . .' she hesitated '. . . to another place where they're needed.' She had become quiet now, and serious, explaining that her parents had upper-class bodies like hers, that their ideas were not at home with their physiognomy (a word I had to ask her to explain), that they would form the revolutionary vanguard to lead the misshapen Lumpen Proletariat (another term I'd never heard before) to overthrow the Fastas and their puppets.

I had a desperate desire to change the subject, to plug my ears, to shut my eyes. I wouldn't have been any different if I'd discovered she was a mystic or a follower of Hiwi Kaj.

'Anyway,' I said, 'you've got a beautiful body.'

'Why did you say that?'

I could have said that I'd spent enough of my life with her beloved Lumpen Proletariat to hold them in no great esteem, that the very reason I was enjoying her company so much was because she was so unlike them. But I didn't want to pursue it. I shrugged, grinned stupidly, and filled her glass with beer.

Her eyes flashed at my shrug. I don't know why people say 'flashed', but I swear there was red in her eyes. She looked hurt, stung, and ready to attack.

She withdrew from me, leaning back in her chair and folding her arms. 'What do you think is beautiful?'

Before I could answer she was leaning back into the table, but this time her voice was louder.

'What is more beautiful, a parrot or a crow?'

'A parrot, if you mean a rosella. But I don't know much about parrots.'

'What's wrong with a crow?'

'A crow is black and awkward-looking. It's heavy. Its cry is unattractive.'

'What makes its cry unattractive?'

I was sick of the game, and exhausted with such sudden mental exercise.

'It sounds forlorn,' I offered.

'Do you think that it is the crow's intention, to sound forlorn? Perhaps you are merely ignorant and don't know how to listen to a crow.'

'Certainly, I'm ignorant.' It was true, of course, but the observation stung a little. I was very aware of my ignorance in those days. I felt it keenly.

'If you could kill a parrot or a crow which would you kill?'

'Why would I want to kill either of them?'

'But if you had to, for whatever reason.'

'The crow, I suppose. Or possibly the parrot. Whichever was the smallest.'

Her eyes were alight and fierce. She rolled a cigarette without looking at it. Her face suddenly looked extraordinarily beautiful, her eyes glistening with emotion, the colour high in her cheeks, a peculiar half-smile on her wide mouth.

'Which breasts are best?'

I laughed. 'I don't know.'

'Which legs?'

'I don't know. I like long legs.'

'Like the film stars.'

Like yours, I thought. 'Yes.'

'Is that really your idea of beautiful?'

She was angry with me now, had decided to call me enemy. I did not feel enemy and didn't want to be. My mind felt fat and flabby, unused, numb. I forgot my irritation with her ideas. I set all that aside. In the world of ideas I had no principles. An idea was of no worth to me, not worth fighting for. I would fight for a beer, a meal, a woman, but never an idea.

'I like grevilleas,' I said greasily.

She looked blank. I thought as much! 'Which are they?' I had her at a loss.

'They're small bushes. They grow in clay, in the harshest situations. Around rocks, on dry hillsides. If you come fishing with me, I'll show you. The leaves are more like spikes. They look dull and harsh. No one would think to look at them twice. But in November,' I smiled, 'they have flowers like glorious red spiders. I think they're beautiful.'

'But in October?'

'In October I know what they'll be like in November.'

She smiled. She must have wanted to like me. I was disgusted with my argument. It had been cloying and saccharine even to me. I hadn't been quite sure what to say, but it seems I hit the nail on the head.

'Does it hurt?' she asked suddenly.

'What?'

'The Chance. Is it painful, or is it like they say?'

'It makes you vomit a lot, and feel ill, but it doesn't hurt. It's more a difficult time for your head.'

She drained her beer and began to grin at me. 'I was just thinking,' she said.

'Thinking what?'

'I was thinking that if you have anything more to do with me it'll be a hard time for your head too.'

I looked at her grinning face, disbelievingly.

I found out later that she hadn't been joking.

3

To cut a long and predictable story short, we got on well together, if you'll allow for the odd lie on my part and what must have been more than a considerable suppression of commonsense on hers.

I left my outcast acquaintances behind to fight and steal, and occasionally murder each other in the boarding house. I returned there only to pick up my fishing rod. I took it round to her place at Pier Street swaggering like a sailor on leave. I was in a flamboyant, extravagant mood and left behind my other ratty possessions. They didn't fit my new situation.

Thus, to the joys of living with an eccentric and beautiful woman I added the even more novel experience of a home. Either one of these changes would have brought me some measure of contentment, but the combination of the two of them was almost too good to be true.

I was in no way prepared for them. I had been too long a grabber, a survivor.

So when I say that I became obsessed with hanging on to these things, using every shred of guile I had learned in my old life, do not judge me harshly. The world was not the way it is now. It was a bitter jungle of a place, worse, because even in the jungle there is co-operation, altruism, community.

Regarding the events that followed I feel neither pride nor shame. Regret, certainly, but regret is a useless emotion. I was ignorant, short-sighted, bigoted, but in my situation it is inconceivable that I could have been anything else.

But now let me describe for you Carla's home as I came to know it, not as I saw it at first, for then I only felt the warmth of old timbers and delighted in the dozens of small signs of domesticity everywhere about me: a toothbrush in a glass, dirty clothes overflowing from a blue cane laundry basket, a made bed, dishes draining in a sink, books, papers, letters from friends, all the trappings of a life I had long abandoned, many Chances ago.

The house had once been a warehouse, long before the time of the Americans. It was clad with unpainted boards that had turned a gentle silver, ageing with a grace that one rarely saw in those days.

One ascended the stairs from the Pier Street wharf itself. A wooden door. A large key. Inside: a floor of grooved boards, dark with age.

The walls showed their bones: timber joists and beams, roughly nailed in the old style, but solid as a rock.

High in the ceiling was a sleeping platform, below it a simple kitchen filled with minor miracles: a hot water tap, a stove, a refrigerator, saucepans, spices, even a recipe book or two.

The rest of the area was a sitting room, the pride of place being given to three beautiful antique armchairs in the Danish style, their carved arms showing that patina which only age can give.

Add a rusty coloured old rug, pile books high from the floor, pin Hup posters here and there, and you have it.

Or almost have it, because should you open the old high sliding door (pushing hard, because its rollers are stiff and rusty from the salty air) and the room is full of the sea, the once-great harbour, its waters rarely perturbed by craft, its shoreline dotted with rusting hulks of forgotten ships, great tankers from the oil age, tugs, and ferries which, even a year before, had maintained their services in the face of neglect and disinterest on all sides.

Two other doors led off the main room: one to a rickety toilet which hung out precariously over the water, the other to a bedroom, its walls stacked with files, books, loose papers, its great bed draped in mosquito netting, for there was no wiring for the customary sonic mosquito repellents and the mosquitoes carried Fasta Fever with the same dedicated enthusiasm that others of their family had once carried malaria.

The place revealed its secrets fast enough, but Carla, of course, did not divulge hers quite so readily. Frankly, it suited me. I was happy to see what I was shown and never worried about what was hidden away.

I mentioned nothing of Hups or revolution and she, for her part, seemed to have forgotten the matter. My assumption (arrogantly made) was that she would put off her Chance indefinitely. People rarely plunged into the rigours of the Lottery when they were happy with their life. I was delighted with mine, and I assumed she was with hers.

I had never known anyone like her. She sang beautifully and played the cello with what seemed to me to be real accomplishment. She came to the Park and Gardens and beat us all at poker. To see her walk across to our bed, moving with the easy gait of an Islander filled me with astonishment and wonder.

I couldn't believe my luck.

She had been born rich but chose to live poor, an idea that was beyond my experience or comprehension. She had read more books in the last year than I had in my life. And when my efforts to hide my ignorance finally gave way in tatters she took to my education with the same enthusiasm she brought to our bed.

Her methods were erratic, to say the least. For each new book she gave me revealed a hundred gaps in my knowledge that would have to be plugged with other books.

I was deluged with the whole artillery of Hup literature: long and difficult works like Gibson's *Class and Genetics*, Schumacher's *Comparative Physiognomy*, Hale's *Wolf Children*.

I didn't care what they were about. If they had been treatises on the history of Rome or the Fasta economic system I would have read them with as much enthusiasm and probably learnt just as little.

Sitting on the wharf I sang her 'Rosie Allan's Outlaw Friend', the story of an ill-lettered cattle thief and his love for a young school mistress. My body was like an old guitar, fine and mellow with beautiful resonance.

The first star appeared.

'The first star,' I said.

'It's a planet,' she said.

'What's the difference?' I asked.

She produced a school book on the known solar system at breakfast the next morning.

'How in the hell do you know so little?' she said, eating the omelette I'd cooked her.

I stared at the extraordinary rings of Saturn, knowing I'd known some of these things long ago. They brought to mind classrooms on summer days, dust, the smell of oranges, lecture theatres full of formally dressed students with eager faces.

'I guess I just forgot,' I said. 'Maybe half my memory is walking around in other bodies. And how in the fuck is it that you don't know how to make a decent omelette?'

'I guess,' she grinned, 'that I just forgot.'

She wandered off towards the kitchen with her empty plate but got distracted by an old newspaper she found on the way. She put the plate on the floor and went on to the kitchen where she read the paper, leaning back against the sink.

'You have rich habits,' I accused her.

She looked up, arching her eyebrows questioningly.

'You put things down for other people to pick up.'

She flushed and spent five minutes picking up things and putting them in unexpected places.

She never mastered the business of tidying up and finally I was the one who became housekeeper.

When the landlord arrived one morning to collect the rent she introduced me as 'my house-proud lover'. I gave the bastard my street-fighter's sneer and he swallowed the smirk he was starting to grow on his weak little face.

I was the one who opened the doors to the harbour. I swept the floor, I tidied the books and washed the plates. I threw out the old newspapers and took down the posters for Hup meetings and demonstrations which had long since passed.

She came in from work after my first big cleanup and started pulling books out and throwing them on the floor.

'What in the fuck are you doing?'

'Where did you put them?'

'Put what?'

She pulled down a pile of old pamphlets and threw them on the floor as she looked between each one.

'What?'

'My posters, you bastard. How dare you.'

I was nonplussed. My view of posters was purely practical. It had never occurred to me that they might have any function other than to advertise what they appeared to advertise. When the event was past the poster had no function.

Confused and angry at her behaviour, I retrieved the posters from the bin in the kitchen.

'You creased them.'

'I'm sorry.'

She started putting them up again.

'Why did you take them down? It's your house now, is it? Would you like to paint the walls, eh? Do you want to change the furniture too? Is there anything else that isn't to your liking?'

'Carla,' I said, 'I'm very sorry. I took them down because they were out-of-date.'

'Out-of-date,' she snorted. 'You mean you think they're ugly.'

I looked at the poster she was holding, a glorification of crooked forms and ugly faces.

'Well if you want to put it like that, yes, I think they're fucking ugly.'

She glowered at me, self-righteous and prim. 'You only say that because you're so conditioned that you can only admire looks like mine. How pathetic. That's why you like me, isn't it?'

Her face was red, the skin taut with rage.

'Isn't it?'

I'd thought this damn Hup thing had gone away, but here it was. The stupidity of it. It drove me insane. Her books became weapons in my hands. I threw them at her, hard, in a frenzy.

'Idiot. Dolt. You don't believe what you say. You're too young to know anything. You don't know what these damn people are like,' I poked at the posters, 'you're too young to know anything. You're a fool. You're playing with life.' I hurled another book. 'Playing with it.'

She was young and nimble with a boxer's reflexes. She dodged the books easily enough and retaliated viciously, slamming a thick sociology text into the side of my head.

Staggering back to the window I was confronted with the vision of an old man's face, looking in.

I pulled up the window and transferred my abuse in that direction.

'Who in the fuck are you?'

A very nervous old man stood on a long ladder, teetering nervously above the street.

'I'm a painter.'

'Well piss off.'

He looked down into the street below as I grabbed the top rung of the ladder and gave it a little bit of a shake.

'Who is it?' Carla called.

'It's a painter.'

'What's he doing?'

I looked outside. 'He's painting the bloody place orange.'

The painter, seeing me occupied with other matters, started to retreat down the ladder.

'Hey,' I shook the ladder to make him stop.

'It's only a primer,' he pleaded.

'It doesn't need any primer,' I yelled, 'those bloody boards will last a hundred years.'

'You're yelling at the wrong person, fellah.' The painter was at the bottom of the ladder now, and all the bolder because of it.

'If you touch that ladder again I'll have the civil police here.' He backed into the street and shook his finger at me. 'They'll do you, my friend, so just watch it.'

I slammed the window shut and locked it for good measure. 'You've got to talk to the landlord,' I said, 'before they ruin the place.'

'Got to?'

'Please.'

Her face became quiet and secretive. She started picking up books and pamphlets and stacking them against the wall with exaggerated care.

'Please Carla.'

'You tell them,' she shrugged. 'I won't be here.' She fetched the heavy sociology text from beneath the window and frowned over the bookshelves, looking for a place to put it.

'What in the hell does that mean?'

'It means I'm a Hup. I told you that before. I told you the first time I met you. I'm taking a Chance and you won't like what comes out. I told you before,' she repeated, 'you've known all along.'

'Be buggered you're taking a Chance.'

She shrugged. She refused to look at me. She started picking up books and carrying them to the kitchen, her movements uncharacteristically brisk.

'People only take a Chance when they're pissed off. Are you?'

She stood by the stove, the books cradled in her arms, tears streaming down her face.

Even as I held her, even as I stroked her hair, I began to plot to keep her in the body she was born in. It became my obsession.

4

I came home the next night to find the outside of the house bright orange and the inside filled with a collection of people as romantically ugly as any I had ever seen. They betrayed their upper-class origins by dressing their crooked forms in such romantic styles that they were in danger of creating a new foppishness. Faults and infirmities were displayed with a pride that would have been alien to any but a Hup.

A dwarf reclined in a Danish-style armchair, an attenuated hand waving a cigarette. His overalls, obviously tailored, were very soft, an expensive material splattered with 'original' paint. If he hadn't been smoking so languorously he might have passed for real.

Next to him, propped against the wall, was the one I later knew as Daniel. The grotesque pockmarks on his face proudly accentuated by the subtle use of make-up and, I swear to God, colour coordinated with a flamboyant pink scarf.

Then, a tall thin woman with the most pronounced curvature of the spine and a gaunt face dominated by a most extraordinary hooked nose. Her form was clad in the tightest garments and from it emanated the not unsubtle aroma of power and privilege.

If I had seen them anywhere else I would have found them laughable, not worthy of serious attention. Masters amusing themselves by dressing as servants. Returned tourists clad in beggars' rags. Educated fops doing a bad charade of my tough, grisly companions in the boarding house.

But I was not anywhere else. This was our home and they had turned it into some spiderweb or nightmare where dog turds smell like French wine and roses stink of the charnel-house.

And there squatting in their midst, my most beautiful Carla, her eyes shining with enthusiasm and admiration whilst the hook-nosed lady waved her bony fingers.

THE CHANCE

I stayed by the door and Carla, smiling too eagerly, came to greet me and introduce me to her friends. I watched her dark eyes flick nervously from one face to the next, fearful of everybody's reaction to me, and mine to them.

I stood awkwardly behind the dwarf as he passed around his snapshots, photographs taken of him before his Chance.

'Not bad, eh?' he said, showing me a shot of a handsome man on the beach at Cannes. 'I was a handsome fellow, eh?'

It was a joke, but I was confused about its meaning. I nodded, embarrassed. The photograph was creased with lines like the palm of an old man's hand.

I looked at the woman's curved back and the gaunt face, trying to find beauty there, imagining holding her in my arms.

She caught my eyes and smiled. 'Well young man, what will you do while we have our little meeting?'

God knows what expression crossed my face, but it would have been a mere ripple on the surface of the feelings that boiled within me.

Carla was at my side in an instant, whispering in my ear that it was an important meeting and wouldn't take long. The hook-nosed woman, she said, had an unfortunate manner, was always upsetting everyone, but had, just the same, a heart of gold.

I took my time in leaving, fussing around the room looking for my beautiful light fishing rod with its perfectly preserved old Mitchell reel. I enjoyed the silence while I fossicked around behind books, under chairs, finally discovering it where I knew it was all the time.

In the kitchen, I slapped some bait together, mixing mince meat, flour and garlic, taking my time with this too, forcing them to indulge in awkward small talk about the price of printing and the guru in the electric cape, one of the city's recent contributions to a more picturesque life.

Outside the painters were washing their brushes, having covered half of the bright orange with a pale blue.

The sun was sinking below the broken columns of the Hinden Bridge as I cast into the harbour. I used no sinker, just a teardrop of mince meat, flour and garlic, an enticing meal for a bream.

The water shimmered, pearlescent. The bream attacked, sending sharp signals up the delicate light line. They fought like the fury and showed themselves in flashes of frantic silver. Luderick also swam below my feet, feeding on long ribbons of green weed. A small pink cloud drifted absent-mindedly through a series of metamorphoses. An old work boat passed, sitting low in the water like a dumpy brown duck, full of respectability and regular intent.

Yet I was anaesthetised and felt none of what I saw.

For above my head in a garish building slashed with orange and blue I imagined the Hups concluding plans to take Carla away from me.

The water became black with a dark blue wave. The waving reflection of a yellow-lighted window floated at my feet and I heard the high-pitched wheedling laugh of a Fasta in the house above. It was the laugh of a Fasta doing business.

That night I caught ten bream. I killed only two. The others I returned to the melancholy window floating at my feet.

5

The tissues lay beneath the bed. Dead white butterflies, wet with tears and sperm.

The mosquito net, like a giant parody of a wedding veil, hung over us, its fibres luminescent, shimmering with light from the open door.

Carla's head rested on my shoulder, her hair wet from both our tears.

'You could put it off,' I whispered. 'Another week.'

'I can't. You know I can't. If I don't do it when it's booked I'll have to wait six months.'

'Then wait . . .'

'I can't.'

'We're good together.'

'I know.'

'It'll get better.'

'I know.'

'It won't last, if you do it.'

'It might, if we try.'

I damned the Hups in silence. I cursed them for their warped ideals. If only they could see how ridiculous they looked.

I stroked her brown arm, soothing her in advance of what I said. 'It's not right. Your friends haven't become working class. They have a manner. They look disgusting.'

She withdrew from me, sitting up to light a cigarette with an angry flourish.

'Ah, you see,' she pointed the cigarette at me. 'Disgusting. They look disgusting.'

'They look like rich fops amusing themselves. They're not real. They look evil.'

She slipped out from under the net and began searching through the tangled clothes on the floor, separating hers from mine. 'I can't stand this,' she said, 'I can't stay here.'

'You think it's so fucking great to look like the dwarf?' I screamed. 'Would you fuck him? Would you wrap your legs around him? Would you?'

She stood outside the net, very still and very angry. 'That's my business.'

I was chilled. I hadn't meant it. I hadn't thought it possible. I was trying to make a point. I hadn't believed.

'Did you?' I hated the shrill tone that crept into my voice. I was a child, jealous, hurt.

I jumped out of the bed and started looking for my own clothes. She had my trousers in her hand. I tore them from her.

'I wish you'd just shut-up,' I hissed, although she had said nothing. 'And don't patronise me with your stupid smart-talk.' I was shaking with rage.

She looked me straight in the eye before she punched me.

I laid one straight back.

'That's why I love you, damn you.'

'Why?' she screamed, holding her hand over her face. 'For God's sake, why?'

'Because we'll both have black eyes.'

She started laughing just as I began to cry.

6

I started to write a diary and then stopped. The only page in it says this:

'Saturday. This morning I know that I am in love. I spend the day thinking about her. When I see her in the street she is like a painting that is even better than you remembered. Today we wrestled. She told me she could wrestle me. Who would believe it? What a miracle she is. Ten days to go. I've got to work out something.'

7

Wednesday. Meeting day for the freaks.

On the way home I bought a small bag of mushrooms to calm me down a little bit. I walked to Pier Street the slow way, nibbling as I went.

I came through the door ready to face the whole menagerie but they weren't there, only the hook-nosed lady, arranged in tight brown rags and draped across a chair, her bowed legs dangling, one shoe swinging from her toe.

She smiled at me, revealing an uneven line of stained and broken teeth.

'Ah, the famous Lumpy.'

'My name is Paul.'

She swung her shoe a little too much. It fell to the floor, revealing her mutant toes in all their glory.

'Forgive me. Lumpy is a pet name?' She wiggled her toes. 'Something private?'

I ignored her and went to the kitchen to make bait in readiness for my exile on the pier. The damn mince was frozen solid. Carla had tidied it up and put it in the freezer. I dropped it in hot water to thaw it.

'Your mince is frozen.'

'Obviously.'

She patted the chair next to her with a bony hand.

'Come and sit. We can talk.'

'About what?' I disconnected the little Mitchell reel from the rod and started oiling it, first taking off the spool and rinsing the sand from it.

'About life,' she waved her hand airily, taking in the room as if it were the entire solar system. 'About . . . love. What . . . ever.' Her speech had that curious unsure quality common in those who had taken too many Chances, the words spluttered and trickled from her mouth like water from a kinked and tangled garden hose. 'You can't go until your mince . . . mince has thawed.' She giggled. 'You're stuck with me.'

I smiled in spite of myself.

'I could always use weed and go after the luderick.'

'But the tide is high and the weed will be . . . impossible to get. Sit down.' She patted the chair again.

I brought the reel with me and sat next to her slowly dismantling it and laying the parts on the low table. The mushrooms were beginning to work, coating a smooth creamy layer over the gritty irritations in my mind.

'You're upset,' she said. I was surprised to hear concern in her voice. I suppressed a desire to look up and see if her features had changed. Her form upset me as much as the soft rotting faces of the beggars who had been stupid enough to make love with the Fastas. So I screwed the little ratchet back in and wiped it twice with oil.

'You shouldn't be upset.'

I said nothing, feeling warm and absent-minded, experiencing that slight ringing in the ears you get from eating mushrooms on an empty stomach. I put the spool back on and tightened the tension knob. I was running out of things to do that might give me an excuse not to look at her.

She was close to me. Had she been that close to me when I sat down? In the corner of my eye I could see her gaunt bowed leg, an inch or two from mine. My thick muscled forearm seemed to belong to a different planet, to have been bred for different purposes, to serve sane and sensible ends, to hold children on my knee, to build houses, to fetch and carry the ordinary things of life.

'You shouldn't be upset. You don't have to lose Carla. She loves you. You may find that it is not so bad . . . making love . . . with a Hup.' She paused. 'You've been eating mushrooms, haven't you?'

The hand patted my knee. 'Maybe that's not such a bad thing.'

What did she mean? I meant to ask, but forgot I was feeling the hand. I thought of rainbow trout in the clear waters at Dobson's Creek, their brains humming with creamy music while my magnified white hands rubbed their underbellies, tickling them gently before grabbing them, like stolen jewels, and lifting them triumphant in the sunlight. I smelt the heady smell of wild blackberries and the damp fecund odours of rotting wood and bracken.

'We don't forget how to make love when we change.'

The late afternoon sun streamed through a high window. The room was golden. On Dobson's Creek there is a shallow run from a deep pool, difficult to work because of overhanging willows, caddis flies hover above the water in the evening light.

The hand on my knee was soft and caressing. Once, many Chances ago, I had my hair cut by a strange old man. He combed so slowly, cut so delicately, my head and my neck were suffused with pleasure. It was in a classroom. Outside someone hit a tennis ball against a brick wall. There were cicadas, I remember, and a water sprinkler threw beads of light onto glistening grass, freshly mown. He cut my hair shorter and shorter till my fingers tingled.

It has been said that the penis has no sense of right or wrong, that it acts with the brainless instinct of a venus fly-trap, but that is not true. It's too easy a reason for the stiffening cock that rose, stretching blindly towards the bony fingers.

'I could show,' said the voice, 'that it is something quite extraordinary... not worse... better... better... better by far, you have nothing to fear.'

I knew, I knew exactly in the depth of my clouded mind, what was happening. I didn't resist it. I didn't want to resist it. My purpose was as hers. My reasons probably identical.

Softly, sonorously she recited:

'Which trees are beautiful?

All trees that grow.

Which bird is fairest?'

A zipper undone, my balls held gently, a finger stroked the length of my cock. My eyes shut, questions and queries banished to dusty places.

'The bird that flies.

Which face is fairest?

The faces of the friends of the people of the earth.'

A hand, flat-palmed on my rough face, the muscles in my shoulders gently massaged, a finger circling the lips of my anal sphincter.

'Which forms are foul?

The forms of the owners.

The forms of the exploiters.

The forms of the friends of the Fastas.'

Legs across my lap, she straddled me. 'I will give you a taste . . . just a taste . . . you won't stop Carla . . . you can't stop her.'

She moved too fast, her legs gripped mine too hard, the hand on my cock was tugging towards her cunt too hard.

My open eyes stared into her face. The face so foul, so misshapen, broken, the skin marked with ruptured capillaries, the green eyes wide, askance, alight with premature triumph.

Drunk on wine I have fucked monstrously ugly whores. Deranged on drugs, blind, insensible, I have grunted like a dog above those whom I would as soon have slaughtered.

But this, no. No, no, no. For whatever reason, no. Even as I stood, shaking and trembling, she clung to me, smiling, not understanding. 'Carla will be beautiful. You will do things you never did.'

Her grip was strong. I fought through mosquito nets of mushroom haze, layer upon layer that ripped like dusty lace curtains, my arms flailing, my panic mounting. I had woken underwater, drowning.

I wrenched her hand from my shoulder and she shrieked with

pain. I pulled her leg from my waist and she fell back on to the floor, grunting as the wind was knocked from her.

I stood above her, shaking, my heart beating wildly, the head of my cock protruding foolishly from my unzipped trousers, looking as pale and silly as a toadstool.

She struggled to her feet, rearranging her elegant rags and cursing. 'You are an ignorant fool. You are a stupid, ignorant, reactionary fool. You have breathed the Fastas' lies for so long that your rotten body is soaked with them. You stink of lies . . . do you . . . know who I am?'

I stared at her, panting.

'I am Jane Larange.'

For a second I couldn't remember who Jane Larange was, then it came to me: 'The actress?' The once beautiful and famous.

I shook my head. 'You silly bugger. What in God's name have you done to yourself.'

She went to her handbag, looking for a cigarette. 'We will kill the Fastas,' she said, smiling at me, 'and we will kill their puppets and their leeches.'

She stalked to the kitchen and lifted the mince meat from the sink. 'Your mince is thawed.'

The mince was pale and wet. It took more flour than usual to get it to the right consistency. She watched me, leaning against the sink, smoking her perfumed cigarette.

'Look at you, puddling around with stinking meat like a child playing with shit. You would rather play with shit than act like a responsible adult. When the adults come you will slink off and kill fish.' She gave a grunt. 'Poor Carla.'

'Poor Carla.' She made me laugh. 'You try and fuck me and then you say "poor Carla"!'

'You are not only ugly,' she said, 'you are also stupid. I did that for Carla. Do you imagine I like your stupid body or your silly mind? It was to make her feel better. It was arranged. It was her idea, my friend, not mine. Possibly a silly idea, but she is desperate and unhappy and what else is there to do? But,' she smiled thinly, 'I will report a great success, a great rapture. I'm sure you won't be silly enough to contradict me. The lie will make her happy for a little while at least.'

I had known it. I had suspected it. Or if I hadn't known it, was trying a similar grotesque test myself. Oh, the lunacy of the times!

'Now take your nasty bait and go and kill fish. The others will be here soon and I don't want them to see your miserable face.'

I picked up the rod and a plastic bucket.

She called to me from the kitchen. 'And put your worm back in your pants. It is singularly unattractive bait.'

I said nothing and walked out the door with my cock sticking out of my fly. I found the dwarf standing on the landing. It gave him a laugh, at least.

8

I told her the truth about my encounter with the famous Jane Larange. I was a fool. I had made a worm to gnaw at her with fear and doubt. It burrowed into the space behind her eyes and secreted a filmy curtain of uncertainty and pain.

She became subject to moods which I found impossible to predict.

'Let me take your photograph,' she said.

'Alright.'

'Stand over there. No come down to the pier.'

We went down to the pier.

'Alright.'

'Now, take one of me.'

'Where's the button?'

'On the top.'

I found the button and took her photograph.

'Do you love me? Now?'

'Yes damn you, of course I do.'

She stared at me hard, tears in her eyes, then she wrenched the camera from my hand and hurled it into the water.

I watched it sink, thinking how beautifully clear the water was that day.

Carla ran up the steps to the house. I wasn't stupid enough to ask her what the matter was.

9

She had woken in one more mood, her eyes pale and staring and there was nothing I could do to reach her. There were only five days to go and these moods were thieving our precious time, arriving with greater frequency and lasting for longer periods.

I made the breakfast, frying bread in the bacon fat in a childish attempt to cheer her up. I detested these malignant withdrawals. They made her as blind and selfish as a baby.

She sat at the table, staring out the window at the water. I washed the dishes. Then I swept the floor. I was angry. I polished the floor and still she didn't move. I made the bed and cleaned down the walls in the bedroom. I took out all the books and put them in alphabetical order according to author.

By lunchtime I was beside myself with rage.

She sat at the table.

I played a number of videotapes I knew she liked. She sat before the viewer like a blind deaf-mute. I took out a recipe book and began to prepare beef bourguignon with murder in my heart.

Then, some time about half past two in the afternoon, she turned and said 'Hello.'

The cloud had passed. She stood and stretched and came and held me from behind as I cooked the beef.

'I love you,' she said.

'I love you,' I said.

She kissed me on the ear.

'What's the matter?' My rage had evaporated, but I still had to ask the stupid question.

'You know.' She turned away from me and went to open the doors over the harbour. 'Let's not talk about it.'

'Well,' I said, 'maybe we should.'

'Why?' she said. 'I'm going to do it so there's nothing to be said.'

I sat across from her at the table. 'You're not going to go away,' I said quietly, 'and you are not going to take a Chance.'

She looked up sharply, staring directly into my eyes, and I think then she finally knew that I was serious. We sat staring at each other, entering an unreal country as frightening as any I have ever travelled in.

Later she said quietly, 'You have gone mad.'

There was a time, before this one, when I never wept. But now as I nodded tears came, coursing down my cheeks. We held each other miserably, whispering things that mad people say to one another.

10

Orgasm curved above us and through us, carrying us into dark places where we spoke in tongues.

Carla, most beautiful of women, crying in my ear. 'Tell me I'm beautiful.'

Locked doors with broken hinges. Bank vaults blown asunder. Blasphemous papers floating on warm winds, lying in the summer streets, flapping like wounded seagulls.

11

In the morning the light caught her. She looked more beautiful than the Bonnards in Hale's *Critique of Bourgeois Art*, the orange sheet lying where she had kicked it, the fine hairs along her arm soft and golden in the early light.

Bonnard painted his wife for more than twenty years. Whilst her arse and tits sagged he painted her better and better. It made my eyes wet with sentimental tears to think of the old Mme Bonnard posing for the ageing M. Bonnard, standing in the bathroom or sitting on the toilet seat of their tiny flat.

I was affected by visions of constancy. In the busy lanes behind the central market I watched an old couple helping each other along the broken-down pavement. He, short and stocky with a country man's arms, now infirm and reduced to a walking stick. She, of similar height, overweight, carrying her shopping in an old-fashioned bag.

She walked beside him protectively, spying out broken cobblestones, steps, and the feet of beggars.

'You walk next to the wall,' I heard her say, 'I'll walk on the outside so no one kicks your stick again.'

They swapped positions and set off once more, the old man jutting his chin, the old lady moving slowly on swollen legs, strangers to the mysteries of the Genetic Lottery and the glittering possibilities of a Chance.

When the sun, in time, caught Carla's beautiful face, she opened her eyes and smiled at me.

I felt so damned I wished to slap her face.

It was unbelievable that this should be taken from us. And even as I held her and kissed her sleep-soft lips, I was beginning, at last, to evolve a plan that would really keep her.

As I stroked her body, running one feathery finger down her shoulder, along her back, between her legs, across her thighs, I was designing the most intricate door, a door I could fit on the afternoon before her Chance-day, a door to keep her prisoner for a day at least. A door I could blame the landlord for, a door painted orange, a colour

I could blame the painters for, a door to make her miss her appointment, a door that would snap shut with a normal click but would finally only yield to the strongest axe.

The idea, so clearly expressed, has all the tell-tale signs of total madness. Do not imagine I don't see that, or even that I didn't know it then. Emperors have built such monuments on grander scales and entered history with the grand expressions of their selfishness and arrogance.

So allow me to say this about my door: I am, even now, startled at the far-flung originality of the design and the obsessive craftsmanship I finally applied to its construction. Further: to this day I can think of no simpler method by which I might have kept her.

12

I approached the door with infinite cunning. I took time off from work, telling Carla I had been temporarily suspended for insolence, something she found easy enough to believe.

On the first day I built a new door frame, thicker and heavier than the existing one and fixed it to the wall struts with fifty long brass screws. When I had finished I painted it with orange primer and rehung the old door.

'What's all this?' she asked.

'Those bloody painters are crazy,' I said.

'But that's a new frame. Did the painters do that?'

'There was a carpenter, too,' I said. 'I wish you'd tell the landlord to stop it.'

'I bought some beer,' she said, 'let's get drunk.'

Neither of us wanted to talk about the door, but while we drank I watched it with satisfaction. The orange was a beautiful colour. It cheered me up no end.

13

The dwarf crept up on me and found me working on the plans for the door, sneaking up on his obscene little feet.

'Ah-huh.'

I tried to hide it, this most complicated idea which was to lock you in, which on that very afternoon I would begin making in a makeshift workshop I had set up under the house. This gorgeous door of iron-hard old timber with its four concealed locks, their keyholes and knobs buried deep in the door itself.

'Ah,' said the dwarf who had been a handsome fellow, resting his ugly little hand affectionately on my elbow. 'Ah, this is some door.'

'It's for a friend,' I said, silently cursing my carelessness. I should have worked under the house.

'More like an enemy,' he observed. 'With a door like that you could lock someone up in fine style, eh?'

I didn't answer. The dwarf was no fool but neither was he as crazy as I was. My secret was protected by my madness.

'Did it occur to you,' the dwarf said, 'that there might be a problem getting someone to walk through a doorway guarded by a door like this? A good trap should be enticing, or, at least neutral, if you get my meaning.'

'It is not for a jail,' I said, 'or a trap, either.'

'You really should see someone,' he said, sitting sadly on the low table.

'What do you mean, "someone"?'

'Someone,' he said, 'who you could see. To talk to about your problems. A counsellor, a shrink, someone . . .' He looked at me and smiled, lighting a stinking Fasta cigarette. 'It's a beautiful door, just the same.'

'Go and fuck yourself,' I said, folding the plans. My fishing rod was in the corner.

'After the revolution,' the dwarf said calmly, 'there will be no locks. Children will grow up not understanding what a lock is. To see a lock it will be necessary to go to a museum.'

'Would you mind passing me my fishing rod. It's behind you.'

He obliged, making a small bow as he handed it over. 'You should consider joining us,' he said, 'then you would not have this problem you have with Carla. There are bigger problems you could address your anger to. Your situation now is that you are wasting energy being angry at the wrong things.'

'Go and fuck yourself,' I smiled.

He shook his head. 'Ah, so this is the level of debate we have come to. Go and fuck yourself, go and fuck yourself.' He repeated my insult again and again, turning it over curiously in his mind.

I left him with it and went down to talk to the bream on the pier. When I saw him leave I went down below the house and spent the rest of the day cutting the timber for the door. Later I made dovetail joints in the old method before reinforcing them with steel plates for good measure.

14

The door lay beneath us, a monument to my duplicity and fear.

In a room above, clad by books, stroked slowly by Haydn, I presented this angry argument to her while she watched my face with wide wet eyes. 'Don't imagine that you will forget all this. Don't imagine it will all go away. For whatever comfort you find with your friends, whatever conscience you pacify, whatever guilt you assuage, you will always look back on this with regret and know that it was unnecessary to destroy it. You will curse the schoolgirl morality that sent you to a Chance Centre and in your dreams you will find your way back to me and lie by my side and come fishing with me on the pier and everyone you meet you will compare and find lacking in some minor aspect.'

I knew exactly how to frighten her. But the fear could not change her mind.

To my argument she replied angrily: 'You understand nothing.'

To which I replied: 'You don't yet understand what you will understand in the end.'

After she had finished crying we fucked slowly and I thought of Mme Bonnard sitting on the edge of the bath, all aglow like a jewel.

15

She denied me a last night. She cheated me of it. She lied about the date of her Chance and left a day before she had said. I awoke to find only a note, carefully printed in a handwriting that seemed too young for the words it formed. Shivering, naked, I read it.

Dear Lumpy,

You would have gone crazy. I know you. We couldn't part like that. I've seen the hate in your eyes but what I will remember is love in them after a beautiful fuck.

I've got to be with Mum and Dad. When I see beggars in the street I think it's them. Can't you imagine how that feels? They have turned me into a Hup well and proper.

You don't always give me credit for my ideas. You call me illogical, idealist, fool. I think you think they all mean the same thing. They don't. I have no illusions (and I don't just mean the business about being sick that you mentioned). Now when I walk down the street people smile at me easily. If I want help it comes easily. It is possible for me to do things like borrow money from strangers. I feel loved and protected. This is the privilege of my body which I must renounce. There is no choice. But it would be a mistake for you to imagine that I haven't thought properly about what I am doing. I am terrified and cannot change my mind.

There is no one I have known who I have ever loved a thousandth as much as you. You would make a perfect Hup. You do not judge, you are objective, compassionate. For a while I thought we could convert you, but c'est la vie. You are a tender lover and I am crying now, thinking how I will miss you. I am not brave enough to risk seeing you in whatever body the comrades can extract from the Fastas. I know your feelings on these things. It would be too much to risk. I couldn't bear the rejection.

I love you, I understand you,
Carla

I crumpled it up. I smoothed it out. I kept saying 'Fuck' repeating the word meaninglessly, stupidly, with anger one moment, pain the next. I dressed and ran out to the street. The bus was just pulling away. I ran through the early morning streets to the Chance Centre, hoping she hadn't gone to another district to confuse me. The cold autumn air rasped my lungs, and my heart pounded wildly. I grinned to myself thinking it would be funny for me to die of a heart attack. Now I can't think why it seemed funny.

16

Even though it was early the Chance Centre was busy. The main concourse was crowded with people waiting for relatives, staring at the video display terminals for news of their friends' emergence. The smell of trauma was in the air, reminiscent of stale orange peel and piss. Poor people in carpet slippers with their trousers too short sat hopefully in front of murals depicting Leonardo's classic proportions. Fasta technicians in grubby white coats wheeled patients in and out of the concourse in a sequence as aimless and purposeless as the shuffling of a deck of cards. I could find Carla's name on none of the terminals.

I waited the morning. Nothing happened. The cards were shuffled. The coffee machine broke down. In the afternoon I went out and bought a six-pack of beer and a bottle of Milocaine capsules.

17

In the dark, in the night, something woke me. My tongue furry, my eyes like gravel, my head still dulled from the dope and drink, half-conscious I half saw the woman sitting in the chair by the bed.

A fat woman, weeping.

I watched her like television. A blue glow from the neon lights in the street showed the coarse, folded surface of her face, her poor lank greying hair, deep creases in her arms and fingers like the folds in babies' skin, and the great drapery of chin and neck was reminiscent of drought-resistant cattle from India.

It was not a fair time, not a fair test. I am better than that. It was the wrong time. Undrugged, ungrogged, I would have done better. It is unreasonable that such a test should come in such a way. But in the deep grey selfish folds of my mean little brain I decided that I had not woken up, that I would not wake up. I groaned, feigning sleep and turned over.

Carla stayed by my bed till morning, weeping softly while I lay with my eyes closed, sometimes sleeping, sometimes listening.

In the full light of morning she was gone and had, with bitter reproach, left behind merely one thing: a pair of her large grey knickers, wet with the juices of her unacceptable desire. I placed them in the rubbish bin and went out to buy some more beer.

18

I was sitting by the number five pier finishing off the last of the beer. I didn't feel bad. I'd felt a damn sight worse. The sun was out and the light dancing on the water produced a light dizzy feeling in my beer-sodden head. Two bream lay in the bucket, enough for my dinner, and I was sitting there pondering the question of Carla's flat: whether I should get out or whether I was meant to get out or whether I could afford to stay on. They were not difficult questions but I was managing to turn them into major events. Any moment I'd be off to snort a couple more caps of Milocaine and lie down in the sun.

I was not handling this well.

'Two fish, eh?'

I looked up. It was the fucking dwarf. There was nothing to say to him.

He sat down beside me, his grotesque little legs hanging over the side of the pier. His silence suggested a sympathy I did not wish to accept from him.

'What do you want, ugly?'

'It's nice to hear that you've finally relaxed, mm? Good to see that you're not pretending any more.' He smiled. He seemed not in the least malicious. 'I have brought the gift.'

'A silly custom. I'm surprised you follow it.' It was customary for people who took the Chance to give their friends pieces of clothing from their old bodies, clothing that they expected wouldn't fit the new. It had established itself as a pressure-cooked folk custom, like brides throwing corsages and children putting first teeth under their pillows.

The dwarf held out a small brown-paper parcel.

I unwrapped the parcel while he watched. It contained a pair of small white lady's knickers. They felt as cold and vibrant as echoes across vast canyons: quavering questions, cries, and thin misunderstandings.

I shook the dwarf by his tiny hand.

The fish jumped forlornly in the bucket.

19

So long ago. So much past. Furies, rages, beer and sleeping pills. They say that the dwarf was horribly tortured during the revolution, that his hands were literally sawn from his arms by the Fastas. The hunchback lady now adorns the 50 IG postage stamps, in celebration of her now famous role at the crucial battle of Haytown.

And Carla, I don't know. They say there was a fat lady who was one of the fiercest fighters, who attacked and killed without mercy, who slaughtered with a rage that was exceptional even in such a bloody time.

But I, I'm a crazy old man, alone with his books and his beer and his dog. I have been a clerk and a pedlar and a seller of cars. I have been ignorant, and a scholar of note. Pock-marked and ugly I have wandered the streets and slept in the parks. I have been bankrupt and handsome and a splendid conman. I have been a river of poisonous silver mercury, without form or substance, yet I carry with me this one pain, this one yearning, that I love you, my lady, with all my heart. And on evenings when the water is calm and the birds dive amongst the whitebait, my eyes swell with tears as I think of you sitting on a chair beside me, weeping in a darkened room.

THE CHILDHOOD GLAND

Gillian Mears

MY SISTER HOLDS OUT her hand to me. For a moment I think the white mice in her palm are sugar mice she has made using beaten egg white and icing sugar. But they're my own dead. Paul and Paulette, I think I named them and only a few days before had sealed up the escape hole they'd gnawed in the fruitcase home that neither they nor I wanted. I cup my hands. Sonya tips in the bodies. She looks at me and her eyes are like watermelon seeds. My little sister's eyes make me cry. I try to pretend I'm crying for my mice that I've murdered through weeks of long malnutrition and general neglect, and Sonya isn't fooled. It is hard to pass a lie to a sister. On my hand the mice feel light and desiccated. My fake grief shines through as clearly as the pink light through their ears.

In the old kitchen that is Sonya's bedroom in the Miller Street house in Grafton, I hear Karin and Sonya talking. Not only do I hate the mouse project, they are saying, but the love I hold for my cat isn't anywhere in the league of love they experience for their dogs. I listen to the companionable noise of my sisters sharing a packet of dog chocolates which taste fine as long as they are straight from the fridge. These are the beginning of the sugar-deficient years, when our mother has begun to make health food cakes instead of sponges. The house, which used to be the Grafton ferryman's, where we live all our adolescent years, smells sour from the lichens that grow up it like it's a tree not a building. I stay a little longer to hear their pronouncements before trailing away to bury the mice under the frangipani outside our parents' bedroom window. Yvonne comes home on the old blue bike we imagine once belonged to the giantess of Grafton it is so tall and the seat so wide. I hear Yvonne fall off. She takes the steps three at a time. I hear her kick down Sonya and Karin's welcoming dogs. I stay hidden in the creamy shadows of the frangipani, digging graves with a stick.

It isn't so much that my sisters mind the mice are dead. They kill their own with scalpels stolen from school. The hostility comes from my approach to the project, which has been lukewarm from the first. As Karin, Yvonne and Sonya devote many hours to breeding, killing, dissecting and tanning the skins of their pet-charges, I've allowed my concentration to wane. I haven't been wholehearted enough. I've betrayed the sisterly allegiance system that binds us still, twelve or fifteen years on.

If I had an ordinary Australian grandma I would run round to her place but Eileen Challacombe is better. She makes me Yorkshire pudding and shows me the piglets just born and doesn't ask too many questions. She is our mother's only real friend. Her laugh happens deep in her throat like singing. I help Eileen fold damask serviettes. She helps our mother clean our house. Her son is flagrantly gay for such a small town and I love him silently for years, from afar, for his exquisite style. She shows me photo albums of her long-ago childhood in Shanghai and makes me forget the disgrace of having erred in the eyes of my sisters. *Margerie was my sister,* she says, showing me pictures of ringleted girls in frocks. *She was much more beautiful.* But no one is, no one could be. Eileen is quite old but she wears her steel grey hair in two long plaits that thump her back when she walks. And we tell each other this is exactly how we will be when we reach that age.

Red leather, yellow leather, red leather, yellow leather. Our project carries the tongue-twisting rhyme from language into production. Yvonne wants enough mouse-skin leathers to make quivers. She makes bows and arrows out of stinkwood and shoots down a magpie. *Redleatheryellowleatherredleatheryellowleatherredleatheryellowleather.* The tanning fluid is brewed using bark from the wattle trees in the back garden. We had a grandmother, we know, who went mad on a wattle plantation in South Africa. It's where the mouse-skin idea comes from. From one of the Natal Tanning Extract Company booklets in one of the old trunks. Betty was our father's mother. Our parents look for signs of her in us, all through childhood and beyond, waiting for a mad child to emerge. *Redleatheryellowleatherredleatheryellowleather.* Red is Karin's favourite colour, yellow Sonya's, green Yvonne's and mine is blue.

In Grafton there is nothing to do and our tongues grow thick with repetitions.

There is something brazen in the way I love my sisters. Yet sometimes, when I am overwhelmed by the extreme way I'm loved back, all I want is to run away. For a while at least, to not be a Mears Girl. Their number is growing. Sonya's boys begin to call themselves Mears Girls, as if it is the name of a type of hero, and have to have it explained.

Perhaps it's because in the sixties, before the move to Grafton, there are four of us under the age of five. Or that our mother believes in reclusiveness to the extent that we're each other's only true friends and hers too.

When I see my sisters I hear how we tend to scream and yell. The noise rises around us faster than any flood. We don't act the way I've noticed other sisters act. We don't hug and kiss. The nieces call us the Indian Arm Wrestling Aunts. We shake hands. They all drive big old cars that burble, and live on hills where they can't be seen. We swap boots. My sisters laugh at the five hairs under my belly button and at my breasts, which remain the floppiest though they've done no baby feeding. *Yes*, they say, *you'll be enormous when you're in milk*. If Yvonne has a long grey hair hanging over her forehead, one of us will pull it free. We'll descend into each other's hair, searching for more signs of age. Because I am childless, is why I don't have any, they think. They suggest who'd be someone good to get sperm from. They can't imagine I won't follow them into motherhood and order me to hurry up about it. If I shut my eyes I can imagine three dazzling queen parrots screeching, as they sift through my hair. We can't hug and kiss and I still don't know why.

If one of us is absent we may find ourselves saying dreadful things about her.

We eat more sugar than the next generation of children. There are nine so far yet we are not Catholic or any religion particularly. I am the favourite aunt. The nieces carry around hexagons I've crocheted which they've stuffed with hair from my brush. They take their hair-hexagons to bed in order to have my smell with them when the visit is over. *Oh the buzzing of the bees and the cigarette trees, the soda water fountains.* I sing what our mother used to sing. There is so much noise I sing around a corner. Everyone is gabbling at once. My sisters sound like birds. It is one of the dangers of trying to write about them. That the details will disappear in the noise.

Our mother used to eat too much sugar too and dies when she is not old. But even as she's dying and we are easing her tongue with a grapefruit flavoured swab and her hat is tipped at a death angle to the pillow, we don't think she can die. She believes in her own invincibility and we do too. When we are little she teaches us how to make quick toffee, heating caster sugar in a pan over high heat. Teaspoons become lollipop sticks. Our mother has an English complexion and few wrinkles. Ours is Australian and when we're tired there are purple-coloured sockets under our eyes. In bright light we can all pass for a decade older than our true age. We scar easily and remember everything. A scratch will still be mulberry a year or more later.

Why will our faces no longer carry fat? I don't know. It's our lantern jaws, Yvonne says, drawing how we'll look if we ever reach old age. She draws four thin skulls. When she was a child her series of monster paintings, which she'd hold down for me to see from the top bunk, gave me nightmares I still remember.

Our real faces are small. They all look like insects if we try to wear sunglasses and grow the same squint wrinkles instead. Our cheekbones make me remember the day our father's stockhorse mare smashed her head against the yards. We could see into her face through bones as fine and fragile as the plywood gliders our father used to buy us to construct and fly. I fainted seeing the eye pop out. Yvonne helped the vet hold it.

We have long arms and long necks. In jumpers, we roll up the sleeves to the elbow. There are muscles in our forearms. One day we'll have to bury a sister. I hope it's me.

Still we don't move. Our mother's calling her four daughters but we keep dipping our hands into a bucket of sunflower seed. The seeds are warm. The parrots wait in the fig tree for us to move.

Although it's a golden afternoon we are no longer children and our mother, who's directing our father to cut down the first ripe pod of bananas, is dying. She's wearing a long dove-coloured dressing gown and a bonnet that makes the garden seem to be the set for a Chekhov play. It's calm weather, the last day of June; Sonya's birthday and she's a quarter of a century old.

– Sunflowers are like chocolate for parrots. Did you know, she says.

A memory of tossing Sonya into the air on my knees, arrives and leaves. White bells are ringing in a white Greek church that make our mother cry with pleasure. Memories that aren't photos. In Greece we live on baby sardines and Coca-Cola. Sonya was plumper then and that encouraged strangers to want to reach out and squeeze her. Once she was so tiny she could hide in the grandfather clock in the hall of the ferryman's house, pretending to chime. For her seventh birthday in Crete our mother bought her a sunflower cake. I think so anyway. In my memory our plates are awash with honey as Sonya unwraps a glass charm to ward off the evil eye. But I know I've always had a tendency to find links and connections where there aren't any – how can there be, when nearly twenty years have passed, we are not girls anymore and our mother is dying?

– Really? Like chocolate? says Karin.

I like how she says their wings seem to be red capes. She is heavily pregnant with her fourth baby, who will be called Little Sonya when she's born two weeks after our mother dies.

– Saturated fat. We're wrecking their livers.

Sonya rattles off facts but bites down on that one, because our mother has a kind of cancer that has moved quickly into her lungs and now her liver. She is calling out for us. Our father is sawing the soft banana wood. Her voice is still her clear English voice though now we remember how last year she would pause for a while if she'd walked up a hill. She'd hold her ribs and say hang on until I get my breath. Karin begins to throw the seed in arcs away from us.

– One day before I went to Africa, I say, she said she could see fireworks in her left eye. But she looked so *well*.

We concentrate a moment longer on the birds. It's safe out here in the garden and it's my little sister's birthday. I begin to recognise my fondness for that expression. My little sister, as if the tenderness it elicits cannot ever be overdone. Our mother's favourite dog has climbed onto the highchair in the sun and stares out across the river.

— If I lived here, says Yvonne, I'd net this fig tree in and write my stories under that.

Her real desk is a door on 44-gallon drums. Budgie wings and bones decorate its surface. Our father's gymnast rings as well as horse paraphernalia hang above. Her crow, Furious, sits watching her work and on each of Yvonne's shoulders are scars from crow claws. Sometimes Furious talks too much and she throws her outside. One day when I am in Yvonne's desk room (which smells of dark feathers and leather dressings), I see a picture of a beautiful woman. The piece of paper's folded over. Hmm, I think, what a beautiful and serene face the painted woman has.

— Well, says Yvonne, coming up behind me. What would you say she's looking at?

— Parchment? Perhaps.

Yvonne gives her manic laugh and unfolds the other side of the painting.

— Judith and Holofernes! she says.

I look down at a gory decapitation scene.

Yvonne is the eldest and the eldest girl in a family of sisters is always the fiercest. But go for a walk with Yvonne through any landscape and you will see things in another way.

— So this is it, this is how it feels sometimes, she observes as our mother is dying. So peaceful and ordinary and unalarming.

— We should go over, I say, but still we stand. I tell my sisters I feel so immobilised I have dreams somebody keeps attaching me to a piece of string to fly me in an afternoon wind away from the hill.

— The air smells of straw, says one of us.

– It's storms and beetles, I reply.

– It's your hat, dumb-dumb.

– I smell citrus blossom.

Who says what doesn't always matter. Our voices are almost perfectly interchangeable, half Australian, half something else. Yvonne's goes faster, that's about the only difference.

– Gillian! There is a call for me. I've always been her favourite.

As we begin to move towards our mother, I notice we all have our hair up. How stalky our necks seem, how vulnerable. Our arms look too long. This is the third house our parents have lived in in Australia and the thinnest. Only Sonya lived here for the tailend of her childhood. There's so much glass you can see clear through the river. This sensation adds to the unreality of afternoons. In our reflections we seem to go all glittery with uncried pain.

I think how Yvonne used to make me do dangerous tricks in the late evening light. How I was her minion. It would grow late and dark but we'd continue to jump our horses over pieces of string or wire. It was like facing yourself and your horse at nothing. The impending death of our mother feels the same. There are no groundlines, rules or precedents and the leap, though fully anticipated, will still come as a terrible surprise. I wish suddenly that I was ten years old again. When I was a child, right up until I was a late developing fifteen-year-old, I was so thin, so bendable, I could walk right under the belly of my mare, following the figure of my big sister wherever she might lead me.

I don't believe it's possible to write about my sisters without writing about our mother too. When we were teenagers, she called herself the fifth sister, but wistfully, knowing she wasn't really.

Through the action of tumours rubbing against her stomach lining, our mother's belly is as big as Karin's nearly full-term pregnancy. The irony is not ignored. Our mother has a string of jokes about full-term babies and often refers to her pain in terms relative to childbirth. Coffee brewed four rooms away causes her nausea.

Karin's life seems the closest to our mother's. Her place is on the edge of a small weatherboard town on a small rocky acreage. She has made a round rose garden, just as our mother did in the sixties, in a very similar northern landscape of empty paddocks and far blue rock candy peaks with edges so sharp they'd cut your tongue. A town hall tin chair in the middle of the circle is turning to rust. Karin sits there with the hose in her hand and there are many small children and dogs running past. Karin and I are the middle girls. The soft centres, our mother says, and we are. We are not as vehement or ferocious or relentless in the way we lead our lives.

— Darling? On my birthday, which is twenty-one days after Sonya's, our mother holds out her now tiny arms. The inscription she has written in the biography is without indication of the gravity of the situation. It's a polite far-feeling inscription. Sometimes, I say to Sonya in exasperation, it's as if she's approaching her own death in the way she used to read biographies: refusing to skip ahead or to look at the pictures before they are arrived at in the text.

I take her arms over my shoulders, waiting for her question before bending towards my knees. In the lift position our eyes can't ever meet and her fingers tap my back like wings. Yvonne comes to help. Our mother orders her away. Yvonne's eyes might as well be my own, the dismay I find in them is so sharp.

— I can't finish my letter with all of you flapping around me, our mother says. All of you, she says, meaning Yvonne, whom she is determined still to paint as a daughter tyrant. There are things at this point that can't be mentioned, that would crack our hearts to acknowledge.

On my birthday our mother is writing a letter on airmail paper with butterflies on the border. It is to her own mother but she has no intention of posting it. At times, the letter seems to cause her distress. She's writing out all her griefs and all the old hatreds. She can remember only two kindnesses, very ordinary ones, such as would've occurred to any one of us on any one day of our childhood. After sleeping on her accusations for a night, she burns them.

Our mother seems glad as well as gentler. One day, she advises me, when we feel ready, we should write out similar letters of grievance. Against her. You can't be a mother, she says, of four girls, without inflicting damage.

For a number of days after my twenty-seventh birthday the remains of our mother's letter stay under a vase of flowers. The vase makes the rose stems look like dancers' legs, says Sonya. The rose stems dancing in spangled green tights. My fanciful little sister.

But the saucepan of ashes begins to unsettle us. Something has died in that saucepan, I think. The afternoons are so quiet we can hear the high tide slapping against the other side of the riverbank. Soon Yvonne and Karin will go back to Queensland and we have to battle the strong temptation to poke the ashes with a twig, to try to work out some of the unburnt words. It's a relief when our mother decides to bury them in a pot underneath some flowers. She can no longer bend so Sonya helps prepare the soil. It is late in the year to be putting in spring flowers but I like to think of the way the freesia bulbs will begin to send their shoots through bad memories; towards light.

My sisters' hands, when I shake them goodbye, are broad and padded, like workers' hands. Sometimes I am amazed when I look at the hands of other girls, to see how delicate they are. None of us have ever had our mother's hands. Whenever I see a sister after an absence I wonder why it's only our fingers and palms that are touching. Their hands are warm; mine are cold. They knuckle-crunch my fingers as if they are not mothers or grown-ups and never will be.

Sometimes we consult each other, trying to find the reasons. We blame our mother. We blame our father. We blame the madness that put fears of it repeating itself on a not very well hidden agenda.

In the ferryman's house there are shadows on the floor in summer. There is a man in our mother's bedroom who isn't our father. In Grafton, summers are long and winters are warm. We all wander round with no clothes on. Our mother banishes our father to the cement bathroom downstairs. The shadows move slowly and take years to decipher. Even now these outlines of old stories seem as if they may never join up.

– I think it was dangerous trying to be friendly to a Mears girl.

– Well, yes in a way.

– There was something sometimes monstrous.

– Is!

(laughter)

– Only in that we didn't need anybody else.

The voices don't matter. Our voices are all the same. Have I mentioned that? Yes. We are always repeating ourselves. Don't boil your cabbages, we tell each other. We still like to trick people sometimes. We can easily trick our father, who calls us by each other's names anyway, or sometimes by the name of a dog or cat long deceased.

We hedge people out.

People who are not sisters say things like: you all begin to act like ten-year-olds when you see each other.

– A crowbar couldn't wedge you apart.

– You're still little gels, aren't you Mummy, says Sonya's four-year-old.

I think it's our gland of childhood, says Karin, on the back of a postcard she has made of her shadow standing in a ploughed field. The shadow is tall and eerie. It takes me months to go in search of what she means.

– High school biology, the thymus, you know, *The Web of Life*, Karin's voice over the phone sounds withering and then she has to hang up.

– Children . . . I hear her voice rising from the middle of the noise, before the phone is put down.

Our mother cries in storms. She sees haloes around storm clouds and her own death occurring in a blaze of lightning. Sometimes she cries if we laugh. On her way to Africa, during a storm at sea, she threw most of her old clothes out the porthole. She is always happy at the beach, in blue swimmers, floating in the shallows.

We grow up being careful not to make our mother cry. We can make her laugh and her laughter is infectious, but nothing we ever say or do can take away the sadness that gives her that smudged and stony kind of beauty. My sisters and I have our father's brown eyes but hers are pale. She hates that they are so deep set. We hate how she tries to smooth wings of eyeshadow out from their corners, using a mixture of blues, silver and mauve on her finger. She trusts no one, not us nor anyone I can remember. She holds her grudges forever. When she cries behind half-closed doors we know it's dangerous to look. After a certain age we aren't allowed to climb into her lap. She runs away twice and says if she kills herself it will be by drowning. The river in flood comes to within three feet of cresting the levee and smells to us of death. Or is it the blood and bone melting down in the wind coming from the tannery on the other side of the river?

At other times, though she never hits us, she smashes china. Karin and I do also. What has been unleashed, I wonder? And what exactly do we do when she's throwing? When we are children? We learn more about invisibility. We eat sugar in our bedrooms, with our noses in books. We have fast metabolisms and are all speed readers. Only Yvonne tries to match our mother's anger with her own. They fight and cry and hate each other. Sweethearts, our mother calls us but there are times when we no longer believe her.

Our mother's anger chooses ancient and irreplaceable china. She throws downwards, so that the vase or bowl or thin Minton teacup moves through the shallowest of trajectories before shattering. Later, after moving to the farm, she has a throwing wall. She hurls her anger against it. One day far into the future, someone's going to end up with cuts all over their hands pulling out the old allamanda vine that grows against that wall, for it is my wall now, though I only ever throw bottles or vegemite jars. Sonya has a bottom drawer full of china she says she's going to mend one day. She's been saying this since she was seven years old.

I can remember my little sister in hand-me-down swimmers, crouched over the kitchen floor the summer after we came home from England. She is so brown her skin has a kind of gloss. She's searching for a piece of parrot head. She's been feeding her honey spiders which is why she's up at the house not down at the river where we spend most of our holidays. Her feet are bare and it seems remarkable to me they are not getting cut. 'Mummy's crying,' she says. I cock my head. Our mother cries all the time since we're back in Australia and we don't know why. For Christmas and her birthday we give her linen and cross-stitch hankies for her tears.

I shake my head. 'Come down and play sardines,' I say. 'Yvonne said to come and get you.'

Not that we'll play sardines. Instead Yvonne and Karin will get us with willow wand whips or we will get them. Or if it's summer, regardless of the deadly bullrout fish who live in the river weed, we'll press our bodies through there in order to continue the weed war we rage against our neighbours. Even our dog Rolf has been trained at a command to bash up their blue heeler Bernie. Sonya is tireless in building booby traps and has ambushed her room with logs that fall when you open her door.

'Here are The Babies,' says Karin, when we reach the pampas grass. Karin is about eleven, Yvonne twelve, I must be nine or ten, Sonya almost eight. It's the early seventies. Yvonne's drawing horses in the circle of white sand dumped by the last flood.

– I hated school, says Yvonne these days. It did me Untold Damage. Only near horses did I feel a hint of infinity.

Yvonne continues to draw horses. Not a day goes by when she doesn't. They are her nemesis. There are her bony headed mares with their ears laid back and often accompanied now by naked women with highly muscled legs. When she draws me, I am always half mare.

– Is there such a thing as a female centaur, Gillian? she phones me after midnight to ask. She lives without sleep to fit in all she wants her life to be. Instead of drinking coffee, she eats sugar and caffeine sandwiches washed down with Coca-Cola. She thinks she'll die on a horse. I have a black and white photo of her from childhood over my desk. She is jumping a raised double gravestone. The horse and the line of a tree cast the shadow of a cross on the marble. When we are children she is always doing one dangerous thing after another with the horses, and I must follow. Sometimes I follow with my eyes shut and my ears clamped tight against the sound of disaster. We jump fire. We jump a barbed wire fence.

– I can't, I say.

– Don't say you can't. You can.

I do. Propelled by an elder sister's ferocity I can do anything.

THE CHILDHOOD GLAND

Yvonne wears Christmas beetles hooked through wire in her ears. Her garden when she is grown, when she is mother, night sister Mears, writer and artist, is full of the surprises of unfinished sculptures. She takes you around to the shed to show you a battalion of small wooden horses she's been tapping out of camphor laurel with a chisel. Often she canters instead of walking. Exhaustion lines hang from her eyes. Over the last few yeas she has bought all of us black thoroughbred mares, full sisters to each other. Her children jump their bikes and fend for themselves. She owns about a hundred chickens and ducks and her garden is caged against them. They are like ballroom dancers, I say, the way they spread out across her paddocks.

– No Gillian, she says, I prefer to think they're the last of the dinosaurs. And says look closely at their eyes and legs.

Her crow makes a noise.

– Don't you love that swallowed cry! I can't write about Yvonne without using exclamation marks.

Sister stories hold a kind of endlessness. They are full of surprises, even now the most familiar ones can cast up something new. We were watching you from Mum's bedroom, Karin told me a little while ago. That's how we knew where you'd buried those dead mice.

Before we went to England we ate our breakfast on the Fallen Tree at the edge of Mr Greenwood's farm, Goonelebah, near Lismore. It's a clear childhood memory. It's the house our parents build after migrating from Africa and they call the rim of the blue Dividing Range the Chimanimanis, as if they still live in Rhodesia. At the Fallen Tree our porridge is cold. We are small. Our father's mother in England, the one who was mad and sick, has died: Betty. Our mother, who Betty refused to believe existed, is singing. *Four little ducks went out one day, over the hill and faraway.* This song makes me forlorn, as if we will be separated from our mother forever. She points out to us that English rabbits in blue and crimson coats hop around and around the edges of our bowls. We're concentrating on the melted brown sugar and on walking as we eat, up and down, up and down, the long tree stretched like a dead grey giant across the paddock. Every now and then our tongues find a small circle of hard sugar. We look for foxgloves: expecting England in Australia and never finding it. Our mother's singing voice is pale. *Oh the buzzing of the bees and the cigarette trees.* Her dress too, that morning down at the Fallen Tree, is some vague colour, a bit like the mist in my memory, rising from the small valley way beyond the boundaries of our parents' land.

We walk up and down, up and down the Fallen Tree each morning until our parents decide to remove us from school and take us with them to England for as long as it takes to sort out Betty's estate. Our father burns bonfires of old mail and ships crates full of things away to auction. We stay half a year and when we come back realise there's no disguising our difference now.

Australia seems too yellow, Honey, says our mother.
And it is.
Honeybun, says our father back. He has no remedies.
It's 1973.

THE CHILDHOOD GLAND

We've moved from Goonelebah to Grafton and it's on every map of the world we ever look at. We even find it on the old shower curtain of the ferryman's house our parents end up buying because, though it's ugly and frail with various rots, it is on the river and the river is to entertain us in the teenage years that lie ahead, that our mother speaks of with a certain hush in her voice.

— There. Grafton, in neat helvetica type, says Yvonne, scraping away a blossom of mould with her thumb.

It's a game we continue to play for years, finding Grafton in neglected shop fronts of Ireland or on a tablecloth in Malawi. A doona cover in Fitzroy, Melbourne.

There is too much yellow in the glare coming through all the new green growth. The new town is flat and in October is said to turn mauve. Our mother spends much time trying to straighten her fine black curls with hot rollers. She's singing along to old Joan Baez and Dory Previn songs She wears dark blue silk blouses. We are always longing to lean forward. To push the button near her breasts back through its silk slit.

— They're as narrow as nails, she likes to say about real Graftonians.

We refuse to have haircuts. Mopheads, our mother calls us. The bits of hair we never brush up on top of our heads bleach yellow too. We all get horses. Our messiness, our horsiness, betray her. To an extent she begins to abandon us and we barely notice. She tells the same unhappy stories of her own childhood until we stop listening.

When does our mother begin to drink and have affairs? Now. The seventies, the vague years, when she favoured long and ugly evening dresses, wooden beads, beige-coloured pantsuits, leather belts with embossed vines and buckles. Later she says it was the horses; the horses and her daughters who made her so careless and sad. But she was sad before Grafton, she was sad before we were born, you can see it in any old photograph. You can see it in the photographs from the Catholic orphanage her mother put her in when she was three years old and where she was left, even when the war was long over, as her father took years to die from multiple sclerosis in a monastery in Yorkshire.

Yvonne can do anything and I am her slave. I fetch and carry and obey her every order no matter how dangerous. Sonya and Karin form a counter alliance and our fights are scattered but steady. Yvonne collects china horses, Sonya and Karin china dogs. Sonya bites into two my most precious potsherd stolen from the Parthenon in my sling. The kittens get put into an esky and are forgotten. No, that's not true. That story is about somebody else's little sister, but it fits. My sisters and I have left scars on each other's bodies that will be with us when we die. That wiggle of white skin next to Karin's eye when Yvonne went charging at her too wildly with a long stick. Sonya's two bottom teeth — brown and shrunken after the day I pushed her down the stairs. Though in a fit of remorse I tried to hurl myself down afterwards, my teeth remain intact.

There seems to be nothing to do at first in Grafton except injure ourselves or other things. The heat makes us scream. We have screaming contests in the bathroom where the acoustics are good and my screams always win.

THE CHILDHOOD GLAND

Sonya and Karin, the dog-girls, drown fleas. Yvonne and I stoop to defleaing Rolf and Bella too. The guinea pigs are eaten by the dog next door. We watch flea legs flail in time to our mother's fast piano records. Each sister employs different methods of drowning and each thinks the other's less efficient. The fleas Yvonne drowns in a glass flask look like they're dancing and cast blue drowning shadows at the bottom of the water jug. We form theories as to why some fleas sink without more than one or two kicks of their legs whereas others last all day, through symphonies and suites. I'm so skinny I'm sure I've accidentally eaten flea eggs left under my fingernails and that inside me is a labyrinth of parasites. I begin to have oil in my hair and my underarms start to sweat. When our father invites some children around to our place to play we make them eat peppercorns, fleas and tadpoles before attacking them from behind with green lemons. We make the son of a soybean scientist, who is now a banker in New York, who later shaved his eyebrows into strange shapes and kissed Karin at the drive-in, howl. Hold him down, you Zulu warriors, hold him down, you Zulu chief, chief, chief, chief. We tie him up with our elastics and stomp around on top of him. Does he ever go near the water trough in our horse paddock when our father suggests his pony stay in our paddock? It's Yvonne's idea that we leave him messages. We write them on bits of old fibro. The messages are mean and mince no words. We prop them at the water trough. It's as if our sisterliness is so intense it can brook no interlopers.

The messages are signs of our malevolence, our mother says, when somehow she finds us out – and blames Yvonne. She blames Yvonne for everything, even her pain, when she is dying and Yvonne is tending to her medically in as tender a way as she knows how.

When we begin to get weekend jobs, I find there is nothing quite as forlorn as a sister in uniform, trapped and restrained and unable to act normally as I go by. I have to turn my face from Karin in the hot bread shop, Yvonne sewing bridles on a stool at the saddlers, Sonya at a Woolworths checkout or my own reflection in yellow polyester uniform, making hamburgers and chips for long distance truck drivers.

Sometimes we hear rumours of Mears Girls. They arrive via Eileen Challacombe, who tells us more stories than she ever sweeps, who's always discovering various bits of pornography round our beds, who remembers how on the second time she came to our place, our mother was about to smash a plate on the kitchen floor. How our mother told her to pay no attention, it was just something she had to do. We barricade our rooms with string and notes imploring her not to enter the messy zone and usually she obeys.

Eileen looks after us while our mother is away and the rumours increase. By then we're older. The woman who owns the richest frock shop in town claims she's seen all four Mears girls copulating on her lawns. We were so drugged, this rumour went, we looked as if we were flying. In retaliation we took our horses out after dark and galloped up and down her turf. Our father made us go back the next day with sackfuls of soil from our own levee bank to fill in the holes. The letters to our mother read with a high strain of worry barely hidden beneath news of school, horses, the dirty washing getting beyond a joke and pictures of the dogs.

Some rumours begin even before we are born. The nurses can't believe we aren't all going to come out with black curls and skin because our parents, though white, are known to have arrived from Africa.

Our mother comes home and has a hysterectomy and, although we see her lying as if dead before she's through the anaesthetic, she is walking the next day.

— I'm a Mears, she says. Mears Girls don't feel pain.

These images and memories. There are so many. They are like a sad face on my wall I want to make laugh. I can feel them sometimes in my dreams, poking towards me like wishbones that haven't yet been snapped.

Our parents drink more. Memories of the Miller Street house recur because they were the unhappier times. Remembering can overwhelm us with distaste. The parties are wilder. The uncertain violence of drunk grownups. Distaste against our parents whose fault it is. Our parents barricade the rooms around their bedroom, around their weekend hangovers, but Sonya knows a route in, through two windows that won't lock, in order to thump at their door and demand a hug.

— They'd send me out to buy the *Sun Herald*, Sonya remembers. And I'd only go because I'd get icecream money as well. Even now, she says, the smell of Sunday paper cartoons can make her feel ill.

The lipstick our mother wears in Miller Street has silk powder in it so that it lasts on the lip longer. She seems afraid not to have it on when she goes out of the house but it makes her teeth look yellow near the gums. Her stomach ulcers bleed. Her nails are red. Kissed tissues float out from the top of waste paper baskets all round the house.

Sonya wears Elizabeth Arden lip-gloss and stops being with us at school. She won't ride with us to school anymore and her betrayal is keenly felt. Yvonne and I read her diary to gather an inkling of what it is all about. Sex. Then Karin too. She begins to kiss the boy we once tied up, who is shaving his eyebrows. Yvonne and I reavow our antimarriage sentiments. We sell our geldings and buy mares. Summer, or it's warming up anyway and outside our window we can smell the Yesterday, Today and Tomorrow trees that our mother hates, but never gets around to removing, turning from white to purple.

We bring monstera deliciosa fruits into our room, eating them so fast our tongues fill with spikes as fine as stings. Under the big brooding leaves of the monstera plants I pray that I will stop blushing. My white mice die and no sister talks to me for ten or fifteen days. They go around with scalpels in their hands, dispatching certain mice of the right wild colour for their skins. Yvonne looks for ways to dye the shrivelled hides and I'm not allowed to help. White mice are pets. My sisters' white mice crawl up and down their bodies and poop in their shirts. They only kill wild mice for leather. Mouse skins tanned in this way are as soft and pale as chamois.

We skip many days of school and our mother always writes good notes. The cakes for after school turn from sponges into frozen oblongs of health cakes that are flat and dense and airless and have barely any sugar apart from a few dates thrown in. I sell a horse and over one summer spend all the money on sweets for myself and my sisters.

Before the ferryman's house in Miller Street was put on pylons the floods used to go through it. The walls when we press our faces into them smell of silt and ribbon weed. When it rains we write our animals' names in the grey mildew that grows on the fibro. I've called my mare Betty after my mad grandma whose photo is never on our father's desk or anywhere else, not even after she's dead and her wealth and belongings are all through the house.

The shapes of my sisters obsess me. I would prefer any one of their bodies to my own. I make my sisters cold, filling a bucket with iced water before creeping into the bathroom, which is ugly with fake gold trimmings, climbing onto the bath and pouring the water onto them in the shower. They scream. Their nipples curl up.

At night Karin comes into my bed following our secret signal of scratches on the dividing wall and we draw on each other's back maps of where we would like to go. She has a large globe from Hamleys toyshop on her desk and is much better at geography than I will ever be. Karin is the least horsy sister but she can give the best horsebites.

Karin's travelling name is Mexican Marigold and I am Nipsy Beetle. She calls the main vein along my left arm Women River, after a river she has noticed in Canada and if her fingers are travelling along that, we are in a boat. Sometimes we take a torch with us under the blankets the better to see our destinations. She horsebites with surprise and they leave marks. If it is summer we turn my pillow over and over, seeking for anything cool. Our mother says she is going to run away to Russia so we never travel to any of the Russian cities with their lovely, icy-sounding names. There is also the game of the Red Trail which involves a more delicate kind of pain.

On wet days, Yvonne cleans our dead grandma's girlhood saddle.

I hover around, ready to be helpful if necessary. I fetch her coffee sugar in a cup and her favourite teaspoon. She allows me to have every second teaspoonful. We promise each other that we will never get married. The English pigskin is as dark as the eggplants our mother's growing in the garden, trying to bring back the holiday in Greece in all the moussakas she's making. The dolmades she composes with the grapevines from the verandah don't work very well but we eat them anyway. We are growing girls. After school we eat two loaves of bread and nearly a tin of plum jam. When Yvonne puts on fresh yellow saddlesoap the pores of leather turn white. I love milk but have stopped drinking it a long time ago so that Yvonne won't smell it on my breath. We eat our cereal, porridge and Milo powder dry. The Inter Dominion is the name of a trotting heat we can hear floating to us in the evenings of the show. In Her Dominion, I think it's called. I think this for years.

We all want to know how Betty had been mad but the silences ring out from her name. Travelling around Europe and England in the back of a van, we play Madness every day. We dress up in our father's jumpers and stuff ourselves full of cushions and fruit until we take on the right proportions of a fat mad grandma.

Her past arrives into our Australian life, one afternoon, in two silver Selby's removalist trucks. The old oak furniture glints with silver and beads and old paintings lurch out of their frames. Many things are broken in the badly packed inheritance from England and all the ring drawers have been robbed. We put our fingers into the empty velvet spaces. Our mother is furious at the lack of care but doesn't mind about the rings. She has never worn rings. And none of us do or have. The smell of Goddard's silver polish enters the house. Suddenly there is silver everywhere. Our father wants us all to eat with the cutlery of his childhood, which is heavy and so large Sonya can't get the pudding spoon into her mouth. Having come from a servanted childhood, cleaning heirlooms doesn't occur to him. Somehow the arrival of all this silver in the house adds to our mother's sadness. She goes to great lengths to keep it gleaming and hides many of the more valuable pieces (she looks up identification of the hallmarks of these in fat silver textbooks she orders from Sydney) in strange places. One day Sonya finds a bundle of fish forks underneath her mattress. Our mother keeps a long pair of sixteenth-century duelling pistols, registered annually as firearms, in the sewing drawer next to the damaged pinwheels we made her in Infants.

We're paid twenty cents per half hour to help with the silver cleaning. Our fingers grow pink and dry with Goddard's products.

On rainy days Sonya and I get out Betty's leather travelling bag with its many secret compartments, silver hairbrushes and half-used glass bottles of perfumes and powders. In the silk lining we find a picture of an old woman in a hat, the powder so thick on her face there is an impression that it is cracking. The face looks like one of Yvonne's earlier monsters. We regret deeply the day our father sells the case to buy Yvonne a new horse; and are kind of relieved, for we'd begun to call it the Madness Case.

Then we all leave home one after the other, fast and doing silly things; and when we return not only does the big square ugly house no longer belong to us, but it's no longer there. Late one evening I go to see the empty block with Sonya. It's been raining. The puddles in the place where our rooms and our noisiness had been are purple and soft. I have to hold back my tears.

— I'm sorry, says Sonya. As if she's responsible. It is as if that particular past has vanished and there has never been the comfort of sisterly hands.

Yet we always say our childhood was happy. Even though in some ways it was only ordinary with ordinary kinds of distress. It is a mixture in my memory, with the same sharp edge as acid drop two-for-one sweets sold in the Oliver Street corner shop.

From one of the never-used lookouts along Old Copmanhurst Road, the farm looks like a big seed pod, floating along a wide stretch of the Clarence River. Or if it's winter, a yellow plover's egg, bobbing up and down. When our mother's dying I sit at the lookout on my way back from town and in my mind the past keeps coming out as the present. Sometimes I wish, as I sit there, that I could dilute the love my sisters have always directed my way because one day they're going to find out things about me I'd rather have hidden. Somehow all the secrets will be dislodged from my guarding heart. To my sisters, who are mothers and have been for seven years, the secrets will sound outlandish. And they will bring to mind the same sense of disappointment a brown egg which turns out to be a floater can cause. Something very wholesome-looking and smooth but certainly damaged inside.

As I sit there thinking about this one overcast day at the lookout

I begin to drink my mother's morphine, which is the sort of thing I mean. The thought of my sisters stops me. I only have a few sips and my mouths goes dry and pink. I hold the flask up to my eye instead so that the farm suddenly reminds me of an egg with the yolk blown out and dyed pink for Easter. I have a shameful memory of the white mice I starved to death by neglect and of how in Sonya's outstretched palm they looked like ornamental meringues for a party. Or when I dropped them into their shallow graves – gardenias in a soil the colour of wedding cake. I think of how I didn't have my baby the year my sisters all fell pregnant.

Our mother begins to die in earnest. Yvonne and Karin travel down again and are home when the big storm of the year hits the hill. The muteness imposed by our mother lies like some soft and heavy and not all tender or pleasant thing between us. The house is full of moths. Our mother calls them death moths. They're ugly, fat and seem blind. The other day one flew out at her and she fell over. She thought it was a mouse. Wedge wings, I call them. Murder moths, says one of Yvonne's children. Killerheads. No, says Sonya, they are in fact sphinx moths. They rest up in the corners of the old furniture and are the same dark colour.

– Moths in our house mean death, says our mother, in a way I can't forget. Oh, don't look at the moon through glass, it is very bad luck, darlings.

Sadness, I think. Salt water growing more salt water crystals. Remembering the city of beautiful chemicals Sonya, Karin and I once built with Yvonne's chemistry set while Yvonne nearly blew her hand off in a homemade explosion.

Each night, whoever is in the house bandages our mother up in a configuration of bandages the medical profession calls The Spike. As we commence this procedure, carried out in the forlorn hope that it will halt the swell of our mother's body, I make sure to turn away from her face. I try to turn down Gillian Fischer singing Purcell's 'When I am Laid in Earth', that is being played on ABC FM, but my mother says to leave it. Remember me. We cry all over her. Her skin is silk – we have to massage. Everywhere, all over, feeling for the knots of small lymph nodes and moving our fingers in a clockwise or anti-clockwise direction, according to charts. I far prefer doing this with a sister than my father.

It grows dark and windows turn into mirrors. In the windows I sometimes catch sight of how we're leant over the poor beleaguered body on the massage table as if over a bier. Our mother lies with her face turned towards the river in the hope of seeing flocks of evening egrets flying from the trees. Egrets grow long filamentous plumes that were once in great demand for ladies' hats. Plumes were collected from egrets killed at their nesting colonies across the river from the house, as the feathers are best when the eggs are being laid. Yet we don't like to tell our mother that her chosen symbol of light and health has such a bloody local history.

For Yvonne, who is a nurse, who has seen such things before, it is hardest. She says she has seen women reach the size of 44-gallon drums.

I see her bending into the fire to warm the circle of massage cream in her hands. Her knuckles burn.

— That storm's coming fast! says Sonya.

— Is it wearing a halo? asks our mother.

Sonya's eyes meet mine. She is twenty-five and full of secrets and I can remember being just like that. When she tells a lie, her eyelashes flutter to the left and her head tosses in the same direction.

I think of sisterly love as being very pure and flowing. If it had a colour, it would be the kind of blue moving out from one of Yvonne's finest paintbrushes into a jar of rainwater.

— When I used to breastfeed, our mother says, the milk coming through was like silk threading out of my body.

Since the chemicals took away her hair our mother wears silk scarves theatrically, tied to give a long wild tail down her back. We look with fear and pleasure at the hair growing back like a little dark cap.

Karin begins to light all the candles in the house. One candle in a gin bottle by a window melts and is blown into the shape of a schoolgirl or an old woman with her legs pushed back at the knees. From one angle she stands the way Yvonne, trying to bow her legs into the appropriate horseriding shape long before she ever had a horse, used to stand. But from the side, the waxen head is cricked forward in a despondent way. Its belly is a poddy kind which could belong either to a girl or her grandmother.

— That's what I look like, says our mother. A little wax crone. A pregnant pygmy. Did you know the Shona buried their tiny children in wet soil but older children under rocks in the hills. I wonder will it be a wet or a sunny day for me? Yvonne! Don't put the dryer on unless you've removed the lint first or the house might burn down.

Our mother has fallen asleep in the chair where she winds her bandages. Her arm stays in the air for some time. When Yvonne goes to take the bandage away our mother wakes up.

– I'm happy doing them myself, darling, she says. You go and talk to your sisters. Within a few minutes she is asleep again, the bandage rolling to the ground this time.

I'm trying so hard to describe my sisters I think I'm failing.

They love me in such a way they fall in love sometimes with the same women I do. They fall in love with my stories of them. They write to my lover and look towards mythical times when we can all spend more time in each other's company. I fall in love with women who are better storytellers than Mears girls.

I find Yvonne looking at the black and white photograph of H rowing, which I've stuck with superglue to my desk next to the shadow of Karin.

– She has beautiful eyebrows, says Yvonne. Just like in this piece of Isak Dinesen I'm reading, her small face, with its grandly swung eyebrows . . . I'd like to try a painting.

My sister can see the same things I see in the delicate and ageing face on my desk. The same mix of age and beauty touches Yvonne as it touches me. We allow our eyes to meet and glance away.

THE CHILDHOOD GLAND

— Do you want to come for a walk to the mail? I ask.

— No. No. I think it really has reached the stage where she shouldn't be left alone. We look away from each other again and then in the direction of our mother's bedroom, as if the walls may become transparent to our gaze.

— I think I could do anything and my sisters wouldn't mind, I tell H. Except disappear from their lives. Vanish.

As I'm approaching the letter box I hear the mailvan and take a cartoon-like leap behind the lantana. I watch the silver ribbons of Double Swamp Creek and its silver sand. I kill hopper ants as I wait. There is the teak tree. We used to paint the seedcases silver and gold and hang them in the she-oak trees at Christmas. Inside the seedcases are the seeds. Thrown into the wind they fly away like little fawn moths. The mailman goes way. Karin too, I've heard via Sonya, has become reclusive: taking off for the gully with her children until the sound of the visitor's car has gone away again. Perhaps reclusiveness is a kind of madness and the exclusive love we reserve for sisters part of that. I begin to fear Karin and I are social phobics. When we speak to other people, we confide, the pulse in our necks hammers so much it hurts. A telephone call from a stranger will leave me drenched in sweat. We talk in a quieter and quieter way. People have to say *What?!* They must lean in towards our faces.

There's a letter from Yvonne at the bottom of the bundle. Mail is always slow from the outer Brisbane suburb where she lives. The envelope's dirty. I keep leaving the track, bumping into trees, concentrating to make out the words, for although Yvonne is only ten minutes away, her letter is full of things it is hard to talk openly about. In between writing to me, her letter details, she's been sharpening knives, and one has just lopped the top off her thumb. Hence the blood. She quotes a few appropriate lines from a Plath poem and urges me to notice how her blood has fallen in diamond shapes onto my letter, describing its colour as well as foretelling that by the time it reaches me it will look like rust.

— You're right, I say to Yvonne, who's still sitting at my desk. Your blood did go like rust.

But we don't talk about what else is in the letter. I look at the sad rowing face of H but can't summon any kind of reality until glancing at Yvonne's face from this height, I suddenly know again, exactly how it would feel to put my lips onto the bone above H's eye. Have I always fallen in love with women who resemble a sister? And if so is this a bad thing? I want to write about my sisters but it is becoming very difficult.

I remember a boyfriend who travelled with a crayon self portrait and hung it in my room for a while.

— He hasn't enough room between his mouth and his nose Yvonne points out one day. And his fate's sealed.

Some would say we are very childish. We laugh like children, our glands of childhood keeping the pitch high. Or someone might say I have never separated sufficiently from my sisters, in a clinical sense, and they would be right. So that we feel silent except in their company, having in a way been robbed of a normal language.

— Is this also H? asks Yvonne, still looking at my noticeboard.

— No, that's Karin's shadow.

THE CHILDHOOD GLAND

Seventeen days after my birthday, our mother's abdomen is drained at the local hospital and her phoney pregnancy fails away from her. She seems to disappear in bed and for the first time in her life, doesn't get up. The next day Yvonne and Karin drive down again. My mother thinks the burble of their V8 engines is a jumbo jet flying overhead.

– I'll always be like another sister, won't I? She says with her hand in my hair.

These are her lasts words for me. She dies early in the morning. My ears seem to grow cold, as if they are being cried on. Our mother's face looks Byzantine and slightly mauve. At the moment, I still cannot look at photographs of Yvonne, Karin or Sonya upside down due to the impression this gives of somebody having taken photographs of my sisters after death.

There is a Tear Tree in Africa, I remember our mother telling us once, or perhaps it was on the Canary Islands, she is dead now and I cannot ever check the facts again, that cries for a week during the hot dry days just before the summer rains. The ground below such trees becomes saturated. The tree tears are large and rolling. This is how we cry, I think. And we cry with hardly any noise wishing our father wouldn't.

The mist is being ripped apart by sun as we walk away up the farm hill and look, look says Sonya, don't the early morning egrets look like tissue paper floating over the river? It is the first time I've ever held Sonya's hand, as opposed to shaken and squeezed it and I'm aware how delicate it is. Even when I was in the labour ward with her when BB her last son was born, she bit her own arm and didn't take my hand.

Later, when the funeral director comes, we all creep to other parts of the house. I watch from the water tank. The stretcher is green and there is the funeral director who is rumoured to drink gin lemonades each evening until he passes out.

Sonya spends the day dyeing all our mother's cashmere jumpers black. The cotton darns do not absorb the black pigment. In the laundry sink the jumpers look like drowned grey babies. She cries as she pokes at the jumpers still at the simmer on the stove. She walks from stove to sink and back again. Her crying sounds like a bird in danger that I don't know how to save.

Somebody takes a photo of us. My hand over Sonya's shoulder looks dead. As if somebody took it off at the wrist and hung it on a sister to drain.

Outside the cathedral is our mother's old car that she sold many years before. The cathedral is full, though only two or three people who were not daughters were allowed to visit her once she was sick. I look inside the car remembering the family dog Rolf as he looked laid out on a picnic rug after being hit by a car. The fleas were still alive. I kept wondering, as he was buried, are fleas on a dead dog like rats on a sinking ship? Would they know to get off before the earth began to go on? Our mother planted strawberries over Rolf, which were always eaten before they were ripe by other scavenging sisters.

Eileen deliberately misreads the reading:

. . . she brings home food from out of the way places, as merchant ships do. She gets up before daylight to prepare food for her family and to tell her servant girl what to do . . .

Servant girl not servant girls as really reads in the Bible. A small pun for us. A small pun from Eileen to make us smile through the crying.

In the church I see how the hairs on Yvonne's legs curl back under the black stockings Sonya lent her and that there are fissures and cracks in the heels of her feet. By the time we reach Copmanhurst cemetery the stockings have laddered on the skin of my sister's feet. Our mother would say dab a bit of nailpolish on, don't throw them out. I can hear her voice. She was frugal and extravagant both at once.

The hole that has been dug, says the funeral director, is big enough to fit a Volkswagen. We carry the coffin again and again I am too tall — unbalancing the rest of the sisters.

We all cry with only our left eyes, so that the gathering of people on the other side of us don't see our tears. I suppose this is peculiar.

– I want to be buried in a sheet, says Karin when it's just us left by the grave. Let the worms get to their work fast.

– Me too, says Sonya.

– Wrap me up in my stockwhip and blanket, says Yvonne.

– You can pop me in a crochet rug. We're really weeping now, both eyes, as well as laughing.

– Don't all just disappear at the farm, will you? says our father. I want you girls to talk to people.

We all disappear.

I dream my sisters die and wake up in sheets drowned in tears. It is the same when reading about the death of Janet Frame's sisters. And on a train journey to Sydney I hear two old sisters talking about the death of their youngest sister.

— Who'd ever have thought, they say to each other, that Eily would be the one to make the first break. They unwrap small squares of fruitcake to eat, oblivious to the tears slipping unhankied from my eyes. I can imagine nothing more painful than the death of one of my sisters and hold onto the selfish hope that like Eily, I will make the first break. This, it turns out, is also the wish of Yvonne, Karin and Sonya. Our mother died young and she was always sad. She had a sad core.

At Central there often seem to be sisters travelling to and from each other. I am sitting near an ancient little man. His wife is growling at him. 'She's just been with her sisters,' he says to me. 'Been visiting them in turn. She always gets like this afterwards. She'll settle down after awhile.'

It's as if nothing can quite match sisterly love. Maybe we hold irrationally tight to its sensations. Perhaps forever. We can't believe our mother has died. We return to the scene over and again. We tell stories to each other, trying to recollect exact sequences of events.

— I'm a Mears Girl, aren't I? says one of the nephews, sitting with his school shoes up against the kitchen counter. 'The Pale Dark', by Hampster Mears, he writes at the top of his picture while eating all the soft centres out of the chocolates our mother has given him to share out.

I have often written about sisters. Whenever writing about these fictional sisters I've found myself battling a sense of phoniness. I continue to wait for someone to point out to me that something is not quite right with the point of view of my sisters. What exactly do I mean? I mean I've always invented Australian voices for them, with retinues of Australian aunts, uncles, friends and grandmothers to prop up their voices. When in fact, the reality was only us. Only Yvonne, Karin, Gillian and Sonya. Take the first letter of each of my sisters, reverse the age order and you can spell the sky. I think of sisterly love as being blue and light or dark and sad, plumbago or plum-coloured, prone to change, affected by weather and mood. And shifts of alliance always rearranging the patterns that bind us. Sequins of shade and light seem to be dancing towards me from the leaves of the old Port Jackson fig. Thinking about sisters can make my sentences seem too tender.

It's dark under that tree. As the paraphernalia of death begins to surround our mother I go out into the garden and open my mouth under the tree to swallow in the cool and thick sensations. Yvonne pushes off a dog and sits in the giant grey padded recliner from the cancer clinic, which Sonya calls the throne. The tick-birds in the willows by the river made those trees look exotic and sad, like magnolia trees. The dark makes me feel like crying. Karin finds the first freesia and we take it in turns, dipping our long noses towards the flower that will accompany our mother to her death. Words desert us. A coolness floats from the flower in a way reminiscent of hanging wet, clean washing in a wind, or putting your face close up to dry ice.

We keep a fire going, so big the grate explodes.

We remember our mother loved fires. She would go out into the cold. I am looking for knubbly bits, she would say. She used to dry lines of wishbones for us above the fire in order that they would snap fairly. In order not to mix chicken grease and wishes. The delicate snap! Sonya used to suck the marrow out of bones. It is the day before Christmas when the ultrasound technician can't conceal his horror in front of our mother's gaze at what he sees in her liver and lungs, but that night she decorates the cake, apologising that the cake is so thin. Confessing that she has been taking off slivers from the bottom since it was made. Taking care not to disturb her icing.

Sonya thinks she will die by a blood vessel in her brain becoming so frail it bursts. Or maybe, she says, it will be a big crash from one of the racehorses she speeds around the Grafton racetrack on, in the near dark each morning. Asthma.

Karin thinks a shark is going to eat her and no longer swims in the sea or the river. Or that she has a slushy pulse and that will be her end.

— Have a feel, have a feel, she will say, placing your fingers to her neck so you can feel the slur of blood that is due to a damaged valve.

Yvonne looks me straight in the eye and says for her it will be a horse accident. She wants nothing less than a dramatic death.

Only when we die will our childhood gland also disappear. According to Karin's university notes the thymus, the gland of childhood, should shrivel and vanish by the time you are sixteen. It is the gland that keeps a child a child. I think we'd find ours still, in under our hearts and fatter than ever.

I write to Karin to tell her of my recurring image of her sitting in the rusting chair in the middle of her circular rosebed. In this image her baby is strapped to the front of her body and she holds a hose towards rose bushes afloat with old blossoms. Past the roses are yellow and green paddocks and beyond them the blue edges of Scenic Rim, so vague with mist they could be painted there in sunfaded watercolours. The baby Sonya sleeps with a mouth like a slightly open rosebud between my sister's breasts.

Karin writes back the same day on the back of an envelope. The grass has grown so high she would disappear if she sat down and only two rose flowers, like white faces, poke out at her over the jungle of grass and castor oil bushes.

— I AM a Mears Girl, says the same nephew, still sitting with his school shoes up against the kitchen counter. Sonya? he asks.

Sometimes I think I know everything there is to know about my sisters but this isn't true. I talk about them too much to strangers and worry afterwards that I've left out everything that is important.

Like the shadows on a sister's neck from an earring. Moving as she laughs. Look! I want to say. I have always wanted people to see everything that is beautiful about them. For the ordinary to be transformed. See their necks so long and swannish when they tip back their heads to laugh. The Mears crest is four English swans. There on all the old cutlery and seals.

And the way they make their children laugh.

How Yvonne urges me to tell my stories sideways. Her mind going at a hand gallop to my steady pace. And she would tell everything differently, faster, with a blare. All my sisters would and there would be different stories, and other memories, less defined, incomplete, mysterious to me – of our childhood – where figures and events keep slipping in and out of focus. Such movement.

See, I want to say.

HALFLEAD BAY

Nam Le

IT WAS SHAPING UP to be a good summer for Jamie. Exams were over. School was out in a couple of weeks – the holidays stretching before him, wide and flat and blue. On top of that he was a hero. Sort of. At assembly that morning, the principal had paused after his name and the school had broken into spontaneous cheering and clapping. Jamie was onstage with the rest of the first eighteen. He could barely make out the faces beneath him – the lights turned off on account of the heat – but what he remembered were voices swelling out of the large, dim hall as though out from one of his daydreams. You couldn't buy that feeling. Still, his dad. Seated in the front row with the other guests of honour – unimpressed as ever. His smile as stiff as his suit.

'Carn, Halfies!' the principal called out. He opened his arms. From the back of the hall students started stomping their feet.

Jamie had scored the winning goal in last week's semifinal. For the first time in five years, Halflead Bay High had a real crack at reclaiming the pennant. All his school years Jamie couldn't recall even having a conversation with Alan Leyland, the principal, but now Leyland turned around from the podium and half bowed to him. Everyone looked at the two of them. Then the cry was taken up – *Halfies! Carn,*

Halfies! – even teachers, parents, joining in, Jamie still and rapt in the hot roar until he arrived, again, at his dad's face. The uneasy grin. Of course. The stomping, chanting, Leyland's theatrical attitude: a faint film of mockery slid over it all. Jamie pushed it aside. His dad was wrong, he thought. He was wrong, and anything was possible.

ALISON FISCHER APPROACHED HIM AT RECESS.

'Leyland was licking your arse,' she said.

He clutched up from the drinking fountain, mouth brimming water, swallowed. 'Hi,' he said. The word came out in a burp and left a wet trail down his chest.

'Hi yourself.'

She stood with her head cocked to one side, hip to the other. Her school dress was stretched so tight it bit into her thigh. He wiped his mouth, looked around. Alison Fischer. It was a morning of firsts.

'Leyland couldn't be stuffed about footy.'

'What?'

'He's thinking about enrolments,' Jamie said. He tried to remember how his mum had put it. 'He just wants the pennant to sucker new parents.'

'Shove over,' Alison ordered. She bent down to the nozzle and pursed her mouth in a glossy O. Her top button was undone – sprung open as though by heat – and he could see the inside line of her breasts. The stripe of sweat gleaming between them.

She said, 'I've seen you down at the wharf.' Her lips bright wet.

'I'm working there these holidays.'

'Nah, the jetty, I mean. Fishing. With that surfie mate of yours.'

'Cale?'

He looked around again. Most of the kids had stayed indoors for recess; others were lying in shade, as still as snakes, under the casuarinas. It was too hot for sport. Off in the paddocks a knot of boys poked at something on the ground. Alison switched hips and smiled patiently at him.

'That was your dad in there, right?'

'My dad?' He laughed weakly.

'With the tie.'

This was how it happened: these girls, they did it for kicks, daring each other to go up to random blokes and act interested. He'd seen it before. A gaggle of them – Alison their leader – sitting apart from everyone else, watching on; they sealed off even their amusement, coughing it around their circle like a wet scrap. Tammie, Kate, Laura – all the rest of them, faces mocked up – they were bored with everything and totally up themselves and every boy at Halflead wanted them.

'He didn't even come to the game.'

'*My* parents,' she said, 'after *that* game.' Her smile went lopsided. 'I reckon they'd adopt you.'

He pretended to wave away a fly, looked around again. None of them were in sight. No Dory either. The sound of a piano started up from somewhere – each note hung – tin-flat, percussive – then evaporated in the heat. So she wanted to talk about the game. No way they'd mess with him, not after last weekend. That assembly. She was alone. She was smiling at him as though she didn't belong to somebody else.

'That'd make you my sister.'

'We couldn't have that, right?'

Whoever was at the piano was a beginner, trying out a new scale: slow, stop-start. Jamie felt himself trapped between the notes, inside the heavy spaces where nothing moved. He realised his whole body was sweating. So she'd talk about his dad – himself sweating in that funereal suit, several sizes too small for him, cuffs up past his wrists – and he'd let her. Applause in his ears. That wry, sceptical smirk.

'So you reckon we can beat Maroomba?'

'I'm there heaps,' he said. His voice came out rougher than he'd intended. 'The jetty, I mean.'

'What?'

'Don't be such a bloody snob. Say hi next time.'

'And then what?'

'What are you after?'

'Alison!' a voice called from the school building. Everyone started moving back inside. The sound of the piano petered out, blaring moments later as passing hands bashed its keys.

She leaned toward him. That band of sweat between her breasts – he wanted to bring his mouth to it and lick it up. He wanted her to giggle, push him away, tell him it tickled. Her smile seemed different now.

'I can teach you how to squid,' he said.

'Fuck,' she said in a low voice, 'you're a fast worker, aren't you?'

He didn't say anything.

'Who would've guessed it. Loose Ball Jamie – that's what they call you, right?'

His face flushed. Someone shouted her name again. The school grounds were almost empty now but he had the overwhelming feeling of being watched. Every window in the building blazed with reflected light.

He inclined his head in the classroom's general direction. 'We should —'

'So is that what I am? A loose ball?' Her voice went weird, slightly off-pitched: ' "Just come down to the jetty and say hi?" '

The sweat on her collarbones, too, burned white in the sun. The back of her hip-cocked arm. That was the problem with Alison Fischer: you never knew which part of her to look at. He looked at her face. She was grinning crookedly, her mouth still wet.

DORY'S GIRL – SHE WAS DORY'S GIRL – but then who knew how serious that was? Jamie had liked her for ever. And not just in the way everyone talked, in the change rooms, about chicks at school: Laura Brescia, who wore a G-string under her school uniform; Tammie K, who gave Nick a head job and then gave Jimmy one as well so he wouldn't dob about Nick to her big-smoke boyfriend. She was gagging but kept going, Jimmy crowed. He mimed it: gripping her long hair, kneading it into her scalp. No– Alison was more than that. She ran with that crowd but kept herself apart, reserving herself, everyone knew, for the thrall of the big city. Where her family – and their money – were from. Where everyone assumed she'd head once accepted into the university there next year. Until this morning, Jamie would never even have thought to lob his hopes that high.

Still. Dory Townsend. You'd have to be a lunatic.

THEY LIVED, THE FOUR OF THEM, on a spur overlooking the sea. Their house must have been one of the most elevated in town. His parents had bought it twenty years ago, back when Halflead Bay was little more than a petrol station and stopover to and from the city. According to Jamie's mum, that was how they'd first met: she was filling the tank of her rented car when his dad's crew traipsed up from the wharf and into the pub. He was the one who walked without moving his hands. Hungry, worn out from her day in an adverse office – she worked, then, as a forensic accountant – she'd decided to go in too, for a counter meal. Two months later – her own car fully loaded, her career resolutely behind her – she returned to seek out the man who'd seemed, all that evening, to stand for a world of simpler details: a big sky, a sustaining sea, a chance to do work whose usefulness a child could understand.

At first they stayed with his dad's folks on the southern prom. A family of fishermen. Then, when they got married, they moved up the hill. Before the advent of all the developers and holiday-homers, the winemakers and tourists. Back then, Jamie's dad said, you could buy property for next to nothing: the town was dying, haemorrhaging people and industry first as the bay was overfished, then again when Maroomba poached its port traffic. Only the few hardy locals stayed behind. For the next fifteen years his parents had lived exactly how they'd dreamed, his dad skippering one of the town's few remaining trawlers, his mum working on her landscapes – seascapes, really – low, bleached blocks of colour settling on a horizontal line. Sky and sea. It was why she'd picked this place. She needed to live in sight of the ocean as much as his dad needed to be on it.

Then, five years ago – the diagnosis. MS. The devastating run of relapses. Despite his wife's protests, Jamie's dad sold his stake in the trawler – started working in the home workshop, knocking out shop fittings, furniture. Jamie and Michael kept going to school. Everyone carried on – working through, around, the illness – as though every moment wasn't actually a dare. As though every word wasn't a word more, every act a further act of waiting.

MICHAEL WAS STANDING at the mouth of the driveway. His body bleared in the heat haze above the bitumen. Coming closer, Jamie felt a spark of affection toward him and almost called out his name.

'Dad wants us,' Michael said first. He didn't look up from his Game Boy.

'I'm gonna head down the jetty.' He hesitated, watching Michael's thumbs wagging on the grey console. 'You can come if you like.'

'They're fighting.'

'So?'

'I just told you, they're fighting.' His voice was too deep for a ten-year-old.

Jamie stopped himself laughing. 'Mum okay?' He peered up the slope. The house was barely visible from the road, blotted out by foliage: ironwoods, kurrajongs, ghost gums bursting up through the brush. The garden was wild. As he started up the driveway, everything described itself as though to Alison: overhanging branches, knee-high grass, yellowed in places by warped, gutted objects – miscarriages of his mum's interest. Sprockets of leaves. Green everywhere plaited with brightly coloured spikelets and bracts. There was his bedroom, the shedlike bungalow. Once his mum's studio, it still gave off an aftersmell of turpentine – faint as something leaked by a body in the dark and dried by morning. And there, a stone's throw away at the top of the driveway, was their double-storied house: a worn weatherboard that seemed choked by bushes and creepers, by the old white verandah that buckled all around it. What would she make of it?

He went round the back and into the workshop. The lamps – they must have made it ten degrees hotter indoors. His dad was bent over a long, slightly curved piece of wood, one end wrapped in tape like a boxer's fist.

'I'm almost done,' his dad said. His shirt clung wetly all the way down his back, right down to the apron string. 'Figured it out. Front struts were too heavy, that's why it wouldn't rock.' Using vice-grip pliers, he clamped down on the taped end with his left hand. With his right he started planing the length of the wood. The top half of the chair – the seat and back – lay tipped forward on the table before him.

'I'm going down the jetty,' said Jamie.

'Storm's coming.'

'Yeah?'

'Day or two. I need you to bring in your mum's stuff first.'

'Okay.'

'Make sure you look everywhere. Her stuff's everywhere.'

'Okay.'

'Hang on,' his dad said. He put down his tools and turned around. His face and neck – except for two white trapezoids behind his goggles – were plastered with a skin of sawdust. It cracked around his mouth when he smiled. 'You should've heard them cheering this morning,' he said. 'For your brother.'

Jamie was confused, then heard Michael's voice: 'What'd they say?' His brother stepped around him into the workshop.

Their father aimed a roughhouse swat at Michael's hair, then wiped his own brow with the back of his gloves, leaving a wavy orange smear. 'Sounds like we missed a big game. But we'll make it next week.' He nodded at Michael, the smile still tight and dry on his face. Was he taking the piss? 'Biggest game of all, right?'

'We're gonna get slaughtered,' said Michael.

'Shut up,' said Jamie.

Michael shied away, out of his reach. 'Everyone says so.'

'Boys.'

'Okay,' said Jamie. 'I'll move the stuff to the shed.' He kicked some dust at Michael. 'Come on.'

'Hang on.' His dad took off his gloves, then his safety goggles. Sawdust swirled in the lamplight. 'I need you boys to do something for me,' he said. 'For your mum.'

He went to the sink. Using the heel of his palm, he pushed open the tap, then washed his hands under the water violently, absorbedly, the old habit of a fisherman scrubbing off a day's stink. He threw water on his face.

'I got an offer on the house,' he said.

Neither of them said anything.

'It wouldn't be till January. But they need our go-ahead by Friday.' After a moment, he reached behind himself and untied his apron, looped it over his head. 'We talked about this.' He glanced at Jamie. 'I know you got that dock job these holidays. Shouldn't clash, though.'

Michael said, 'I don't wanna move.'

Jamie corked him just beneath the shoulder. He felt his knuckle meet bone: that one would bruise.

'Don't,' said Michael.

'Don't be such a little dickhead then.'

Their dad frowned at them, blinking water, rust-coloured, out of his eyes. Michael massaged his arm and muttered, 'That was a good one.'

'But Mum wants to stay here,' said Jamie. He was thinking about Alison.

'Last month,' said his dad, 'when me and your mum went to Maroomba.' He inhaled noisily, the sawdust jiggling on air currents in front of his face. 'We talked about this,' he repeated. 'Everything's in Maroomba. All the facilities. Your mum – right now – she needs to be there.'

'What's that mean, "right now"?'

His dad sighed. 'Come on, Jamie.'

Earlier that year he'd seen his mum naked, slouched back, knees spread, in the bathtub and his dad kneeling over her, holding a sponge. The water was foamless and he saw everything – most of her body the colour of the water except for two large dark nipples, her pubic hair. Dark spots wrinkling under the liquid skin. That time, her eyes were closed.

'I need you boys to talk to her. Tell her you don't mind. Moving, I mean.'

'She doesn't want to, but.'

'Not if you boys keep acting like this. Like you don't want to either.' He ran his hands through his hair, orange sweating down his forehead.

Her body a ghostly rippling film of her body. Ever since the diagnosis she'd been separating, bit by bit, from her own body. His dad hadn't even fully turned around from the tub. *Come on, Jamie* – he'd said that then too.

'What'd the doctors say?' Jamie asked at last. He remembered, before they'd left for Maroomba a few weeks ago, his mum's familiar protests – she was okay, she didn't need to go, not this time.

'Jesus – what's so bloody complicated about it, son?' His dad was blinking hard now, as if to bully his eyes into some new clarity. 'You can't just do what I tell you?'

Michael, still caressing his arm, didn't look up.

His dad went to the sink and washed his face again. A stool beside him was stacked high with creased linen and he used a corner of the top sheet to towel off. His face in his hands, he said, 'You know what she's like.'

'Sorry,' said Jamie. His voice sounded too loud. 'I'll talk to her.'

After a few moments, his dad nodded. 'So you going down the jetty.'

'Probably the flats first.'

'Sandworm?'

'Yeah.'

'We need to let the buyers know by Friday.'

'I know.'

By then – Friday – the sheets would be washed, hanging from lines that zigzagged across the backyard. They'd fill with light and puff themselves up like curtains. She'd be upstairs, on her reclining couch, looking the other way. Out toward the water.

'You know what she's like,' his dad repeated.

HE'D FALLEN OFF THE JETTY ONCE. He was with a group of mates, chucking rocks at the moored boats. Longest throw won, loser was a poofter. His turn: one moment he was doing a run-up and the next he was dead – what death must be like – a thrown switch, a fizzling of the senses, the sound sucked out of things. Your eyes a dark cold green hurt.

He'd come into his mum's studio and offered her his head.

'This is what I mean,' she said in her clear voice. His dad was by the window, leaning heavily with crossed arms over the top of an easel, a sandwich in one hand. Underneath him a canvas was set and stretched and primed – this was years ago, when she would work on several paintings at the same time.

'I better go, Maggie, I'm late. What happened?'

Jamie looked up. His dad's forearms seemed as dense as the wood they rested on, scored with scabs, sun lesions. He stuffed the last of the sandwich into his mouth and came closer.

'You okay, son?'

His mum poured Dettol on the wound, rubbed it in with her sleeve. The thin, toxic fluid leaked down Jamie's face and into his mouth. In his spit, still, the gagging memory of seawater.

His mum slapped her palm against his dad's cheek as he was leaving, pulled it in for a kiss. 'Of course he is,' she said.

At first she kept it to herself. There may have been minor episodes but Jamie and Michael were both at school, their dad out on the trawler all day. She worked alone. Her city life a lifting impression. By that time she was beginning to make a name for herself painting with big steel spatulas, smearing and scraping her compositions over broad canvases. She mixed her own paint. The house and studio and yard were cluttered with the junk of her labour: glass panes and book dust jackets used as makeshift palettes, improvised seashell slabs as mullers. Every window she passed was thrown open – for ages afterward she'd come across sketches and enigmatic notes to herself crammed between books, weighted down under tins of pigment powder, turps, and binding oils. Even before the diagnosis, her work – and it was heavy work – seemed driven by mania.

As if she knew. As if before it all, she already understood how it would happen: one moment you were bunching up the full strength of your body for a throw and the next you lost your purchase on everything, you'd slipped on squid guts and woke up drowning in paint, your body a hurt, disobedient in paper-thin sleeves. After all, what was to say it shouldn't hurt? – to feel, or move; to push a hand or eye across a plane? If your body endured for no real reason, what was to say you should feel anything at all?

SEAGULLS, HUNDREDS OF THEM, wheeled and skirled overhead. Jamie lay down on his back and followed the light-dark specks against the sunlight, tuning out Cale's voice.

'Easy, big man,' Cale was saying. 'Easy.' He was talking to Michael, his speech already slurry with pot.

'The backpackers too.'

'Nah, big man, they're not the enemy,' said Cale. 'Them and the blackfellas, they just mind their own business. They're all right by me. It's the holiday-homers, those rich wankers. And the local bogans.'

'Yeah.'

'And the Asians, hey,' Cale added.

The line tweaked under Jamie's fingertips. He sat upright, fumbled with the rod, but already he could tell the tension had slipped out of it. Seaweed, probably. He sucked down a couple of deep breaths to ease the head rush.

'Some of them are okay,' mumbled Michael. 'At school.' He was playing with a scuffed cricket ball, sending it into elaborate spins from right hand to left.

Cale turned his attention to Jamie. 'Monster bite, hey?'

Jamie couldn't remember how they'd become mates. Cale had

blown into town a couple of terms ago and started hanging around the beach. Just another shaggy-blond layabout in his vaguish twenties. One day he ran up the jetty and helped Jamie gaff a big banjo. They clubbed it dead and Cale held it up under the gills, both of them gape-mouthed, then introduced himself: he was from out west, a surf-chaser: he'd surfed off the coast of Tassie, in Hawaii, around the Horn in South Africa. That leather topaz-studded necklace had been souvenired from his girlfriend's body, wiped out in Europe. He'd glazed his eyes, letting that sink in. Sure, he'd teach Jamie to longboard.

'You're stoned.'

Cale nodded, almost shyly, then his face sank into its usual easy, thick-lipped smile. 'Those Israelis, man. Always farkin stashed.' He teetered up in his red boardshorts and reeled in his line. After prolonged examination, he set a fresh worm on the hook.

'You seen them?' he asked Jamie. 'Out near the heads?'

'The Israelis?'

'The Asians, you dimwit.'

'What about them?'

'The reef. That's where they poach now.'

He had, of course, from a distance. Everyone had. Sliding in and out of rubber dinghies, slick-faced – indistinct even about town where they banded together, laughing in low lilts. An impudence in their laughter. And why not? thought Jamie. They pretty much ran the fishing racket in town now – they'd bought out the fish plant when it was going belly-up years ago. He vaguely recalled being dragged to those rowdy town meetings – all the tirades against those money-grubbing Chinks – his parents arguing on the way home.

'Makes sense,' Jamie said. 'Hundred bucks a kilo.'

Michael looked up. 'A hundred bucks?'

'That's right, big man. Flog it off to posh restaurants, don't they? And those restaurants, they flog it off to posh wankers — for ten times that much.'

'Ten times easy,' said Jamie.

'Farkin abalone.' Cale grinned. 'A month's pay, hey?'

Jamie's parents, finally, had agreed to his getting a job over the break. He'd have cash of his own. He'd be able to buy things. He was starting at the fish plant, where Cale worked as well, but secretly he hoped to get a spot on a commercial boat before too long. He was his dad's son, after all.

Michael started whistling, then stopped. Jamie lay down on his back. The wooden planks seared his skin for a second, then eased their heat throughout his body. He closed his eyes: a dark orange glow, shadowed fitfully by gulls. He felt, in his bones, the slap of Michael's cricket ball against his palm. Muzzy with warmth, he allowed himself to relive that morning's assembly: the gale of applause . . . Alison . . . but each time, at that point, his mind looped back around. He found himself thinking about Dory. That huge, mean body — the man's face on top of it. He'd been held back a couple of years. He'd been full forward for Halflead four years running. From the sudden silence, the irregular scuffing of feet, Jamie could tell Michael had tossed the ball high into the air. He pictured it arcing slowly up, out — over the water. The dangerous thought came; he brushed around it, then let it in: What if they — Alison and Dory — weren't together any more? When was the last time, anyway, anyone had seen them together? Michael caught the ball. Then, against the planking . . . *thump* . . . *thump* . . . each bounce a mottling shape in the sunglow.

'Cut it out,' Jamie murmured.

The bouncing stopped. Cale wet his lips loudly. Water lapped against the pylons.

'So,' said Cale. 'What the fark.'

Jamie remained quietly on his back.

'Look who's in a good mood lately.' He said it accusingly. 'Alison Fischer. She got anything to do with it?'

'What?'

'Yeah yeah.' His mouth made more slopping noises. 'What a shifty cunt. You, I mean.'

Jamie sat up, opened his eyes – the world bursting yellow and vivid – and gestured his head toward Michael. His brother's shape crouched over the tackle box.

'Sorry.' Cale lowered his voice. 'He's always around so I forget.'

'What'd you hear?'

'Nothing.' He smirked. 'She's a bit all right – that's all.' He licked two fingers and held them curled upward, then glanced dramatically at Michael. 'Remember Stevo . . . Stefan? That Danish show pony? He reckons he got a finger in – you know. After that school play in April.'

Jamie rolled over onto his stomach. He hadn't expected word to come round so quickly. Who was where, with who, how far they got – a town like this spread gossip like the clap. Cale, despite being older, hung out a lot with high-schoolers – couldn't hack being out of the loop. He was looser-lipped than any girl. But it'd only been a couple of hours since Alison had come up to Jamie . . . and – he kept reminding himself – nothing had happened.

Cale paused. 'Good thing Dory never found out . . . that time.'

'Shut up.'

Of course what Cale meant was: Remember those other times? Jamie remembered. The whole town remembered. There was an element of community ritual in remembering all the things Dory was known or suspected to have done. The worst, of course, being the to-do with the Chinese poacher. Never cleared up. He was only twenty but he stood in as the town's hard man. And Alison – the girl with the silver spoon, the girl with the reputation – was known to give him plenty of reason for it.

'So?' said Cale.

'You don't know shit.'

Cale nodded in satisfaction. 'Ahh,' he said. 'If only you truly believed that.'

Jamie laid one eye up against a crack between two timbers, felt the old, beaten wood on his face. If he could choose a place – if it could be all his – this was it. Strange how trying to think and trying to forget amounted to the same thing here. Cale was still talking about Alison. The sound of his voice familiar, pointless, in keeping with the complaint of the mooring lines, the metal creakings from the wharf's gantry crane across the bay. He was talking about Alison and Jamie wasn't listening but then something dislodged itself from the craw of his memory and the incident was undammed, clear and natural as breathing: last summer – sun-white day – Jamie crabbing on the flats when word was sprinted down from town: *Fight*. The thrill in his blood as he raced up the main street. Kids streaking in from every direction, breathlessly swapping accounts on the way: Dory – him and some bloke – Vance Wilhelm, that was his name – who'd been spending time with Alison. Sirens started up to the south just as Jamie veered into the main carpark. Through the mayhem he took in the whole scene at once: a black jeep, its windshield smashed, keeled back at an odd uphill slope; people limping off, nursing arms; the flash of a blood-slagged face. He was about to scatter as well when he saw, on a grassy strip, two bodies asprawl one another – elbows bloody, pebbled with glass – one finally hoisting, shunting its knee into the other's back, wrenching the head up into an armlock. The face looked full at Jamie. It was Lester – Dory's best friend. *Jamie,* it gasped, *get him off me.*

'Hey, Romeo,' Cale called out.

Always he returned to this. *Get him off me.* And – weak in the legs – he'd frozen. A heavy shape barrelled across his vision and lifted the body clean off Lester and drove it hard into the ground. Trapped beneath Dory's weight, it gave out an odd creaking sound. Jamie circled around for a last look, saw Dory holding down the head, then saw the stranger's face – it could only have been Wilhelm – his mouth agape and crammed over a steel sprinkler head, cheeks streaming and shuddering. His face a picture of drowning. Lester staggered to his feet and glared at Jamie, then Dory looked up at him too. Lester made to speak but Dory stopped him. His arms still bearing down on Wilhelm's head, he'd said: *You're rubbish.*

But that was a year ago. Now, things were different. He was a hero now.

'Hey, Jamie, wake up.' Cale's voice sounded as though it had risen a metre.

'Hmm.'

'Your girlfriend's here.'

'Piss off.'

Bit by bit his thoughts tailed off; he began to feel the knurled wood jutting into his hip bone. His back roasting. He gazed down. Small schools of baitfish inflected the clear water. Old squidding lines and sinkers caught on the crossplanks, bearded with kelp.

'Nothing you wanna say to her?'

Jamie reached behind himself and pulled down his boardshorts, flapping one bum cheek open and shut: 'Piss . . . off.'

Michael sniggered.

'Piss . . . off . . . Cale . . . y.'

'Any luck?'

A girl's voice – he spun over, shielded his eyes. It couldn't be. She was standing at the head of the jetty with Tammie, both decked out in their netball gear. Alison still wearing a bib that spelled 'GA' – goal attack – in large lettering. Cale, next to him, cracking up.

'Nope,' reported Michael. 'No fish.'

'What'd I say?' said Cale.

'You're a fuckwit,' said Jamie.

'I'm a fuckwit? Whose knickers are down?'

Even Michael couldn't conceal his smile. Tammie laughed, a squeezed sound like the yapping of a small dog. She was playing with her camisole straps, studying him.

'You told me to come,' said Alison.

He got up, face burning. He felt suddenly naked in front of them. Even though everyone, all summer, went around in just their boardies, he felt naked. 'We're actually heading back,' he said, gesturing to Michael. Why had he said that?

'Cool,' said Alison. 'Carn then.' She turned to address Cale: 'There's a party on Thursday. Slogger Tom's place – you should come too.'

'What's in it for me?'

For a second Jamie was thrilled by his friend's boldness, then he felt strangely uneasy.

'You're Cale, right?'

'Yep,' he said, grinning broadly.

But Alison didn't fall for his act. Her voice turned clerical, polished: 'This is Tammie.' Tammie smiled dutifully. She was hot all right, thought Jamie, but when she smiled there was something puddled about her face.

Cale said, 'So *this* is Tammie.'

The whole way, Michael walked in front of them, lugging the gear in one hand and his cricket ball in the other. He kept his head bowed and never looked back. By some instinct he led them a roundabout route – avoiding the foreshore, the main street with its drab, dusty stretch of shops – and cut across the edge of the tidal flats. The afternoon was cooling fast.

Still plenty of people around.

When they reached the asphalt Alison touched her hand to the back of Jamie's elbow. She crossed the road and started hiking up the scrubby slope. Jamie watched his brother trudge the other way, up the road to their house. Then, without a word, he followed Alison. The ground beneath them skiddy with shell grit. As they climbed, the sun absorbed itself into her body: calves, hamstrings, the belt of skin above her skirt, the backs of her golden arms. The glaring nylon letters on her bib. She scuffed through the saltbush and mulga, kicking up little plumes of dust, and he stepped hypnotically into them.

They reached the clearing. At the centre of the bluff – on its highest table of land – was the old stone courthouse, long ago ruined. It was arched with white, oxidised columns, reared against a low sky. The seaward wall had been torn away by the weather, creating the impression of a great stage overlooking the ocean.

Alison led him around the jagged masonry and leaned against a wall, bouncing on her heels.

'What's the saddest place you know,' she said, 'this is mine.'

He didn't speak. Baffled by her question. Still catching up to the fact of being there, alone, with her. Then he said, 'Why?'

Before her sickness, his mum had often dragged him here in the dark of first morning. She liked painting the sea before sunlight came up and flattened the water. He'd cart her stuff along the ridge, trying to stay awake, and she'd talk, sometimes to him, sometimes to herself. She'd always been fascinated by the courthouse's history. How, more than a hundred years ago, the town council, flush with fishing money, had commissioned a series of public buildings – of which the courthouse was to be the first – and how, a week after the naming ceremony, a storm had rolled in and ripped it apart. According to the legend, the chief benefactor, after whom the courthouse was named, had packed his wife and five children into a skiff the very next day and rowed them out to sea – never to be seen again. The story appealed equally to his mum's senses of the romantic and the absurd. The town had abandoned its building program, closed off all the access roads. Too many bad omens all round. As she laughed to herself he'd see the courthouse ahead, floaty and blue-glowing – hinting at a past that seemed, at that hour, still very much present.

'Have you ever . . ?' Alison began. 'Nah, that's stupid.'

Below them sunlight lay over the whole bay. The sea breathed against the lip of the pale shore. Back from the water's edge, flats and dunes encircling it, the town glinted like a single eye.

'What?'

'Nah.'

He looked around, listened. So exposed up here. The wind loud and brackish. He made out somewhere nearby the clickety sound of skateboarders, the high-pitched drone of jet skis out on the water. Human voices skimming like mozzies across its surface.

He turned away from the sea and pointed out his family's house on the adjoining spur, along the winding saddle.

'That's you guys?' she asked.

'My mum used to come here to paint.'

She let it pass. She said, 'Your brother looks like you,' then, noting his lack of enthusiasm, went on, 'You'd think you'd get an awesome view from up here – of all places, right?' It came out in a single quick exhalation: 'But you look and you look and everything's just shit-house.' Skating her hands down the side of her pleated skirt: 'Your friend, Cale, is he always high?'

'He's a good bloke.'

She didn't seem happy with that.

'His girlfriend died in Europe,' he added lamely.

'Europe?' Her voice twisted up.

'Yeah, he's been everywhere. Hawaii and Africa and everywhere, before he came here.'

She chortled. 'Why would anyone come here?'

Now she'd stopped bouncing, now she was brushing her hands together. Both of her hands were within reach.

'I mean,' she said, 'there's not even fish here any more.'

With other girls, it was just the next thing – hands, neck, pash, fingers under their tops. But with her, for him, nothing was next.

'Carn, then,' she said softly.

She eased forward and leaned her body into his bare chest. Her smile lopsided, bigger and bigger. Then her mouth sprang open and then they were kissing. He was kissing Alison Fischer. There was a mineral tizz on her tongue, the smell of wet rock. He lifted his hand to her hair.

'Ugh.' She stepped back, soles crunching on broken glass. 'It stinks in here.' She skipped over to the opposite wall, standing beneath a deep, high crevice that might once have held a window. The wind even choppier in that corner.

'Animals come here for shelter,' he said. Who'd told him that? The musty smell seemed familiar.

'Well, they stink.'

She kissed him again. He felt the start of a hard-on, pressing through the mesh lining of his shorts – then quickly wilting. Maybe thinking about it. Maybe thinking about Dory. An awful lag behind this happening and the idea of it. She lifted her bib and wiped her mouth.

'Okay, then,' she said.

'Sorry.'

Wordlessly they looked out of the broken wall over the bay. The sun full in the sky. There was a blue kite on the wind and far below, way out on the ocean coast, the black half-bodies of surfers, ducking into early-breaking waves or standing, slewing across the tall steep faces until they dropped into white slag. Every ride ended in failure. He'd never noticed this before.

'I'm not scared, you know.'

He didn't say anything.

'Me and him aren't really together.'

'Who, Dory?' He tried to sound nonchalant.

'Everyone just assumes.' She smiled into the open, blustery air. 'So how well do you know him? Are you guys, like, friends?'

'Dory?'

'No, the fucking postman. Yes, Dory.'

'I mean,' Jamie said carefully, 'we play on the same team. He's a good ruck.' He paused for a moment. 'A good bloke.'

'A good bloke,' she mimicked.

He fell silent. The water of the bay seemed, if possible, to bulge. In that light it seemed as though the courthouse was tilting, about to slide into the ocean.

'See that?'

The kite hung in the high wind, still and full. Then a slip of colour again. Way out a ship coughed up black smoke ever more feebly. He realised she was looking off to one side – past the dunes, past the old rock pier, even – to the low, wet lines of swale behind. Deep where it was dark, shallow where pooled with light.

'That's where he lives,' she said. 'With his uncle.'

'Good fishing out there.' Immediately, the rock pier imagined itself into his mind. Black and slick, lathered with surf. He'd managed, for so long, not to think about it.

'Their place, though – you wouldn't believe.'

But it, too, was clear to him: one of those fibro, tin-roofed affairs, a single naked bulb shearing light through planked windows. He'd seen it from the boat. Stray dogs ganging outside.

'How much cash you got on you?' she asked abruptly.

'Cash?'

She stepped out from the stone recess and a breeze snapped up a fistful of her hair, suspended it above her head.

'We could go to the bottle shop,' she said.

He thought frantically for a moment. 'What about ID? Do you have – I know, we could get Cale's ID.'

But she was already somewhere else in her head. It struck him she was bored with him. Without warning she came over and leaned into his shoulder and, slowly collapsing her knees, traced her upper lip – inch by inch – all the way down to the tips of his fingers. He stood there inside the stone walls, suffused in sun, shock-still, the hot tension through his body almost painful. What happened now?

'It's you!' She crinkled up her nose. 'You! You stink of fish.'

His cheeks flared red. 'Shit,' he said. He brought up his fingers and smelled them. Bait. 'You're right. Shit, sorry.'

She hopped back with a childlike little scowl. He struggled for an excuse and she watched him, letting him struggle, saying nothing. Finally he slinked off. Now she was saying something but he was too busy with shame to take in the words. The easterly gusted up. Then, at the edge of the granite ruin, he forced himself to turn around.

'There's tonight,' she called into the wind's low howl.

'What?' He cupped his ear.

'Thursday night,' she was saying. 'See you Thursday night.'

HIS MUM WAS DYING and seemed torn between ignoring it and rushing toward it. She wanted to meet it in the middle of many arrangements. After the first relapse – the scans, the taps, the tests – she sank back into her work, her only concession to the diagnosis being a switch from spatulas to paintbrushes. She spent even more time outdoors, painting, gardening. She was always a physical gardener, sporting Blundstone boots and a singlet, gloves up to her elbows and her ginger hair scrunched back with anything at hand – a rubber band, a torn strip from a plastic bag. She was indefatigable. If asked, she'd say it was just like pins and needles. What was the phrase people used? – she refused to become her illness. She beat it back.

Then, two years ago, the second major relapse. She claimed, afterward, that she didn't remember any of it. But she'd seen him. They'd seen each other. She'd lain on her side, the easel also knocked on its side. It was as though she'd been dancing with it and they'd tripped over together. Her face was compressed against the floor, strands of hair streaked diagonally across it, captured as though in a thrash of passion. Everywhere there was bright cerulean blue paint, the entire floor slick and sky-coloured, a centimetre deep, leaching into her arms, her scissored legs, her smock and boots. Her palms were vivid orange.

'Mum,' he said.

But she couldn't speak. The blue paint coated her lips – through it he saw the tip of her blue tongue – it matted her hair, enclosed her right eye like a face mask. That eye was open. It didn't blink. You could see. It was nightmare in her head.

'Mum?'

Never – it'd never been this serious. Once before, he'd come upon her slumped on the kitchen lino. Just dizzy, she'd said. She'd made him promise not to tell Dad. He knelt, now, watching her. He put out his hand but it seemed incapable of touching anything. Her eye roved, jerkily, like a puppet's, around the room – to him – away – to him again. She was frozen in the middle of her mangled sidestroke, the paint frothing in front of her mouth. Slowly it hardened into a lighter blue paste. He felt as if he were breathing it as well. Then the footsteps, the bottomed-out growl of his dad's voice – what happened, how long, how long – *how long* – the dark form crouching down, standing up, crouching down again and cutting off her hair, the crunch of the scissors, then stripping her up, limb by limb, out of the dry blue muck. A long pause.

Come on, Jamie.

Once, he'd seen her in front of the bathroom mirror. She was plunging a bone-grey comb again and again into her hair, as though punishing it. Arms trembling. She caught his eye in the mirror and smiled. Here, she said, holding it out. Help me.

He washed the sand off his feet at the outside tap. When he came into the living room she shifted in her reclining couch, in his direction. She looked shrunken, he thought, diluted somehow. The red of her hair slowly ashing.

'I could see you,' she said, 'at the courthouse.' A mischief in her voice, even through its slow woolliness.

He kissed her on the right side of her face. Then he stuck his head out her window, dodging the potted plants and flowers and trailing philodendrons. She wasn't lying. There was a clear view the whole way.

'It was nothing,' he said.

'Didn't look like nothing.'

'I was fishing with Michael.'

'Yes, I know. He came home an hour ago.'

An electric saw revved up from the workshop downstairs. Despite himself, Jamie started smiling. Silly with the memory of kissing Alison. He recalled his dad's instructions.

'How're you feeling, Mum?'

'You're avoiding the question. Do you like this girl?'

'Yeah.'

No other answer occurred to him. Her illness had had the effect of completely opening up their conversation.

'And she likes you?'

He hesitated. Summoning back the smell of her, the smell on your hands after scaling a wet chain-link fence. He smiled again. Then he remembered her reaction when she smelled his fingers. 'I dunno,' he said. 'It's more complicated than that.'

'One more reason for us to stay here.' The right side of her mouth edged upward; automatically he gauged the bearings behind the effort. Too much. During the worst spells, her face lost most of its sensation. 'Yes,' she went on, 'I know why you're here.'

'Dad said to tell you —'

'Tell your father,' she said, 'he can stop having his secret meetings.' Her breath was coming out serrated now, in little huffs, and he realised she was trying to clear her throat. 'Tell him to tell those bankers, and real estate agents, and all those others . . .'

She stopped. He wasn't used to seeing her this bad. Speechless — almost entirely immobilised. Not so long ago she'd have never run short of a few choice words for real estate agents. The scum of the earth, she called them. Nor would she have been able to get out of her chair — any chair — fast enough. But she'd already been a couple of weeks in this one. She'd missed his semifinal in this one.

He shook his head. 'I'm with Dad,' he said. 'We'll go to Maroomba and come back when you're better.'

'Live with the enemy? You kids.'

'They need to know by Friday, Mum.'

She attempted another half-smile. 'Look at you now,' she said. She scrutinised him for some time, then turned back toward her window. She said, 'It's more complicated than that.'

He left the house. Partway down the drive he saw Michael sitting on the bungalow steps. Jamie went over to him and yanked out his earphones.

'Hang out in your own room, will you?'

Michael shrugged.

'Go tell Mum you wanna move to Maroomba.'

'What? I don't, but.'

'I don't care. Go tell her.'

Michael slouched up from the concrete steps, sheaves of hair – he cut it himself, using kitchen scissors – hanging over his brow. He was too skinny and his arms too long and every part of him that bent was knobbly. No way they looked alike.

'I hate Maroomba, they're all posh there.'

'Would you rather move to the city?'

Michael jerked his head up. 'Do you think she'll get better if we go?' At one point his voice dipped into a lower register and sounded like their dad's. The earphones still buzzing around his neck.

Jamie tsked impatiently. 'Why else would we go?'

'Cale said he'd teach me how to surf.'

'Cale won't teach you shit.' He instantly felt bad for saying this. 'Look, it's not till next year anyway.'

Michael put his hands in his pocket.

'Go,' said Jamie.

Michael pursed his lips as though readying to whistle.

'Go!'

'Lester saw us. Before – with Alison Fischer.' He glanced up questioningly. 'Just past the service station.'

For a moment Jamie felt booted outside himself. His voice spacey in his skull. He heard himself say, 'So what? Stop following me around.'

Michael shrugged again. 'I saw him, and he saw us,' he said.

Jamie came at him and punched and pushed him against the doorjamb. 'You better shut up.'

'Sorry,' Michael cried out.

'I mean it.'

'I'm sorry I'm sorry.'

At teatime, Michael ate by himself in the kitchen. Sooking in front of some TV show. Jamie joined his parents, who'd already started, in the living room. As soon as he walked in he could tell they'd been fighting. His mum sat facing the window under her striped blanket and his dad was angled opposite, feeding her. They ate in silence. A light breeze rumpled the curtains. Jamie watched the dull green of eucalyptus leaves bleed into the darkening sky. His mum started coughing.

'Are you okay?' his dad asked.

Once she'd fetched her breath she said, 'Jamie.'

'Yeah, Mum.'

'You know what no one ever asks me?'

His dad stared straight ahead, over her shoulder. 'Ask her,' he said.

'What, Mum?'

'Everyone always asks me if I'm okay. No one ever asks me if I'm happy.'

The sound from the kitchen TV faded, then amped into the voice-over for a commercial. His dad put down his plate and left the room.

She'd already made her instructions clear. She wasn't timid about these things. She didn't want a machine breathing for her, nor her body grafted into a computer. She didn't want any hoohah. She wanted to be cremated and then planted in the soil under the waratahs. Part of this was slyness — they'd be more likely to keep the property. She wanted this, and she wanted his dad to buy back his stake in the trawler. Jamie remembered their conversations, after her second relapse, about moving. Money. Dim voices and lamplit silences. One night he was in the driveway and glimpsed a slice of his dad's face through their bedroom window. It was hard and tear-smudged and sneering with hurt. Then he saw a dark shape flit in front of the window in the next room. Michael. Both of them, sons, watching their parents. One handful, his mum said, she wanted brought to the bluff, where she watched the storms come in, and she wanted it scattered — she said the word cheekily — into the ocean.

She was in fine form when his dad came back in. Teasing Jamie about incredible views at the courthouse.

'Jamie was up there today,' she explained.

'Got some free time, has he?'

'That reminds me,' she said. 'Your holiday job, Jamie — when you get a chance, go talk to John Thompson at the wharf. Word is he's got a spot on his boat.'

His dad made as though to say something, but didn't.

'Tell him I sent you. He might even start you straight away.'

'The final's coming up,' his dad broke in. 'Can't it wait till after then?'

'Fishing and football.' She let out a dramatic sigh. 'That's all this town cares about.'

The room lightened, loudened, as Michael barged in from the kitchen. His expression anxious. 'Thirty percent chance of thunderstorms tomorrow,' he said. 'But higher on the weekend.'

His mum looked at him intently. She said, 'Thank you, sweetie.'

'I'll have your rocking chair done by then,' said his dad.

It was dusk outside now – the window a square of black, brooding colours. Waratah shrubs lifting their scent of honey into the room. Hundreds of kilometres away the ocean streamed into itself, careening its mass over and over, sucking even the clouds down.

'Shall we open a bottle?' his mum asked.

'You sure, Maggie?'

'Let's open a bottle.'

THE NIGHT WAS WINDY. Clouds hung low and fat, lit up by the massive bonfire in the backyard. People were feeding it anything they could toss a couple of metres: furniture, textbooks, beer cans and bottles, even their clothes. Farther back from the fire the darkness was crumbed with cigarette ends, glowing, fading, each time seemingly in different spots. People might have been dancing out there.

Cale quickly ditched him for some surfie mates – the bloke could trace a sniff of mull through a dust storm.

'Hey, Jamie!'

Someone lifted a bottle to his mouth. Jamie hurled his head to the sky.

'Jesus,' he said, coughing, laughing as a hand thumped his back.

He spun around and saw Billy Johnson – left half-forward flank, an ordinary player, but one of those blokes everyone got along with.

'Hell's that?'

'Bourbon, I think,' Billy said, teeth gleaming widely.

'Fuck you,' said Jamie.

'Stole it from my sister's room.' He held it out like a handshake. 'Have some more.'

Jamie took another swig. The burning rushed through him, mixing with the fumes from the fire. He felt deeply awake.

'Thanks,' he said. 'Thanks a lot, man.'

'Ready for the game next week?'

He tossed the bottle back to Billy. 'What game?' he jeered.

By midnight, the party was peaking. She hadn't arrived. He sat in a tight pack with the other Halflead High kids, drowsing in their cheap deodorant. Norsca and Brut and Old Spice. They had the next day off – curriculum day – and everyone was going balls out. They drank. They drank and talked about the upcoming game. Jamie watched the bonfire, gusts of wind playing havoc with the smoke, people gliding in and out of its thrown light.

Cale rocked up, off his face. He started making toasts – to footy, to cunt, to mates, to getting fucked with your mates – each word swerving in the smoke-dark wind. At one stage he threw himself to the ground. Everyone watched as he did a strange, simian dance across the lawn.

Jamie drank. The wind moved through the tall purple grass, sifting the light of an arriving car's high beam. Like the wind was made of light. Next to him one of those UV bug lights thrumming purple above a pit of carnage: skeletal legs, carapaces, wings.

Cale held something up: 'Got it!'

Then he saw her. Trying to light a cigarette, her face in the brief flare of a struck match. White skirt and a boob tube. She looked somehow smaller-figured in the night. On an instinct she turned and met his gaze and then, bold as you like, started walking up to the group. Tammie and Laura close in behind her.

He looked away.

'Got a light?'

But she was talking to Cale, the twenty-dollar bill flapping between his fingers. Billy rifling through his pockets, striking, restriking the wheel of his lighter, hands cupped, body swivelling to shield the flame.

The girls waited and then walked off, giggling.

Cale whispered to him: 'So?'

But he couldn't speak. His head teemed. It was late and he sensed all around, in the shadows, mouths straining against each other as though to breach, to break through to a clear feeling.

'So what?'

'So you gonna score with her?'

'What, are you stupid too?'

She was waiting out front. Cross-legged on the trunk of an old Holden, cornered by a chaotic blockade of cars and bikes. Someone next to her in the darkness. As he came closer, he saw that it was Tammie: she flicked down her cigarette, whispered something into Alison's ear before leaving. Under the cloud-strained moonlight Alison's skirt was hitched up past her gleaming thighs. Her two legs interlocked.

'You look different,' she said.

'You too,' he replied. He wasn't lying. Closer up, the light wasn't kind to her face. Makeup moved like a tight gauzy screen on top of her skin.

'Most of these things,' she said, 'no one even talks to me.'

He nodded. Laughter spilled from the backyard. Then the smash of a breaking bottle. He spun around.

'Dory's not here tonight,' she said.

He deflected it, the cold edge held up to his warm drunken cocoon. From the house came the rising scud of voices. Then the wind shifted. They were alone again.

'He hates these high-school parties.'

He said, deliberately: 'You can talk to me.'

She looked at him without smiling. 'You're funny,' she said. 'But seriously, all me and him do is talk. How his uncle's gonna get an abalone licence one day. How he's got friends in Fisheries. Remember that time with the Chinese poacher?'

The chill came back, darting through every fissure in him. He remembered. The young woman's body they found in the swale – within shouting distance of where Dory lived with his uncle. Its blank, salt-soused face. The cops at school, pulling Dory, and later Lester, out of the classroom. After they were released from questioning, Lester had pantomimed the whole thing in the school paddocks. Jamie was too far away to hear anything, but saw the circle of boys reshape itself as Lester knelt down – he was Dory now, straddling the woman's body. Punching the ground like a piston. Dory himself standing aside, watching on without a word.

Alison soured her face. 'His uncle – he's a nasty piece of work.'

She quickly looked behind her, then swung back around. His heart pounding his skull as she considered him. He took a long breath.

'So are you and Dory together or not?'

She bounced her shoulders. 'Honestly, sometimes I wonder if he's a poofter. Seriously, Tammie cracked on to him once, the slut. And, you know.'

'Yeah?'

'You know. He didn't do anything.'

'He didn't do anything.'

'I even asked, but you know him. Won't talk to save his life.'

Her conversation was like surface chop, trapped in the same current, backing over itself. It made him seasick. He realised she hadn't answered his question. He was about to ask again when he heard her name being called out. The front door of the house banged open and a figure surfaced from the red rectangular glow, coming straight at them, trailing a small wake of commotion.

'Fuck,' Alison muttered.

'*A*–lison.' A singsong tug, stretching out the first syllable.

His stomach rose up thick and rancid. He swallowed, breathed it down. Here it came. 'Who is it?' he asked, as if he didn't know – as if asking were proof he didn't care. Always there were the rules, plying, pressing in around you.

'Alison?' The voice affected surprise now. Two black shapes – then another two – their shadows scrambling ahead of them across the yard. One by one the faces came into sight. 'Dory's been worried about you.'

'Fuck you, Les,' said Alison evenly.

In response Lester dipped his head and lifted his bottle above it.

Then he turned and leered to the person who'd accompanied him out: a tall, lanky mullet-head who'd dropped out of school last year.

A few steps back Tammie tottered against Cale. They seemed engrossed in their own windy drama. Both held their beers out in front of them like candles.

'I'll pass that along,' Lester said.

'Sure,' said Alison, 'once you pop his cock out of your mouth.'

Lester's tall mate started snickering. 'Slut,' said Lester. He was unfazed. 'You think you're top shit now? After one fluke goal?'

In a single moment Jamie realised that Lester was talking to him and that Alison was watching. He prepared himself to say something. The words, however, snagged deep inside him.

'We'll see you at training on Monday,' Lester went on. 'He's gonna fuck you up.' He shook his head in amazement. 'You're fucked.' He turned to Alison: 'Remember your old loverboy, Wilhelm?'

Alison stayed quiet. Her face stern, narrowed, like she was trying to light a cigarette. Cale took a step forward. 'Come on, man.' He sounded unsure – and unsure who he was talking to. Lester's mullet-headed friend watched him steadily.

'Fucked,' repeated Lester.

What should he say? He felt sickened by his words – hollow, soggy-sounding – before they even came out. He said, 'Whatever, mate.'

Lester laughed. 'So fucked.'

And it was true: each iteration struck Jamie with its truth, drained his body cold. The sick dread soaking and the worst was how familiar it felt. Too late to turn back. You'd think it was too much for one person but no, he'd already made room for it. He was rubbish.

Alison watched, then nodded. 'Let's go, Jamie.'

'See you Monday,' Lester sang out. 'Have a good weekend!'

She led him off.

For a while they walked without speaking. There was a shape to the silence between them: unfolding, contracting in the night. At the end of the street Alison reached out her hand. He held it desperately but there was no exhilaration in it. He wondered if she could feel that it wasn't his hand at all – that it wasn't he who was connected to it. They ducked under a fence and then his knees gave way beneath him.

'Sand,' she said.

They skirted the edge of a caravan park. Light and music wafted over from the lots, carrying the day-old scent of sunscreen, charred barbecues. Early summer tourists. Finally they reached a shoulder of cliff. There was a steep drop-off behind it, and, behind that, the bay.

'You wanna keep walking?' she asked.

'Okay,' he said. A strange formality had arisen between them.

'You know a spot? I'll follow you.'

He continued on the same track. Along the headland, abstracted from any thought of direction, through the mulga scrub, and paddocks of wild grass, and fields stubbled up to burn marks delineated by dark trees. Maybe he could just keep walking. Just not stop. And what if he did? Would he want her to follow him? The wind was sharp, and salty, and then there was water on it.

'It's cold,' said Alison. She hugged her bare arms. 'Where are we going?'

He was dazed, for a moment, by the trespass of her voice. He looked out. In the high moon the water was sequined with light. Muted flashes from the freighters past the heads. Beyond that, stars. But directly beneath him – that, there, was the real shocker. The black stub in the black bay. He'd brought them right to the rock pier.

'You wanna go down there?' Her tone was a little impatient.

'It's gonna rain.'

'Carn,' she said. 'It'll rain up here too.'

She swayed and shimmied down the dark slope. He followed her down and then onto the rocks, almost sprinting across them until they reached the tip of the pier. Water boiling over its edge. Vertigoed, he looked back – saw, across the long darkness, the foreshore thinly threaded with lights. Then, breathing hard, he turned around again and looked out into the deeper black, toward the heads where the water came in strong and deep and broke on the raised table of the reef.

'I haven't been here for ages,' he said.

Alison found a curved rock on the lee side, long and canoe-narrow. The pier a heap of shadows in the night. 'Lester's just a dickhead,' she said. She drew her legs beneath her.

'Yeah.'

'You should have seen him when he first met Dory. Talk about arse-licking.'

He sat down opposite, shivering. It was like the wind was greased, he thought, it slid right against you, leaving your skin slippery where it touched. The mention of Dory triggered something inside him and he reached for her.

'Come here.'

He heard himself say it. He saw his arm stippled by cold. The smell of kelp and metal dissolving on his tongue. She fended the hair from her face as he hauled her in, his hands up and down her body, claiming as much of her as he could. She responded at once, then drew herself upright.

'I just don't get why he hangs out with him,' she commented.

'What?'

He rocked back, hugged his shins tight. Looked at her. Her hair silver in the pale spill of moonlight. Her makeup worn down and somehow, in this light, accidental – as though she'd been rehearsing on a friend's face. She looked like a complete stranger.

'I mean. He doesn't even like him.'

'Will you shut up?' He realised, suddenly, that it pissed him off: that strange, settled face of hers. 'Please? Fucking Dory this and Dory that.' Words gushing up in him, frothy and cold, but he couldn't give body to them, not fast enough. 'Why were you even with him? Don't you know what everyone says? What everyone thinks?'

Her expression was level. 'Go on.'

It occurred to him instantaneously that this was her real face, and that it was the same as Dory's – the same blankness of expression – and that that was what had been drawing him in. *That* was what he wanted to break himself against. As quickly as it came, the heady anger began to seep out of him.

She said: 'So what does everyone think?'

He didn't answer.

'Carn,' she said. She leaned into him again, almost aggressively, urging his hand with her own, up over her shoulderblade. Her lips muzzling his neck.

'Carn.'

'Just that you could do better than him.' His voice came out as if by rote. 'Like . . . he's slow or something.'

She pulled back, teeth flashing, and then she was laughing, liquidly, into the night. He waited, watching her. Sensing, deeper and deeper, how profoundly her laughter excluded him. In the distance he heard metal rings clinking against masts. The creaking of stretched wood. He would stay quiet. He'd say nothing and maybe she'd say something – one thing – that would release him for good.

Alison's face remembered itself. 'Sorry,' she whispered. She crawled forward on all fours and put her hands on his knees.

'Hey.' He was holding her shoulders. Vance Wilhelm had been hospitalised with internal injuries – whatever that meant. Had she crawled on her hands and knees for him? Had he afterward regretted letting her? The pier, buffeted by rising waves, felt as though it was beginning to list from side to side. She looked up.

'I'll go if you want.' How she said it – the words running one way and the meaning another. After a while, her mouth opened disbelievingly. 'You gotta be joking.' She threw his hands off her. 'But okay. If that's how it is. You're up for it and Lester Long shit-talks you and then you're going every which way.'

The wind grieved louder. Cutting off his every tack of thought.

'All year you're up for it —'

'It's not fucking Lester,' he spat, 'and it's not fucking shit-talk.'

She exhaled, her eyes shining.

'Anyway,' he said, fetching in his voice with effort, 'you're moving.'

'What?'

'Next year. To the city.'

Alison ignored him. 'Stuff it,' she said. 'They were right about you.'

'We're moving too – but just to Maroomba.' He was flustered by her comment. *Who?* he wanted to ask. *Right about what?* He said, 'It's my mum.' Then he stopped himself. Just saying it felt like some sort of betrayal.

'Look,' Alison said. Now he breathed in, primed himself for the inevitable questions. But once again she acted as though she hadn't heard him. She said, 'You're scared of Dory – fair enough.' Her brow knitted together. 'I just thought . . .' She paused. 'It's different with you.'

He didn't say anything.

'I just thought it'd be different with you.' She crouched up, onto her feet. He turned toward her and she was smiling, lips pressed tightly together. Something about that smile. 'But I'll talk to him,' she said. 'He'll leave you alone. Promise.' She made a half-choked sound like a chuckle. 'Don't worry – Dory listens to me.' She held still for a moment, then started across the rocks.

Jamie turned around to face the water. Years ago he'd swum out there heaps – out where the coral was. It was easy to forget, past the reef, that you were on the edge of the great continental shelf until a rip drifted you out and one of those cold currents snaked up from the depths and brushed its slightest fringe against your body. Then you remembered. She was almost out of sight when the recognition arrived. That smile – her smile – it wasn't one-way. There was a question in it.

'Alison!' he called out.

The cry passed his mouth and coursed back into his body. Tons and tons of water moving under you. She stopped. Her body was slim and pale, a trick of light, against the black rocks.

'How's it different?' he said.

'What?'

'How's it different with me?' he shouted.

She stood in the half-dark, then shrugged. When her shoulders didn't stop shrugging he realised she was crying. Jesus. He got up and scrambled toward her.

'All that time – you don't know what it's like for me all that time,' she said. Her voice sounded older. She lifted her head and searched toward him with her open face. 'He likes to hold my hand when he's drunk,' she said. Even over the wind he could hear the bitterness. 'The rest of the time – you look and you look and there's nothing there. Fucking zilch. With you, it's different.'

'Okay.'

'It just is.'

'Okay.'

'I'm sorry.'

He watched as she stood there, hugging her ribs. You couldn't turn back from something like this. You saw it through and it ruined you.

'Don't go,' he said.

WHEN HE WAS LITTLE he used to follow his dad down to the wharf. Watched him cast off the hawser, chug out ahead a rimy trail of grease bubbles, the chorus of curses from the wharfies. In time Jamie was allowed, on school holidays, to come along. But usually his dad would be gone by breakfast and it never felt like a missing – more like he brought the sea into their house and it braced the rest of them to know where he was, what it looked like where he was, the sea around him. Before Michael was born, before his mum's sickness. Best was when they went out in the little runabout with the two-stroke, him and his dad, and sometimes his mum as well – she'd be cradling a basket of barbecued chicken and some beetroots, sitting on rolls of butcher's paper as long as her legs – and he'd dip his fingers behind the stern and draw a white gully into the darker water.

Then Michael. When he was old enough they took him along and together they explored the whole bight of the bay. They fished for King George whiting off the southern promontory and snapper and trevally in the deeper waters. His great-grandfather had skippered one of the first trawlers in Halflead Bay: back then he could go out for six weeks over Christmas, dip in, and make enough money to fish for sport the rest of the year. Jamie loved it – the idea of his family having worked that body of water for generations. He caught his first fish when he was six – a mako – he'd never forget its spearlike snout, the long cobalt gleam of its back. His dad's hands cupping his on the reel. They gaffed it twice, behind the gills, and even when its tail flayed his arm he could barely hold in the rapture. Gulping down his dad's praise – *Not a bad effort*, he kept saying. *Not a bad effort, a shark your very first time.*

His last time, though. Over five years ago. Early evening: no luck – nothing – they'd only stayed to make it worth the long hike. The rock pier was a tricky spot: you couldn't moor a boat and it was on the undeveloped side of the dunes. No tourists out there. The nearest road was an hour off – you had to cart all your gear along the headland. They'd been about to leave when Jamie's rod bowed forward.

He grabbed it, hauled back until the rod made a tight arc.

'What is it?' asked his dad.

The resistance was strong but even. 'Snagged, I think.'

Michael looked back down, continued packing the tackle away. Jamie reeled in his line. It was getting dark, the sea glass-coloured. The tide was coming in fast, too, washing higher against the rocks and leaving a frothy train. His mum, foraging through the lower rock pools, planted her feet – freezing her posture – every time the water surged in, and it seemed to Jamie like a private game.

'Okay,' said his dad. 'Pull her in and let's go.'

Jamie continued reeling in. Then his line jerked hard. He leaned the rod back again – probably the reef, or a bed of sea grass – but then he felt it, there, and there – the unmistakable give and drag of a fish.

'Got one,' he cried out.

'You sure?' His dad observed the weight on the line and climbed to his feet.

'Got one,' Jamie repeated.

It was fighting now, weaving and twisting. The line went slack. When the charge came he was pulled forward and almost lost his footing. He looked down: browny yellow lichen. Spume churning over his ankles.

His dad grinned. 'Set the drag,' he said. Jamie set the drag. They watched over the grey water together. Too dark to see anything. He fought the fish, tracking its every tension, tugging and reeling, imagining its flight through spindling reefs and sand and meadows of sea grass. This was it – this was why you waited. His dad next to him, fired up, talking him through it.

The line went spastic. It convulsed in short bursts. Jamie gripped the rod with excitement – he'd never felt a fish do this before. He glanced at his dad, who was squinting out to sea. Michael and his mum too. The sea was like this. You could wait all day and then, just when you were leaving, it might offer something up – the rubbery back of a whale, the glass-sharp glint of jumping mackerel – something. You wouldn't even know you were waiting till it came and you missed it. In the distance, something disrupted the surface of the glazed water – it was beautiful – beautiful to think it connected to him.

He tugged, reeled, tugged. His mum said, 'Oh my God.' He couldn't make anything out in the greyness. When she said it the second time he saw it. Wings beating furiously. A seagull. Then he heard the high-pitched screeching. It sounded human, the intonations of a baby girl throwing a tantrum. He continued reeling, the rod stooping lower and lower as he dragged the bird across the water, through the chop and, at last, to the rocks. Now it was quiet.

'Oh my God.'

His dad said, 'Where's it hooked?'

It had stopped moving. Jamie tried to lift the line but its body was wedged somehow, stuck in the rock scum.

'It's dead,' he said.

It was enormous. Blood dyed the top of its plump breast, banded its neck – impossibly red against its white neck. Its webbed feet, limp in the wash, floated like old orange peel. He stepped toward it. The water shook its body. Then he saw, behind it, the sinuous, steely torso of a fish.

'There's a snapper too,' he said, twisting around. His mum was staring at him, her face peaked but utterly focused.

'Bob,' she said.

'It's on the fixed hook,' said Jamie.

'Let him do it,' said his dad.

He took another step. Bent down, saw the second hook, the long shanked keeper sunk in above the wing. Barbed into its shoulder and still letting blood. He reached out and suddenly the gull lurched up, screaming, flailing its big wings. Its beak gaped open: he could see right down into its pink, tattered innards. The bird was terrified – leaking something that smelled like dog piss gone off, its shrill squawks corrugating in its throat. He looked into that violent white rush and knew he couldn't touch it. No way. He jerked back and pointed the rod, trying to poke it onto the rocks, but the pliant fibreglass tip spooked the creature even more.

'Stop that,' said his dad.

'I'll unhook it,' he said, but he didn't move.

Michael stared at the bird, whose cries were tapering now to a dry rattle.

His mum repeated, 'Bob.'

His dad took the fishing rod from him. He squeezed Jamie's shoulder. 'It's suffering, son. You understand?'

He nodded, but he didn't know what he meant by doing that – nodding. The bird's wings were half splayed. He watched it for a long time, churning in the water's guts. He didn't move.

A minute passed. Then he heard Michael digging around in the tackle box, mumbling to himself. He picked things up and threw them back in, metal-sounding. 'Nope,' he whispered under his breath. 'Too blunt.' A little later he handed something up to Jamie: a pair of scissors.

His dad watched silently.

So he'd have to hold it. With one hand. Should he hold its head or body? Those huge wings. The fish-flesh writhing behind it. He opened the scissors – so flimsy, with his fingers inside them. He crouched down and then it saw him – the yellow eye with its black heart – and let out a coarse shriek. That smell, that secretion of terror.

'Come on,' said his dad.

'I could just cut the line,' he said, not looking up.

'You will not just cut the line,' said his mum. She said it so scathingly he immediately pictured the bird flying with the nylon leader hanging from one wing, the ball sinker running up and down between the swivel and hook, weighting its body into a sinking spiral.

'For Chrissake, Bob.'

'He's gotta do it himself.'

'Look at it.'

'It's his catch.' His voice firmed. 'He has to do it.'

Jamie bent down again. Then he stood up and backed off.

'Jesus,' said his dad. There was a weariness in his tone Jamie had never heard before.

'He's crying,' Michael pointed out to their parents. His voice was matter-of-fact but his face seemed itself close to tears.

His mum didn't say anything to Jamie. She didn't look at him at all as she climbed down to the water's edge. She bent over and picked up the gull with both hands and laid it on a flat rock. Then she sucked her lips into her mouth, lifted one of her Blundstones, and stomped down on the gull's head, once, hard.

The morning was blue when he awoke. Alison gone. Had she even been there? Somewhere on the water a radio dispersed its sound. Translucent sand crabs, the size of his fingernails, scurried over his shins. It was a dream. Last night had been a dream – her skin moving against her ribs, so thin over her body he could see the laddering of it. She rocked above him, coaxing her face out of the shadows. The star-drenched sky reeling. I got you, he said, when she slipped.

Now, in the shock of early morning, he was wrenched back into his body. The rocks slimy with moss. The water ice-cold and molecular. Late in the night there'd been thunder, and heat lightning – all night it had felt like it was minutes away from raining – but it hadn't rained. Already you could feel the day hotting up again. From some dark crevice the smell of a dead animal, rank and oversweet. That evening they'd laid the gull on the water and it was borne out, mutilate, into the grey drift. For hours – every time he'd looked back – he'd seen other gulls, dozens of them, circling in a silent gyre. Making black shapes out of themselves in the dusk sky. Then the light had failed. Here, he thought. He stood up, the soreness returning to him all at once. Here is the saddest place I know.

IT WAS AFTERNOON by the time he got home. All morning he'd wandered the dunes and tidal flats – too spent to think – then, strange to his own intentions, he'd set eyes on the courthouse before him. He'd climbed all the way up the cliff. He went in, sat down in a cool, dim corner.

At home there was a strange car in the driveway, a new-looking four-wheel drive. Out-of-towners. He watched from his bungalow as his dad came around the side of the house with two men. One wore mountain boots and a red polar fleece around his waist and walked quickly, keys in his fist. The other was a suit. His Brylcreemed hair cracking in the thirty-plus heat as he kept pace. They got into their car and did a three-point reverse and dusted down the driveway. His dad still standing by the front verandah. Two beer bottles sweating on the railing. He wore a short-brimmed hat and Jamie couldn't see his face.

Tea was a quiet affair. Every now and then Michael looked at him furtively but otherwise they kept to themselves. Afterward, Jamie plastic-wrapped the leftovers and washed the dishes. Michael dried and stacked. They worked silently, waiting to see if their parents' voices would start up. Michael's studied silence beginning to get on Jamie's nerves. Their dad came out of the living room, grabbed two bottles of wine, and went back in.

'They turned down the offer on the house,' whispered Michael.

'Who, Mum?'

'Nah, the buyers.'

'Why?'

But he wouldn't say any more. Jamie didn't push. Once, he'd caught Michael at the caravan park, wagging school, and hadn't said anything – he never knew whether it was out of loyalty or laziness. Once, he'd hit Michael in the mouth harder than he'd meant to and broken a tooth. *I hate you,* Michael had said, blood darkening the arches of his gum. It had only struck Jamie later that his brother might actually have meant it. That he might actually hate him. That he'd have reason. But Michael had calmed down, his face settling into an expression as smooth, cloudy as sea glass. He hadn't dobbed him in. They didn't talk to each other much, maybe, but they kept each other's secrets.

The dishes were done and then there was nothing to do.

At eleven that night his dad knocked on his door. He was holding an open wine bottle. His teeth shone chalky in the dark.

'Your light's on,' he said.

'Sorry.'

He stood on the concrete steps of Jamie's bungalow, swaying a little. His shadow stretched out long behind him and hung over the acacia shrubs. 'Looks like no one's sleeping tonight,' he said. 'Not your mum either.' He looked up the drive at the dark house and smiled broadly. He only smiled like that when he was drunk. 'She can probably hear us.'

'Dad.'

'I thought I might just . . .' he patted the air above the steps. 'Do you mind . . .' now hoisting his bottle – the staggering of statements confusing Jamie.

They both sat down on the steps. His dad didn't seem to know what to do with the bottle: he clamped it between his two straightened palms, rolling it forward and back, then set it down with a loud chink.

'Big game next week,' he said at last.

Jamie nodded. Unbidden, his mind cast back to the school assembly – he'd been onstage – could that really have been him onstage four days ago? That person seemed unrecognisable.

His dad said, 'Well, at least you won't have to move.'

'Those the buyers today?'

His dad laughed. 'We're all set, right? Then she tells them to bugger off. Calls the guy a tight-arse, says they can't even wait another couple of months.'

'A couple of months?'

Jamie regretted it as soon as he said it. You couldn't talk about that. Not without talking about after. There was no after.

'Sorry,' he said.

But this time something came into his dad's eyes. 'No . . .' he said, 'no, you should know.' He glanced at the house again, then stared out into the garden. 'A matter of months. That's what they told us in Maroomba.' He spat on the ground away from Jamie. 'It's her kidney. They can map it out like that. They're useless to fix anything but they can give you pinpoint bloody timelines.'

Jamie froze – it was as though he'd stalled. He heard his dad's words. He'd expected them – he'd hoarded himself, day after day, against them – but now, when they came, all he could think about, obscenely, was Dory. The black tablet of his face. He hated it. He hated himself for it.

'I thought you should know,' said his dad.

He could tell him: Dad, I'm in trouble – it'd be that easy – Dad, it's Dory Townsend. He wanted to, but there was no way. He knew what his dad thought of him.

'Does Michael know?'

His dad shook his head. Finally he said: 'It's tough enough for him already.'

The smell of wine was strong on his breath. They each waited for the other to speak. How did people speak about these things?

His dad said: 'You know you can't work these holidays.'

'Yeah, I know.'

'I need you around the house.' He fell silent. 'Good boy.' After a time he said it again. 'Good boy.'

'Dad?'

'Yeah, son.'

But the distance was unthinkable. His dad took a swig from the bottle and patted Jamie's knee. He stood up, teetering with undelivered advice.

'You been fishing.'

'Yeah. With Cale.'

His dad's face momentarily betrayed his distaste. Then he frowned. 'I been thinking. We should do that again. Michael too. Would you boys like that?'

Jamie nodded. He saw, now, how the conversation would spin itself out.

'We could take the two-stroke.'

When he was little, he used to run down ahead and start the outboard motor. Turn the water over, pump out the bilge. Good boy. Now, his dad looked dead ahead whenever they drove past the wharf, its silent throng of boats.

'And your mum, she'd probably like us out of her hair.'

'Yeah.'

'We'll have someone come over.'

You couldn't think of after, you only thought of now, and come to think of it, you didn't do that either – you were left with pools of memory, each stranded from the next by time pulling forward like a tide. *The two of you,* his mum had told him once, *you thought you were so smart – sneaking out on your secret fishing trips. You'd both come home reeking of diesel.* Her first relapse had come a matter of weeks after that trip to the rock pier. The seagull. No more time for fishing. After that, Jamie sensed a difference – a dilution – in how his dad treated them; though with Jamie, and to a lesser extent Michael, his attention turned offhand, buffered by wary disappointment. With their mum his behaviour took the form of an impeccable courtesy. He moved her studio into the house. He quit his boat, started full-time woodworking. He laundered her sheets. Now, when you looked at him, five years on, and tried to see him without her, there was almost nothing left. What he'd given her, Jamie understood – what he was giving her still – he knew he'd never get back.

CALE CAME OVER THE NEXT DAY.

'Tammie told me to tell you,' he said. He closed the bungalow door behind him.

'What?'

'Lester said Dory'll meet you after training on Monday.'

'*Meet* me?'

Cale shrugged. 'She told me to tell you.'

Jamie stood up. It was Saturday: he had two days left. He guided himself, as though measuring distances, all around the small room. He made himself breathe. 'I'm fucked,' he said.

Cale didn't meet his gaze. 'The final's next weekend,' he said.

'So?'

'You know,' he groped for the right words. 'He might...' He trailed off.

'What about Wilhelm?'

Cale looked at a complete loss.

'And that Chinese chick,' Jamie said. 'What about her?'

No charges had ever been laid. No evidence, or the evidence was inconclusive. Some Maroomba authority came down and said so. What no one said was that Dory and his uncle – a notorious flag-waver – had taken recently to assaulting Asians in that part of the bay. The town turning a blind eye. This body, belonging as it did to a faceless, nameless poacher, was just another case of no one's business. More than anything, what Jamie remembered was Lester's reenactment: the sheer joy of his punches – their appalling regularity.

The conversation faltered. Cale grim-faced. Jamie felt a sudden longing to talk to him, tell him everything – he was three years older, after all, had seen that much more of the world – then all at once he wanted Cale to leave him alone. They stayed quiet for a while.

'She said they weren't even together.'

'Yeah,' Cale replied instantly. 'Tammie said that too.'

Jamie hesitated, then said, 'What should I do?'

'You're fast. Use your speed.'

'What?'

'Throw sand in his eyes. Then get him in the balls when his hands are up.'

Jamie stopped, shook his head. The conversation was unreal. 'Fuck off. I'm serious.'

Cale considered him, his face rough with the effort of understanding.

'I'll do a runner,' said Jamie. 'Like you. Travel around.'

Cale put his hands in his pockets glumly. 'Nah,' he said. 'I don't farkin know.' He sat down on Jamie's bed. 'You want some mull?'

'Jesus.'

Cale puffed out his cheeks, sucked them back in, then said, in a low, hurried breath, 'That's why I ran away. My old man used to beat me up.' He brought out his hands, rubbing his knuckles. 'And I kept telling myself. That every time he hit me, he was telling me he loved me that much – that much.'

Jamie tensed. It clouded him, hearing this.

'Shit, man.'

Cale closed his hands into fists. Then, doubtfully, he banged them together. The mattress bounced up and down. 'Fark. That's bullshit. He never did. I don't even know why I said that.'

Jamie watched on, confounded, as Cale fingered the beads on his necklace. He lumbered over to the window. 'Look,' Cale said, facing away from him, 'I've never been any of those places either.'

'What?'

'But my ex did give me this.' He added quickly, 'She's alive. In Cairns. Shithole of a place. She's a horoscopist or horticulturist or something.'

'You're fucking hilarious.'

'Easy, big man.'

He straightened up and came over to Jamie and nudged his shoulder, the gesture itself ambiguous – neither playful nor solemn. 'It'll be over soon, man.'

Jamie pushed past, suddenly flooded with an intense rage toward his friend.

'You fucking stink of fish,' he said.

Cale chuckled mournfully. 'You kidding? This whole town stinks of fish.'

SUNDAY AFTERNOON. All day he'd kept to himself – morning he'd spent behind the bungalow, in a lean-to built against the back wall. Hidden from the house's view. He'd sat there holed up and boxed in by his mum's old painting supplies – oil bottles, brushes, wood panels crammed into milk crates – listening to traffic along the coastal road, chatter lifting from the beaches: the stirrings of tourist summer. He'd stewed under the aluminium sheeting. The fight was tomorrow. The thought almost too much to contain, his mind recoiling between that and the thought of Alison, each contorting – neither providing respite from – the other. When the midday humidity got too much he went back inside and lay down.

Someone knocked.

'Storm's coming,' said Michael through the door.

'Where's it coming from?'

'Umm, from the west. I mean, the east.'

Jamie opened the door and Michael slouched in.

'Does Mum know?'

He shrugged.

'Let's go get her.'

The house was empty. The reclining couch in front of the window unoccupied. 'Probably at the bluff,' Michael said.

'Is her wheelchair here?'

His brother checked the closet.

'Nope.' A stirring on his features: 'I'm gonna go look for them.'

Alone, Jamie lowered himself onto the couch. The striped blanket crumpled at his feet. He nestled into the indentation of her body – so shallow – and imagined he could feel her residual warmth.

He looked out of the open window. So this was what it was like. He looked through the green foliage, over the ocean, and felt around him the heat massing in the air, the current of coolness running through it, taking form in the thunderheads. He saw the black energy becoming creatured from a hundred kays away, roaring toward shore, feeding on itself. On the headland, trees bending to absorb the weight of the forward wind.

'It's coming in,' a loud voice said.

Startled, he turned to take in the room. No one. Then he sat up, craned his head out of the window. A raindrop as large as a marble plopped on his bare neck.

'Yes.' That was his mum's voice. 'Thank you, Bob,' she said. 'It's lovely.'

Silence, then his dad's voice: 'It's a good chair.'

They sounded scrappy, as though coming through radio static. Jamie realised they hadn't made it to the bluff; they were nearer to the house – probably on the shaded verandah below – and the wind was reconstituting the sound of their voices, carrying it to him.

Now their conversation was unintelligible. Then his mum said, 'Darling,' just as half the sky darkened. 'It's coming in,' she said again.

And she was right, the storm was coming in – it was streaking in like a grey mouth snarled with wind, like a shredded howl, rendering the land into a dark, unchartered coast. The bay turning black. For centuries, fleets had broken themselves against the teeth of that coast.

'I can almost feel it on my face,' his mum said.

Her voice was strangely amplified, then voided by a detonation of thunder – it shook the house; the remaining daylight dipped and then, with a rogue gust of wind that rocked the couch backward, it was raining – heavy and straight and stories high.

Jamie sat by the window. The sky dark yellow through the rain. The baked smells of the earth steamed open, soil and garden and sewage and salt and the skin of beasts. Potted music of water running through pipes, slapping against the earth; puddles strafed by heavy raindrops until in his mind they became battlefields, trenched and muddy. The wind swung westward and whipped the hanging plants' tendrils into the room. Wetting his face. He could hear them again.

'Ask me now,' she said.

Sheets of water sluicing the other windows. The wind rattling them.

His dad's voice, so low as to be almost inaudible: 'Are you happy, Maggie?'

A breaking of thunder ran through the sky and into the ground. Her answer blown away. Jamie sat in the shape of her body and closed his eyes and imagined the feel of the weather against her numbed face. He felt the sky's cracking as though deep along fault lines in his chest. He tested the word in his mouth: 'Yes.'

'I'm sorry,' someone said. 'Forgive me.' Whose voice was that?

'Yes,' said Jamie, 'I'm happy now.'

'Oh, you know there's nothing to forgive.'

He got up from the chair. This wasn't right, listening in like this — he'd go downstairs.

Michael burst into the room, hair pasted on his forehead and streaming with rain.

'Where are they?' he wheezed. 'I can't find them.'

'They're downstairs,' said Jamie.

'But I checked downstairs.'

Michael moved closer to the window. Water dripped from his chin, his sleeves, logging at the bottom of his shorts.

'Listen,' said Jamie.

Soft, shapeless, their mum's voice wafted up. Michael turned and smiled tentatively at Jamie. 'Bet Mum's getting a kick out of this,' he said. The storm crashed around them. Michael seemed, in that moment, caught up simply in the anxiety of having Jamie agree with him.

Jamie smiled and nodded. He was always forgetting how it had once been between them.

'Come on,' he said.

At the door, there came a louder voice – their dad's – broken up by the unruly wind. He was talking about finding something, saying they found something —

Their mum's voice: 'That Townsend kid.'

Michael glanced at Jamie.

Their dad's voice went on, scratchy and sub-audible. Then the wind lifted the words clearly. Findings. Findings at the coroner's inquest.

'What's a coroner?' asked Michael.

'Shut up.'

'Something wrong with that kid,' his mum's voice said.

'I'm worried.' His dad's voice. 'Know why they call him Loose Ball Jamie?'

The sky raining through the rising wind. Clay pots swaying, tapping against the window frames.

'It means he doesn't go in hard. For the fifty-fifties.' A fresh agitation in his dad's voice, laying open the folds of his feeling. 'I'm not saying he's gutless – but he freezes.'

Jamie turned toward Michael, who shrank back, face already crimped in fear.

'Let's go,' he said.

'Don't,' said Michael. 'Please don't.'

Before they left, his dad's voice floated into the room, loud and raw and plain: 'You should remember.'

In the kitchen he got Michael in a headlock. 'How'd they find out? You little shit.'

'I can't breathe!'

'You told them, didn't you?'

'Everyone knows.'

'What? What'd you say?' He shoved Michael's head against the sink washboard, forced it along the metal ribbing, then dropped him to the floor. Michael's body shivering. The storm muted in here. Slowly, he felt the remorse bleeding into him. Always it came, immediately afterward. He said, 'Everyone knows what?'

Michael curled into a cupboard corner. He lifted his hand to feel the side of his head. He was breathing hard when he looked up, and he didn't look at Jamie's face but at some indistinct point beneath it.

'That you're gonna fight Dory,' he said in his deep voice. 'And that he's gonna slaughter you.'

ALL NIGHT HE COULDN'T SLEEP.

He threw on some clothes and wandered outside. The rain had stopped. Branches shuddered the water off themselves. The moon was still bright, caught in their wet leaves.

His mother had fallen asleep on the reclining couch. She was snoring softly. The moonlight poured in from the window and buoyed around her as though to bear her up. It seemed unreal. He pulled the blanket snug beneath her chin. Her mouth dropped open as though its hinges had snapped, and she snorted.

'Darling?'

'Sorry, Mum,' he said. 'I didn't mean to wake you.'

It was as though she were swimming up from some distant pit of herself. The drugs awash in her – he saw it now. With sudden clarity he understood how lost she must feel in her body.

'God, I'm sorry,' she said. Her voice was drawn thin. 'I was wrong. Who gets to choose where they die?' Her eyes were barely open, one of them darting about quick as silverfish.

'Mum, wake up.'

'But the boys love it here. You too.' Her face loosened. She said, 'You wouldn't believe.'

'Mum.' He shook her shoulder.

'The things I see now. But my hands.'

'Mum.' A pulse in her eyes and then her mouth moved. It jerked, then spread slowly into a smile of recognition.

'Sweetie.' She fell quiet. They listened together to her breathing. All through her the odour of bleach, bleach sopped and smeared with a used rag.

'What is it?' she said.

A nauseous rush of answers rose up in him but he said nothing.

'The girl?' She didn't wait for his response. 'And that horrible boy. Are you scared?'

He nodded.

'You're my son,' she whispered. A strange shifting in her eyes, as though grass moved behind them. For a moment she looked lost. Then she said, 'My son does anything he wants.'

Gradually her head drooped forward. The muscles around her mouth went slack and he realised she was lapsing back into sleep. This was where she lived most of the time. He felt toward her an immense quantity of love but it was contaminated by his own venom, made sour. He wanted it to stop. When? Monday, after training? What would be enough – what commensurate with his lack? And what if he couldn't? She had come back from the hospital and the first thing she said to him and Michael was, *This won't happen to you. I promise.* He was rubbish. Whatever he did or didn't do now, he'd hate himself later – he knew that.

A truck raced by on the coastal road, ripping skins of water off the bitumen.

Her head still bowed, she said in a slurred voice, 'James?' He slid his fingers into the pouch of her right hand. He'd never before noticed how loose the skin around her knuckles was.

She said, 'My wine.' After a long silence she said, 'Will you pass it to me, please?'

'Mum.'

'Your father and I love you very much. No matter what.'

'Okay.'

'Okay?'

It wasn't until a minute later he realised she might be squeezing his hand. 'Okay.'

He dreamed he was alone. The glass was cold against his fingers and forehead. He shrank away, went to the next black, steamed window, and the next, calling out as he searched. His voice sounded as though trapped inside some metal bladder. What if the paddocks were empty? And the long white corridors, too, with their waxy floors, and the dark slopes of the dunes he clambered up and down as though drunk? What if he couldn't find him?

The ocean seethed and sighed in the dark. So this was where you ended up, sick in sleep. Your night a beach and all sorts of junk washing up on shore.

AT SCHOOL NEWS OF the fight had spread. Monday at last. Everyone watched him and no one looked him in the eye. Even the teachers seemed to leave him to himself, steering their voices around. The semis, the assembly — all of it seemed long gone, preserved elsewhere. He was being quarantined. He'd seen it before. You were dead space, you were off limits — until afterward. Nothing malicious in it. What made it strange for him was the incongruous buzz around school — everyone getting fired up for the holidays and, in particular, the grand final that weekend. First time in five years, and against archrivals Maroomba too. The tension brinking on hysteria.

Recess he spent in the C-block toilets. What was the grand final to him? He tried to throw up but couldn't.

Lunchtime he saw her. Her friends clustered in the concrete corner of the downball court where, as one, they turned to look at him, opening apart, unfurling like some tartan-patterned flower, and there she was, leaning against the wall with large concentric targets painted in white behind her. She held his eye for a second and then the circle sealed shut. He realised he was holding his breath.

Vague impressions of classes rolled on. Each period ending with teachers saluting the team, rallying everyone for the big game. Jamie felt exhausted. Time pushed him forward. His mind wound out, one point to the next.

'Carn, Halfies!'

He spotted Dory just before final period. Taller than everyone else. Like a dockworker in his school uniform – shirtsleeves high on his biceps, shorts tight across his quads. His eyes too close together, his hair flaxen, floppy. Like some sick cartoon of a dockworker. The corridor packed and noisy. A few people saw them, made space, straggled, but Dory disappeared into a classroom. Lester was behind him, of course, and from a distance Jamie could see his face, pinched up in anger, yelling something out.

'Fucking retard!' he seemed to be yelling.

Jamie opened his mouth.

'Fucking retard mum!' he was yelling.

Of course he couldn't be saying that. Jamie shook it off – the bog-like feeling that accompanied the thought of his mum. There was his mind again, groping at anything but what was right in front of him. In front of him – wherever he went – Dory. Huge and hard, a thing of horror. He'd been dumped on the beach by his folks. He'd bashed up this guy, hospitalised that guy. He'd killed a Chink with his uncle.

The teacher talked on as Jamie watched the clock.

You had to shut it out. You could see it on players' faces, how they approached him, ready to take damage. You could hear it in your parents' voices. You had to shut it all out, otherwise it would sprout in you like weeds.

The bell rang.

He was headed for the lockers when his geography teacher flanked him, escorted him wordlessly to the principal's office and dropped him off there.

'Go on,' said the secretary. She looked up. 'Go *on*. Mr Leyland's waiting.'

Jamie knocked, cracked open the door.

'There he is,' a voice boomed. Coach Rutherford. He was wearing trackies and a Halflead T-shirt, a whistle around his neck. He stood behind the principal's desk. Where was Leyland?

'I was just coming to training,' Jamie said.

'Good,' said Coach. He waved him inside. Then Jamie saw Leyland – on the couch obscured by the door. With him was Jamie's dad. His mum in her wheelchair. His mum – what was she doing here? Jamie stood in the doorway and didn't move. All these people. All day he'd been waiting – all those days since Thursday night's party – and now it felt as though time had pushed him forward too far, too hard. Everything collapsing into one place.

Coach said, 'But today, you get a rest.' He smiled curtly and closed his fist around the whistle, shaking it like dice. Jamie's dad stood up and thanked him. He was wearing work clothes, his jeans smeared with oil and sawdust. Then he turned and thanked Leyland.

'Well,' said Leyland, also rising to his feet, 'our students, our business.'

Coach left the room. Jamie didn't say anything. He was thinking of Dory, the rest of them, waiting for him on the oval. What they must be thinking. He felt airy in his own body. What they must be saying. He remembered Lester's words in the corridor.

'It's not your business,' his mum said quietly, but Leyland didn't hear.

His dad moved to stand behind her chair. 'Come on, Jamie.'

'It's between the boys. It's not their business.'

'Maggie,' his dad said under his breath, 'we talked about this already.'

Jamie couldn't bring himself to look at them. He sensed that to witness a drama between his parents here, now, might wreck him completely.

'Jamie,' said Leyland. His voice took on added weight: 'I've talked to Dory. He understands – there's to be no trouble whatsoever.'

His dad pushed the wheelchair out of the room.

'All right?' Leyland asked. He held the door open. 'It's over.'

Even from the car he could see Dory. Even at that distance. Tallest in a line of green guernseys, the one moving slower, as though to a separate beat, while the others jogged in place, ran between the orange witches' hats between whistle bursts. Sprint exercises. All the way home Jamie said nothing.

When they pulled up, he got out and unfolded the wheelchair.

His dad said, 'Help your mother into the house.'

'Bob, I'm okay.'

His dad looked at Jamie and then at the house. 'I said help your mother.'

The front door opened and Michael came out. He stopped – transfixed and tense – as soon as he saw Jamie, staring at him without any of his usual bashfulness. Something like concern, deeper than concern, all through his expression. Then he went over to their mum and took hold of the wheelchair handles.

'I'm going down the jetty,' Jamie told his dad.

His mum turned to him with a strange, clear-eyed face. 'You're allowed. You're allowed to go. You can go.'

HE WALKED, ALONE, down to the jetty. It was clogged with tourist families who'd arrived over the weekend. All along the walkway were canvas chairs, Eskies, straight-backed rods thick as spear grass. A mob of fluoro jigs hopping on the water. He found a spot and sat. Someone had a portable radio and music streamed into the air in clean, bright colours. The bay a basin of light.

Could that really be the end of it? Leyland talking to Dory? What would he have said to him? That the school needed Jamie fit for the final? That Jamie's dad had begged Dory to spare his gutless son? That his mum, in that wheelchair, was dying? He sat in the midst of the jetty's hurly-burly, watching and listening. He felt the need of explanation. Here's what he could say to Dory – no, he could say anything, all the right things, and it still wouldn't be enough. Maybe things could be normal again. He'd finish school, run onto the field on Saturday and run off two hours later. He'd take up the job at the fish plant, or, better yet, he'd talk to John Thompson. His dad would take the sheets in. *Stop.* They'd pot the ashes under the waratahs; leave a handful for the bluff, throw it up and the wind would probably shift and putter it into their faces. She'd like that. No – you didn't think of that.

He got up and started walking. He'd sat there long enough – training would be done by now. He walked down the main street and past the wharf. At the tidal flats he took off his shoes and kept going. He had an idea where he was going but nothing beyond that. Sand spits sank into ankle-deep shoals. The night had been cold and the water chilled his feet. The sky flat and blue with mineral streaks. He passed the rock pier and started picking his way through the sedgeland – sharp, rushlike plants grazing his legs. At every step he dared himself to turn around, but he didn't. He followed a rough trail marked with half-submerged beer bottles, clearings where blackened tins from bonfire rockets were set into the dirt like sentinels.

And Alison. How would he have any chance with her otherwise? He stepped on solid-looking ground and sank to his knees. The bile rose up in him. Roundabout here was where they'd found the poacher's body. Half stuck, half floating in the marshy suck. No – nothing was worth that. And in that moment he realised, deep as any realisation went, that that wasn't what he was afraid of at all. He had to see it through.

He came to the shack in the middle of a muddy clearing. A man sat out front on a steel trap doing ropework. He was surrounded by other traps and old nets, dried and sun-stiffened in the shapes of their failure. It must have been Dory's uncle. He didn't look up.

'Dory,' he called out. 'One of your little friends is here to see you.'

Jamie moved closer. The sides of slatted wooden crates were laid end to end over the mud – a makeshift path – and he stepped onto them. He saw the man's hands, shot with swollen veins and spidery capillaries. The waistband of his shorts cutting deep under his beer gut.

'Dory!'

'I'll come back,' said Jamie.

The screen door opened and there was Dory, his body blocking almost the whole space, eyes narrowed in the sun. Hair over his eyes. He was wearing trackies and a stained singlet. He rubbed the bristles on his chin and cheek. Then he came partway down the crate-board path.

'You're here,' he said. He sounded surprised.

'Offer him a drink,' said his uncle. 'And get me one while you're at it.'

'We're out,' said Dory.

His uncle looked up and chortled, his face orange and unevenly tanned like an old copper coin. Then Jamie heard a whoop from inside the hut. He saw movement behind the boarded-up windows where the wood had rotted off.

'The fuck you doing here?' said Dory in a low voice.

Jamie stared dumbly at him. 'The fight,' he managed to say.

Dory surveyed the entire clearing behind Jamie. 'It's off.'

'Why?'

A disgusted look came over Dory's adult face. 'Why?' He glanced, almost involuntarily, over his shoulder, then came a step closer to Jamie and said, 'You dunno what the fuck you're doing, do you?'

Lester appeared at the door. 'This fucker,' he shouted, his face splitting into a grin.

'Jamie?'

Alison – that was Alison's voice. She emerged from the hut in her school uniform like some sort of proof. Even here – deep down in this plot of filth – her dress was clean. The mud didn't touch her. She looked at Jamie with an expression of dark intensity.

'I thought . . .' He tried to make his voice firm. 'There's squid now, down the jetty,' he said.

She hesitated, then walked toward him, then stopped beside Dory. Her face still amok. Then she put her mouth to Dory's ear and after a moment he laughed, a deep, throttled hack of a laugh.

'See,' said Dory's uncle. He lowered the greased rope onto his lap. 'Here's what I don't get.'

'Alison,' Jamie went on. He spoke only to her. But his voice faltered, undercutting what he wanted – what he was trying to say.

'Don't you boys go to school together? Why come all the way out here?'

'Can't hide behind his retard mum here, that's why,' said Lester.

Dory gave out another guttural laugh. Then, turning his back, he said, 'Just fuck off, Jamie. Okay?'

It wasn't as though he'd planned anything. He hadn't known exactly what to expect. But this – Alison, her shoulders neatly narrowed as though pinned back, spinning Dory around and hissing now into his ear, the old man leering on a crab trap in a crater of mud – this wasn't part of it. He stepped up to Dory.

'Okay then,' Dory said.

Jamie held up his arms but the first pain came in his stomach – he could feel the air being forced up, spraying out of his mouth. He cradled his stomach and then there was a heavy knock to the side of his head. He sat down. The ground tramped with mud like a goal square.

'Fuck you up!' Lester hooted.

'Right,' said Dory's uncle. 'Now I get it.'

Alison stared at Jamie with a stunned expression. Then slowly, stutteringly, she started laughing too, a thin, uncertain trickle into the air.

Was that enough? The air felt hot in his lungs. He waited for his breath to come back. He stood up. He looked at Dory and realised he'd never looked at another body – not even Alison's – so closely: the hard-knotted chest, the scabbed shoulders. The face a hide stretched over a seat of stone. When it came, he swung at it but his own head whiplashed back.

Seated again. His throat burning. His vision broken into scales. Stay down. Someone's voice – a whisper – he looked over to where Alison had been standing but she was no longer there. On the rock pier that night, under the hot stars – she'd said it into his mouth. She'd been there with him, watching the water wink, moonlight on the surface and then underneath, too, the glow of shucked abalone shells . . . *It's different with you.* He could still hear her laughing, and Lester yelling – he sounded angry, too angry – as though by proxy for Dory. When his sight returned he saw Michael drop his bike and wipe the sand from his eyes.

'That's enough!' His dad – breaking through the sedge into the clearing. Of course, thought Jamie, slogging through the mire of his mind – Michael. Michael had followed him.

'Stay down.'

But who was speaking? The voice was too soft.

'You all right, son?'

'Just stay down.' Jamie twisted around and realised, with mild surprise, it was Dory muttering to him.

His dad arrived at his side.

The only sound left was Alison's laugh which, somewhere along the line, had turned inside out, into a sequence of hollow sobs.

'Let's go, son.'

He searched his dad's face – he was ready, now, to accept all its familiar reproaches. But the face he saw was different: shaken loose from its usual certainty. Frowning, though without heat, Jamie's dad bent down, picked Jamie up. At his dad's touch a tremor ran all through him.

'Boys, ey?' offered Dory's uncle with a smile.

Jamie's dad looked at him flatly, then turned away. 'Come on, Jamie.'

Alison was still standing halfway down the crate-board path, next to Lester. Her arms were crossed low over the front of her school dress, over her stomach, as though it were she who'd just been gut-punched. Her sobbing had subsided. Jamie half made to approach her when his dad squeezed his shoulder.

'Son,' he said in a low voice. He shook his head.

Alison's mouth, her eyes – now turned toward them – seemed slowly to shape themselves into a leery cast. She rushed up to Dory. 'Wait!'

Dory said something back to her.

'What I wanted?' she cried out.

Dory turned toward Jamie and his dad. The expression on his face – a mask concealing another mask, and behind that – what? Minutes ago, Jamie would have said there was nothing: a dark gale thrown into a room and trapped. Now, he didn't know.

Dory gripped Alison's forearm but she flung his hand off.

'Rubbish is rubbish,' muttered his dad. 'Wherever it comes from.'

'You're letting him off!' She was tiny next to Dory, furious. 'You know. You *know* what he said! What he did!'

Everything became quiet. An ocean wind swept over the swale, heavy with salt, carrying the faint shriek of seagulls.

'I told you,' Dory replied. His tone was impersonal. It occurred to Jamie unexpectedly that Dory might be talking to him. He looked and looked at Dory but could no longer induce himself to feel anything.

'Come on,' said Jamie.

He reached up to touch his face and the touch came earlier than he'd expected. His face was numb. This was how it felt. His mouth tasted of mud, and blood, and it was smiling.

'Jamie?' murmured his dad.

He felt them all watching him, felt the sun warm on his face. A gold-tinged rope of spit dangled from his lips. Dory squared his body around. His demeanour was slack, drained of intention, like a sprinter's after crossing the finish line.

'I'm still here,' said Jamie. 'Come on.'

It hurt to speak: his jaw felt locked and he was pushing, pushing down on it.

'That's enough, son.'

He stepped clear of his dad. 'I said I'm still here!'

Dory was stumped, you could tell. It didn't make sense. He took a deep breath and then came at Jamie, his arm outstretched. Something grainy about his face, unfocused. Something sounded like balsa wood breaking and suddenly Jamie's dad was on the ground, lying on his elbow, his face flecked with dirt. Everything froze. Then Dory hit Jamie as well: it felt like pity, and Jamie was down, too, in the midst of the mud and the shattered light. Bursts of colour so bright they must speak, surely, for something.

No one talked. Then Dory's blunt, blurred voice: 'It was an accident.'

Alison's voice started up: 'Stupid . . . stupid . . .'

Lester: 'Shut up, cunt.'

'I didn't mean to hit his dad – he jumped in. He just jumped in.'

'Jesus,' said Dory's uncle.

But what if this was all of it? What if, when you saw things through, this was all that waited for you at the end? He lay on the ground and saw the black line of mud and the yellow lines of sand and sedge and then the bottle-green ocean. How wonderful it would be to be out there on the water. The wind scoured in and stung his eyes until they were wet. He'd watched her paint, once, at the courthouse. It was before dawn and he was half asleep. Blue and blue-green and then dark blue. A hasty white swath. He watched as she turned the bay into a field of colour. Then he looked out and, in his grogginess, saw it all through her eyes – the town, the dunes and flats, the foreshore with its man-made outcrops, the bay, sandbars, reef and deep sea. All of it motionless – slabs of paint, smeared on and scraped off, just so, fixed at a time of day that could never touch down. And here was his father, picking himself up from the black sludge, his face in its old grief. Here was Dory, who, despite everything – his emptiness – seemed uninterested, or incapable, of holding Jamie's hate. Michael, who still could. Alison. Watching from within her immaculate uniform. Only Lester's face brimmed with epiphany – a line had been crossed – and nothing had changed.

His dad got to his feet. He was shorter than Dory but spoke straight up into his face.

'That's enough.'

They looked at each other and then Dory looked away. A second later, Alison coughed into her hands and ran inside the shack. Michael waded into the mud and helped pull Jamie up. His face, Jamie realised, bore the same clear, graceful expression Jamie had last seen on their mum's face – his hands on Jamie's wrists surprisingly strong. Again – despite everything – he'd chosen to come. Jamie felt himself falling apart. Now, as Michael hauled him up from the ground, he braced his pain against his brother's strength. His dad held him under the armpits. Now, for the first time, Jamie gave over his weight to them entirely.

His dad tightened his embrace. He said, 'You okay?'

Michael, face tracked with mud, went to pick up his bike, steered it around. He wheeled it close by them. Jamie held fast to his dad's shoulder. At the edge of the clearing his dad stopped, turned, as though to kiss him on the head, then said, 'You're okay, son.' They started the long walk home.

NOTES ON THE AUTHORS

Peter Carey

Peter Carey's 1985 novel *Illywhacker* was shortlisted for the Booker Prize. His next (*Oscar and Lucinda*, 1988) won. Later, in 2001, *True History of the Kelly Gang* made him the second writer in history to be awarded the prize twice. In 1998 he was awarded the Commonwealth Writers' Prize for *Jack Maggs*, and again in 2001 for *True History of the Kelly Gang*. He has received the Miles Franklin and the National Book Council Award three times each. His most recent novel is *His Illegal Self* (2008). Born in Bacchus Marsh, Victoria, he grew up in the years when the dunny man made shocking visits in the early morning. Peter Carey now lives in New York where he is the Executive Director of the MFA Creative Writing program at Hunter College.

Helen Garner

Helen Garner was born in Geelong in 1942. She has worked extensively as a journalist, reviewer and scriptwriter, and has published numerous works of fiction, non-fiction and short stories, including *Monkey Grip* (1977), *The First Stone* (1995) and *Joe Cinque's Consolation*

(2004). Her most recent book is *The Spare Room* (2008), her first work of fiction for fifteen years. She lives in Melbourne.

PETER GOLDSWORTHY

Born in Minlaton, South Australia, in 1951, Peter Goldsworthy divides his time equally between writing and medicine. His novels have been translated into many European and Asian languages, and his numerous literary awards across many genres include the Commonwealth Poetry Prize, the FAW Christina Stead Prize for fiction, and a Helpmann Award for Best New Work shared with Richard Mills for the opera *Batavia*. *Three Dog Night* and *Honk If You Are Jesus* have been adapted for the stage, the latter winning the 2006 *Advertiser* Oscart Award for Best Play and the 2006 Ruby Award for Best New Work. Five of his novels are currently in development as movies, and two more for the stage. His most recent novel is *Everything I Knew*, published in 2008.

ELIZABETH JOLLEY

Born in England in 1923, Elizabeth Jolley was one of Australia's most celebrated writers, with a formidable international reputation. She was recognised in Australia with an AO for services to literature and was awarded Honorary Doctorates from Curtin University (1986); Macquarie (1995), Queensland (1997) and the University of New South Wales (2000).

Although she wrote all her life, it was not until she was in her fifties that her books started to receive the recognition they deserved. She won the *Age* Book of the Year Award on three separate occasions (for *Mr Scobie's Riddle*, *My Father's Moon* and *The Georges' Wife*), the Miles Franklin Award for *The Well*, and many other awards. Her last two novels were *An Accommodating Spouse* (1999) and *An Innocent Gentleman* (2001). Her non-fiction collection, *Learning to Dance*, was published in 2006.

Elizabeth Jolley died in 2007.

Nam Le

Nam Le was born in Vietnam and grew up in Melbourne. He is currently the fiction editor at the *Harvard Review*. His work has been published in *Overland, Zoetrope, A Public Space, Conjunctions* and *One Story*, and anthologised in *The Best Australian Stories 2007, The Best American Nonrequired Reading 2007, Best New American Voices 2009* and *The Pushcart Prize 2008*. His first book, *The Boat*, was published in 2008 and won the Dylan Thomas Prize.

David Malouf

Since his first collection of poetry in 1962, David Malouf has published novels, short stories, collections of poetry, opera libretti, a play and a volume of autobiography. His novels include *An Imaginary Life, Harland's Half Acre, The Greta World*, winner of the Commonwealth Writers Prize in 1991, and *Remembering Babylon*, shortlisted for the 1993 Booker Prize and winner of the inaugural international IMPAC Dublin Literary Award. His most recent novel is *Ransom*. Born and brought up in Brisbane, David Malouf lives in Sydney.

Gillian Mears

Gillian Mears was born in 1964 and spent much of her life in or around the northern New South Wales town of Grafton. Her first novel, *The Mint Lawn*, was awarded the *Australian*/Vogel Award in 1990. A second novel, *The Grass Sister*, won the regional section of the Commonwealth Writers' Prize. Short stories remain her love, however, and her latest collection *A Map of the Gardens* won the Steele Rudd Award in 2003. She lives and writes in the Adelaide Hills.

Louis Nowra

Louis Nowra is a playwright, novelist, screenwriter and essayist. His latest work for the stage was *The Boyce Trilogy* and he also co-wrote the documentary series *First Australians*. His novel, *Ice*, was published in 2008. He lives in Sydney and is married to Mandy Sayer.

Tim Winton

Tim Winton has published twenty books for adults and children, and his work has been translated into twenty-five languages. Since his first novel, *An Open Swimmer*, won the *Australian*/Vogel Award in 1981, he has won the Miles Franklin Award four times (for *Shallows*, *Cloudstreet*, *Dirt Music* and *Breath*) and twice been shortlisted for the Booker Prize (for *The Riders* and *Dirt Music*). He lives in Western Australia.

ACKNOWLEDGEMENTS

My thanks to publisher Robert Sessions for contracting this book within a week of my proposing it. Thanks also to publisher Ben Ball for introducing me to the work of Nam Le, and for his editorial suggestions. Thanks to Jo Rosenberg for her detailed production and editorial work. And thanks to Murray Bail for facilitating author contacts and for sharing his thoughts on the Australian short story.

The editor and publisher are grateful to the following writers, agents and publishers for permission to reproduce their stories in this anthology:

'The Valley of Lagoons' from *Every Move You Make*, copyright © David Malouf 2006. Reproduced by permission of the author c/o Rogers, Coleridge & White Ltd., 20 Powis Mews, London W11 1JN.

'Jesus Wants Me for a Sunbeam' from *Little Deaths*, copyright © Peter Goldsworthy 1993. Reproduced by permission of HarperCollins Publishers (Australia).

ACKNOWLEDGEMENTS

'Ten Anecdotes About Lord Howe Island' from *A Sea Change, Australian Writing & Photography*, Adam Shoemaker, ed. (Ultimo, Sydney Organising Committee for the Olympic Games), copyright © Louis Nowra 1998. Reproduced by permission of the author.

'Honour' from *Honour and Other People's Children*, copyright © Helen Garner 1980. Reproduced by permission of Penguin Group (Australia).

'Boner McPharlin's Moll' from *The Turning*, copyright © Tim Winton 2004. Reproduced by permission of Pan Macmillan (Australia).

'Grasshoppers' from *The Travelling Entertainer*, copyright © Elizabeth Jolley 1979. Reproduced with the permission of The Estate of Monica Elizabeth Jolley.

'The Chance' from *War Crimes*, copyright © Peter Carey 1979. Reproduced by permission of the author c/o Rogers, Coleridge & White Ltd., 20 Powis Mews, London W11 1JN.

'The Childhood Gland' from *Collected Stories*, copyright © Gillian Mears 1997. Reproduced with permission of the author.

'Halflead Bay' from *The Boat*, copyright © Nam Le 2008. Reproduced by permission of Penguin Group (Australia).